T0285031

PUPPET FLOWER

MODERN CHINESE LITERATURE FROM TAIWAN

For a complete list of titles, see page 298

PUPPET FLOWER

A NOVEL OF 1867 FORMOSA

YAO-CHANG CHEN

TRANSLATED BY

PAO-FANG HSU, IAN MAXWELL,

AND TUNG-JUNG CHEN

Columbia University Press   New York

Columbia University Press wishes to express its appreciation for assistance given
by the Chiang Ching-kuo Foundation for International Scholarly Exchange and
Council for Cultural Affairs in the preparation of the translation
and in the publication of this series.

Columbia University Press
Publishers Since 1893
New York   Chichester, West Sussex
cup.columbia.edu

Cataloging-in-Publication Data available from the Library of Congress
LCCN 2022032805
ISBN 978-0-231-20850-5 (cloth)
ISBN 978-0-231-20851-2 (paper)
ISBN 978-0-231-55746-7 (electronic)

Columbia University Press books are printed on permanent
and durable acid-free paper.
Printed and bound by CPI Group (UK) Ltd, Croydon, CR0 4YY

Cover design: Chang Jae Lee
Cover image: Part of "Kangxi Taiwan Map" (康熙台灣輿圖, 1699–1704),
with the Puppet Mountains in the background.
Courtesy of National Taiwan Museum

CONTENTS

FOREWORD

MICHAEL BERRY

I n the field of contemporary Taiwan literature, Yao-Chang Chen 陳耀昌 is something of an anomaly. Born in 1949, he didn't publish his first novel until he was in his sixties, yet he would go on to become one of the most prolific and impactful novelists of the past decade in Taiwan, winning several major literary awards. The importance of Chen's fiction lies in its opening new literary sites for reimagining Taiwan history and in the process, renegotiating issues of cultural identity during an era of tumultuous change.

Yao-Chang Chen spent the majority of his professional career as a physician, professor, and medical researcher. A graduate of the College of Medicine at National Taiwan University, he spent time at St. Luke's Medical Center at Rush Medical College in Chicago on a hematology fellowship (1978–1981), then returned to his alma mater in Taiwan as a professor of medicine and became one of Taiwan's leading specialists in blood cell diseases. After many years as a physician in the Department of Hematology and Oncology, Dr. Chen is recognized as a true pioneer in his field: in 1983 he completed the first bone marrow transplant in Taiwan, where he also established the first bone marrow database. He also served as director of the Stem Cell Research Center at the National Health Research Institutes, trained many future leading doctors in Taiwan and Vietnam, and published numerous groundbreaking studies on hematology.

Dr. Chen has also been active in politics: he served as a represen-tative for the Democratic Progressive Party in the Taiwan National Assembly, and after charges of corruption were brought against Chen Shui-bian 陳水扁 in 2006, he took part in anticorruption activities as a leading activist alongside Shih Ming-teh 施明德. In 2007, Dr. Chen even established his own political party, the Red Party (Hongdang 紅黨), for which he served as chairman.

Given his extraordinary achievements in medicine and contribu-tions to Taiwan politics, Dr. Chen's fictional turn comes as a surprise. His transition to writing began in 2006 with a series of nonfiction works, culminating in the popular 2015 book *Island DNA* (*Daoyu DNA* 島嶼 DNA). Through a synthesis of his knowledge of medical sci-ence and history, he put forth new discoveries concerning the DNA of Taiwan's indigenous peoples. Eventually, however, he began to devote his attention to fiction.

From 2012 through 2021, Yao-Chang Chen would publish five major works of historical fiction: *The Three Tribes of Formosa* (*Fuermo-sha sanzu ji* 福爾摩沙三族記, 2012), *Puppet Flower: A Novel of 1867 For-mosa* (*Kuilei hua* 傀儡花, 2016), *The Lionhead Flower* (*Shitou hua* 獅頭花, 2017), *Bangas* (*Kulian hua* 苦楝花, 2019), and *Dawn of Formosa* (*Dao zhi xi* 島之曦, 2021). *The Three Tribes of Formosa* begins in 1647 with the story of Maria, a Dutch girl who arrives in Formosa at the age of six-teen with her missionary father, and culminates in 1661 with the violence unleased by the arrival of the Chinese general Koxinga (Zheng Chenggong 鄭成功). *Puppet Flower: A Novel of 1867 Formosa* homes in on the year when an American vessel shipwrecked off the coast of Kenting in southern Taiwan set in action a series of events that would reverberate throughout Taiwan history. In *The Lionhead Flower*, the focus is on the 1875 Battle of the Lionhead Tribe (Shi-toushe zhi yi 獅頭社之役); the novel juxtaposes a violent military conflict between Qing forces and the indigenous Tjakuvukuvulj tribe with an interracial romance. *Bangas* continues Chen's exploration of

Taiwan indigenous history with a plot set against the 1877 Cepo Incident (Da gangkou shijian 大港口事件), when members of the Cepo, Kiwit, and Amis groups resisted the Qing policy of expansion into indigenous mountain regions; the uprising ended with a brutal slaughter of indigenous people at the hands of Qing troops. And in *Dawn of Formosa*, Chen pushes his historical field of vision forward to the 1920s during the period of Japanese colonial rule.

Over time, these novels have revealed a collective ambition that has rewritten and refocused our attention on some of the most overlooked incidents in Taiwan history, focusing primarily on the period predating the Japanese colonial era. Chen's fiction also reveals a deep commitment to a nuanced and sustained exploration of Taiwanese indigenous cultures and a series of little-known conflicts between Taiwanese indigenous groups and outsiders.

While Yao-Chang Chen's work stands out for its bold intervention into Taiwan history, it should also be looked at within a broader context of epic Taiwanese historical narratives in fiction. This tradition is normally referred to as *dahe xiaoshuo* 大河小說, or "great river fiction." The term originates from the French *roman-fleuve*; however, in the context of modern Taiwan fiction, the genre has taken on a distinct nativist tone and style in the hands of writers like Wu Zhuoliu 吳濁流, Zhong Zhaozheng 鍾肇政, Dongfang Bai 東方白, Li Qiao 李喬, and Chen Lei 陳雷. These *dahe xiaoshuo* typically involve sprawling multigenerational narratives that span multiple volumes, focus on working-class protagonists, and emphasize local Taiwan history (especially the Japanese colonial period) and Hokkien and Hakka language and culture. Although the tradition of *dahe xiaoshuo* seems to have waned during the 2000s, Yao-Chang Chen's "Flower Trilogy" (*Puppet Flower: A Novel of 1867 Formosa, The Lionhead Flower, Bangas*) marks an important contribution to this once robust genre of writing Taiwan history. With the exception of an abridged version of Li Qiao's *Wintry Night* (*Hanye sanbuqu* 寒夜三部曲), the vast body of *dahe xiaoshuo* also remains largely unrepresented in English-language translations, which makes this edition of *Puppet Flower* all the more important.[1]

Puppet Flower: A Novel of 1867 Formosa is significant not only because of the work's multilayered narrative but also for the author's meticulous attention to reconstructing historical details. Drawing extensively from historical sources like Charles W. Le Gendre's *Notes of Travel in Formosa* and his 1874 *Is Aboriginal Formosa a Part of the Chinese Empire?*, Chen's novel is informed by in-depth historical research, including many historical figures and even incorporating elements from period-specific texts and documents. In the process, Chen also attempts to challenge and deconstruct the ways this era of Taiwan history has been previously rendered. When discussing the impetus for writing the novel, he made clear that he was engaged in an effort to rescue history: "The strange thing is that, for most people in Taiwan today, the year of 1867 carries no particular significance for them. History textbooks in Taiwan hardly ever even mention what occurred in 1867."[2] For Chen, however, 1867 marks a crucial turning point in Taiwan's interaction with the world, and it also marks the date of the first major treaty signed between Taiwan and the West. Significantly for Chen, the treaty involved not the Qing government but the American Charles Le Gendre and the chief of the Tuillassock tribe, Tauketok. So many stories of Western soldiers, traders, and missionaries encountering "the native other" have been narrativized from the perspective of the colonizer cum oppressor, but *Puppet Flower: A Novel of 1867 Formosa* presents a narrative that highlights a multitude of perspectives, with particular attention to the indigenous point-of-view. Chen's narrative also reveals an almost

---

[1] Like *Wintry Night, Puppet Flower: A Novel of 1867 Formosa* was adapted into a twelve-episode miniseries for Taiwan Public Television by veteran film and television director Tsao Jui-yuan under the title *Seqalu: Formosa 1867* (2021).
[2] Yao-Chang Chen 陳耀昌. *Kuilei hua* 傀儡花 (*Puppet Flower: A Novel of 1867 Formosa*) (Taipei: INK, 2016), 443–444.

Rashomon-like strategy, allowing the reader to see this unique page in Taiwan history unfold from the triangular perspective of foreigners, the Chinese population, and the indigenous population.

But even that triangular relationship among Chinese, Westerners, and Taiwanese indigenous groups is, in reality, rendered in a much more layered manner. Within each group is a more complex cross-section of ethnicities, languages, and identities at play; for instance, among the broader group of Chinese characters there are Hokkien, Hakka, and Qing officials; among the Westerners are Americans, British, and Dutch; and among the indigenous groups highlighted are the Tuillassock, Tjaquvuquvulj, Tjaliunay, Siraya, Uwaljudj, Ping-puzu, and Koalut tribes. Further complicating any attempt at categorizations and generalizations is the author's attention to *tushengzi* 土生仔, or "half-breeds," which develops the notion of hybrid identity. Of course, cultural hybridity is most powerfully articulated through the novel's main protagonists, Butterfly and Bunkiet, siblings born to a Hakka father and a Tuillassock mother. Even the novel's main Western character, Charles Le Gendre, a French-born American spending most of his life in Japan, Korea, China, and Taiwan, seems to raise questions about cultural identity. By inundating the narrative with issues of cultural and ethnic allegiance and characters who embody the complexity and fluidity of identity, Yao-Chang Chen introduces a much richer and true-to-life portrait of what Taiwan was like during this pivotal phase in its history. At the same time, he also challenges hegemonic Han Chinese-centric views that dominated decades of official narratives of Taiwan under the Nationalist regime beginning in 1949.

Dr. Chen brings an element of historical realism into his approach to fiction in the way he renders dialogue, his portrayal of disease (clearly drawn from his rich background in medicine), his keen attention to military strategy, and, most notably, his loyalty to historical truth over narrative conventions and convenient resolutions. At the heart of the novel is the "relationship" between Butterfly and

Charles Le Gendre, but it is certainly not a typical love story—the male protagonist does not appear until halfway through the narrative, and then the relationship that emerges is marked more by awkwardness, waiting, and misunderstanding than the typical literary tropes often employed in stories of intercultural romance. Clearly this is not a "love story," but a more complex and subtle exploration of intercultural exchange. If we look at the relationship between Butterfly and Le Gendre instead as a metaphor for Taiwan's negotiation with the world, we begin to appreciate Chen's larger project of cultural and historical translation. In addition to the layers of identity inscribed onto the characters, Butterfly's role when she first accompanies the Westerners on their mission is that of translator. It is highly symbolic, as Butterfly straddles two or more worlds that often seem impossible to truly bridge. Yao-Chang Chen is also a translator of sorts, synthesizing forgotten pages of Taiwan history into a grand narrative that skillfully juxtaposes the epic with the quotidian. But in some sense, *Puppet Flower: A Novel of 1867 Formosa* is also a novel about the impossibility of translation. It is a novel about what happens when peoples, cultures, histories, and languages rooted in completely different traditions and ways of looking at the world meet and clash. Chen explores the misunderstandings and the obsessions that arise, the histories that have unfolded, and hypothetical histories that could have been.

Another iteration of one of those hypothetical histories was realized in 2021 when *Puppet Flower: A Novel of 1867 Formosa* was adapted into a twelve-episode miniseries for Taiwan Public Television by veteran film and television director Tsao Jui-yuan 曹瑞原 under the title *Seqalu: Formosa 1867* 斯卡羅 (2021). The series drew heavily from Yao-Chang Chen's original source material while also venturing into bold new territory as it reimagined plot points, embellished conflicts, and created a new mythos for this era of Taiwan's past. *Seqalu* became the single most talked-about Taiwan television drama of 2021; a veritable cultural phenomenon, the series also triggered widespread controversy, debate, and discussions about how Taiwan history is portrayed in popular culture. This runaway success is in part a result of renewed interest in Taiwan's multiethnic history and complex international connections (which had been long suppressed in favor of Han-centric macronarratives), but also a result of Yao-Chang Chen's literary imagination, which has taken lost memories and broken fragments of history and brought them back to life.

PREFACE

K enting National Park, on the Hengchun Peninsula at Taiwan's southern tip, boasts beautiful beaches, which are
now favorite destinations for domestic and international
tourists. Few people, however, know that this area was a battlefield
where U.S. soldiers and Taiwanese indigenous peoples clashed
about 150 years ago.[1]

The battle broke out on June 13, 1867, when Rear Admiral
Henry H. Bell, commander of the United States Asiatic Squadron,
sent a troop of 181 officers, sailors, and marines to land on a beach
in Kenting. The American force was, however, defeated by the warriors of the Paiwan people. Major Alexander Mackenzie, lieutenant
commander of the troop, was the first officer to sacrifice his life in
America's first military operation in Asia after the Civil War.

This American expedition to Formosa originated from an accident
on March 12, 1867, when the American merchant ship *Rover* was
shipwrecked near Kenting. Fourteen survivors managed to row small

---

[1] On April 13, 2019, at a conference on the history of Liangkiau, I had the honor of
meeting Dr. William Stanton, former director of the American Institute in Taiwan. When I mentioned to him the 1867 American Expedition to Formosa,
Ambassador Stanton was greatly surprised, because he had never heard of this
incident. He acknowledged, however, that it was certainly an important event in
the history of U.S.-Taiwan relations.

boats to a beach close by. All except one were killed by local aboriginals. This "*Rover* Incident" not only triggered Bell's invasion but also
set the stage for the future engagements of Charles W. Le Gendre
(1830–1899) with Taiwan. Le Gendre, a French-born American diplomat, would later become a legendary figure in modern East Asian
history.

The fact that only a very limited number of people know about
these historical events and their successive repercussions in Taiwan
motivated me to write a historical novel featuring Charles Le Gendre, with the Hengchun Peninsula (formerly "Liangkiau") as the
main backdrop and the *Rover* Incident as the pivotal event. The novel
I had in mind aimed to illuminate the long-neglected and little-
known aspects of Taiwan; to manifest the ethos, lifestyles, social
structures, religious practices, and worldviews of Taiwan's inhabitants at that time, and to highlight the island's distinct and unique
culture, its intricate multilingual and multiethnic elements, and its
cross-connections with the outside world. *Puppet Flower: A Novel of
1867 Formosa* is the result of my efforts.

Ever since its publication in 2016, *Kuilei hua*, the Chinese-language
edition of *Puppet Flower: A Novel of 1867 Formosa*, has been luckily well
received at home and abroad. It won the Golden Award for Taiwan
Literature in 2016 and was selected by Taiwan's Public Television
Service to be adapted into a twelve-episode drama series, aired and
streamed in August 2021, with the title *Seqalu: Formosa 1867*. Professor Shimomura Sakujiro of Tenri University, Nara, has rendered my
novel into Japanese, and his translation was published in 2019.[2]

The present English-language version was conceived specifically for English-speaking audiences, academic and nonacademic.
Through the dramatic narrative of the *Rover* Incident and its subsequent developments, I hope to give readers a glimpse into the

---

[2] The Japanese title is フォルモサに咲く花 (literally, "Flowers Blooming in Formosa").

variegated life of that era and to entice them to further explore the vibrant and pluralistic culture ever present in Taiwan society.

While preparing this English edition, I found it not easy to transliterate the names of the historical figures, aboriginal tribes, and geographical locations associated with the story, because variants abound. In 1860s Taiwan, various ethnic groups used such languages as Mandarin, Hokkien, Hakka, and local aboriginal languages to interact with each other. Ways of transliterating proper names differ from author to author. Since the novel is set mainly in the latter half of the nineteenth century, I decided to adopt some of the proper names used by Charles Le Gendre in his *Notes of Travel in Formosa*, with a view to re-creating an aura of the era. For other names, I elected to use the pinyin system for transliteration, with some exceptions.

This is admittedly *not* a verbatim translation of my original novel; it has been deliberately tailored for English-speaking audiences. However, I have taken special care to present historical facts as accurately as possible and to craft the novel artfully so as to make it at once interesting and informative.

The term *Liangkiau* used to refer to the area south of present-day Fangliao Township, Pingtung County, Taiwan. Like the rest of the island, this was once a territory solely inhabited and controlled by Taiwanese indigenous peoples (formerly "Formosan people" or "Taiwanese aborigines"). Their ancestors had been living on the island for a very long time before the major migrations of Han people from mainland China. As Jared Diamond, author of *Guns, Germs, and Steel* (1998), pointed out, their ancestors started to migrate out of the island about 5,500 years ago and consequently had historical connections with the Maori and other Pacific islanders. Polynesians may have originated from Taiwan's indigenous peoples. Languages of the Austronesian peoples are spoken from Taiwan to Hawaii to Easter Island to New Zealand to Jarkata to Madagascar. According to Robert Blust, a Hawaiian linguist, among the 1,200 Austronesian languages, nine of the ten subgroups (containing twenty-six languages) are spoken only by the non-Chinese aborigines of Taiwan. They are truly Taiwan's precious gift to the world.[3]

The migration of Han Chinese people to Formosa began in late 1500s or early 1600s, no more than 500 years from the present. In 1867, the eastern half of the island was outside of Qing China's administrative control.

For centuries, Taiwan's indigenous inhabitants have experienced economic competition and military conflict with a series of colonizing newcomers. Through trade, intermarriage, and other intercultural processes, they have gradually suffered the loss of their tribal languages and cultural identity. Officially, there are sixteen indigenous peoples or groups in Taiwan, living mostly in the rugged mountains or alluvial plains. Nowadays, more and more people move out to work and live in the urban areas. Currently the indigenous people number around 569,008, constituting roughly 2.38 percent of the population.

During the Qing dynasty, Taiwan's aboriginals were categorized into two kinds: raw savages (*sheng fan*) and cooked (tamed) savages (*shou fan*), based on the degree of their adoption of the Han Chinese lifestyle. Those living in the high mountains were generally marked as "raw" and those on the plains as "cooked."

Liangkiau was once part of the Qing Empire and yet not exactly under its jurisdiction. Its inhabitants enjoyed autonomy, without being levied taxes by the Qing government. In 1867, Taiwan was actually divided into two parts: immigrants from mainland China living on the plains and ruled by the Qing Empire, and self-governing Formosan mountain aborigines. Not until the Japanese expedition to Formosa in 1874 (the "Botan Tribe Incident") did the Qing government start to take fuller control of the island.

---

[3] See Jared Diamond, "Taiwan's Gift to the World," *Nature* 403 (2000): 709–710; https://doi.org/10.1038/35001685.

The name *Liangkiau* can be traced back to the Dutch colonial era (1624–1662), when both the Dutch and the Han Chinese called this place Liangkiau. Interestingly, the name could also have come from Paiwan, referring to a species of orchids. It was believed that Han Chinese immigrants had used it to refer to a plant native to that area: the butterfly tail flower.

"Puppet Mountains" and "Puppet Savages" were official terms used on Qing-dynasty maps and bureaucratic literature. The ancient maps show that to the east of the Hengchun Peninsula was the Pacific Ocean; to the south, across the Bashi Channel, was Luzon Island. In the center of the peninsula were the Puppet Mountains, now the Dawu Mountains, home to the "Puppet Savages" (*kuilei fan*).[4]

In this novel, the term "Puppet savages" is used for the indigenous groups living in Liangkiau, nowadays called the Paiwan and the Rukai. When Han Chinese immigrants saw them running through the mountain forests as if on level land, they thought the aboriginals' nimble movements resembled those of bouncing puppets they remembered from their homeland. That might be the reason they called them "Puppet Savages."

However, the term may also have a different derivation. When Han Chinese immigrants were still small in number, the indigenous would greet them with an enthusiastic "*Kaliyang.*" The sound of this greeting led the newcomers to call the natives "Ka lei" or "Ka lyi a."[5] Unfortunately, as more Han Chinese people arrived and settled down, they began cheating the aboriginals out of their land and

---

[4] From a present-day perspective, it is of course offensive and inappropriate to use the term "savages" (*fan*) to refer to Taiwan's indigenous peoples. Yet, when writing this historical novel, I elected to use terms in line with those appearing in the official documents or maps, such as "Kangxi Taiwan Map" (*Kangxi yutu* 康熙台灣 輿圖). I beg readers' indulgence if they feel offended.

[5] Han Chinese immigrants used to call aboriginals "Ka lei" or "Ka lyi a," which is rendered into Chinese as 傀儡 (*kuilei*), 嘉禮 (*jiali*), or 加禮 (*jiali*), all pronounced "Ka lei" in Hokkien. "Kalees" is the term used by the Paiwan people, meaning "friends."

property. Thus, the aboriginals' opinion of them turned sour, and they started to take revenge through the practice of beheading. The immigrants in turn started to call Ka lei people "Puppet Savages," as the two terms sounded similar in Hokkien.

Over the centuries, Taiwan has experienced a series of colonial periods. Starting in the sixteenth century, Han Chinese immigrants came to settle on the island in increasing numbers. The Spanish colonized the northern part of Taiwan from 1626 to 1642, and the Dutch occupied a large part of it from 1624 to 1662, when Koxinga (Zheng Chenggong) led an army to attack the Dutch in Tainan and drove them away. Koxinga's was the first government founded by Han Chinese in Taiwan. In 1683, his grandson was defeated by troops sent by the Qing government, which annexed the island into Fujian Province.

In the nineteenth century, the Qing government forbade people from crossing the Black Water Channel (i.e., the Taiwan Strait) to Formosa. To avoid being caught, Han Chinese people (mostly Hokkien and Hakka) smuggled themselves and landed in Liangkiau, a safe haven for them then. With the influx of these immigrants, Liangkiau became a habitat for diverse ethnic groups. In addition to the original inhabitants, there were Hokkiens, Hakkas, Peppos (or plains aborigines), and *tushengzi* (or "hybrids," to use Le Gendre's term, referring to the half-Peppo, half-Hokkiens). Coming from different backgrounds, they started to develop intricate relationships among themselves.

With the signing of the Peking Treaty in 1860, Taiwan was forced to open its ports to Western merchant ships. From then on, more and more Westerners came to the island, bringing with them—among other influences—Christianity and Western medicine. The Formosa of 1867 was thus full of exciting scenes, with foreigners mingling with local officials, landlords, businessmen, peasants, and others. Charles Le Gendre apart, there was, for instance, a British physician

Dr. Patrick Manson (1844–1922), who worked at the Customs House in Takao (present-day Kaohsiung). Because of his great contribution to the study of tropical diseases, he was later honored as the "Father of Tropical Medicine." There was also a well-known English businessman, William A. Pickering (1840–1907), who wrote *Pioneering in Formosa: Recollections of Adventures Among Mandarins, Wreckers, and Head-Hunting Savages* (London, 1898). He could speak Cantonese, Hakka, Hokkien, Mandarin, and some Formosan aboriginal languages, among others. These foreigners, who worked in the public or private sector, appear in the novel as main or minor characters.

Le Gendre was born in France in 1830. He became a naturalized U.S. citizen after marrying a daughter of a prominent New York lawyer. He joined the Union Army to fight in the Civil War and was promoted to brigadier general when he was honorably discharged. After the war, he was stationed in Amoy (present-day Xiamen) as a U.S. consul. It was he who helped resolve the complicated issues surrounding the *Rover* Incident, and it was he who signed—along with Tauketok, a great leader of Formosan aboriginal peoples—the South Cape Agreement, which henceforth safeguarded all sailors navigating the Taiwan Strait.

The South Cape Agreement was signed by Le Gendre and Tauketok on February 28, 1869, sixteen months after their historical meeting at Volcano in Liangkiau in 1867. As recorded in Le Gendre's *Notes of Travel in Formosa*, its text goes as follows:

TERRITORY UNDER TAUTEKOK
Village of the Sabarees February 28, 1869

At the request of Tauketok, the ruler of the eighteen tribes south of Liangkiau, and between the range of hills east of it and the Eastern Sea, including the bay known as the Southern Bay of Formosa, where the crew of the American bark Rover were murdered by the Koaluts, I, Charles W. Le Gendre, United States consul for Amoy and Formosa, give this a memorandum of the understanding arrived at between myself and the said Tauketok in 1867, the same having been approved by the United States Government and assented to, I believe, by the foreign ministers at Pekin, viz:

Cast-aways will be kindly treated by any of the eighteen tribes under Tauketok. If possible, they are to display a red flag before landing.

Ballast and water.—Vessels requiring supplies are to send a crew on shore, displaying a red flag, and must not land until a similar token has been shown from the shore, and then only at the spot indicated. They are not to visit the hills and villages, but, when possible, are to confine their visit to the Tuiahsockang, being the first stream on the east coast, north of the southeastern cape of South Bay, and to the Toapangnack, to the west of the rock where the Rover's crew were murdered, the latter being the better watering-place in the northeast monsoon. Persons landing under other than these conditions do so at their own peril, and must not look, I believe, for protection from their government if molested by the natives, who, in such case, will not be held responsible for their safety.

CHAS. W. LE GENDRE
United States Consul.
Witness: I. ALEX. MAN, *Commissioner of Customs for Southern Formosa*
Witness and interpreter: W. A. PICKERING[6]

Le Gendre later became a well-known expert on Taiwan and the Far East. Nevertheless, by 1872 his attitude toward Taiwan had

---

[6] The Library of Congress in Washington, D.C. now houses a sizeable collection of Le Gendre documents and letters. In July 2019, I made a special trip to this library and saw many letters and documents in the files labeled *Le Gendre*, but for some reason was unable to look at the original copy of the South Cape Agreement.

changed from hopeful expectation to disappointment. In December of that year, on his way back to the United States, he stopped over at Yokohama, Japan. While there, he decided to accept the Japanese government's invitation to serve as their diplomatic consultant. In this role his chief mission was to help Japan draw up a plan to attack and occupy Taiwan. Some historians even claim that he was the initiator of Japan's ambitious scheme to develop a "Greater East Asia Co-Prosperity Sphere."

For the following twenty-seven years, until his death in Seoul in 1899, Le Gendre lived in Asia. Eighteen of these years were spent in Japan and nine in Korea. He never again set foot on American soil.

Seven years after the 1867 American expedition to Formosa, a similar expedition was launched—by Japan. It too was a failure. The details of this 1874 Japanese expedition can be found in *The Japanese Expedition to Formosa* (1875) by Edward Howard House, the only foreign journalist who accompanied the Japanese forces. Not until 1895 did the Empire of Japan defeat the Qing Empire and take control of Taiwan, remaining there until the end of World War II in 1945.

The *Rover* Incident and the consequent American expedition to Formosa, the Japanese expedition to Formosa, and Taiwan's annexation by Japan in 1895 at the end of the first Sino-Japanese War all might well be attributed to the "butterfly effect" caused by this germinal figure, Charles W. Le Gendre.

When writing *Kuilei hua*, I tried to give historically faithful accounts of the diplomatic negotiations, international wars, and love-hate relationships among various ethnic groups in Qing-dynasty Taiwan. For dramatic effect, however, I deliberately fictionalized the complex interracial connections between Le Gendre and Butterfly.

The relationship between Le Gendre and Butterfly is complex. One is a handsome, urbane, and powerful foreign diplomat, the other a young, brave, and intelligent local girl. As the plot develops, a subtle mutual attraction slowly evolves. Le Gendre at the age of thirty-seven is obviously very much charmed by Butterfly. Readers may be disturbed (or even upset) by a scene in which Butterfly is forced to have an intimate relationship with him. It is on the eve of his first meeting with Tauketok. Like a new recruit about to join combat, Le Gendre feels much agitated and anxious, yearning to have Butterfly's company. On that evening, Butterfly, however, is desperately attempting to seek peace and save her people's lives. After some hesitation, she braces herself to enter Le Gendre's tent and beg him not to engage in war against the local aboriginals. After consenting to her request, Le Gendre loses control of himself and takes Butterfly's body by force, despite her protests. This scene is devised to dramatize Le Gendre's complex feelings and intense yearnings at that moment in a remote southern Taiwan village. It clearly demonstrates the unbalanced but likely power relations between them. Having grown up in a family strongly influenced by her Chinese-educated Hakka father, Butterfly, under the dictates of Confucian ethics and religious beliefs, is unwont to expressing her true feelings publicly. After this crucial incident, she eventually chooses to take the middle-of-the-road approach and accept her lover Chinya as he is, despite his previous misdeeds and flaws.

In the novel, Butterfly, a woman of mixed ethnic heritage, time and again demonstrates that she is a strong person with such laudable qualities as diligence, resilience, intelligence, modesty, adroitness, resourcefulness, self-sacrifice, and stoic dignity. In a sense, she is an avatar of Taiwan. In view of the supreme significance of the role she plays, I decided to use her nickname, *Kuilei hua* (literally, "Puppet Flower," meaning "demure or admirable young lady from the Puppet Mountains") as the title for the Chinese-language version. For the English-language version, I chose *Puppet Flower: A Novel of 1867 Formosa* with the same view to highlighting Butterfly as the female protagonist in this historical novel.

ACKNOWLEDGMENTS

In preparing *Puppet Flower: A Novel of 1867 Formosa* for publication, I am very fortunate to have had assistance and support from many friends, colleagues, and organizations. First, I would like to thank the Chiang Ching-kuo Foundation for International Scholarly Exchange for its support of this publication project. I also wish to thank Dr. Pao-fang Hsu 許寶芳 for preparing the first draft of this translated work, Ms. Ginny Jaramillo for proofreading Dr. Hsu's draft, and Ms. C. J. Anderson-Wu 吳介禎 and Mr. Chieh-Ting Yeh 葉介庭 for helping me seek a possible publisher in the initial stage. My sincere appreciation goes to Mr. Ian Maxwell for revising the draft to make it more accessible to Western readers. It is very kind of Professor Jerome C. Su 蘇正隆 to have proofread portions of the manuscript. I am deeply indebted to Professor Tung-jung Chen 陳東榮, who not only translated my preface and prepared the list of principal characters and glossary but also edited the manuscript professionally with his keen eye and attention to detail.

Professor Thomas H. C. Lee 李弘祺 of the City University of New York and Professor David Der-wei Wang 王德威 of Harvard University deserve my special thanks, because they have been most generous in giving their sagacious advice here and there and in liaising on my behalf with Columbia University Press and the Chiang

Ching-kuo Foundation for International Scholarly Exchange for the publication of this book. I am most grateful to Professor Michael Berry of the University of California at Los Angeles for giving me valuable comments and suggestions for amendment and for writing a succinct and insightful foreword.

A word of thanks goes to Mr. Jasper Huang 黃旭憲, who has produced maps of nineteenth-century southern Taiwan and East Asia. My special gratitude goes to Mr. A. H., whose encouragement and financial support have made this project possible. I also wish to thank Ms. Christine Dunbar of Columbia University Press for guiding this book through production. The anonymous outside readers of my manuscript have favored me with valuable suggestions for improvement; I am very grateful to them.

Many other friends and colleagues—too numerous to mention here—have pushed me to bring this project to fruition; I wish to thank them all.

To my dear family, I lovingly dedicate this book.

LIST OF PRINCIPAL CHARACTERS

MAIN CHARACTERS

Bunkiet (文杰)—son of Lim Mountain Products and Majuka; younger brother of Butterfly; adopted son of Tauketok

Butterfly (蝶妹)—daughter of Lim Mountain Products and Majuka; disciple of Dr. Patrick Manson; wife of Chinya; owner of a medicine shop in downtown Tainan

Chinya (松仔)—second son of Bamboo Yang in Sialiao; husband of Butterfly

Charles Le Gendre (李讓禮；李仙得)—French-born American; brigadier general in U.S. Army; U.S. consul based in Amoy (or Xiamen); advisor to Japan's Ministry of Foreign Affairs and to the Emperor of Korea

Mia (棉仔)—elder brother of Chinya; leader of Sialiao

Tauketok (卓杞篤)—chief of the Tuillassock tribe and Big Head Chief of the Confederation of Eighteen Tribes of Lower Liangkiau

OTHER CHARACTERS

Taiwanese Indigenous People

Isa (伊沙)—chief of Sabaree

Majuka (瑪珠卡)—daughter of the chief of Tuillassock; wife of
Lim Mountain Products

Paljaljaus (朴嘉留央)—chief of Tuillassock; brother of
Majuka; yielded his Big Head Chief Seat to his brother
Tauketok

Payarin (巴耶林)—chief of Koalut

Zudjui (朱雷)—son of Paljaljaus; later chief of Tuillassock

Hokkien People

Mr. Chen (陳廟祝)—manager of Ciji Temple in Fungshan
Koo-sia; Yao Ying's son out of wedlock

Yizhen (乙真)—abbess of Guanyin Ting, a temple in Fungshan
Koo-sia

Hakka People

Lim Mountain Products [Honest Lim] (林山產，林老實)—
Fukien-born Hakka settler; worked for Bamboo Yang in
Sialiao before moving to Tongling Po; itinerant tradesman;
father of Butterfly and Bunkiet

Lim Nine (林阿九)—headman of Poliac, a Hakka village

Tushengzi

Bamboo Yang (楊竹青)—headman of Sialiao; father of Mia and
Chinya

Qing Government Officials

Liang Yuangui (梁元桂)—*daotai* (intendant) of Taiwan *Dao*
(Circuit)

Liu Ming-teng (劉明燈)—regional commander of Taiwan *Zhen* (Defense Command)

Wang Wenqi (王文棨)—subprefect in charge of Formosan aboriginal affairs

Wu Ta-ting (吳大廷)—*daotai* of Taiwan *Dao*

Yao Ying (姚瑩)—government official; later *daotai* of Taiwan *Dao*

Ye Zongyuan (葉宗元)—prefect of Taiwan-fu

Foreign People

Joseph Bernard—interpreter for Charles Le Gendre

Charles Carroll—British deputy consul in Taiwan

James Horn—British merchant, commissioned to recover the remains of murdered Americans on the *Rover*

Joseph W. Hunt—captain of the shipwrecked American barque, the *Rover*

Mercy Hunt—wife of Captain Hunt, decapitated by a Formosan aborigine during the *Rover* Incident

Alexander S. MacKenzie, Jr.—lieutenant commander of the American troop, killed in combat during the 1867 American expedition to Formosa

Patrick Manson—British doctor at the Customs House in Takao; mentor of Butterfly; later honored as the "Father of Tropical Medicine"; founder of London School of Tropical Medicine

James L. Maxwell—first British missionary and physician to Taiwan; founder of hospitals in Taiwan-fu [Tainan City] and Takao

William A. Pickering—British merchant-adventurer, fluent in Mandarin, Hokkien, Hakka, and some Formosan aboriginal languages

Robert Swinhoe—British naturalist, specializing in Taiwan's birds; British consul in Taiwan

1

A PYRRHIC VICTORY

1

The rain that had drenched the village for an entire night and morning finally let up at noon. Payarin, Chief of Koalut, looked out from his house. Sunlight cut through layers of heavy clouds; finally, an afternoon with fine weather.

Payarin was delighted. He knew that big game would now be feeding, and he looked forward to a day spent hunting in the valley. He hoped to bring back boar or goat, maybe even sika deer.

He stood and stretched. Although the rain had stopped, the wind blew up from the ocean undiminished, bringing with it something of the sea.

Payarin glanced down the mountain toward the coast and then shouted in alarm; two boats were approaching the shore. Without a second thought, he issued five calls of the gray-faced buzzard. Before long about twenty warriors, male and female, arrived carrying knives, javelins, bows and arrows, and muskets. He waved a hand, and they ran toward the foot of the mountain.

Dense acacia woods and then screw pines covered much of the ground between the village and the water, and as they moved through the woods, the warriors could see the shore more clearly.

Some of the people on the boats wore white, which from a distance dazzled incoherently in the sunlight, and some of them had blond or red hair, which made the approaching warriors think of the story told first to them and then by them countless times since their birth.

Once, long ago, their tribe had been invaded by a red-haired people. Those "Red-Hairs" fired guns that could kill at impossible distances. Not more than twenty of them had killed nearly all of the people in Koalut; those who survived did so by hiding. After the Red-Hairs left, the villagers started rebuilding their homes and lives. Many years had since passed, and the Koalut had needed much of that time to return to a normal life; such a heavy blood debt weighed yet on their hearts.

Payarin stared at the people securing the boats on the shore and knew that they were Red-Hairs. Rage and the furious necessity of revenge boiled his blood. Why, after such a long time, had they returned?

"Please, bless us with the power to defend Koalut and destroy the Red-Hairs!" Payarin was sweating as he addressed the ancestral spirits. Mercifully, their ancestral spirits were protecting the Koalut and had alerted them in good time.

When Payarin and the others reached the edge of the screw pines they stopped and looked out from behind cover. Although some of the people from the boats were indeed red-haired, others had black hair, or hair that seemed to be of no color at all. They all looked exhausted. Some were sitting, some were lying on the ground, and others were stumbling as they got to their feet to walk. One or two had removed their shirts, exposing hairy chests.

The Red-Hairs were repulsive as well as terrifying, and Payarin was in no doubt that those who came with them on the boats were also enemies. He let out a cry, and one of his men fired a musket. Others followed suit, shouting and firing their guns or shooting their arrows or casting their javelins. Two of the foreigners on the beach fell heavily into the sand and were still. Those unhurt screamed and scrambled to find shelter or otherwise ran in disorganized fear.

It seemed they were too tired to run fast, and perhaps that was why Payarin was able to catch up so quickly with a tall Red-Hair and then knock him to the ground. They fought. In the scuffle the Red-Hair bit Payarin, who reeled in pain. Soon after, two of his men rushed over and grabbed and then beheaded the Red-Hair, who died with a voice that sounded to Payarin like a woman's. Victorious whooping. The invaders were conquered.

But then, Payarin turned over the bloody sailor-suited corpse and saw a necklace of sparkling beads. And the man who held the severed head found it covered with long streaming hair. This Red-Hair was a woman.

Their thrill vanished. According to tradition, any Koalut man who killed a woman would be doomed and cursed, unworthy of being called a warrior. Payarin felt his blood chill, and the man with the knife was so frightened that he threw the head far away from where he stood. However, buoyed by the cheers from the other warriors, they pretended to be happy, and, hoping to be forgiven, decided that they would ask the shaman to hold a ritual of communication with their ancestral spirits.

Payarin and his warriors returned to the tribe carrying several heads. The woman's skull was left where it landed. Breaking waves tore over the reef and then slapped the shore. Blood stippled a beach strewn with headless corpses, clothing, and two empty boats. Everything was ravaged. The sun sank beneath the horizon, as if it could not bear to look at such a tragedy.

Hours later, after nighttime had dusted itself over the world, something crawled out from the screw pines and sat trembling on the ground for a long, long time. Finally, it stood and walked away, vanishing with pain and great solitude.

2

Butterfly and Bunkiet raised their incense sticks and bowed three times in front of their father's tomb; then they knelt and kowtowed to bid farewell.

"Mr. Lim," Mia too raised his incense sticks to the newly finished tomb and said, "you planned to visit us in Sialiao, but instead I have come to see you. Do not worry about Bunkiet and Butterfly. I will take them to live with me."

Drizzle fell at an angle from the overcast sky. Autumnal winds sent from the Puppet Mountains swept over the wilderness of Tongling Bo. The sound of the weather, together with the rolling Liangkiau River—swollen from the rain—combined to increase the afternoon's sadness.

Mia looked around; there were only three or four houses. Upstream, he could vaguely make out Flea Mountain and Mount Wuchongxi. He knew that beyond that mountain was the realm of the fierce Puppet Savages (*Kuilei fan*).[1]

How could Lim stay in such a remote place for twenty years?

Mia inserted the incense sticks into the censer in front of the tomb, put away the offerings, and then said to the sister and brother, "It's time to go."

The two of them stayed in place for a moment longer, reluctant to leave their father. The rain was getting heavier; Chinya spread an oil-paper umbrella and held it over Butterfly's head as she whispered some final words.

---

[1] *Kuilei* 傀儡 means "puppet" literally, but its meanings go beyond that. The term "*Kuilei fan* 傀儡番" (literally "puppet savages") appeared in the official documents of the Qing government. From the perspective of chauvinistic Han Chinese, Formosan aborigines were "uncivilized savages." Historically, Han Chinese used to view non-Han people as "barbarians" (*yidi* 夷狄 or *manyi* 蠻夷) or "savages" (*fan* 番). In this novel, the term is used in its historical context, without any disrespect to Taiwan's indigenous peoples.

Butterfly looked gratefully at Chinya, then turned to Mia. "Mia, we cannot go just yet; we need to say good-bye to our *yina.*"

They entered the house. In one corner of the living room was a large stone slate set higher than the rest of the floor. Butterfly had prepared a plate of betel nuts and a plate of freshly picked flowers to place in front of the slate. This time they carried no incense sticks, and sister and brother spoke to their mother in the savage language. While Mia was watching them, it dawned on him that Butterfly and Bunkiet's mother was buried inside the house, in accordance with Puppet Savage customs.

Mia sighed, thinking that no immigrants from mainland China would ever take over such a house. *Lim really sacrificed everything for his Puppet Savage wife,* he thought, as the four turned and walked outside into the persistent gray rain.

3

It was dark when Charles Le Gendre opened his eyes, which meant that he had slept through the entire afternoon.

Exhaling slowly, as if trying to avoid aggravating a mortal wound, he realized that he had again been dreaming of Clara. For over a decade he had loved her without reservation, but then she had betrayed him while he was away fighting for her country. How could flesh and blood put up with this?

He had worked so hard, often risking his own life to prove himself a loyal hero and to shape himself into someone of whom she could be proud. Judging from his accomplishments, he could count his work as a success. But her betrayal had nearly destroyed him, and in truth, that was why he had come here—with a broken heart—to Amoy, this alien Oriental place.

He entered the study and lit a lamp. Official documents lay on the desk awaiting signatures. For more than three months he had put his life into his work. His new position, that of Consul General, representative of the United States in China, had been announced the previous summer, in 1866. His old boss, General Ulysses S. Grant, had made the arrangements.

Smiling, Grant had told him, "Charlie, I hear that Amoy has pleasant landscapes and warm weather. You can take your son with you and convalesce while traveling around the mysterious Orient. When you have fully recovered, I will arrange for you a better position."

Indeed, Le Gendre had been wounded many times during the American Civil War, in part because he was so desperate to prove his own worth. His wounds had forced him to leave the army sooner than expected, but before leaving he was granted the brevet rank of a brigadier general—a title won at the cost of an eye, a fractured chin, a broken nose, and many scars.

But how can one recover from a broken heart? he wondered, submitting for a moment to his more melodramatic instincts.

His mind wandered back to May 12, 1865. The war had not yet ended, but General Grant nevertheless attended and spoke at the promotion ceremony: "By way of a conclusion, let me say simply that Charles Le Gendre has demonstrated, and, I might stress, demonstrated repeatedly, the bravest in-battle fortitude of any soldier that I have met ever in my life."

Standing on that podium, Le Gendre had looked composed and dignified, but his heart had rung out in pain. One month before the ceremony he had received Clara's letter, in which she told him that she had given birth prematurely to a second baby boy. The child had died soon afterward, and Clara was declared physically and mentally wretched and sent to a sanatorium for rehabilitation.

Since joining the army in late 1861, Le Gendre had returned to New York to stay with Clara for just ten short days in September 1862; clearly the baby was not his. Moreover, Clara had written in the letter that the baby was born six weeks premature, enabling Le Gendre to calculate that it had most likely been conceived during the time when he lay hospitalized in Maryland with his most serious injuries. It was such a humiliating disgrace! Throughout the war he had written to Clara, telling her how much he missed her, and then, when he was at his weakest, she had betrayed him. The victories, his medals— everything was suddenly without meaning.

He had met Clara in Brussels when he was twenty-four years old. He was a confident young Frenchman, born into a well-connected family, who had recently graduated from the University of Paris. It was 1854, and she was on a trip to Europe with her parents. It seemed at first that the young couple were made for each other. Her father, a renowned New York lawyer, consented to their marriage on the condition that Le Gendre relocate to America after the wedding. They got married in October, and soon afterward Le Gendre moved to New York. The following year they had a son, William.

However, after they married, the couple did not always get along. He practiced law in New York, but he was a stranger to the city. It upset him that he remained under the influence of his wife's family, and Clara herself was overbearing and very hard to please. As a young man Le Gendre had been quite dominating, but over time he gave way to her completely. Once, in an attempt to impress her, he traveled all the way to Central America on a long-shot mining endeavor.

In 1861, when the Civil War broke out, he felt a sudden longing to make his name as a soldier. Clara was against his joining the army. She maintained that, with the support of their esteemed families, Charles needn't take part in any battles. And anyway, she said, he was a Frenchman, so it wasn't his war to fight. Right before he set out to enlist, he and Clara clashed terribly. In a later letter, he joked that he had been lucky to escape with his face intact; he had assumed such teasing would make her happy, but Clara's terse reply made it clear she didn't find it at all funny.

But despite these altercations, he never imagined that Clara would do something to him like this. She was nowhere to be seen after his discharge from the army, and he did not visit her at the sanatorium. As a Catholic, he would not seek divorce, but for now there was no possibility of his loving her as he once had done.

Le Gendre had originally intended to take up his position in Amoy the previous summer. With William and a Chinese teacher, he had set off from New York on a ship bound for Liverpool. From there they sailed to France to visit his mother. While in France, however, he tripped, fractured a leg, and was immobilized for the duration of his recovery. It was December when he arrived in Amoy.

While recuperating in bed in France, he read many books about Formosa. He learned that Anping and Taiwan-fu[2] were established in the seventeenth century by the Dutch East India Company, and that at that time Anping had been called Zeelandia, and Taiwan-fu had been known as Provintia. It turned out that he would be supervising an area related in name to Europe—a fact that cheered him up immensely during a difficult rehabilitation.

He was to be in charge of five of the treaty ports open to foreign commerce in China. Only Amoy (where the consulate was located) was on the Chinese mainland; the other four lay across the strait in Formosa. Originally, there had been only two treaty ports in Formosa: Tamsui and Anping. Anping was the port of Taiwan-fu, the largest city on the island; Keelung and Takao had been added later.

Amoy was a beautiful place. But he nevertheless felt an unshakable despondency in the gloomy depths of his heart; he could not stop thinking of Clara and her disloyalty. What brought him further displeasure was that his work in Amoy had almost nothing to do with diplomacy. Instead, he was dealing with slavers. Surely this was not his destiny.

---

[2] Present-day Tainan. "Fu" is "prefecture," a division in the Qing's local administration.

But then, after more than three months in Amoy, he opened a letter to learn that something had happened to the *Rover*, an American barque, in Formosa. Though appalled by the violence, Le Gendre felt a secret thrill at the prospect of a new challenge.

4

Payarin was angry. He just had lost another of his men. For an athletic man to fall out of a betel-nut tree and hit his head on a rock: unimaginable!

Ten days after the killing of the Red-Hair woman, the tribe had already lost three men, a woman, and a dog. The first man was the warrior who had cut off the foreign woman's head. The second had fired the first shot that day. The two had been good friends, but they quarreled after drinking, and each killed the other in a knife fight.

The woman who died had stolen a bracelet and necklace from the corpse. Later, fishing by the sea, she hooked a never-before-seen, slender silvery-white fish. She was happy at first, but then the fish stung her finger. Soon her entire arm became infected and then rotten; she died a few days later.

And as for the dog, it was said to be the one that had found the woman in the bushes and flushed her out of hiding. It died with a strange white lather around its mouth.

The shaman explained that the Red-Hair's ghost, acutely agitated and filled with hatred, was now exacting revenge. People in the tribe were appalled. The shaman said that if they still had the woman's head, she could attempt to communicate with the ghost to appease the spirit. But alas, the head was gone.

So instead Payarin took the shaman and several lesser chiefs to the top of Turtle Nose Mountain to pray for the blessing of their ancestral spirits. According to the shaman, the ancestral spirits were of the opinion that, since the Koalut were avenging their ancestors, the tribe had done nothing wrong. The shaman reminded them that when the Red-Hairs had last attacked the tribe, not even the children were spared. Only the few young boys and girls who had been playing at the river were able to hide and escape death. The ancestral spirits expressed relief that this time the tribe had taken their revenge, and promised that if they chanced upon the Red-Hair demon, they would tell her that all was now even because her people had in the past killed many Koalut women.

When Payarin and the tribal warriors heard this, the anxiety that had been tormenting them was finally dispelled. One warrior suggested to Payarin that they pass along news of the ancestral spirits' judgment to Tauketok, Big Head Chief of Seqalu. Koalut did not belong to Seqalu, but Tauketok was widely respected. They might well tell him about this, and also of their victory, of the killing of more than ten Red-Hairs. Yes, quite right, Big Head Chief should be informed of that as well.

2

THE TRAGEDY THAT BEFELL

THE *ROVER*

5

The ox cart rocked slowly across the wooden bridge and then headed downstream to the outskirts of Sialiao village at the foot of Turtle Hill. The Sialiao River had its headwaters in the Puppet Mountains; it flowed northwest through the large Hakka village of Poliac, becoming a wide river before finally meeting the sea. Turtle Hill stood on the left side of the Sialiao River estuary, blocking the onshore winds.

As soon as the ox cart arrived at the house, Chinya jumped down and shouted, "Mia, Mia, something's happened!"

But it was Bunkiet who came outside. "Mia is not home. He's away acting as a mediator in a dispute. Chinya, what happened?"

Chinya's voice lost its momentum. "Some savages killed some foreigners. Anyway, we'll wait till Mia comes home."

Bunkiet began helping Butterfly, who was quietly unloading the cart. "Did you sell them all? Our peanuts, sesame oil, the fabric you wove. All sold out?"

"Yes, business was good today." Butterfly opened the bamboo basket in excitement. "Here, try these pastries we bought in Chasiang. Tomorrow we'll bring back apricot kernel drinks.

"The winds were so strong today that I was unsteady on the cart coming back. It was so uncomfortable."

Bunkiet noticed Butterfly's wrist was swollen. "And what happened to you?"

"Your sister is tough!" Chinya exclaimed. "A Hokkien guy tried to take advantage of her, but she knocked him to the ground."

"Be quiet. This is nothing to be proud of," said Butterfly.

Bunkiet asked again, "What happened?"

Chinya replied, more sincerely this time, "We were eating at a place in Chasiang. Sitting across from us was a table of about ten people. All of them were loud and excited. They were talking about how a tribe of raw savages killed some foreign sailors. Some of them blamed the savages, saying that they were cruel and ignorant. One of the men leaned over and teased Butterfly for dressing like a raw savage. Then he reached out to touch her. Butterfly only meant to bat away his hand, but she used so much force that she knocked him down from his chair. The man stood up, really embarrassed, and then he got angry and shook his fist at Butterfly. He was shouting, 'Savage! Savage!' It was when Butterfly hit him that she got hurt. I think her arm swung into the table or something after hitting him. Afterward I kicked him, but he was the one who started the fight, and those around us also thought he was the one to blame, so they pulled him away."

Ever since Butterfly had come to Sialiao, with the exception of a new headscarf, she had continued to dress exactly as she had done in Tongling Bo. She wore a vest patterned with red diamonds and stripes, which looked like the one her mother had often worn. Below this she wore a pair of Hakka pants.

Chinya frowned. Now that he had finished his story, he was keen to admonish Butterfly. "It's like I said on our way home. How many times have I told you? You can wear that vest at home. But why do you insist on wearing it around the streets of Sialiao? Even Mia said it would do you no good. And in Chasiang?! You know that the Hokkien guys there look down on Puppet Savages."

Butterfly snorted. "*And?* My mother was a savage. That is the truth. Are Hokkien guys really better than people like me and Bunkiet?"

Chinya sighed. "Getting angry won't help. To them, even *I* am half savage, and I was born here. Hokkien guys just look down on Hakka people." As he was talking, Chinya noticed the house cat eating some crumbs of food from the floor. He cursed the animal and kicked at it, sending it skittering away to take refuge on the roof.

After the commotion had died down, Mia's voice sounded from outside, and he stepped into the house. "What's all this noise?"

His appearance was similar to that of other plains aborigines or Peppos, though his white headscarf was particularly refined, as was the shiny red string he used to bind his long braid, and the thick silver bracelet around his wrist certainly added to an air of magnificence.

Chinya stuttered with excitement, "I was just about to tell you, brother! In Chasiang today we ate at a shop . . . we heard these, these Hokkien guys talking about Puppet Savages . . . these Puppet Savages killed several people. This time they killed different people . . . foreign sailors. . . ."

Mia interrupted him. "Foreigners? Are you sure?"

Chinya answered, "Well . . . I. . . ."

Mia turned to Butterfly. "Tell me what you heard." He clapped his hands impatiently. "There will be great trouble if this is true."

Butterfly spoke slowly. "Those people in Chasiang said that two days ago a stranger came into town. His arms and legs were badly scratched. They said he was the cook hired by a foreign vessel sailing from Chaozhou. The ship met a storm near Vele Rete Rocks and sank. About ten people from the ship rowed day and night to get to South Bay, but when they got there, they were killed by Puppet Savages. The cook survived, and he walked until he reached Bayaken, where people found him. . . ."

"Wait a second. How many foreigners were killed?"

"They said that more than ten people were killed, but I don't know how many of them were foreigners. Do foreigners really have red hair?"

Mia ignored Butterfly's question. "If all this is true, foreigners and foreign vessels will be here soon."

"How do you know, Big Brother?"

"And among them will be military vessels, not just ordinary freight ships." He paused for a second and then answered Chinya, "Whenever something happens to foreign ships, foreign military vessels come to investigate."

"Have they been here before?" Bunkiet asked. Butterfly and Bunkiet had arrived to live in Sialiao just the previous autumn, and this was all new to them.

Mia tossed a betel nut into a mouth of blackened teeth. He chewed for a while and nodded. "You've never seen foreigners, right? Well, they came to Sialiao for the first time sixteen years ago. It was when I was getting married, so I remember it quite clearly. The shipwreck happened around South Bay. Some of the foreigners were killed by Puppet Savages. Two of them fled to Chasiang, and from there they were sent to Taiwan-fu. A few months later, a cannonball ship came to find the killers. Anyway, this is not the first time the savages have killed foreigners."

Bunkiet cut in, "What do they look like, the foreigners?"

This time Chinya was impatient enough to volunteer an answer. "They are much taller than we are, with a fair complexion and a lot of hair. They have moustaches, and tall and narrow noses." He stopped to laugh. "It's funny, their noses are not round, but down-turned triangles. They are so tall that whenever I look up, I can see their triangular nostrils." He was gesturing profusely, proud and excited to have seen foreigners.

Mia took over, chewing his betel nut as he talked. "They don't nec-essarily have red hair. Some have hair the color of a sparrow's feathers, and foreigners from different places all look quite different. I have seen foreigners with very dark skin.

"The foreign chief who impressed me most has been here twice. The first time was nine years ago, when he came to look for some foreigners who he believed were being held captive by raw savages. But the second time, this was three years ago, he seemed to be here for fun. The chief's name is Swinhoe,[1] and the second time he spent a night here with several of his men. During that visit he asked us about a ship, but the shipwreck was far from here. In my opinion, he showed more interest in birdwatching and sightseeing than in finding foreigners. He said he wanted to see our leader, but Father was away. He wanted me to find him some local guides."

Now it was Mia who was getting excited. "We set out before daybreak. Three followers of his, who were foreign sailors, all had guns with them. Their guns were much better than our muskets. They didn't need to light them, and they could shoot continuously. The two other guides were a Hokkien guy from Chasiang and a Hakka man from New Street. We looked around Chasiang, and then Swinhoe said he wanted to see the inland savage tribes. We walked along the Sialiao River valley and up into the mountains. I have never seen anyone so interested in birds. Whenever he heard a bird chirping, he would stop to look for it. He sketched a bird whenever he saw one. Just a few strokes, and the bird looked real.

"We walked all the way up to Bayaken, to the savages' tribe. He kept asking questions, like, why do we carry weapons with us all the time? I remember he referred to the Hokkien guys in Chasiang as Chinese. But he called the Hakka people Hakka people. He knew that Hokkien people and Hakka people do not speak the same language and don't often intermarry. He also asked how much rent the Hakka had to pay the raw savages for their crops, whether the Hakka people

---

[1] Robert Swinhoe (1836–1877), an English naturalist who worked for a time as a consul on the island of Taiwan.

got along with raw savages, whether Hakka people ever married us *tushengzi*,[2] and whether they married raw savages. He looked around, asking all sorts of questions. He asked about whatever came into his mind. He was particularly interested in sketching. Whatever he drew looked like the real thing. It was like I said, just a few strokes, and things came alive. Very impressive.

"When we reached Bayaken he kept on sketching—people, houses, crops, and utensils. He was extremely interested in how the raw savage women dressed themselves. He sketched a lot of them, but he sketched only a few men."

Mia withdrew a dagger from his bag, saying triumphantly, "He gave this knife to me. It is beautiful and sharp."

Bunkiet and Butterfly were completely engrossed in what he was saying. Butterfly said, "You seem to have a pretty good impression of the foreigners."

Mia nodded. "Well, Swinhoe at least gave me a good impression. Foreigners are quite kind, as well as generous. Every time they come here, we get something. And those who come here to take shelter from the storm or to find supplies are also friendly. Humph, they are better than those Hokkien guys in Chasiang, that's for sure."

6

William A. Pickering whistled as he approached the British consulate in Takao. Consul Charles Carroll had summoned him from Prefectural City (present-day Tainan) to attend the meeting. Being called for by name, he thought as he whistled yet more loudly—it was almost as if he was competing with the birds—surely meant the

---

[2] Literally, "native born kids," referring to the half-blood offspring of Peppos (plains indigenous peoples) and Hokkien immigrants. Le Gendre used the term "hybrids" to refer to them.

consul thought highly of him. However, his good mood was to prove rather short lasting.

The consulate was located inside the building of McPhail & Co., the first Western-style building to be built in Formosa. In the consulate, Pickering noticed a nervous-looking Qing man, whom Carroll introduced to those present as a Cantonese cook called Tok Kwang. He had been one of the crew on the *Rover*, a barque with three masts. The ship was wrecked near South Bay, and Tok Kwang was the sole survivor. According to Tok Kwang, there had been others aboard the ship. Thirteen of them, including Captain Hunt and Mrs. Hunt, had made it ashore, only to be killed by the local savages.

Tok Kwang said he had stayed hidden for hours. Even though his skin was scored by the screw pine leaves and his whole body itched, he dared not move. Only in the full dark of night did he finally leave his hiding place. He moved slowly and with great anxiety until he met a kind-hearted Hokkien guy who took him to Chasiang, where he waited another four days until a ship took him to Takao. He shook his head and shrugged when asked whether there were other survivors.

Pickering dominated the meeting. He was something of a polyglot, and wherever he went he endeavored to learn the local language. In the five or six years since he first came to China, he had mastered Mandarin. In 1863, he requested a transfer to work in Anping Customs House on Formosa. When he arrived, he discovered that what the Qing government called the "savage realm" was in fact inhabited by several tribes of Formosan aborigines. By now he could understand Hokkien along with some of the aboriginal languages. There were so many of them that it was impossible for him to master them all, but with his diplomatic skills, he felt able to navigate the different cultures.

Pickering explained to Carroll what had happened to the many crews shipwrecked in recent years. "Ever since the Peking Treaty was signed in 1860 and the Qing government opened ports to foreign commerce, many more ships have sailed these waters. Last year alone there were seven shipwrecks. The crews of those ships have often been maltreated or even robbed by islanders."

He gave the date of each shipwreck, the name of each ship, the number of sailors involved, and a summary of what had happened; he conveyed the information in laconic detail, as if reporting business accounts. "Twelve. A record high. Fortunately there was a survivor. Otherwise, this tragic accident may very well have remained untold."

Pickering had spent time as a sailor, and he grew visibly agitated as he said to the whole room, "Each time we negotiate with Qing mandarins, we impress upon them the importance of not allowing their citizens to commit such vicious atrocities. And though they offer us their word, these tragedies happen again and again." He thumped the table. "This time, the Qing government *must* do something!"

This was Carroll's first time dealing with a shipwreck. He smiled faintly. "There is perhaps something good to be found in the midst of this terrible news. Word has just now come from Canton that the *Rover* did not belong to us. Rather, it was an American ship. As the United States has not stationed any diplomats in Formosa, we ought to follow regular diplomatic practice. We should inform the Qing officials in Taiwan-fu and then present our report to Rutherford Alcock, our minister in Peking. He will then inform his American counterpart, Anson Burlingame. We should let the American diplomats themselves negotiate with the Qing government."

Before the meeting ended, Dr. Patrick Manson, the Takao customs doctor, posed a question. "Since the cook was able to escape, could it be that there remain other survivors, but they have simply gotten lost? Or perhaps not all the sailors were killed? Maybe some were taken captive by savages?"

Pickering exhaled loudly and said, "Such things have happened in the past. If there are hostages, we should pay their ransom, even though it was not a ship belonging to Great Britain. I suggest that we send a vessel to search near the shipwreck site to determine if there are other survivors."

Carroll agreed, and he ordered that a ship be sent to South Bay. The *Cormorant*, anchored in Anping Port, would take up the mission.

7

Le Gendre put away the documents he had been examining and got up from his desk. He walked to the window, breathing deeply the fresh air of the islet Gulangyu off the coast of Amoy. The morning's light threw long shadows across his room; everything felt good. For too long, he had been deprived of energy and sunlight.

He had spent the night before conducting research. He read about the Tientsin and Peking Treaties, and he read about shipwrecks in China. He came to understand the manner in which the Qing government negotiated with Western countries. Afterward he spent another two hours in deliberation, considering how best to deal with the *Rover* Incident.

Le Gendre felt a great force summoning him. He had read the history of Formosa, an island with a once-glorious past. For thirty-seven years in the mid-seventeenth century, Formosa was the hub of Dutch settlements in the Orient—the place where the Dutch made some of their greatest fortunes. He had read that, at that time, Formosa had been known in Europe for its abundant products and attractive landscapes. He was taken by what he saw as certain parallels between the history of this so-called "beautiful island" and his own adoptive nation: the Dutch had landed on both places in 1624; both were countries of immigrants; and a great expanse of each belonged to indigenous populations. He wondered what else might be shared between the two countries.

The man who eventually defeated the Dutch, driving them away and changing the island's name to Taiwan, was Koxinga. He had based himself in Amoy, and Gulangyu, where Le Gendre's consulate was situated, was the very place where Koxinga trained his navy.

Le Gendre looked out to the east. He thought of Koxinga and imagined him looking out at the same sea, strategizing for an impending invasion. Le Gendre could not see Formosa, but he knew that it lay directly across from Amoy, and he longed almost physically to be there.

3

ORPHANS OF MIXED BLOOD

8

Neither Butterfly nor Bunkiet knew much of their father's history. They knew nothing of his background in mainland China, his family over there, or the reason for his coming to Formosa. All they knew was that, some twenty years ago, their father boarded a boat and crossed the Black Water Channel.

Immigrants from Canton mostly gathered in Poliac, but for years their father, whose surname was Lim, stayed in Sialiao. The first job he found was as a hired hand for the village chief, Yang Zhuqing. This man, known as Bamboo Yang, was Mia's father. Mia was about twelve years old when Lim arrived in Formosa. Although Lim was eight years older than Mia, they got along well and often spent time together.

A few years later, Lim had saved enough money to set off on his own. He opened a small shop in Chasiang, but the business wasn't profitable, and he was forced to close it. He left Chasiang and went upstream along the Liangkiau River to Tongling Bo, where the slopes of the Puppet Mountains were reflected beautifully on the river's surface. Beyond Tongling Bo lay the territory of Botan raw savages. They were feared by some, but in truth they got along fairly harmoniously with the Hakka people in Tongling Bo, as the two groups' hunting grounds were delineated with a known and rarely crossed border.

Lim, like most Hakka people in Tongling Bo, made a living by farming and hunting. Boars, muntjacs, deer, and pheasants all lived close by, so the profession was a natural choice. He carried live animals, hides, and food to sell in Chasiang. People began to call him Lim Mountain Products after the provenance of his wares, a name he merrily accepted.

Once he had sold his items, he would buy clothes, ironware, tools, salt, gunpowder, and weapons from other Han people, which he then sold to the raw savages of the Botan tribe. Lim was diligent, capable, and amiable. The mountain foods he sold were fresh and delicious, and the goods inexpensive.

Ordinarily, when raw savages wanted to buy things from Hokkien merchants, they had to travel long distances to meet them. Lim, however, would take raw savages' orders and carry the goods up the mountain to the tribe. He cheated neither Han people nor savages. Hokkien guys, Hakka people, Peppos, and Puppet Savages: everybody liked him.

At first, Lim did business with the raw savages living in the mid-Liangkiau River area. But he was soon so well-liked that people from farther downstream—Seqalu tribes such as Ling-nuang, Baya, Sabaree, and Tuillassock—placed orders with him. They called him "Honest Lim."

At some point, Lim got married to a pretty girl, who wore flowers on her head and dressed like a raw savage. Nobody knew where she had come from, and Lim never mentioned it himself. When people asked, he just smiled. It was sometimes said that she was a princess, but those familiar with the customs of raw savages were skeptical, knowing that the tribes stuck to a rigid social hierarchy. What they did know was that after Lim got married, he almost never went to the four tribes of Seqalu. He did business solely in the mid-Liangkiau area.

Lim and his wife had four babies, but only two survived, a girl and a boy. Lim named his girl Tiab-moi, a Hakka name meaning "sister butterfly," after the butterflies he loved so much. He had not received a good education, but he hoped his little boy could be strengthened by knowledge, so he named him Bunkiet, meaning "brilliant scholar." Before Bunkiet turned eight, Lim began teaching him how to read and write. Bunkiet was smart; he studied diligently, perhaps to live up to his name. At all times he carried the books, pages yellowing, that his father had brought from mainland China.

Anyone, if they were asked, would say that Lim worked without rest to support his family. However, tragedy makes a habit of calling unexpected.

Early one morning, after the previous night's typhoon-brought rain had unexpectedly stopped, Lim left with Bunkiet to go hunting. Despite his insistence that Bunkiet be literate and numerate, Lim maintained that hunting be an integral part of his son's education. For all his father's encouragement, Bunkiet seemed more interested in studying than hunting, but on this morning he followed his father out of their home without complaining.

After the rain, the air in the valley was particularly fragrant, and everywhere there were butterflies; this region was host to a great diversity of species. Appropriately—considering her name—Butterfly was fond of these creatures. Swallowtails beguiled with their charming colors, but the small butterflies flying in swarms were her favorite. When they were near her, she felt as if she had become one of their number.

"Butterfly," her mother said, "the bamboo must be thriving after all this rain. Let's go out to get some."

Butterfly's mouth watered. The bamboo shoots her mother cooked were so good; the whole family loved them.

Outside, butterflies filled the air like airborne flowers. It would be wonderful to watch them while picking bamboo shoots, Butterfly thought as she walked, carrying a basket on her back, humming to herself popular Hakka folk songs.

The green bamboo shoots had indeed emerged from the soil; their tips remained wet with beading dew, which looked crystalline in the early morning sunlight. Her mother took out a knife and began working. Butterfly followed her example, but she had yet to master the technique. "Don't worry. Take your time." Her mother stretched an arm into the undergrowth and then screamed.

Butterfly was bending to pick up her knife when it happened. She snapped around to see a green snake—or perhaps it was brown—about as long as a forearm, slinking away into the grove. Her mother's wrist was punctured with two marks. Red oozed.

"Damn it!" Her mother cursed, but she looked unpanicked. "I should have been more careful. I think it was a bamboo viper."

"A bamboo viper?" Butterfly repeated. The words hurt with disturbing implications. "Aren't they venomous?"

Her mother wiped her wrist and then began to suck fiercely at the wound. She turned sideways to spit out a mouthful of bloody saliva. Butterfly looked at her but said nothing.

"Don't worry. Let's go home. A bamboo viper won't kill me." She forced a smile, but it seemed clear that she was now only pretending to be calm.

The short walk back seemed lengthened today; neither mother nor daughter spoke as they made their way through the forest.

When they were home, her mother picked some leaves from a varnish tree, rubbed them together, and then placed them on the wound. Butterfly found a cloth with which to dress her mother's wrist. Her mother seemed exhausted; she fell asleep as soon as she lay down. Butterfly sat by the bed, apprehension rising. After a while, blood appeared on the bandage as a slowly expanding stain.

Darkness fell, and her father and brother were nowhere to be seen.

It was time to cook dinner. Her mother had regained consciousness but was still half asleep. Butterfly peeled the bamboo shoots and cut them into small pieces. She made a soup, cooked millet, cut some salted pork, and poured a small glass of millet wine.

These were her mother's favorites, but today she wouldn't eat; she felt only thirst and the cold. Finally she forced herself to sit up for some hot soup. When she was finished, she poured the millet wine onto the cloth and pressed the damp rag against her wound.

She said that she needed to use the toilet, so Butterfly gave her an arm and they walked there together. Her urine was dyed pink with blood. Her mother trembled; Butterfly sank into panic. Even though their nearest neighbor was not far away, she dared not leave her mother alone. All she could do was chant the Buddhist mantra *Namo Amitabha* and ask the Goddess of Mercy for her blessings. Once she was back in bed, Butterfly's mother pointed at the floor, repeating, "Bamboo basket . . . Bamboo basket . . ."

Eventually, Butterfly realized that she was referring to a basket that was kept underneath the bed. She bent down to take it out, and her mother gestured for her to open it. Inside were an elegantly woven shawl and a necklace made with dazzling glazed beads of various colors. Butterfly remembered her mother wearing the shawl and necklace once a long time ago. Back then, her mother had smiled radiantly, but now her lips were pinched thin; she asked Butterfly to put the things on.

After Butterfly obliged, her mother forced a grin. She had something to say, but she coughed through the words until blood patterned the floor. Sweat flecked on her forehead. She closed her eyes and seemed short of breath. Butterfly's father and brother were still not home, and she knew that they would now have to wait until tomorrow to come back. Her mother seemed to have fallen asleep. Butterfly, exhausted, soon joined her.

She dreamed that her father and brother had captured a Formosan clouded leopard and were almost back home when, through an
act of negligence, they let the animal escape; soon, everybody was
screaming. She woke from the nightmare's peak to find day broken
and her mother strangely still. When she touched her mother's hand,
it was icy cold. She was suddenly overcome by a limitless fear, but
she found no voice with which to cry out. All she could do was sit by
the bed, tears streaming, mumbling, "*Mom, Mom . . .*"

Her father and brother arrived home just as the sun was reaching its full force. They draped themselves over the body and cried.
It had occurred to Butterfly that it might be rude of her to be wearing
her mother's shawl and necklace, and her father was indeed surprised, but he said, "If Mom wanted you to be dressed like this, then
you did right to do as she said."

Lim buried his wife according to raw savage customs. Butterfly
combed her mother's hair, wrapped it in a headscarf, tucked betel
seeds into the folds, and then bent her mother's limbs into the
required crouching position. She swathed the body in white cloth,
leaving the head exposed, and they buried her in a corner of the
house. Butterfly kept the necklace but put the shawl in a basket in
the grave. Lim said they needed to make sure her head faced Big Puppet Mountain, because that was where her ancestral spirits resided.
He broke down as he admitted that he had been unable to keep so
many of the promises he had made to his wife, but then he pulled
the grief back inside and stood looking in silence at Butterfly. He
clapped once, knelt on the ground, and used his hands to fill in the
hole with soil. Afterward, he covered it with a piece of slate.

Butterfly's instinct told her that her mother's shawl must have
originally belonged to a chief's family, for it was very well-made.
At home, they spoke Hokkien, Hakka, and "raw savage" languages
in a mix-and-match way. Ever since she was little, Butterfly had
known that her father was a Hakka man from mainland China and
that her mother came from a raw savage tribe in the mountains.

But Lim and his wife had never told the children which tribe was hers; neither had they mentioned anything about her family. Sometimes, when he was in a good mood, Lim would jokingly call his wife a "savage woman," and at such moments she would label him a "con man." Butterfly and Bunkiet never really understood these interactions, but neither parent was ever annoyed by the names.

After the burial, Butterfly found the courage to ask, "Which tribe did Mom come from?" Lim was about to answer, but then he went quiet. Finally he said, "Wait until you and Bunkiet are adults." He walked over to his wife's grave, where he put his hands together and bowed three times. Butterfly did not ask him again.

After their mother's death, their reticent father spoke even less. Butterfly noticed that he would often stare at them as though his mind had gone blank; perhaps everything worth saying had already been said.

At noon on the day of the Dragon Boat Festival, their father prepared rice dumplings wrapped in bamboo leaves to offer to the deities and the ancestors. Though from a savage tribe, their mother had learned many Hakka customs from her husband. She had known how to wrap the rice dumplings, and—like the Han people—she worshiped ancestors, deities, and the Buddha. Lim stressed the importance of these Hakka customs, but he was very respectful of his wife's raw savage practices and never broke their taboos.

In the past, their father would play his bamboo recorder after dinner to accompany their mother's singing, but after she died, they did not know what became of that instrument; their father never again played it. Now, after dinner, they did things on their own. Butterfly did some household chores or needlework. Bunkiet would read or write. Lim dealt with the hunted animals.

Although he had not returned to mainland China in over twenty years, in the months after his wife's death, whenever Lim awoke in the night, he would be thinking of his past. In his hometown, first a drought and then a plague had taken away his parents and brothers. When there was nothing left, he crossed the Black Water Channel to Formosa; those in the boat barely knew each other. In the subsequent decades he had made a life in Taiwan, and he thought he should feel nothing—certainly no yearning—for his homeland. But after years of farming and hunting, he was exhausted. He looked at his worn hands and decided to move back to a thriving town, hoping his son could carry on the scholarly career of his ancestors.

Lim's grandfather had passed the Imperial Civil Examinations at the county level and was ready to serve as a government official. But he had died prematurely, and the whole family had subsequently fallen apart. Who could have imagined that Lim would embrace nostalgia in his old age? He couldn't explain it, and yet the feeling was real.

One evening, the three of them were eating dinner when their father started to talk slowly. "My poor children, you have been in bad hands since your mother died. I want to move. I am old and tired, eager to retire. Bunkiet, you have grown up. There's nothing more I can teach you. You need a proper tutor. I don't want you to work as a pioneer or a hunter like me. You should study and take the Imperial Civil Examinations so that you can grow up to be a government official. Of course, there is no scholar in Tongling Bo. So I want to move to Chasiang, where there are good schools and good teachers."

Although Lim had left Chasiang when he was young, he wanted to give life there another try. He did not have much money, but he believed that he should move for the sake of Bunkiet. Besides, he had many customers in the town.

A couple of sleepless nights then passed for Lim to firmly make up his mind. He asked his two children over breakfast, "Do you still remember old Master Yang? How long has it been since you last saw him?"

"At least two years!" Bunkiet answered, excited at the prospect of a visit.

"Yes, we haven't seen them for a long time," Lim said. "We will visit them this Mid-Autumn Festival. When we move to Chasiang, perhaps we will ask Master Yang for help."

9

After the Dragon Boat Festival came the seventh lunar month—the so-called Ghost Month. During this month, people were particularly wary, as nothing seemed right. Lim had always been a pious man, and throughout every Ghost Month he followed strict rules. He would not venture out before daybreak, and he would always return home before dark. Midway through the month, when the Hungry Ghost Festival took place, he would prepare offerings not only to worship his ancestors but also to comfort the spirits of the many animals he had killed. Although they were not as intelligent as human beings, animals still had spirits, Lim often said, and he felt he owed them something. He would hold a small ritual to redeem their wandering souls so that they could be reborn in the next life, and throughout the month he would consume no meat.

In the corner of his otherwise austere house he had a great worshiping table. Apart from his ancestral tablet, there were three wooden statuettes of deities. These he worshiped at the beginning and the end of each day with incense sticks bought in Chasiang. For their entire lives, Butterfly and Bunkiet had observed their father's religious practices, and they too worshiped their ancestors and showed respect to ghosts and deities.

However, as pious as he was, Lim still encountered the inevitable.

It was the last day of the Ghost Month. Lim set out in the early morning in a good mood. He hoped he could catch a couple of Mikado pheasants to give to Master Yang as a gift. The previous afternoon, he had caught a splendid male pheasant, but the female had escaped. Today, he hoped to make up for the loss.

It was just after the high point of the day when brother and sister heard the hunting dog barking anxiously. They wondered why their father was home so early, but when they looked out the door, they saw him limping, dragging his right leg across the ground.

They ran to help support him. "Damn it!" Their father never cursed, but on this afternoon he swore freely, in great and obvious pain. He had found the female pheasant, but instead of firing his gun he had begun quietly following the bird, wanting to catch it alive. As he got close, when the intensity of prolonged concentration combined with a deep silence to overtake the rest of his faculties, he stepped without looking onto a trap somebody had set in the grove. He almost fainted from the pain, howling as he tore himself free from the grip of the spring-shut jaw. His two children looked down and saw that a big piece of flesh was missing from a foot caked in mud and clotting blood.

The two of them wiped and cleaned the wound, then dressed it with the herbs their father stored in the house. As his pain eased, he said, "Don't worry. Don't worry. A few days of rest and I will be strong again." He struggled to his feet and lit an incense stick to hastily worship the deities before lying back down.

But the wound did not get better. It became red, swollen, and increasingly painful. On the third day, they noticed a yellow pus. After that it became rotten and emitted into the room a putrid smell. Their father began suffering from a fever and soon lost all lucidity. Bunkiet and Butterfly knelt by the bed, chanting Buddhist sutras. On the tenth day, Bunkiet walked to Chasiang to send for a Hokkien folk doctor. The doctor felt Lim's pulse and frowned. He said their father was immensely weakened. He took out a cloth onto which he rubbed a dark ointment; he heated this over the fire and then placed it on the wound. Lim, who had been lying down, sat up and screamed in pain. Afterward, the doctor administered some herbal medicine, telling the two children to give their father one portion in the morning and another in the afternoon. Lim seemed initially to get better, but two days later, he was out of bed less often, and he seldom ate.

Butterfly noticed that her father was urinating only infrequently, and that the color of his urine was becoming darker and darker. His entire body was swollen. His fever refused to subside. His breaths were short. He talked nonsense in his sleep. Bunkiet walked once more to Chasiang to find the doctor, who followed him reluctantly back up the mountain. After looking at Lim, he shook his head and told the two of them, "I'm sorry. Your father is beyond praying for. He is strong, his mind and body are both strong . . . that's why he's lasted till now." He refused their payment, saying that all he could do was bless them and hope for a miracle.

Butterfly's face was wet, and she could not stop sobbing. Bunkiet, however, stood up suddenly and wiped away his tears, forcing his face into a taut expression of resilience. It occurred to him that if his father died, he would be in charge of this family. He was the eldest son. He was a man. His father would not want to see him crying.

After another two days, their father lost the battle to stay conscious. His mouth was agape, and when he breathed, although the muscles on his chest heaved and trembled, his breaths were short and inconsequential. Toward midnight, with a final twitch of his body, his nostrils flared, and then he was still.

After their father died, the two children traveled to Sialiao and brought the single pheasant with them to the Yang family. A few months earlier, old Master Yang had had a stroke; he was still sentient, but he was now paralyzed along one side of his body and spoke with a mouth that blurred most of his words. Mia was put in charge of the family and its business, and he accompanied Butterfly and Bunkiet to Tongling Bo to arrange Lim's funeral. Afterward, Butterfly and Bunkiet moved to Sialiao and began living with the Yang family, just as their father had done when he first arrived in Liangkiau more than twenty years before.

4

IDENTITY REVEALED

10

Dr. Patrick Manson leaned on the side of the *Cormorant*. The ship was soon to set sail for Liangkiau Bay, and the final few items were being carried aboard. He closed his eyes, letting the sea winds pass gently over his cheeks. He cherished Formosa's warm weather, its green mountains and waters, its white clouds and azure skies; it was as if God himself had sent him here.

Two years ago, his eldest brother had gone to Shanghai to work at its customs office. Manson had originally intended to join him in Shanghai after graduating from the University of Aberdeen, but Dr. James Maxwell, a friend of his father's, had persuaded him to go to Formosa instead. Dr. Maxwell had arrived at Taiwan-fu two years earlier; he was the first Western doctor and Christian minister to come to the island since the Dutch withdrew in 1662. To him, Formosa was as beautiful as it was unique. It possessed multiple intriguing cultures, and there were pristine, untouched pieces of nature existing alongside cities with deep cultural legacies. James Maxwell's first year, however, had not gone smoothly. The Hokkien people in Taiwan-fu were quite hostile toward Western medicine and Christianity, so he left to establish a hospital at Chihou Port in Takao.

Although the Qing government had established customs houses in the ports open to foreign commerce, there were but a few Chinese professionals qualified to serve as customs officers. Therefore, the government turned over the management to Europeans and Americans. From that point onward, the number of Western professionals working in trade, finance, and medicine—as well as missionaries—increased greatly.

By the time Manson arrived, the British consulate had relocated from Tamsui to Takao, so he worked in the Customs Service of Formosa in Takao, where he was in charge of quarantine.

As for Maxwell, he took to proselytizing in Takao, so in addition to providing his services at Takao Customs, Manson found himself managing Maxwell's hospital in Chihou.

In Manson's eyes, Formosa was a biological paradise, with an abundance of beautiful flora and fauna. He enjoyed the island's warm sunshine as well as the delight to be had in seeing and treating patients. In the course of his work he encountered numerous diseases not described by British medical textbooks, and he came to understand that many were caused by tropical parasites. Indeed, in the Orient there was a great variety of creatures and pathogens that people in the West had never seen.

These were what fascinated him. Unlike Maxwell, Manson cared little for preaching. His focus was on medicine, especially in the emergent field of parasitology, and Formosa was an ideal location for this kind of research. A magnifying glass accompanied him always, and with it he would examine patients' feces, blood, body fluid, and tissue in search of parasites and their eggs. He recorded what he found assiduously, establishing the parasites' life cycles and their impacts on the human body. Maxwell joked—prophetically, as it would turn out—that someday Manson would have many parasites named after him, just like Swinhoe with all those birds.

As the *Cormorant* was about to set off from Takao, Pickering ran aboard the ship in a great hurry, telling Consul Carroll that something had gone terribly wrong in McPhail & Co., and he would consequently be unable to join them on their journey south. Carroll was annoyed to be losing the company of the renowned Formosa expert, but there was little he could do to keep Pickering on deck.

As the vessel moved out of the harbor, Captain George D. Broad of the *Cormorant* looked up at Saracen's Head and Ape Hill, two mountains that protected the port, and marveled at the great natural blessings bestowed upon Formosa.[1] He told Carroll that he had traveled all over the world, but rarely had he seen such a naturally perfect port as Takao.

The vessel passed by a large heart-shaped rock. Here the water was shallow, and they steered the vessel cautiously. "See? The port is protected by high mountains on both sides, and with this rock," Broad pointed as he spoke, "no enemy vessels can easily enter. As for the harbor Anping, which was built by the Dutch, I hear that so much mud and sand has been deposited there that it will soon go out of service."

Carroll looked at the shuffling sails in the harbor and at the green fields on the land. He sighed. "In the future, Takao will undoubtedly become a diamond of Formosa. And Formosa will be a precious gem in Asia. How fortunate the Qing government is to have such a beautiful island!"

Manson could not agree with him more.

As the *Cormorant* sailed south, Manson was thrilled to have the rare opportunity to observe the western coast of Formosa up close. The vessel made swift progress, and soon they saw a wide estuary.

---

[1] The two mountains are present-day Qihou Hill and Shoushan in Kaohsiung City.

Manson said, "Dr. Maxwell told me that up the river is Lakuri, which is home to the savages. The landscape there, he said, exceeds description."

"Whenever Pickering talks to me about what he sees in the savage tribes," Carroll replied, "he becomes highly enthusiastic. But something has always puzzled me. He hates the Chinese, but he likes tamed savages and raw savages. He tells me that the Chinese are self-conceited liars and cheats, but the savages are kindhearted and straightforward. Perhaps I would grant him tamed savages, but raw savages? Aren't they ferocious cannibals only too inclined to sever heads from shoulders? Those who killed the *Rover*'s sailors, aren't they raw savages?"

Manson shrugged. "Maxwell does not have a good impression of the Chinese either. The Chinese have thousands of years of their own beliefs and medical practices, and they reject our religion and medicine. But in my opinion, we must grant that the East and the West each have their own cultures and moral systems. And anyway, our firms teach the Chinese to smoke opium, while we ourselves outlaw the practice. Now that is a sly and wicked trick!"

Carroll smiled and said nothing in reply.

After the Tangkang River, the vessel passed a large settlement. From his map, Manson determined that it was Tangkang, a town with five thousand residents. Over an hour later, he saw another large town. Manson looked again at his map, then told Broad, "This is Ponglee, the southernmost Qing post."

Soon another estuary came into sight. Manson yelled in excitement, "This must be the estuary of the Shiwen Creek. Pickering told me that Tjaquvuquvulj lies to the south of here. That tribe defeated even the Dutch. You know, it's fascinating. Pickering said the aborigines in Formosa live in tribes, but they have a social system similar to that of a kingdom. Various tribes pay taxes to the chief. And do you know what else? I think it was Swinhoe who said that Hokkien and Hakka farmers here also have to submit five percent of their crops to the chief of Tjaquvuquvulj."

"Yes," Carroll said, "the Qing Imperial Court regards the territory south of Chalatong as the realm of savages. Qing citizens are not supposed to go beyond the pass there, and the raw savages are not permitted to enter the pass either. The notion is that they live separately, without bothering each other."

Captain Broad, who had come to Formosa for the first time, asked, "So this place is not within Qing territory?"

Manson answered, "The Qing government does not extend its rule over raw savages. Although the savages combined are in possession of a great deal of land, they are divided into hundreds of tribes that live individually, like the city states in ancient Greece. Most tribes have just two or three thousand people, and the smaller ones have fewer than a hundred."

Broad laughed dismissively. "The city states of ancient Greece reappear as raw savages' society in Formosa. How perfectly amusing!"

The vessel continued south, and before long they came across another estuary. Manson spoke mostly to himself now while he stared at the map. "This must be Hongkang River and Hongkang Village."

Their Hokkien interpreter explained, "Hongkang means wind harbor. When the winds grow strong, fishing boats can take shelter here. This estuary splits Upper Liangkiau from Lower Liangkiau. Upper Liangkiau, from Shiwen River to Hongkang River, belongs to Tjaquvuquvulj. The tribes of Acedas and Uwaljudj are called the 'Lionhead' tribal group, named after that mountain."

Manson looked to where the interpreter was pointing. From this angle, the mountain did indeed look like a crouching lion leaning against the sea.

"Lower Liangkiau," the interpreter continued, "which is south of the Hongkang River, is home to the eighteen tribes of Lower

Liangkiau. But most people never bother to tell them apart. They just call them 'Puppet Savages.'"

The mountains, which earlier in the journey had disappeared into the clouds, were smaller here as they approached the shore. The seaside plain was quite narrow, and some of the crags dropped directly into the water, forming sheer cliff faces.

Eventually the *Cormorant* came to a bay with a small mountain head stretching a little way into the water. This mountain was labeled as Turtle Hill on Manson's map, and its peak was no more than 100 meters above sea level; nevertheless, it formed an effective natural shield for the bay.

Captain Broad shouted, loud enough that all aboard could hear, "Here we are, Liangkiau Bay!"

Manson saw two rivers feeding into the sea. He figured one was the Liangkiau River and the one farther south, quite close to Turtle Hill, was Sialiao Creek.

Broad turned to Carroll. "We can anchor the ship either in the north or in the south."

"Then let us follow in Swinhoe's footsteps and berth the vessel to the south, in the estuary of the Sialiao Creek."

It was approaching noon. The sun bore down upon the ship, heating its deck to a scorching temperature. Manson started to sweat. At the foot of Turtle Hill, the Sialiao settlement could clearly be seen. Although Sialiao and the nearby Chasiang were close to each other, Manson noted that many of the houses in Chasiang were made of bricks and roofing tiles, whereas most of the houses in Sialiao were made of bamboo and had thatched roofs.

On the shore stood several Peppos wearing headscarves and skirtlike pants. This was the first time Manson had seen a Formosan aboriginal tribe; they appeared quite different from the Hokkien villagers with whom he was familiar.

This was it, the remote Lower Liangkiau; excitement and thrill flamed in Manson's heart.

11

Barely ten days have passed, and this time they come in a cannonball ship, Mia thought as he looked at the approaching *Cormorant. In the past, they waited for months before coming to look for their own people.*

Mia had broadcast his expectation of the foreigners' arrival throughout the village, and he and his neighbors had taken to gathering by the shore whenever they saw a foreign ship coming from the north. They were quite familiar with the Union Jack, because ships carrying this flag had moored in Liangkiau Bay on several occasions. Sometimes they stopped merely to fetch fresh water, but they had fully disembarked three or four times. Whenever they landed, they would bring gifts. The items were not many, but they were novel to the villagers, so most people looked forward to each arrival of a foreign vessel.

As the ship neared, residents of Sialiao stood on the shore and waved enthusiastically. Those on deck waved back; they were dressed in a uniform of navy-blue shirts with double buttons and white pants. Standing next to them was someone dressed like a Hokkien man; when the ship came nearer, the villagers could see he wore his hair in a Qing queue—the front half of his head was shaved, and a braid dangled at the back.

When the ship had moored, four sailor soldiers carrying guns got off, followed by the Hokkien interpreter. Mia approached them, reaching out his hands to show hospitality. Four or five finely dressed foreigners then disembarked in single file. The interpreter spoke loudly. "Listen up! This time, foreign government officials have come to seek your assistance."

Mia instructed Butterfly and a couple of young women in the village to offer the foreigners water, towels, and some fruit. He said to the interpreter, "You must be tired. Please, make yourself at home." The foreign soldiers stared at the wood-cutting knives carried by the villagers. Their hands gripped tightly to their rifles.

Mia noticed this and smiled. "Please, tell these honorable officers that we carry knives to use as tools. There is nothing to worry about."

The interpreter turned around and said something to a middle-aged gentleman with a stubbly chin, who appeared to be the leader of this group. The gentleman nodded and smiled, and the soldiers relaxed.

The interpreter spoke again. "This honorable gentleman is the highest-ranking government official assigned by Great Britain stationed in Formosa."

Mia bowed deeply, then spoke to the official in English. "Sir, my name is Mia Yang. You can call me Mia. I have met Mr. Swinhoe before."

The foreigner seemed surprised to hear English; he reached out to shake Mia's hand, and his tone became quite friendly. "I am Carroll, consul from Great Britain. That is to say, I oversee almost everything related to British people here in Formosa."

Carroll then recovered his stately composure and spoke seriously, with the Hokkien interpreter translating for the assembled crowd. "A vessel with a Star-Spangled Banner was wrecked near here. About ten foreign sailors were killed by raw savages. Do you know anything about this?"

The crowd had no idea about what a Star-Spangled Banner was, so the interpreter took some time to explain to them that foreigners came from several countries, and that Great Britain was the strongest among them. America, whose ships carried the Star-Spangled Banner, was another country quite far away from Britain.

Mia answered, "About ten days ago, a cook from that ship escaped to Chasiang. We heard that people there sent him back to Takao." He paused. "I am the son of the village chief. I speak on behalf of our village. We had nothing to do with it."

Carroll took out a document, and the interpreter announced loudly, "We seek help from the people in Liangkiau. If there are survivors and you report this fact to us, we will reward you handsomely.

You will also be rewarded if you help us find the remains of the sailors or their personal effects.

"But I warn you, do not think lightly of Great Britain. If anyone has robbed the bodies of those shipwrecked sailors, the foreign official will certainly bring them to justice, relentlessly."

Mia replied, "We haven't seen any foreign vessel or foreign people. No outsiders have shown up here."

Carroll chimed in, "Then please send word to the raw savages. This will be your reward." He took out a heavy bag—from within sounded the clattering of metal—and gave it to the interpreter, who in turn offered it to Mia. Mia, however, hesitated. After a moment's deliberation, he said, "Your honor, we had nothing to do with the shipwrecked crew's slaughter. The raw savages in the south coast are to blame. But we haven't had any direct contact with them."

Carroll asked, "Which raw savage tribes live along the coastline?"

"Down south there are three raw savage tribes, Ling-nuang, Koalut, and Tuillassock. But, as I said, we have no contact with them, and we don't know which tribe killed the sailors."

"Tell us more about those raw savage tribes by the sea."

"Of course, sir. We people living here in Sialiao are mostly *tushengzi*, or half-breed aborigines. From here, heading south along the coastline are some hills with just a few inhabitants. The southernmost tip is Tossupong. A long time ago this was a Hokkien settlement. Some Peppos live there, and some Hakka people have moved there recently. Beyond Tossupong is the realm of the raw savages. Close to Tossupong is Ling-nuang, and then Koalut. To the northeast is Tuillassock. In Ling-nuang, some Hakka and Peppos mix with raw savages, so we sometimes deal with them. As for Koalut, which is farther east, it is truly a tribe of raw savages. They are quite hostile, and few outsiders dare to venture into their territory.

"Ling-nuang, Tuillassock, the inland Baya, and Sabaree, together they are called 'Seqalu.' People say they moved here several generations back from northeastern Puyuma. The chief of Tuillassock is their Big Head Chief, the leader of all four tribes. Koalut does not belong to Seqalu, but they are in close contact with them."

Captain Broad asked, "By the seaside, there is a high mountain with a peculiar shape, and a big rock lies in the sea. Which tribe lives there?"

"The coast there is mostly rocky, and there are many big rocks in the sea. The mountain with a peculiar shape may be Turtle Nose Mountain. That mountain is in Koalut, not far away from Ling-nuang. Tuillassock is also by the coast. But it is beyond Turtle Nose Mountain, quite far from here. As for Baya and Sabaree, they do not face the sea."

Carroll said, "It doesn't matter. Please send word to Ling-nuang and Koalut and announce to them what I have said on behalf of Great Britain."

"It will not be hard to send word to Ling-nuang and Tuillassock," Mia replied, "but I have no confidence in my ability to deliver a message to Koalut. They are often aggressive to people from outside their tribe. My feeling is that they might be responsible for the recent killings, but I am not sure."

Carroll said, "We will give you ample time to communicate with them."

The interpreter handed the bag of coins to Mia, who accepted it reluctantly, knowing that he could not reject it a second time.

The brief meeting appeared to be over. Carroll was walking away with the others when he turned around and asked, "You mentioned a 'Big Head Chief' of those raw savages. Is his name Tauketok?"

"Sir, you know Tauketok?" Mia said, surprise affecting his voice.

"I read the record Swinhoe kept of his time here. He mentioned Tauketok as a leader in Lower Liangkiau and identified him as the one with the greatest authority. You should send word to Tauketok. Surely he can command Koalut?"

At that point, a moan floated out from inside a nearby house. The British men looked concerned.

"That is my nephew, Red Cedar. He was bitten while out hunting boar and, alas, has had a fever since the day before yesterday," Mia said, sounding somewhat embarrassed.

A good-looking gentleman who stood by Carroll suddenly spoke in Hokkien. "I am a doctor. Can I see him?"

Carroll smiled. "Oh, how lucky you are! This is Dr. Manson. He treats patients in Takao. Dr. Manson is an excellent doctor. Everyone speaks highly of him."

Mia concurred. "Yes, how lucky indeed to be treated by a foreign doctor. This way, please."

As they were ducking through the entrance, Carroll mentioned, "Our doctors from Europe are very good. I once read a book that claimed that Koxinga, after sustaining an injury in Amoy, sent for a Dutch doctor to treat his wounds."

To Manson's surprise, it was quite cool inside the house. The furniture—the bed, table, chairs, shelves—was all made of bamboo. The patient lay coiled on a bed in the corner of the room. Outside, a crowd gathered and waited with interest, never before having seen a foreign doctor treat a patient.

Manson checked the wound, which took up much of the man's calf. The entire appendage was swollen, and the cut itself was an angry red. Pus discharged as a mixture of blood and another fluid. The stench of infection thickened the air.

Those inside the room covered their noses and kept at a distance. Carroll and Broad quickly left the house. Only the young lady who had served them tea upon entry remained standing by Dr. Manson's side.

"Good. Lady, please help me."

Manson took out a metal box from his suitcase. "Please, how may I address you?" He took out the tools and spread them evenly on a small tray.

"You can call me Butterfly."

"Good, Butterfly. Now get me a basin of water. Hot, if possible."

Butterfly, like the other villagers, was astonished that this doctor spoke Hokkien. Nevertheless, she readied the water.

From his suitcase, Manson took out a piece of round-belly glassware. He removed the cap; the mouth of the bottle was stopped by a rag of burned yellow cloth. He then produced a second bottle, which contained a transparent liquid that he decanted into the first piece of glassware. Butterfly recoiled at the smell.

Manson smiled. "This is alcohol."

He lit the burner and held his tools in the flame one by one. Afterward he arranged them into some kind of order and then took out a section of thin fine white cloth; this he dipped in hot water and then began using it to wipe the leg very carefully.

The wound seemed to grow as the doctor cleared it of blood and scab and pus. Butterfly joined the others and covered her nose with a folded arm; only the doctor seemed entirely unaffected by the smell. The patient, Red Cedar, had been trying to remain quiet, but he cried out as Dr. Manson used a small pair of scissors to cut pieces of rotten flesh from the wound. After cleaning the wound several times, Manson found some yellow pus still oozing from one corner, where the flesh was especially red and swollen. He paused for a moment before asking Butterfly to take out a small knife from the metal box. He held the blade on the flame for a long time and then used the knife to cut into the corner of the wound. He pressed firmly on the flesh and a large amount of pus and blood burst forth. Butterfly exclaimed, but Red Cedar seemed relieved.

As Butterfly watched the doctor continue to deal with the wound, she remembered her father's groaning in the days before his death. His wound was not dissimilar to Red Cedar's. But back then, the two of them, Butterfly and Bunkiet, knew nothing of cleansing or disinfection. All they could do was apply herbal paste. Neither did the Hokkien doctor from Chasiang know any of this. Butterfly looked at the foreign doctor: needle and stitches moved fluently through his hands; sweat gathered on his forehead, but he didn't wipe it dry.

Dr. Manson sighed deeply. He put some yellow ointment on the wound, covered it with gauze, and then said, "Done!" He smiled at Butterfly, thanking her in Hokkien.

It was Butterfly's first encounter with Western medicine, and she was indescribably impressed.

Butterfly followed Dr. Manson out of the house. Mia, Chinya, and some important figures in the village were discussing things with Carroll, the Hokkien interpreter, and Captain Broad. The Hokkien interpreter was making lavish use of body language to help convey the messages, but all involved looked strained. Butterfly saw Bunkiet in the crowd, so she asked her brother what had happened.

"The foreign vessel will sail to South Bay to find those ship-wrecked sailors. The white chief hopes that someone from Sialiao, someone who can speak both Hokkien and the raw savage language, will serve as an interpreter. But nobody is willing to take the job. We're worried we'll misunderstand the savages, and we're afraid that once we get on the whites' ship, we may not be able to return to Sialiao. The white chief promises that they'll send the interpreter back, but nobody trusts him."

The foreigners kept talking, and the Hokkien interpreter kept interpreting, but it looked from his expressions like he did not quite understand the conversation. Captain Broad became impatient, saying angrily, "Perhaps it would be better to take one with a gun pointed at him." Carroll glared, and the captain was quiet.

Mia did not know what to do. He was growing anxious. Suppose nobody was willing to go? He would have to either appoint someone or get on the ship himself.

But then came Butterfly's voice. "Mr. Interpreter, please tell these ministers that I am fluent in both Hokkien and the language of raw savages, and that I am willing to serve as an interpreter, only on one condition." She met Dr. Manson's gaze and pointed at him. "I want this doctor to be my teacher. I want to learn his medicine."

People reacted with shock and conversation. Bunkiet widened his eyes, looking at his elder sister in disbelief. Manson did not need the interpreter to clarify what Butterfly had said. He was surprised, but he smiled broadly as he responded, "Young lady, do you wish to return with me to Takao? In that case, welcome!" The other foreigners, however, did not appear so happy at that prospect.

After a moment's consideration, Mia decided that Butterfly was indeed the best choice. She was quite fluent in the raw savages' language, and she could speak both Hokkien and Hakka. Moreover, Dr. Manson seemed a decent person; he could ensure her safety.

After all was agreed, Butterfly, sensing his unease, said to her brother, "Bunkiet, I witnessed this doctor treat Red Cedar's wound. If we had been able to do what he did, perhaps Father would be alive now. Trust me. Give me some time. I can learn from him, and I will be able to save many lives. When I finish learning, I'll come back here. And even before then, I'll try to come back at least once a month."

She finished talking, and there was a pause before finally Bunkiet nodded in agreement, his eyes welling with tears. It was only when Butterfly turned to walk toward the ship that he cried out, "Take care!"

12

When the ship had sailed out of sight, Mia held a meeting at his house. Everybody sat in a circle, but Bunkiet crouched in a corner alone, his eyes red.

Mia gestured outside to where the ship had been moored. "I really don't want to get involved in their dispute."

"Can't we just leave them alone? I guess it was done by the savages in Koalut."

Mia shook the bag of coins and said, "But we accepted this, so we can't just leave the matter be. And anyway, Butterfly is on their vessel. They've already sailed south and will arrive at Koalut before dark. If we don't warn the raw savages, they will be in great trouble. The foreigners seem really offended this time. And if Koalut decides to blame us, especially if we don't tell them about all of this, we'll be in great trouble, too."

"But didn't the white chief want us to send a message to Big Head Chief? Why not just let him spread the news to Ling-nuang and Koalut?" Chinya suggested.

"We don't have time for that," someone answered. "It's more sensible to go to Koalut directly than to go to Tuillassock."

The circle nodded and made sounds of general agreement. "Quite right. All that we are responsible for is the sending of the message. As for the life or death of those raw savages, that's not any of our business!"

Someone burst into laughter.

Chinya agreed. "As long as they are informed of the situation, we will have done our part."

Mia was about to speak when Bunkiet's voice came from beyond the circle. "I will go to Ling-nuang and Koalut."

Everybody turned to look at him. Mia wondered what had happened to the two of them. Sister and brother had each acted unexpectedly today.

Bunkiet looked angry as he got to his feet. "If we don't tell people in Ling-nuang and Koalut as soon as possible, many will die once the whites start attacking them. If any savages are injured or killed by the whites, they will blame my sister, and they will also blame people in Sialiao for not telling them about the attack in advance. They will hate us for it." Mia and then Chinya nodded as Bunkiet spoke.

"We don't want to anger the whites," suggested Chinya, "but we don't want to offend any raw savages, either."

One member of the circle laughed. "Sialiao is by the sea. How could raw savages come here to fight us? Perhaps Bunkiet is still too young to think things through?"

Bunkiet, undeterred, replied, "No. If the raw savages hold a grudge against us, and that grudge causes them to kill any Hokkien or Hakka people, then those deaths will be our fault."

"Bunkiet is right." Mia spoke authoritatively. "We cannot allow disaster to befall the raw savages, even though it is true that they were the aggressors and acted first.

"We will send two groups of three people. The first group will go all the way to Koalut. They must get to Ling-nuang as soon as possible. The people living there should be able to inform the savages in Koalut quickly.

"The second group will inform Tauketok in Tuillassock. Though they are not as pressed for time as the first group, they too will need to walk through the night to get to Big Head Chief as soon as possible.

"Bunkiet. It is brave of you to volunteer, but you are not a fast walker, so you are not suited for the first group. Instead, you will go to Tuillassock to inform Big Head Chief."

Mia assigned people their roles. The first group would be headed by Pineapple; they set out immediately. Those who were bound for Tuillassock would be led by Chinya. Before leaving, Chinya hesitated a little and asked, "If Big Head Chief is not available, or if he doesn't want to see us, what can we do?"

Mia thought for a minute and said, "Hurry first to Sabaree. It is on the way to Tuillassock. The chief there is Isa, Second Head Chief of Seqalu. He is related to Tauketok. I remember our father met him once in Poliac. He must have heard of the village chief of Sialiao. Whatever the situation, he should be able to make some arrangements for you to see Tauketok."

13

Chinya, Bunkiet, and Melon left Sialiao to hurry south. In the beginning the land was quite flat, and the wide streets were lined with an abundance of flowers, lush plants, and trees. Ox carts occasionally passed them. The homes of Peppos, as well as new settlements and farmhouses, could be seen everywhere. Evidently new settlers were migrating south from Sialiao and New Street in increasing numbers.

The three of them walked so fast that they reached Monkey Cave (present-day Hengchun) within two hours. They then turned east to enter the domain of Seqalu. Here were mountains, and the road soon narrowed. It kept rising but remained smooth. As they walked uphill, they spotted animals in the valley far below, and the rustle of unseen creatures in the shrubbery by their feet let them know that more were nearby. Birds too were everywhere, singing a splendid natural chorus.

Twilight approached. They rushed on until they came to a clearing, at the edge of which stood a wooden watchtower. The roof was low, but some figures could be sighted in the fading light. This, they presumed, was a Sabaree tribal lookout post. They waved at the figures, signifying that they had come in goodwill. A guard climbed down and approached. He carried a musket and was clearly on edge. "Where do you come from? What do you want?" Bunkiet noticed another warrior in the post looking down at them.

The three from Sialiao raised their arms to show that besides their knives, they carried no weapons. Bunkiet was the most fluent in the language of raw savages, so it was he who spoke. "We are from Sialiao. We have something important to tell your chief."

The guard loosened his posture. "What's wrong?"

"Did you hear that some foreign sailors were killed around here?"

"That was people from Koalut. It had nothing to do with us."

"At noon today, a foreign ship came to Sialiao to find out what had happened. There were cannons on it. We saw them with our own eyes."

The guard sneered. "Cannons? Then go tell Koalut's chief. What does this have to do with us?"

"If those people were killed by Koalut people, then the whites will take their revenge using those cannons. There will be a great number of casualties. Don't you have any relatives or friends in Koalut?"

The guard thought for a while. "Follow me."

They were led through a place where the forest was a tangle from root to sky. Bamboo houses were scattered here and there. Deeper in the woods, the houses were arranged in an orderly circle. In the center was a field where flowers and fruit grew. Surrounding the houses was a circle of bamboo trees acting as a natural shield. Through the middle cut a main road, wide enough for ox carts and livestock to pass side by side. Wandering freely throughout the village were several chickens. Children played and climbed trees. The guard told them the chief's house was right in the center. Bunkiet thought, *This village is impressive. Does it really belong to raw savages?* The buildings were at least as good as those built in Sialiao.

Chinya sighed, his relief audible. "We've made it to Sabaree. Our mission is half done!"

14

Isa, chief of Sabaree, was standing in front of Chinya, Bunkiet, and Melon. "Thank you for coming all this way to tell us." He turned to his people. "Koalut is in great trouble. Although we have disagreements with Payarin, Red-Hairs are our common enemies. We can't let people in Koalut think we look on without caring."

"Chief," said Bunkiet, "I didn't say they were Red-Hairs."

Isa cut back, "All foreigners are Red-Hairs."

Bunkiet kept his mouth shut.

Isa gave an order and then, just as night fell, a group of warriors rushed off to Koalut.

It was about the same distance from Sabaree to Koalut as it was from Monkey Cave to Sabaree, but the route involved the crossing of several hills. Sabaree warriors could walk as fast along mountain trails as they could on flat land. However, the only trail was meandering, and it would therefore take some time to get to Koalut.

Back at the village, Isa was talking. "They should get there in the middle of the night. But at that time Koalut may think we are launching an attack. We have some signals for communication. Hopefully it all goes to plan.

"It's quite late now. There's no hurry to interrupt Big Head Chief. Let's relax and drink some millet wine. We will set out at daybreak tomorrow. Tuillassock is just a couple of hours from here."

Chinya thanked him.

Isa continued, "We will ride in an ox cart. I want to bring some gifts for Big Head Chief."

He turned to Bunkiet. "Young man, aren't you from Sialiao? How can you speak our Seqalu language so fluently?"

Chinya laughed and said, "Chief, he does not belong to Sialiao. His father was a Hakka man, and his mother came from a tribe, so he is quite good at both languages. After his parents passed away, he moved to Sialiao with his sister."

Isa was interested. "So which tribe did your *yina* belong to?"

"I don't know."

Isa eyed him up and down; he spotted Bunkiet's knife. "Let me see that."

Bunkiet removed the knife from his waist and showed it to Isa. Isa inspected the wooden handle; it was carved into the shape of a snake.

He looked grave and serious. "Has this knife always belonged to your family?"

"It belonged to my mother. Then when my father died, I inherited it."

Isa raised his head and said slowly, "I spent a whole day carving the head of this viper. Of about a dozen knives I carved, this was my favorite. I could never forget its pattern. When I married Saliling, we gave three knives to Tuillassock as a part of the wedding gifts." His face grew red, and his voice became hoarse. "Are you Honest Lim's son? Are you the son of Honest Lim and Majuka?"

Bunkiet nodded.

Isa threw the knife to the ground. He turned to the guard who had shown them in. "Amo, for Big Head Chief's sake, give them a place to sleep tonight. But send them away when there is light tomorrow."

"Aye!" And Amo took them to another house.

The atmosphere had changed so suddenly that the three of them did not know what to do. It was clear that Isa hated Bunkiet's father, but Bunkiet had no idea why; his parents rarely spoke of the past.

The sky held a crescent moon whose light barely touched the earth. Chinya dared not ask Bunkiet anything. Truthfully, it changed little; the three of them were determined to leave for Tuillassock as scheduled. They had to try their luck, with or without Isa's company.

Long after his companions had fallen asleep, Bunkiet remained deep in thought. His mother was called Majuka? He had never heard of Saliling, and he did not know whether his mother was related to her. Bunkiet's father had occasionally called his wife "savage woman," but mostly he called her "Aniang" or "mother" in Hakka. Butterfly and Bunkiet had known from early on that she came from a savage tribe, but they did not know which was hers. It seemed clear that she was closely related to Tuillassock, but much else was still unknown.

Bunkiet tossed and turned, feeling sure that day would break before he found any rest. But he did, eventually, drift off to sleep.

15

At dawn, the three of them got up quietly. They were ready to move on from the previous night's strange turn, and it was a surprise to all when Amo came in, gave them some breakfast, and said cheerfully, "Isa has decided after all to take you to Tuillassock. Just wait here a while."

Isa showed up as they were eating. He did not look angry, but neither did he appear cheerful. Slowly he started to talk. "Last night I thought it through. Our generation's feud need not be passed down to you. Furthermore, for you to have come all this way to tell us, it must be an arrangement of the ancestral spirits. You seem to know nothing of the past. And since your parents are no longer alive, let's allow it to pass."

Bunkiet did not know anything about the feud, but he lowered his head in gratitude.

Isa continued, "It really is virtuous of you to have come such a long way for the sake of Seqalu. I cannot hold a grudge against you. In any case, I will take you all to Tuillassock. Amo, did you get the ox cart ready?"

Amo nodded.

Isa patted Bunkiet, a clear fondness developing. "So you really don't know where you came from? Honest Lim and Majuka must have kept it from you to save Seqalu's face. Well, I will tell you what happened when we are on our way to Tuillassock. In fact, Tauketok is your uncle. Yes, it must be the ancestral spirits' blessing for you to come back to your tribe."

As the cart moved leisurely along the trail out of Sabaree, Isa looked at Bunkiet closely. "How lucky for you that you look like Majuka and not like Honest Lim; otherwise Big Head Chief wouldn't believe my story."

"My sister has a necklace left behind by my mother. Is it related to Tuillassock?"

Isa smiled. "If I see it, I will know. How many brothers and sisters do you have?"

"Just one sister. She's older than I and looks more like my father."

Isa became serious. "Now you need to know the family history of your mother. We are a part of Seqalu. A few generations ago, our ancestors moved first south and then west to this area, where we divided into four tribes.

"The chief of Tuillassock is Big Head Chief. We Mamaliu in Sabaree have Second Head Chief. Chalingjilu in Baya is Third Head Chief. And Rofaniao in Ling-nuang is Fourth Head Chief. In Tuillassock, Big Head Chief traditionally comes from the Garuljigulj family. According to Seqalu customs, noble people of the four families get married to each other. Women from Big Head Chief's family are unlikely to marry ordinary men, not to mention Hokkien or Hakka men. It was unimaginable for Majuka, a princess, to get married to your father, a *nana*. When that happened, everything was thrown out of order.

"At that time, the Big Head Chief of Tuillassock was Tauketok's elder brother, Paljaljaus. My father was our chief of Sabaree. He had had two sons and one daughter. I am the eldest, and Lalakang is my younger brother.

"That year, I married Princess Saliling from Tuillassock. To celebrate our wedding, my father led all of us in the tribe to bring betrothal gifts. Tauketok was the elder brother of Saliling and Majuka. Back then, he was not yet Big Head Chief."

Isa sighed. "Over twenty years ago, that knife was part of the betrothal gifts. As I told you yesterday, I carved its handle myself.

"Our wedding ceremony was completed, and then the two tribes sang and danced. Paljaljaus presented an impressive feast, and a large swing was on the grass. Only on a princess's wedding day can people play on a swing. The ritual started, and the bride took first turn. Majuka and other girls from both tribes surrounded the swing. I and several other men stood in the center. The female shaman announced each of the betrothal gifts and then handed them to the bride's family. We sang songs and took turns pushing the bride higher and higher, demonstrating our never-ending love and the seamless cooperation of the two tribes. The bride held on tightly. The higher the swing went, the higher our spirits were raised. It was a perfect marriage. That day, Majuka's enchanting smile, her figure, her elegant movements . . . she charmed Lalakang."

Isa looked ahead, as if reliving that day.

"Some two hundred people danced around the bonfire. Two big boars were grilled. There was endless millet wine for the guests to enjoy. Lalakang could not take his eyes off Majuka. She wore canna flowers and wild lilies on her head. When she danced, sometimes she swirled like a snake, sometimes she hopped like a sika deer. She stood out in the crowd, more attractive even than her sister, the bride.

"To attract Majuka's attention, Lalakang performed a dance that simulated fighting with a boar. He circled, turned, and charged. Everybody agreed that his performance was outstanding.

"Although the two families had yet to discuss it, after the wedding dance, many people believed that the next couple to wed would be Lalakang and Majuka.

"A guest from the plains also attended the wedding. Tuillassock had ordered many items, wine and pastries and the like, from your father, Honest Lim. Those were the things that plains settlers prepared for their weddings. And Sabaree too had ordered things, like red cloth, mirrors, combs, buttons, sewing needles, and cosmetics. Those were to be used as betrothal gifts. For the two weeks preceding the ceremony, Lim had frequently traveled to Tuillassock. The bride happily chose from what he carried to the tribe—a privilege that belonged to her alone. Her sister could only look on.

"But Honest Lim must have noticed how much she envied her elder sister for having things common to plains settlers, and he seemed able to read Majuka's mind, knowing which items she favored and giving them to her in private. He must have made quiet advances when helping her fasten a bracelet, or when telling her how to wear perfumed powder. When Majuka was dancing, some people noticed that she exchanged longing looks with Honest Lim.

"I later found out that after the wedding, Honest Lim came to Tuillassock whenever possible, but he did not enter the tribe. Instead, he and Majuka met at a secret place in the valley, where they embraced and did things lovers do. I think what attracted Majuka to Honest Lim was not the gifts he brought her, but the way those gifts showed her the immense outside world. She must have wished that someday Honest Lim would take her there. He once gave her a china vase with an imprint of a beautiful blue landscape. She was fascinated with the pattern on the vase's glossy surface. She always preferred colorful pottery and porcelain to the carvings typical of her tribe."

Bunkiet mused. "No wonder Mom sometimes called Dad a 'liar' or a 'con man,' even if it was in an affectionate way. Poor Mom! As I was growing up, all she did was work. She didn't have much of a chance to see the big world outside. During the New Year, we visited Chasiang or Poliac. That was all she got."

Isa made a small noise of acknowledgment and then went on with his story.

"Later, Lalakang began visiting Majuka at Tuillassock. Mostly he brought with him whatever he had hunted. It would be unfair to say Majuka did not like these gifts, but to her they were nothing new. She must have been aware that he liked her, and she was always polite to him, but she felt no passion.

"She was a sister of Seqalu's Big Head Chief. As you know, Seqalu noble people marry other noble people. Some of the Hakka bachelors had married Seqalu women, but they were ordinary people and not from noble families. Even so, those women were scorned by their tribes. She and Honest Lim. . . . Alas! That was a coupling beyond imagination. If she even raised the idea of marrying him, well, there would have been much uproar. Besides, she knew her Big Head Chief brother held Lalakang in high regard.

"For his part, Lalakang was a straightforward man, but he could not reach Majuka's heart. Nevertheless, he presumed, perhaps naïvely, that Majuka would marry him.

"Anyway, more and more plains settlers were coming to Sabaree to farm the land. Little by little, they encroached on our hunting ground and our remote farming lands. Those plains settlers were mostly Hakka males. As payment for the land, some of those Hakka farmers would give some of their harvested crops to the chief. Still, conflicts were not unheard of.

"As far as we in the tribes were concerned, neither *painan*[2] nor *nana* were to be trusted. Most of the tribes in the high mountains have some taboos about animal carcasses. Seqalu is no exception. Dogs are our loyal friends. Hakka people, however, love to eat them as medicine, and they often set traps to capture our dogs. Afterward, they might discard the remains in a Seqalu field. Because of the taboo, we must then give up our land, which soon is occupied by the settlers. Naturally, when this happens we become enraged and sometimes attack the *painan* and the *nana*. For this, they hate us. However, Honest Lim was an exception in all this mess. He was indeed an honest man, and besides, we liked the goods he sold."

One afternoon, all those years ago, Isa revealed to Paljaljaus and Tauketok, Majuka's two elder brothers, that Lalakang wished to marry their sister. Big Head Chief of Tuillassock was pleased and said he looked forward to the day that their families were even more closely related. They spent the evening drinking together in celebration.

---

[2] Taiwan's indigenous peoples called Hokkien immigrants *painan*, which means "bad guy" in Hokkien. They used *nana* to refer to Hakka males.

It was almost noon the next day when Lalakang awoke and left his house to find the guests already gone. Again he drank for much of the day with his friends. When he returned home it was dusk, and the corpse of a wild cat was hanging on a tree across from his house. He was horrified. Not only was this his favorite jambu tree, but it was heavy with ripening fruit.[3] He had intended to pick some to give to Majuka. But now, with the dead cat, who would dare eat the fruit? This tree was as good as destroyed. Whenever he stepped out of the house, he would think of the cat hanging there. Terrible! Of all the jambu trees, this one was the biggest and bore the sweetest fruit. They offered its fruit for worshiping during the Five-Year Festival. To choose this one. . . .

A Hakka man had recently settled in the creek valley. Lalakang had seen him farming. He had not stopped him, nor had he asked for any rent. He wanted nothing to do with him, but he hoped that they could live alongside each other in peace. He never expected that this new neighbor would be so brutal as to force him to give up his best jambu tree; perhaps he hoped to steal the land.

Lalakang's anger soared without any possibility of restraint and soon, hunting knife in hand, he was crossing the valley to the small hut, shouting as he approached, "*Nana*, get out. You will never see sundown here again."

It didn't occur to Lalakang that the Hakka man would fire at him until a bullet hit his calf. He shrieked and attempted to charge at the Hakka hut, but greater even than his rage was the pain that rang from his leg, a long echo of the gun's bang. He stumbled and fell to the ground.

The Hakka farmer rushed out of the house and ran toward Lalakang, holding a heavy-looking hoe high above his head. Lalakang, propped up on one knee, blocked the attack with his hunting knife,

---

[3] Jambu, also known as wax apple, bell fruit, water cherry, or champoo, was introduced to Formosa by the Dutch in the seventeenth century.

but the hoe hit his left shoulder. Injured for a second time, he was in grave danger.

Lalakang let go of his knife and whipped the man onto the ground by grabbing his ankles. The Hakka farmer flailed and lost his hoe. The two men wrestled for a while on the ground before finding themselves fighting in the shallow creek. Lalakang came close to drowning as the Hakka farmer pressed his face into the water. His free right hand scrambled around until it found a heavy stone. Somehow, as his breath faded, he leveraged the few available angles to smash the rock against the Hakka farmer's skull. The body above his went limp and dropped.

Lalakang struggled to get up, lightheaded and close to fainting, his blood escaping into the water. He blinked heavily, swaying, taking note of the fallen Hakka man at his feet, and staggered out of the creek, where he retrieved his knife and returned to stab it into the man several times. With this final gust of energy, he lurched over to the bank and collapsed. The next day, some men from his tribe found him and carried him home.

That evening, as Lalakang was fighting, the warriors of Tuillassock hunted a boar, and the whole tribe gathered around a bonfire to eat grilled meat and rice cooked in bamboo tubes. Big Head Chief Paljaljaus—who was seated at a table with his younger siblings Tauketok and Majuka—was known for his propensity to drink. After finishing a few cups, he leaned over and said to his sister, "Once the Five-Year Festival is over, we will need to prepare for your wedding with Lalakang."

Majuka answered grimly, "Who said I want to marry Lalakang? And anyway, he has not proposed."

Paljaljaus sneered, his eyes red and unfocused, "That can be settled easily. Lalakang often visits you, right? Next time, give him a hint."

"I don't want to marry Lalakang!" Majuka shouted, breathing heavily.

Paljaljaus jumped up. "How dare you!"

Tauketok knew there had to be a reason for the uncommon strength of Majuka's reaction. "Brother, don't get angry. As for you, Majuka, you shouldn't behave like this. Anyway, it's quite late, and we are all tired. Let's talk about this tomorrow."

He took Majuka by the hand and led her out.

"Tell me, Majuka. What's going on?"

"Brother . . ." Tears shimmered in Majuka's eyes. "I don't *dislike* Lalakang, but I can't say I *like* him, either!"

"Just now you said he didn't propose. Well, this is only partially true."

"How so?" Majuka's bewilderment was obvious.

"Yesterday, while we were in Sabaree, they proposed the marriage, but they haven't yet come to our tribe to make it known."

"Big Head Chief has already said yes?"

Tauketok nodded.

Majuka lowered her head and began to cry silently.

Tauketok patted her on the shoulder. "Majuka, are you in love with someone else?"

Majuka nodded.

"Which warrior? Tell me. It doesn't matter if he is not a nobleman. Perhaps I can talk to Big Head Chief for you."

"I can't tell you. You will be furious."

"Speak it out. I promise I won't get angry."

"What if he's a *nana*?" Majuka whispered.

"A *nana*?" Tauketok almost cried out in disbelief.

He thought for a moment. There were just few Hakka men who came to the tribe. It occurred to him that he had seen Majuka and Honest Lim talking and laughing together several times.

"Honest Lim?"

Majuka's silence said yes.

Tauketok controlled himself and spoke in a biting whisper. "Majuka, they all cheat. *Nana* or *painan*, they are all liars."

"But I love him."

Tauketok was appalled. "Fine. As you wish. But this time, even I won't help you!"

And with that he walked away.

The next day, Majuka was nowhere to be found. Someone said they had seen a girl who looked a lot like her near Monkey Cave, but they couldn't be sure. Tauketok discovered she had left, taking with her only a few pieces of clothing, some small gifts he had given to her, and a necklace from her deceased mother. According to her friends, she had recently finished weaving a beautiful shawl that she said she would use at her wedding.

Big Head Chief Paljaljaus had just decided to keep Majuka's departure a secret when he was informed that Lalakang had been seriously injured.

Lalakang's calf bone was broken, and he soon developed a high fever, but he survived. He lay in bed for two months before he was well enough to walk, and even after he fully recovered, he limped and could no longer run. The tendon in his left shoulder was permanently wrenched; he could barely control his bow to shoot an arrow. It was such a horrible blow.

Rumors started. Some said Majuka rejected the marriage proposal because of Lalakang's injury. Others said that Lalakang could no longer perform a man's duty, so Tuillassock's Big Head Chief was unwilling to marry his sister to Lalakang and had instead hidden her away.

All those in Sabaree, especially Isa and his sister Isi, blamed Tuillassock for not keeping their word. The tie between the two largest tribes in Seqalu was put under a severe strain. Only a few people in the family knew the truth. Tuillassock's elders accompanied Big Head Chief and Tauketok to Sabaree to apologize and explain, bringing with them many gifts.

Half a year later, Paljaljaus quit his position as Big Head Chief and turned it over to Tauketok. Accepting the role, Tauketok vowed to the ancestral spirits that he would someday give it back to Zudjui, Paljaljaus's son.

Although the bond was indeed weakened, little by little, the two tribes recovered.

Isa finished recounting the story. He swallowed hard and then cleared his throat to sing a love song.

My love for you has consumed me;
how I long for your handsome return of my passion.
In the depths of my heart
you are the rainbow across the sky.
No matter where I am,
you are the most beautiful,
but do I have a place in your heart?
Like the toxic fruit on your head
you think nothing of me.

The song moved Bunkiet. Isa explained, "Lalakang sang that all the time. He sang and drank, drank and sang, until eventually that was all he ever did. He hated one Hakka man for taking away his love, and he hated another for taking away his health. He hated them all."

Lalakang had died, disabled and drunk, about ten years after the incident. Even Saliling—Isa's wife, Majuka's sister—had left the world. So much had changed, and those involved in the incident were mostly gone.

Isa sighed. What reasons were there for him to cling to such a timeworn feud?

16

They had reached Tuillassock.

The ox cart turned onto a wide road. Ahead was a hill with a large house at its top. In front of it stood a brawny man who held a bronze sword in his right hand. He looked magnificent.

"We never expected Big Head Chief would greet us in person!" Isa thanked him sincerely.

Chinya was delighted. Bunkiet looked at the hills around them and breathed deeply. The house was located at the highest point of the tribe's land; the view it commanded was beautiful.

Tauketok stared at the three young men dressed like Peppos. He asked Isa, somewhat guardedly, "Who are these men?"

Isa held Tauketok's hand. "I've come all the way to bring them here." He turned to Bunkiet. "This is your uncle."

Tauketok was puzzled. "Whose child is this? How is it that I am his uncle? And who are these other two? Aren't they plains people?"

"Big Head Chief. I have found Majuka's son for you. Doesn't he look good? He is talented and learned as well!"

Tauketok seemed for a while to be incapable of speech. He squinted at Bunkiet. "Are you really Majuka's son?" He inspected him closely. Bunkiet's face was indeed a reproduction of Majuka's, especially the thin, wide lips.

Bunkiet nodded in embarrassment.

Tauketok crouched down. "Ancestral spirits above! Ancestral spirits above!"

He got back up and posed Isa several questions back to back. "How did you meet him? Where's Majuka? Is there evidence that he is really her son? Does she have any other children?"

Isa smiled. "Big Head Chief, there is no hurry. Let him tell you. But we are here today for another reason. A foreign ship has sailed to Koalut and will certainly cause us great trouble. These Peppos say that the foreigners tasked them with informing you of this. Please, tell us what to do."

Once Bunkiet had finished describing how the *Cormorant* had come to Sialiao, Tauketok nodded and said, "I too have heard that Koalut killed some foreign sailors. Payarin was immensely upset that his people killed a woman by mistake."

Isa nodded. "I've heard some strange things are happening to Koalut."

"Is their cannonball ship strong?" Tauketok asked. "Do they know people in Koalut are to blame?"

"When they arrived at Sialiao yesterday, they were not sure. But as they travel south, I guess they will know sooner or later." Bunkiet offered.

"We are afraid of their fury, so . . ."

Tauketok cut Chinya off and turned to Bunkiet. "I will deal with it. What happens to Koalut is our concern. Though they are not a part of Seqalu, we remain closely related. Your aunt, my wife, comes from Koalut. In the meantime, I will take you to see your eldest uncle and aunt, and also your cousins."

He patted the chief's seat. "Isa has probably already told you, but this seat belonged to your eldest uncle. He quit because of the guilt he carried after what happened with your mother."

Chinya tried again, "Big Head Chief, the foreigners' bombs are very destructive. Our chief in Sialiao, my elder brother Mia, he is worried. He wanted us to tell you to take precautions. I hope I've made this clear."

Tauketok sneered disparagingly. "It is indeed wrong for Koalut to kill. But . . . wait a minute. Weren't some of our ancestors also slaughtered by Red-Hairs?" He spat a mouthful of betel nut juice onto the ground.

"Go back to your chief. Tell him we thank him kindly." He stood up and stabbed his sword forcefully into the ground. Isa straightened his shoulders instinctively.

Tauketok smiled. "Last night, Isa, you sent your warriors to inform and aid Koalut. Good! Payarin must have made some preparations. I know them well. If they cannot face the enemy, they will flee. Once they are into the woods, the foreigners won't find them." He smiled. "But still, I will send fast walkers to see what happened."

Isa looked pleased. "My men have instructions for one of them to return to report the situation every half day. In case of an emergency, word should come much sooner. This morning, when I left Sabaree, I told my men to relay all the news to Big Head Chief. We will hear from Koalut by dusk today at the latest."

Tauketok patted Isa, clearly pleased with how the situation had so far been handled. After a little deliberation, he said, "You sent warriors to Koalut. In that case I too will send warriors to Sabaree as backup. They can report to me." He smiled again at Isa. "Okay. This is dealt with. Now we have time to talk about my family affairs."

Bunkiet was impressed with the speed and confidence of this resolution.

Tauketok asked Bunkiet to tell his own story in as much detail as possible, leaving nothing unsaid.

So Bunkiet, starting from his childhood, spoke about his parents, their daily routine, what they did for a living, how his mother was killed by a venomous snake, how his father died from a hunting accident, how he and Butterfly had been living with Mia and Chinya, how the foreign bomb vessel came, and how he volunteered to come to Seqalu. Toward the end, Isa took over and added to the story with vivid descriptions and gestures. It was clear that he was very proud of his having recognized Bunkiet.

After the two of them had finished, Tauketok sat motionless on his chief seat with his eyes closed. He remained silent, appearing composed but for the heaving of his chest. After a long while he stood up, poured himself a big glass of millet wine, and drank it dry. He wiped his mouth and spoke. "I let Majuka down. It was Majuka who sent you back to inform us. She must be worried about her people and their safety." He looked at Isa. "Thank you, Second Head Chief. Thank you for bringing my nephew back to me. Thank you for letting go of the past and accompanying them here. Tuillassock will forever be indebted to you."

Afterward, they saw Isa off, and then Tauketok asked Bunkiet to change into Tuillassock clothes. Seeing Bunkiet dressed in this way, Tauketok couldn't help thinking of his sister. He stood with his back to Bunkiet. "Do you know why your mother hid her name from the world, why she never told anybody that she came from Tuillassock?"

Tauketok walked to a big brown urn placed in the corner of the house. Its opening was quite uneven, as though pieces of it had been deliberately chipped away. Tauketok reached his arm into the urn and withdrew a piece of shattered clay the same color and texture as the urn itself. He told Bunkiet, "When Seqalu women marry, their parents break off a piece of their familial urn and hand it to them, reminding them that they are a part of the family. When you see this urn, it is like seeing our family, the Galu-jiguji family.

"That morning, when Majuka went missing, only I knew why she had run away. I regretted it at once. It took great courage for Majuka to tell me that she wanted to marry Honest Lim instead of Lalakang. I let her down. That night, she must have been lost in despair. Running away was her only choice.

"She took *yina*'s necklace and the shawl she had been weaving. But she didn't take a piece of our urn. She must have thought she was expelled from the Galujiguji family. I believe that's why she never revealed her identity to you. She could not bear to talk about it."

Looking at the piece of urn in his hand, turning it over carefully, Tauketok said, "That first morning, with everything in a mess, the whole tribe went looking for Majuka. I chipped off this piece from the urn and then rushed out, hoping I could catch up with her. I thought it would be best if I could get her back. But if not, I wanted to give her this piece so that she knew she still belonged to our family. I spent the entire day looking, but I found no trace of her anywhere, so I came back here and returned the broken piece to the urn. She never came back to the tribe, but I didn't believe we would be separated forever. And now, now I can never see her again.

"Even your father, he never showed up in Seqalu, perhaps to save our face. Alas! Majuka was so stubborn, as was I back then. But now you are returned. Thanks to Majuka and the ancestral spirits' arrangement, you are back in your mother's tribe." Tauketok looked up to the sky and blinked heavily.

"Come with me." He patted Bunkiet on the shoulder. "I will show you around the tribe. We will meet your elders and your cousins." He turned to Chinya. "As for you, you can go back to your place. Our ancestral spirits have led Bunkiet home. He should stay here for a few more days. Do not worry for his safety. I will get someone to see him back."

Bunkiet agreed. "Go home. I will come back in a few days."

"But I'd feel guilty leaving you here. Maybe Melon can report to Mia."

Tauketok laughed. "Okay. Since you have taken care of Bunkiet, you can stay here. And I would also like for you to meet my niece."

Chinya instructed Melon to return to Sialiao and report to Mia.

Tauketok told Bunkiet, "I have two daughters, no sons. They are several years older than you."

He called his two daughters in to see Bunkiet, then led them all into a house next door. A plump woman stood up. "This is your aunt, wife of Paljaljaus. She comes from Koalut."

When Tauketok told her that they wished to see Paljaljaus, the aunt was evasive, eventually admitting that her husband and son were both already drunk. Tauketok insisted that he would see them, and they soon found the two men. Paljaljaus lay on the floor, sleeping. Zudjui was too drunk to stand; when he saw Tauketok all he could manage was to mumble something incoherent.

"Zudjui, how is it that you are already drunk? It is not yet noon." Tauketok dragged his nephew up off the floor; the young man's head lolled at an unconscious angle. "From now on, you are not to drink until sundown."

It seemed Tauketok had had enough. He returned to his house alone, leaving his daughters to show Bunkiet around the tribe.

17

Back at Sialiao, the *Cormorant* sounded a loud whistle and continued its journey south toward Koalut. Butterfly made her way onto the ship's deck and leaned out over the water to wave good-bye. A few minutes passed, and then Manson approached and began chatting with her. He was not sufficiently fluent in Hokkien to express subtle feelings and thoughts, so he called frequently upon the help of the interpreter. Butterfly never expected she would be talking to a foreign doctor in Hokkien, and neither did Dr. Manson expect that such a clever girl would request that he teach her medicine. Nevertheless, both were cheerful.

Manson asked Butterfly why she wished to learn medicine. She told him about what had happened to her parents and expressed her belief that perhaps, if they had been treated by him, both would still be alive.

Manson was touched. He felt instinctively that Butterfly would be a good student, and he reiterated that he would teach her at his hospital in Takao. He said, "It will take at least a year, and you will have to learn some English. Some medical terms can only be expressed in that language. Hokkien falls short in this regard." Butterfly displayed an interest in learning English, as well as medicine, but she told Manson she wanted to go back to Sialiao occasionally. To this he agreed.

Manson also told Butterfly that, even in Britain, there were but a few women learning how to take care of patients, though things were now starting to change. Manson suggested that one day

Butterfly might travel to London to continue her study of medicine, but to this Butterfly just made a face; such a prospect seemed to her impossible.

About an hour into their journey, they spotted a spectacular mountain ahead, appearing just as the cook from Canton had described. The peak formed a triangle that was unusual for its geometric regularity. Many sailors on deck uttered spontaneous words of admiration; some even took out paper and pencil with which to sketch the mountain. A while later, the *Cormorant* reached the southernmost tip of Formosa. Turning around a cape, they saw South Bay.

All those in possession of binoculars raised them to their eyes and looked toward land. The beach was in parts sandy and in others rocky. Boulders dotted the shoreline. Not far from the beach were hills and mountains that rose to a height of perhaps four hundred meters. By the seaside were trees with distinct trunks and long thorny leaves. These Manson recognized as screw pines, a plant peculiar to the Formosan coast. When the Dutch first came to Formosa, he had read, they mistook the fruit borne by these trees for pineapples. He considered the cook's description—a sail-shaped rock was indeed on the shore—and felt that this surely was close to where raw savages had killed the ship's crew. After they passed a small peninsula, several people cried out. Two small rowboats, worn by sea and salt and wind, lay on the beach. This was it.

The beach was deserted—empty except for the boats. The woods in the distance were quiet. It was late afternoon; the sun shone, and the air was clear.

Captain Broad told Carroll, "If we send a few boats, they will land by five o'clock and still have an hour or so to search before sundown."

Although Carroll respected Captain Broad's military expertise, he expressed some reservations. If the savages initiated a fight, then those on the beach would not be able to make it back to the ship before dark. Furthermore, not being familiar with the land, would they be in increased danger?

Broad said that they should not be afraid of any savages. Besides, hadn't they recently defeated the much more formidable Qing army at Dagukou in Tianjin City? If the savages dared show themselves, the soldiers would make shrewd use of their guns, and they could be backed up by artillery fire from the vessel; the raw savages would be sent running for their lives.

Butterfly was unable to follow the discussion, but she guessed that they were planning to attack. She easily managed to obtain Manson's attention. "Didn't Mr. Carroll want the Sialiao chief to send word to the raw savage tribes? It takes time. Getting there will take at least an afternoon, perhaps even a whole day. I hope you can keep your promise. If you land now, things could easily go wrong!"

Manson thought for a while, then relayed the message to Carroll, who promptly—since the sentiment matched his own—instructed Captain Broad to wait till the next morning. Broad complied, but he was clearly annoyed.

So the Cormorant moored at a distance from the big rock, and Carroll and Broad inspected the land formation, considering how best to land.

Later, Manson leaned on the side of the vessel to watch the sunset. A circle of fire was reflected in the water, bouncing rays of crimson sunlight that returned to beautify the skies. Seagulls flew low, flapping their wings just above the sea's surface, squawking dissonant cacophonies. Though in truth it was the same body of water and the same sun, this was something he had never seen in Aberdeen, where the sea was icy cold, and the sun did not blaze its sunset glory. The mountains by the sea in Scotland were mostly bare; here they were almost impossibly lush. Manson marveled at Formosa, a beautiful island worthy of its name. Yet it appalled him as well, to think of the cannibals living in the mountains. From this angle, the mountain looked even more bizarre. A strange mountain, cannibals, shipwrecking rocks—it all made the sailors uneasy.

18

Butterfly lay awake, unable to sleep. When she volunteered to serve as an interpreter on the vessel, she had not anticipated there being any conflict and had imagined herself helping the foreigners and the tribes to communicate with each other. Perhaps, she thought, shifting her position again on the cot, that was a naïve understanding.

Eventually she admitted that sleep was for the moment impossible, and she moved to sit on the deck, gazing up to the stars, trying to map her own thoughts.

She heard footsteps and turned around to see Manson approaching. "You can't sleep either?"

Butterfly shook her head. She looked around at the ship and then out at the infinite disappearing sea. It all seemed so calm. Being there, on the deck with Manson, she hardly felt able to tell if the world was real or not.

They remained together in silence for some time, him standing behind her, until eventually Butterfly got to her feet and walked away.

Manson sighed wistfully, breathing from an ocean air that no longer registered as salty. "What a beautiful night."

At dawn, Butterfly watched as Captain Broad examined the shore through his binoculars. The previous night, after the sun's final traces had faded, she had looked at the mountains—the forest lost to inky silhouettes—and prayed to the Goddess of Mercy, hoping that the foreigners would not initiate an attack against the raw savages. Manson had consoled her, telling her that the vessel was meant to save the people. After all, he had said, why else would he, a doctor, be on board?

According to Carroll, if there had been any survivors, they would likely now be living in the woods, rather than on the shore or on the beach. The slaughter happened fourteen days ago, and the chances of anyone staying put for that length of time were quite slim—unless, of course, they were too badly hurt to move. He believed that if there were sailors held captive by the raw savages, he could get them back through some form of negotiation. If there were injuries, Manson and the other doctor on board would treat them. If no one had survived, then they would at least bring back the deceased's remains and personal effects.

Broad reported to Carroll that nothing was left behind on the beach except the boats. No human beings could be sighted, but farther along the beach there were seven or eight wild boars. Carroll asked, "Do savages really live on that mountain?"

Broad looked into the mountain's dark green forest—its floor completely invisible—and shrugged his shoulders. "I cannot see clearly, but I would say that nobody could live up there." He smiled arrogantly. "I do hope to meet some raw savages. I'll be sure to bring any we capture on board. . . ."

After breakfast, preparations began for the landing. Broad ordered his men to dispatch three boats. He and Carroll, along with the Hokkien interpreter, were to go on the first boat. The second boat would carry a navy officer, a ship's doctor, and Butterfly. Manson was to travel on the third boat. The first two boats would land, while the third would patrol the waters. Should the enemy attack, the third boat would be ready for relief work. Once they were on the island, if they chanced upon any raw savages, the Hokkien interpreter would translate the English into Hokkien, and then Butterfly would in turn translate Hokkien into the savage tongue, and vice versa, as the conversation dictated. Carroll asked them to speak carefully, stressing that he did not want conflict to arise from misunderstanding. As they approached the shore, Butterfly craned her neck to look for Manson; she found him staring back at her.

It was a hot day. The beach was deserted, and the hills and mountains remained motionless; the world was quiet and still enough that the scene seemed bizarre. The sailors steered their boat cautiously around the black reef and then, when in the shallows, the crew disembarked, ready to move forward.

They had taken about ten steps when a long shot snapped through the air and struck the beach ahead of them, raising a fume of fine sand that lingered for a moment like a heavy gas. Curls of white smoke rose from inside the woods, and then more shots struck the sand. Butterfly, terrified and trembling, immediately squatted down and crunched herself into a tight ball.

The gunshots stopped. After a while those on the beach stood up cautiously; they looked at each other but did not move, waiting instead for a command. Back on the third boat, Manson was also startled; this was the first time he had found himself on a battlefield.

"Damn!" Broad cursed. "How is it that these savages have guns?"

"Let's find shelter. Be careful," said Carroll.

They were still hesitating when another volley of musket fire rained down onto their exposed position. This time, however, the smoke came from a different part of the forest. The British men began their counterattack by firing into the forest. Up close, their guns were so loud that Butterfly dashed backward, trying desperately to get away from the noises; she hid behind a big rock and sobbed, covering her ears with her hands.

The soldiers squinted up into the woods. Carroll knew the odds were against them, as they did not know precisely where the enemies were hiding and were themselves exposed on the beach. Intriguingly, because the shots fell repeatedly on the same patch of sand, he believed they were meant as a warning; if he insisted on pushing forward, many of his men would surely be killed. He waved his hand to signal the retreat.

At first, Butterfly found her legs incapable of supporting her own weight, but she managed somehow to get to the boat. The savages continued to fire. A shot fell not far from Carroll, ricocheting off the side of the boat. Moments later the ship's doctor screamed and began clutching at his arm.

When they were back on the *Cormorant*, Captain Broad raged. How could Great Britain be forced into retreat by a bunch of wild and uncivilizable savages? And they left without even knowing what their enemies looked like! It was a disgrace!

"We need to show them who we are!" Broad snarled.

Two minutes later, the main artillery gun of the *Cormorant* shook the boat and sent a large shell sailing in a beautiful parabolic curve into the side of the mountain. Rock and earth were violently displaced in the explosion. Trees fell. Screams and shrieks of raw savages were heard; perhaps they were hurt. Broad kept snarling, grinning as if gripped by madness. "Again. Blow them all up!"

The second bomb cut the same graceful curve, but upon landing it failed to detonate. Broad appeared sullen.

"That's enough," snapped Carroll.

Butterfly had grown up in a household of hunters, so she was no stranger to gunshots. But hunting was very different from battle. She shivered with worry for the safety of those people on the mountain.

The *Cormorant* changed its course, turning to head back to Takao.

Manson stood on the deck. Yesterday, standing in the same spot, he had been in a particularly good mood, feeling invigorated and ready to treat whichever maladies were presented to him. Not today. It dawned on him that, even though he regarded himself as mostly removed from politics, he could not, as a subject of Great Britain, extricate himself fully from the military dispute.

The ship passed Liangkiau Bay; Sialiao appeared in the distance. Manson thought of the Peppos with their headscarves. They looked so kind, so hospitable. He looked at Butterfly, who was slumped on the deck, and wondered, *They are all Formosans. Will they someday all become our enemies?*

19

In Tuillassock, in the dusk of that same day, Tauketok hosted a simple feast.

When everyone was seated, he said, "This feast is to thank our ancestral spirits and Majuka for returning Bunkiet to us. Majuka and Bunkiet belong to this family again."

Since stepping down as Big Head Chief, Paljaljaus had never interfered with tribal affairs. He just drank all day long. Now he looked at Bunkiet, smiling idly. "Good! Good!"

His four sons were not close with Tauketok; they drank their own wine.

During the feast, someone from Sabaree arrived and reported to them that the Red-Hairs had landed and been defeated at Koalut. The Red-Hairs had shot twice from the vessel as they retreated. Two Koalut men were injured, but not seriously. The whole tribe was overjoyed, and they were ready to celebrate.

The news made Isa stand up and cheer. Chinya and Bunkiet felt relieved. But Tauketok just smiled slightly without saying anything.

Feeling a little awkward, Isa sat down again and scratched his head, but Tauketok patted him on the shoulder and toasted, "It is good, the news about Koalut, it is very good. But I want to thank you properly for bringing back my nephew."

And thus the feasting continued.

Tauketok enjoyed getting up with the sun and sitting by a small pool near his house, where he would meditate while the series of small tumbling waterfalls transported water down the mountain. Sometimes he would stand and call out into the forest.

On the morning after the feast, he sat by the pool for an especially long time, not moving until all the dew had disappeared.

A few days later, after a ceremonial ritual and with the shaman's blessing, Bunkiet had two tattoos inked on his wrists, icons of the Seqalu Head Chief family.

He was now the adopted son of Tauketok.

20

Tauketok brought his newly adopted son to Sabaree to examine the battle's trophy. To get it there, Payarin and his men had dragged the unexploded shell through the forests, over the hills and mountains; to thank Isa for helping them, Koalut was to give the shell to Sabaree.

Payarin was waiting for them on the trail outside the tribe's area; Bunkiet was a little surprised when they met him. Payarin turned out to be a very slight man. He did not look strong at all. He was short, with a small face and a small nose. He wore a crown wreath made of flowers in various colors, with a long hawk's feather in the middle. He moved with a brisk agility, and his eyes shone brightly. His looks and his mannerisms, along with his shrill voice, reminded Bunkiet of the voles that were rampant in the mountains.

As they walked into the village, Payarin could not wait to show off, and he began telling the tale of how he had defeated the Red-Hairs. He said that long before word was sent from Sialiao, he had observed the vessel from a watchtower in the mountain. He was certain that the ship had not come on a goodwill mission. He said it was huge, with thick-barreled cannons. In no time he summoned all the warriors in the tribe, assigning them to various combat positions. Some hid themselves in the woods, others climbed trees.

"At dusk, when the Red-Hairs' vessel showed up, we watched them closely, never breaking focus. The vessel kept circling around at sea, and I judged they must be waiting for the next morning to act. All through the night, we took turns watching, but they didn't once move after dark."

He made a gesture of gratitude to Isa. "Thank you, Second Head Chief. Toward midnight, your warriors came from Sabaree, and each of them carried a musket. That really cheered us up!"

So far, Tauketok had made no response; he continued looking straight ahead as Payarin spoke.

"The next morning, the big ship sent out three boats. Six people landed. I guessed these were forerunners. There had to be at least sixty or seventy sailors on board, and they certainly outnumbered all the warriors in Koalut. I think they must have come on account of those Red-Hairs we killed recently. I was sure that we would be able to kill those six, but to do so would provoke dozens of Red-Hair soldiers to land and attack us. That would be terrible. And there was something strange. Of the six, one was dressed like us and looked like a woman. Last time, as you know, we killed a Red-Hair woman by mistake, so of course this time we were particularly cautious. I ordered my men to shoot at the ground about thirty steps in front of them, just to intimidate them and prevent them from coming any closer. The most important thing was that we should not injure the woman. It was when they fired directly at us that I ordered my men to fight back. One or two Red-Hairs seemed wounded, and they were carried back by their companions."

Still Tauketok refused to make any comment; his cold expression remained fixed.

"The Red-Hairs retreated, but as they went away, they fired the big cannon. It's really amazing that they could shoot the bombs so far, all the way up into the mountain. Really amazing!" Payarin made a face to match his astonishment.

"The first bomb blew up several big trees and set them on fire. A few rocks and plenty of earth fell, and the roots of many big trees were suddenly exposed. Thanks to our ancestral spirits, only one warrior was injured. Another rolled down the hill because of the deafening sound, but both were only slightly hurt.

"Then the Red-Hairs fired a second bomb. Thanks to our ancestral spirits, this one did not blow up. It was quite like nothing! The bomb is as heavy as a boar. We carried it here for Big Head Chief to admire. Ha ha ha!"

Payarin was overtaken by the joy of his own description. Bunkiet stood by, wondering how he could be so talkative. He thought raw savages did not like to talk; his mother hadn't even revealed to her children that she was a Tuillassock princess.

Now Tauketok opened his mouth in reproach. "Why did you kill the foreign sailors?"

Payarin was so startled that he stopped walking. "I thought they were Red-Hair soldiers! We looked down from the mountain and saw two boats coming ashore. How could we know they were survivors of a shipwreck? We thought they were the first boats from the Red-Hairs' army. Our ancestors tell us that Koalut was once attacked by Red-Hairs from the sea. We were almost wiped out. I thought that they were attacking us again!"

Payarin felt stung, and he spoke with words that balanced on the edge of anger. "You people in Tuillassock and Sabaree have never suffered a disaster like that. You cannot understand! And anyway, we asked our ancestral spirits for advice. They said we had done nothing wrong!"

"Okay, but why did you kill that woman?"

Payarin thumped his head with his fist. "We didn't know she was a woman. She was much taller than me, and she was dressed like a sailor. It was only when her head was off that we realized she was a woman. We regret it! After she died, many terrible things happened to Koalut, so we sent for our shaman to pray, to ask for forgiveness. . . ."

Tauketok cut in, "Did the foreigners bring weapons with them?"

Payarin shook and then lowered his head.

"Then you should have held them captive instead of killing them. This time you got lucky, but things are not over yet. Foreigners are different from *painan* or *nana*. Now tell me, will they come again?"

Payarin opened his mouth but found nothing to say.

Tauketok sighed. "Alas! Anyway, it has come to this, and we need to brace ourselves to confront the foreigners. Fortunately, you did not go too far this time, and things have not yet got out of control."

The group entered the village and saw the shell.

Bunkiet marveled, but Big Head Chief remained composed. Though the bomb had been dragged and pushed across hill and mountain, it remained intact, and its surface had been polished into a glowing shine. Bunkiet reached out slowly to touch it. Big Head Chief bent forward a little, his two hands locked together behind his back. "Good, good."

Abruptly, Big Head Chief turned and walked into the woods. He did not stop until he came to a small pool. There he sat down, dipping both of his feet into the water.

Bunkiet and Isa dared not disturb him. Several long moments passed. Without turning his head, Tauketok made a gesture, and they both sat down by his side.

The water in the pool was very cold. Bunkiet shuddered. "Do you want us to do anything?"

Tauketok turned to Isa. "This time, thanks to the blessing of our ancestral spirits, we were lucky."

"Will the foreigners come again?"

"Of course."

The three of them fell silent.

Suddenly, Tauketok jumped up. He bent down to pick up a pebble and then skimmed it across the pool's surface. Bunkiet and Isa applauded.

"Okay, let's figure out how we can win!" Big Head Chief laughed, his pessimism evaporating like water on a hot stone.

"Warriors," he said vehemently, "even a pack of dogs can defeat a boar. Though the foreigners are strong, we still have a chance!

"Isa, we haven't had an assembly for a long time. Let's invite all the tribal chiefs from Lower Liangkiau to celebrate. After all, it isn't every day that we force a foreign ship to retreat. They too can come to see the bomb. Ha ha!"

But as they left the pool, Bunkiet sensed that there remained a little bitterness in Tauketok's laugh.

Tauketok was a determined and accomplished leader; the four tribes in Seqalu respected him and for the most part obeyed his commands. To the north of Seqalu and to the south of Tjaquvuquvulj there were more than ten tribes of all sizes. The most renowned of them was the Botan tribe, which had a large population known for the ferocity of their fighting. They were closely related to Seqalu, but the relationship was not always harmonious. Tauketok was not sure if these tribes would attend the assembly, so after Isa sent out the invitations, he decided to visit them in person, heading first to Mantsui.

Long ago, when the ancestors of Seqalu moved south from Puyuma, they went down along the coast and then headed inland, into the hills and mountains. When they passed by Mantsui, they had a fierce battle with that tribe, which Seqalu eventually won because of their magic. People in Mantsui died in large numbers, and when the corpses decomposed, the smell permeated throughout the entire forest. From then on, people in Mantsui were terrified of Seqalu; even though the two lived close to each other, they did not get along.

People in Mantsui never expected that the Big Head Chief of Seqalu would stoop to visit them with gifts. They were pleased, and quickly agreed to attend the proposed gathering.

Mantsui's chief gave a feast before they left. He saw that Big Head Chief had adopted a Hakka man as his son, and he recognized that Bunkiet was truly a learned young man. At the feast, he told Tauketok, "The world has changed so much! The land is not like what it used to be. It no longer belongs to us alone. It seems we need to learn how to get along with Hakka people and even with Hokkien people."

After he had finished gulping his millet wine, Tauketok took the chief's hand and said, "I agree. I came here to share my experience with you. I too feel that times are changing. Not only do *nana* and *painan* come in great numbers, but foreigners like Red-Hairs may soon arrive. If the Hakka is a mouse that steals from the pantry, and the Hokkien are the boars in the fields that eat the crops, well, the foreign army is a far more horrible demon. It may devour us all. Three hundred years ago, Red-Hairs came to these lands and killed half of our ancestors. The other half were forced to leave their homelands to settle elsewhere. The Red-Hairs left, and then the *nana* came, followed by the *painan*. They took our women, stole our land. But at least we still cling to ancient traditions. However, should foreigners come, it will bring tumult and calamity to us all."

The chief of Mantsui decided then that he would accompany Tauketok to Sihlinge. Tauketok was moved; his gratitude appeared almost beyond expression.

At Sihlinge, the chief there also joined Tauketok.

With the company of the chiefs from both Mantsui and Sihlinge, Tauketok's visits to Kuskus and Botan were stately and impressive. The two tribes greeted him and honored him, and they promised to help form an alliance to unite all the eighteen tribes in the fight against the foreigners. They agreed to attend an "alliance feast," to be held on the next full moon in Sabaree. Kuskus had long been on friendly terms with Botan; the two were the strongest tribes in mid-Liangkiau. With their support, the alliance of all the eighteen tribes in Lower Liangkiau seemed inevitable.

21

For perhaps the first time in tribal history, after the multiplying effects of two shells fired by the British *Cormorant*, all eighteen chiefs from Lower Liangkiau were together in Sabaree.

They sat by a bonfire under a full moon and a clear sky. In front of them were big pieces of boar meat and several vats of millet wine. The fire was at its peak; shadows danced across faces, and light burned inside eyes. Though at first the atmosphere was somewhat cool, as the guests drank, intimacies soon developed. Someone cried out, "Don't be afraid. With millet wine we will have enough spirit to defeat the foreigners!"

Payarin yelled, "Big Head Chief. Your orders are ours to obey."

Tauketok stood up and looked around pointedly. The feast soon gave way to silence. He cleared his throat and then gulped a mouthful of water. "It is true. We must have confidence in ourselves. But we should not act recklessly. We should not attack preemptively. We must stand together. A dog cannot defeat a boar, but ten dogs can hold it to a stalemate. And if there are eighteen dogs, they can wear it out until it is dead from exhaustion."

The chiefs shouted in agreement.

Tauketok continued, "We must stand together, all eighteen tribes. We must form an alliance. Outsiders will know that the eighteen tribes of Lower Liangkiau act as one!

"Long ago, Tjaquvuquvulj defeated the Red-Hairs in this way. Of about a hundred Red-Hairs that entered Tjaquvuquvulj, only three survived.

"If they come, we won't fight immediately. If they fire first, we should stand united. Now, there must be a commander in chief. He will act on our behalf when we encounter people from outside. Among ourselves, however, the tribes will remain what they are."

The chief of Kachilai stood up and said, "Let's have Aruqu, chief of Botan, as our commander."

But Aruqu was quick to pull him back down. "Nonsense! Tauketok will be our commander in chief."

People cheered.

Tauketok raised his hands, "Now we are all here, our courage will burn like the flames of this fire, and our hearts will stand firm like the immovable Turtle Nose Mountain. Thank you all for supporting me. I believe we are blessed by the ancestral spirits. I promise in battle to walk ahead of you, to defend our eighteen tribes, our land, and our glory!" Again everybody cheered, and the shaman offered them cups filled with millet wine. The chiefs joined their arms to drink and then sang at the top of their lungs, their cheering and yelling vibrating throughout the valley.

Bunkiet retreated to a spot beneath a tall monkey bread tree. During the day you could see Turtle Nose Mountain from here. Around him were many meliosma trees; they had blossomed early this year, and their fragrance was hanging like a light mist in the night air.

Not even a month had passed since Bunkiet had first learned that the raw savages had slaughtered the shipwrecked sailors. Back then, he had thought them atrocious and uncivilized, but now he was standing with them, discussing how best to fight off the foreigners, and he could not decide which side was more sensible.

Everything had changed so quickly, and much else continued to change. When he heard Payarin say that of the six people who had landed, one was a young woman dressed like a plains aboriginal, Bunkiet had been sure that that person was his sister; he told Tauketok so in private. "So peculiar! Like mother, like daughter."

He looked over at the eighteen chiefs sitting together. They cheered and drank and cheered and drank. After some time, they started drifting away. The fire had faded, but the fizz of charring wood remained. Bunkiet stared into the night, alone, hoping for an answer to any of his many questions.

22

At that approximate moment, Butterfly was in a place unimaginable to her brother. She was not in Sialiao, nor even in Takao, but in the most prosperous town in Formosa, Taiwan-fu, where the Hokkien elite gathered alongside Qing-dynasty mandarins. It was known also as Prefectural City, or Fu-cheng, and to many people, it exhibited a kind of magnetism. Butterfly was on the outskirts of the city, in the warehouse office of McPhail & Co. in Anping. Manson and Pickering were with her.

Just over twenty days ago, as Manson helped the pale, trembling Butterfly back onto the *Cormorant*, Captain Broad had offered her a hostile glare, looking very much as if he wished to throw her back onto the beach. Manson hurried to take care of his wounded colleague, and Butterfly pulled herself together and worked as Manson's aide.

On the return journey, Captain Broad was frequently overheard by many of those on board, cursing the Formosan raw savages, his unabating rage readily apparent.

At Dagukou, he had defeated the great Qing general Senggerincin, and he had commanded his men to invade Peking as if it were an unguarded city. Now, he had been forced to retreat by raw savages who remained invisible and who used only bows, arrows, and muskets. Such humiliation!

Carroll tried to calm him. They had come not to fight but to save people. And anyway, the shipwrecked vessel was an American ship. They could not justify fighting on Qing territory. "We have done what can be done," he said. "From now on, this is a matter for the United States. When we return to Takao, the consulate will send an official letter to the ministers in Taiwan-fu and Peking. We will request that the Qing government discipline their subjects, especially those raw savages."

Before long, Liangkiau Bay was in sight. Butterfly knew that the *Cormorant* would not stop to moor there, and she swallowed back tears watching the quickly passing Sialiao. Oh, how she missed Bunkiet. She looked up and saw Manson, who told her again that in order for him to better teach her, she would need to understand a little English.

When they arrived at Takao, Manson accommodated Butterfly in a small room at the back of Chihou Hospital. The hospital faced the street, and the backyard extended up a hill. Butterfly was delighted that there were so many trees around, and there were some Hokkien aides and lackeys working at the hospital, so she did not feel too estranged by the new environment.

To begin with, Manson gave her three tasks: first, she had to learn to clean the surroundings, including putting the ward beds and the equipment in order and sterilizing the instruments; second, she was to learn English, not only to listen to and speak but also to read; third, when he treated patients, she was to stand close by to listen and learn.

Butterfly had hoped she would be able to go back to Sialiao for a few days every month, but she soon discovered that there were no ferries serving that route. Freight boats did travel irregularly between Takao and Chasiang, and fortunately these would often accept passengers. As for getting to Sialiao by land, civilians were not allowed through the Chalatong Pass, so she would need to detour through mountain trails.

Manson looked at Butterfly. "You can't walk all the way by yourself!"

"Aren't I half a savage?" Butterfly grinned. "What do I have to be afraid of?"

At the hospital, Manson found Butterfly to be an intelligent girl who learned quickly. Upon arrival, she already understood Hakka, Hokkien, and the Formosan languages spoken by plains aboriginals and mountain tribesmen. To add to that, in just a few weeks she had picked up a few useful English phrases.

One day, Butterfly was putting the utensils in order when Manson ushered in a finely dressed gentleman.

"Come here, Butterfly, and meet Dr. James Maxwell."

Seeing Dr. Maxwell, of whom she had heard so much, Butterfly bowed and offered her greeting in English. "Good afternoon, Sir."

After looking around the hospital, Maxwell told Manson, "Something serious and quite desperate has happened to the Taiwan-fu branch of McPhail & Co. The McPhail brothers risk bankruptcy. That was the reason for my staying there. I wished to see if I could help in any way."

McPhail & Co. was a company established by two brothers, Neil and James McPhail. Neil had once served as British consul, and later as French and then Dutch consul, all the while maintaining a good relationship with the bureaucrats of the Qing Empire. McPhail & Co., as a foreign firm, carried a Chinese name, Tianli, meaning "God-granted profits." Its headquarters was in Takao, and they had a branch office in Taiwan-fu. It was the biggest foreign firm in southern Formosa. Recently, the company had suffered a significant loss when their ship was wrecked near the waters of Penghu. They enlisted the help of Pickering, who had served in Anping customs, hoping that he could revive their business, but things did not go as planned. Barely half a year had passed before an even more serious disaster threatened to destroy the company.

McPhail's most recent crisis was caused when a Hokkien comprador stole tax money intended for the Qing government. Further disaster then struck when the company was charged with embezzlement. The Hokkien comprador took with him his assistants, leaving behind just two local employees. Except for Pickering, nobody could understand the paperwork. The company warehouse was in Anping, but the comprador had lived in Chihkan, near Taiwan-fu's West Gate. Pickering had, therefore, to move frequently between the company warehouse and the comprador's house, while also liaising with the Qing government because he alone could understand both Mandarin and Hokkien. Dealing with this mess was the reason he had been unable to join the *Cormorant*'s expedition.

Soon after the crisis was discovered, the McPhail brothers came to Taiwan-fu. They needed to negotiate with their creditors and were eager to ask other foreign companies for loans. The two brothers and Pickering asked Carroll for help, but all Carroll could do was write a letter to the prefect of Taiwan-fu, imploring him to do his best to capture the comprador and to push back the date by which McPhail was to pay its taxes. Should McPhail go bankrupt, Carroll reasoned, it would do nobody any good.

The prefect of Taiwan-fu promised to delay the payment deadline, but Pickering could not figure out how much money had been lost. He asked Maxwell for help, and then he thought of Manson. But, if Manson moved from Takao to Taiwan-fu, a replacement would be needed for his medical services. Under such circumstances, Maxwell agreed to return to Takao to take care of the hospital, freeing Manson to go to Taiwan-fu to help Pickering.

Despite some initial reservations, Manson felt obligated to agree, since it was his mentor asking him for help. He asked Butterfly to accompany him; he was sure that with her help he could deal with everything more efficiently.

Butterfly had planned to board a freight boat to go back to Chasiang; the ship's owner had suggested a reasonable price. She was so looking forward to seeing Bunkiet and Chinya! Manson's request surprised her.

But, the chance to visit Taiwan-fu was an irresistible temptation. Of all the people she knew in Sialiao, only Mia's father had been there. Even Mia had never set foot in the city. Taiwan-fu had existed for over two hundred years, and the population was said to be one hundred and twenty thousand. Only around five thousand people lived in Chasiang. How incredible! She gave it some thought, then nodded her consent.

The route from Takao to Taiwan-fu carried the heaviest traffic on the island. On a road not especially wide, pedestrians, ox carts, and coaches traveled in both directions, with palanquins among them. Butterfly, Manson, a Hokkien lackey, and a carter sat on an ox cart, looking out at the rice paddies that lined the road; the countless sprouts of lush green bent gently to the breeze.

They spent a night at Arcontien (present-day Gangshan) and then set off again the following morning. At noon they arrived at Taiwan-fu. The South Gate was magnificent. Though Manson had been there several times, he still marveled beneath it. Butterfly was yet more thrilled. Its size, its opulence: spectacular. She thought suddenly of her mother. She had left behind everything to elope with Butterfly's father, hoping to see the outside world, but instead ended up in Tongling Bo. How lucky she herself was; she had been to Chasiang, Takao, and now Taiwan-fu!

On entering the city, they saw straight roads lined with tall buildings. The houses here were spacious, decorated with ornate columns and painted roofs. Butterfly was delighted by their red doors and well-kept gardens. They turned onto a much larger road, and the ox cart struggled up a hill. At the top was a splendid temple; the cart stopped, and they dismounted.

Inside, woody sweetness from burning incense made the air viscous. Butterfly gasped when she saw the flying roof with phoenix tails, and again when she noticed the carved dragon columns; it was all so exquisite. The deity inside held a sword in one hand; one of his feet stepped on a snake, the other on a turtle. Perhaps this was what her father had called the "stance of the magnificent government official," Butterfly thought.

They climbed back into the cart and soon passed another large temple, then a tower said by the carter to have been built by the

Dutch. A little while later he said, "We are entering the Five Channels Zone. This is the city's most prosperous business area."

Butterfly scanned the great variety of food for sale. Restaurants lined the road, their smells fighting desperately for attention.

As they rolled by, Manson commented, "It is said that the snacks here are more than delicious. Let's find something to eat." So they stopped and entered a shop.

There were so many dishes! Butterfly had a hard time choosing from the menu. In the kitchen, a flame leaped out of a wok and climbed toward the ceiling; Butterfly was sure she could feel its heat on her face. Noticing her shock, the carter laughed and said, "It takes great skill to stir-fry eel. Only the best chefs in Taiwan-fu are able to cook it this way!"

The flame subsided and was replaced by a smell that floated over to their table. That helped her make the decision; Butterfly ordered this eel dish. It turned out to be tastier than almost anything else she sampled.

Afterward, they continued on their way through narrow streets until the cart came to a rattling stop in front of a house that appeared unoccupied. Manson stood at the closed door for a while, as if considering his next action. The shopkeeper next door saw him and waved. "Hello, Dr. Manson. It's been long time. How are you? And how is Dr. Maxwell? When will he return to reopen the hospital?"

Manson smiled at the shopkeeper. "Thanks. Dr. Maxwell is busy building a church in Pitau. When he is finished, he will return."

Surprised, Butterfly asked, "Dr. Manson, the people here are very friendly. Why did you close the hospital?"

"Our neighbors *here* are quite friendly, but some scholars and traditional herbalist doctors incited other locals to surround this place. It turned quite unpleasant."

An elderly woman dressed in Chinese-style clothes with a knot of bun-shaped hair approached them. Her feet were small and bound, so she carried a cane and limped unsteadily. "Doctor, you must be Dr. Maxwell's friend. Is Chang with you?"

"Mr. Gao Chang is with Dr. Maxwell, helping him build the church in Pitau."

The woman sighed, "Chang is such a good man, as is Dr. Maxwell. Something went wrong with my grandson's belly last year. He was rolling with pain until Dr. Maxwell cured him."

Here she paused for a second before saying, "Alas, you doctors should just take care of your patients. Why bother telling us to worship Jesus? What's wrong with our ancestors? No wonder they would pull down your sign. Anyway, come, have some food at my son's stand. We have the best angelica duck and fried pork ribs in town."

Manson smiled. "Thank you for your kind offer, but we have already eaten." The woman, however, insisted, and began pulling him by the arm. Afraid that she might trip, Manson walked with her. Butterfly eagerly joined them. "Are the residents here especially hospitable?" she asked with a wink. "Or is it that foreign doctors are very well-liked?"

It was approaching dusk by the time they reached Anping. McPhail & Co. was not far from Zeelandia, the fortress built long ago by the Dutch. Pickering was delighted to see Manson, but the delight seemed to fade once he was introduced to Butterfly.

For the next few days, Manson brought Butterfly with him wherever he went. With the assistance of the two Hokkien employees, he dealt with the affairs of the company. Butterfly had learned to keep books, and she was thrilled to discover her reading ability was improving rapidly.

The McPhail brothers had decided to sell the company. When they thought of the Hokkien comprador who had cheated them, they were dismayed; it was on his account that they were charged with "cheating the government." Now the enterprise they had worked on for more than a decade was over.

Pickering snorted when he heard of the charges. "Humph! No Chinese can be trusted. They are but cunning mice waiting to steal our food."

After working hard for about a week, Manson and Butterfly had finished combing through the terrible bookkeeping and other tedious affairs in McPhail & Co., but Pickering was not having the same luck; the deficit he was managing appeared bottomless. Meanwhile, the Qing government had given them only another five days to clarify the situation. The McPhail brothers despaired. The deadline loomed and all seemed lost, until Pickering strolled into the McPhail & Co. office, crying out, "The savior has come! The savior has come!"

Bewildered, Manson asked, "The savior? What business has Christ in Taiwan-fu?"

Pickering poured and then promptly finished a rather large glass of whiskey. "Consul Le Gendre will arrive in Taiwan-fu the day after tomorrow. And he will stay here in McPhail & Co."

5

REPULSE OF THE FOREIGN FORCES

23

Le Gendre was what one might call a man of action, and he brought his soldierly style with him to the diplomatic stage. On hearing news of the *Cormorant*'s southern expedition, he contacted Henry H. Bell, Commander of the Asiatic Squadron, and secured from him the use of a ship.

On April 8, he boarded the *Ashuelot* and sailed to Foochow, capital of Fukien Province. There he visited Governor-General Wu Tang and Governor Li Futai, two officials who were the direct superiors of the Taiwan *daotai*.[1]

The *Ashuelot* left Foochow on April 10, and two days later it arrived at Tamsui (present-day Danshui), a port in northern Formosa. After he landed, Le Gendre paid a visit to John Dodd, the most famous foreign businessman on the island. On April 15, he visited the island of Penghu. On April 18, he arrived at Taiwan-fu and headed directly to McPhail's.

---

[1] A *daotai* is an intendant in charge of a *dao* or a circuit, an administrative division in the hierarchy of territorial administration. This was the highest-ranking civil official in Taiwan from 1727 to 1885, subordinate to the governor of Fukien Province.

Manson looked closely at this "God-sent savior." Le Gendre was by every measure of medium size, and he spoke with a permanently hoarsened voice. Though his face had been injured many times—cuts, bruises, and breaks had certainly left their various marks—he was still very good-looking. A moustache covered his upper lip, a patch his left eye. His right eye radiated determination, and his posture expressed much the same.

He comforted the McPhail brothers, telling them that he would help, that he was on friendly terms with their largest creditor, and that he would negotiate on the brothers' behalf. However, he also told them that his chief point of business, his main reason for visiting Formosa, was related to the sinking of the *Rover* and the killing of its crew.

Le Gendre had intended to visit the prefect's office the following morning, but word was sent that Regional Commander Liu Mingteng had been busy with bandits in Changhwa; it was daybreak when he arrived back in Taiwan-fu, and he needed some time to rest. The meeting was therefore rescheduled for the afternoon.

That day, Le Gendre did not come back until ten at night. He was somewhat drunk and went to bed soon thereafter.

The next morning, he got up early and handed an official letter to Neil McPhail, who became excited upon reading it. It was a search warrant signed by Taiwan *Daotai* Wu Ta-ting, allowing Pickering to travel to Penghu in search of the criminals. Word had spread that the criminals boarded a ship at Anping that left for Penghu, from where they could, of course, have departed for Hong Kong, but there was still a chance that they had stayed on that island. Le Gendre gave Neil a copy of another letter written by the Taiwan *daotai* to those in charge of Penghu, requesting that they help Pickering arrest the escaped comprador and his men.

The subject of their conversation then turned to the *Rover* situation.

"It went smoothly!" Le Gendre said triumphantly. "Not one of the Qing bureaucrats denied that the *Rover* was wrecked in Qing waters. Nor did they deny that the mariners were killed on Qing territory. Moreover, they were willing to shoulder the responsibility. The prefect said that before I even arrived, he had taken it upon himself to command local officers to deal with the incident. Wu Benjie, Magistrate of Fung-shan District, is the civil official in charge, while Ling Dingbang is the military commander.

"Toward myself the prefect is quite friendly, but he was critical of Carroll. He mentioned that in not informing the Qing government of their endeavor, the British displayed considerable recklessness. He hoped we would not act so irresponsibly, for they would feel great regret should anything happen to us. Of course, such concern was but a veiled warning.

"I asked when they might take action. General Liu Ming-teng answered that the perpetrators are raw savages residing on Koalut Mountain. Theirs is an extremely remote tribe, accessible only through rough and winding mountain trails. In addition to carrying provisions, the army will need to be familiar with the challenges inherent to mountain combat. That is to say, it will take time to prepare for such an expedition. But the general emphasized that his army consists of seasoned soldiers. He believes they can equip themselves well, without the need for foreign help."

Neil nodded. "Wu Ta-ting and Liu Ming-teng are both disciples of the famous Qing leaders Zeng Guofan and Zuo Zongtang. They conquered the Taiping rebels.[2] They were transferred to Formosa last year and are comparatively young and extremely capable. They belong to the Hunan Army, which is widely acknowledged as

---

[2] Taiping Tianguo (the "Kingdom of Heavenly Peace," 1851–1864), a rebellious force that tried to overthrow the Qing government. The incident is generally referred to as "the Taiping Rebellion."

the best of all the Qing armies. Consul, how much time will you give them?"

"At the very latest, they should send out their army by June."

But Pickering was pessimistic. "It'll be to no avail! Be it the Hunan Army or the Anhui Army, old or young, Qing governments are all the same. If you don't keep pressing them, they will never take action. I do not believe for one second that we will see their army leave by June."

Le Gendre eyed Pickering in disapproval and said, "We Americans ought to respect the promise of the Qing government. After all, we have just suffered through a civil war, and ours is not half as imperious a country as yours.

"Even though I have promised them that we will not take military action, there is still the need to rescue any survivors and retrieve any remains. The *Ashuelot* will sail to the shore of Koalut Mountain. I will visit Carroll in Chihou tomorrow to ask for his opinion."

Pickering added, "Dr. Manson from Chihou was also aboard the *Cormorant*. Presently he is in Anping. But I believe he has left the hospital this morning to treat a sailor with an acute injury. When he returns, you might ask him to tell you everything in detail."

"Good!" Le Gendre was pleased. "You know, Qing officials in Taiwan-fu have a peculiar way of dealing with diplomatic affairs. Inside their office, they give no direct response. But then after the official call is concluded, they bring out a meal that reaches our hearts by way of our stomachs. I have to admit that of the many I have eaten, yesterday's feast was perhaps the most unforgettable. The dishes were more exquisite even than those I had in Amoy. And gentlemen, I come from France. It is not easy to please my palate."

Everybody burst into obedient laughter.

Le Gendre's words seemed to touch Pickering, who said, "You all know I don't like Qing mandarins, but I love Formosa's food, its weather, and its environment. In truth, that's why I have stayed here for so long. Formosa is not only beautiful. It is also bountiful. The camphor oil produced here is excellent. The coal mined here is good, and maybe there is also gold to be found. I think the tea leaf here will also make itself famous. You know, two hundred years ago, when the Dutch first arrived, they just wanted to make it a harbor for the transportation of china and silk. Indeed, gentlemen, everything is good in Formosa, with the glaring exception of the safety of its waters."

He could not hold back his discontent, and the intensity of his speech increased. "In the seven years since 1860, more than twenty vessels have been shipwrecked. But still the Qing government allows its subjects to ransack the ships and mariners. It is not only raw savages who are capable of such things. Swinhoe negotiated with the Qing government several times to ask for compensation. But as you have witnessed, those government officials are devilishly good at securing exemptions from such expenditures. Swinhoe simply could not put up with it anymore. His decision to send ships to patrol the coast along Formosa, this so-called 'gunboat diplomacy,' truly was necessary."

Le Gendre changed the subject. "When I was in Tamsui, I met with John Dodd, and we drank Formosan tea. You are right to believe it will make this island famous, for it is much better than any Fukien tea I drank in Amoy. Dodd told me he intends to export Formosan tea to Europe. He predicted that, in the foreseeable future, its tea will compete with Assam from India."

Pickering sighed. "Formosa is indeed a fabulous place, and yet it is ruled by the incompetent Qing government. What a waste!

"Moreover," he continued, "the Qing Empire did not want this island! Over two hundred years ago, when they defeated Koxinga's grandson and destroyed his army, they wanted to give up on Formosa. The Qing court discriminated against the islanders. All the Qing nobility and officials came from Manchu. Manchurians looked down on Han people, who in turn looked down on Formosan aborigines. Under the rule of Emperor Kangxi, they segregated

Han people from savages and ruled them differently. They didn't want anything to do with the aborigines. But Hokkien guys from Fukien and Hakka people from Canton kept smuggling themselves into Formosa, coming into conflict with the aborigines. Until now, the Qing government would rather ignore the matter, saying that the savage tribes are external to its empire.

"Indeed, Qing officials come to Formosa for a term of three years. But as their saying goes, 'Three years of the official position are done in two.' They just focus on the first two years, then idle away the third year as if here on vacation. They are all waiting to return to the mainland, where they can get a promotion and live in retirement. When they are in Formosa, they don't explore this place, nor do they care about how the people here live. They are but passersby. Few officials really think about how to cultivate the land, nor how to improve it.

"Those officials are well educated and learned. They distinguished themselves in the Imperial Civil Examinations, yet they know nothing of modern science. Their duty is not to develop the infrastructure but to flatter their supervisors. Look! The Chinese ancestors were both intelligent and creative. How is it that their descendants are so incompetent? What's worse, the high-ranking officials of the Qing dynasty are immersed in the dream of their past imperial glory. They may flatter us, but believe me, they hold us in great disdain."

Pickering looked at Le Gendre and asked, "Suppose they take no action after June, what will you do?"

Le Gendre smiled.

"We must follow Swinhoe's example," Pickering suggested. "We can depend only on ourselves."

Le Gendre considered for a moment and then replied, "If they have taken no action by the end of June, then I may send my army. But I wonder what Washington would say to this. Strictly speaking, that would violate international laws."

Pickering shook his head. "Your senators do not have the slightest idea about the Qing government and its officials. You should follow the British example of dealing with Qing China. Without 'gunboat diplomacy,' without armed forces, the Tientsin and Peking Treaties would still be unsigned. Without these, how could you be stationed in Amoy and Formosa as consul?" He grinned. "General, have you heard of an ancient Chinese saying, 'When a general is in battle, he does not have to take the emperor's order'?"

Le Gendre hesitated. "Your country resorted to war to force the Qing government to agree to the importing of opium for your own profit. This behavior is internationally notorious, and that reputation is not unjustified. It is not only the Puritans in my country who judge your wars unjustified. The French also frown upon what you have done. And as for burning down the Yuanming Garden, the Old Summer Palace in Peking? We rightly feel you've gone too far."

Pickering laughed away the accusation. "The French? Their colonies do not grow poppies, nor do they produce opium. And you Americans? It was but a short while ago that you were owning slaves. And, I might add, how we Europeans envied you for that! Anyway, morality has nothing to do with it. We helped the Qing government defend Nanking. And we helped them recruit and train the Anhui Army. Without General Charles Gordon's help, how could the Hunan Army have defeated the forces of the Taiping Rebellion in Nanking and recovered the lost land from the rebels? But for the help of the British Empire, the Qing Empire would have ceased to exist. What matters a summer palace? All things considered, the Qing government owes Great Britain a debt of gratitude."

In the preceding few minutes, Pickering seemed momentarily to have lost his head. Finishing, he snapped back into a more fitting register. "You must forgive me for being so straightforward. Had your country not been engaged in the Civil War and your railroad system to the Pacific coast not been completed, you would have sent an army to share our profits in the Far East. Now it is time for your country to catch up with ours. If you are willing to change policy in the Far East, your name will certainly go down in history. You were once a lawyer. Now you are a general. You excel at both scholarly pursuits and military feats. Few can be as talented as you. I believe you are much more forward-looking than those short-sighted politicians in your homeland."

Le Gendre appeared lost in deep thought; he remained silent.

Neil changed the subject. "Consul, you have come all the way to Anping. The Dutch-built Zeelandia is quite nearby. Would you like to visit it?"

Le Gendre rubbed his right eye—a habitual gesture—and said, "Of course. Besides, I want to meet with Dr. Manson, provided he is back at the hospital, and discuss with him the trip to South Bay. Tomorrow I will go to the British consulate in Takao to make an official visit to Consul Carroll, where I will thank him for his help and ask for his advice."

That morning, a British mariner was unloading goods in Anping port when he fell and hit his head. Dr. Manson was sent for, but the mariner was so seriously injured that he died in the early afternoon. When Manson and Butterfly returned to McPhail & Co., Le Gendre had already left for Zeelandia.

In the evening, Le Gendre returned and was delighted to see Manson; he quickly began inquiring as to the details of his trip to South Bay. Manson mentioned that Butterfly, interpreter of the savage tongue, was in McPhail & Co., a fact that excited Le Gendre to no end.

After they met, Le Gendre asked Butterfly many questions about Sialiao, South Bay, tamed savages, and raw savages. He laughed a lot, but Butterfly felt uncomfortable and slightly confronted by the long periods of unbroken eye contact upon which he seemed to insist.

Le Gendre told Manson and Butterfly that he would visit Carroll in Takao the next day and intended to repeat the *Cormorant*'s journey.

He would board the *Ashuelot* to leave for Liangkiau, then carry on south for further exploration. He was willing to take Manson back to Takao. As for Butterfly, she could go all the way to Sialiao.

Butterfly had not seen Bunkiet for almost a month, and she was overjoyed when presented with the opportunity to visit Sialiao. That night, sleep was almost impossible; she tossed and turned and wondered how to tell Bunkiet and Chinya of her adventures.

24

On April 21, Butterfly boarded the *Ashuelot*. Le Gendre continued to stare at her. Butterfly could not understand quite why it was that she felt entirely at ease when with Manson, but so uncomfortable around Le Gendre. In any case, she decided to avoid the consul's looks as best she could. Manson, who was likewise aboard the ship, was also aware that Le Gendre was interested in Butterfly; it was plain to see.

The ship pushed quickly through the water, and soon they arrived at Takao. The British consulate had sent men to greet them at the pier, and a coach was waiting to take Le Gendre to see Carroll. As he was leaving, Le Gendre told Butterfly that the *Ashuelot* would depart for Liangkiau Bay the following afternoon. The ship would moor there for a while before continuing on to South Bay.

Butterfly and Manson thanked Le Gendre and then started their walk back to the hospital. Butterfly hummed an aboriginal song, anticipating her trip to Sialiao. They turned onto a small trail that wound its roundabout way to the hospital. It was a beautiful day; Butterfly's happiness and excitement seemed reflected perfectly in the weather.

They were nearly at the hospital when someone yelled at her, "Butterfly! Butterfly!" Knocked from her daydreaming, Butterfly stopped abruptly. The voice was familiar—but no, it couldn't be.

Surely not here . . . But yes, yes it was! Chinya! How did he . . . ? She ran toward him and burst into tears.

When Butterfly had first decided to board the *Cormorant*, she had done so in such a hurry that she had been unable to spare much time to bid proper farewells, and she was not able to offer any good-bye at all to Chinya. She had expected that the *Cormorant* would stop again at Sialiao on its return journey, but things did not go that way.

Back in the village, Chinya kept thinking of Butterfly, and he came to realize that time spent with her had been the happiest of his life. For weeks, although he heard nothing from Butterfly, he could think of little else but her.

One day, the waiting became too much, and he hastily boarded a boat heading for Chihou. Less than half an hour after arriving in Takao, he had located the hospital. A Hokkien guy at the door told him that Butterfly and Dr. Manson had left for Taiwan-fu on an ox cart; he did not know when they would be back.

That very afternoon, Chinya found a job laboring at Chihou Port. For each of the next few days, after finishing work, he stopped by the hospital to see if Butterfly had returned. When he became sufficiently tired, he would lie down to sleep beneath a tree in the nearby woods; on those April nights, the temperature remained comfortable right through to daybreak. Even with the insects that buzzed and bit, he could bear it. He passed three nights this way before seeing Butterfly on the fourth day.

"Butterfly, you look so different in a foreigner's dress. I can hardly recognize you! It's nice, though."

Butterfly smiled back at him. "Thank you, Chinya. I'm glad you like it."

Chinya turned to Manson and bowed. "Dr. Manson, how are you? My cousin has almost completely recovered. My family thank you. I thank you."

"Not at all." Manson was pleased. He turned to Butterfly, "Your friend has come to see you? How nice! Feel free to spend the afternoon with him."

Butterfly led Chinya to her room. "How is Bunkiet?" she asked immediately.

"That's what I wanted to tell you. Bunkiet has left Sialiao. He was adopted by Seqalu's Big Head Chief Tauketok."

Butterfly was taken aback, and she listened intently as Chinya explained to her what had happened. She felt pleased for Bunkiet, but it was a response tinged with sadness; from then on, she would have fewer chances to see her brother.

Their father had intended for Bunkiet to take the Imperial Civil Examinations, and although Bunkiet was indeed intelligent, Butterfly understood that theirs was a poor family living in a remote place, far away from the centers of government bureaucracy; just taking the exams would be difficult for Bunkiet. But now he was the adopted son of a savage chief, and for that change she felt relieved. Perhaps, she considered, since Bunkiet was living with her mother's family, she would inherit her father's legacy. It was an interesting thought.

In a short time, she and Bunkiet had each gone through such drastic changes, and the two of them seemed to be traveling in quite different directions. For the second night in a row, Butterfly tossed and turned, unable to fall asleep.

25

The morning of the next day, April 22, Butterfly and Chinya stood beside the moored *Ashuelot* waiting for Le Gendre. Finally, at two in the afternoon, he arrived in an inelegant hurry.

Butterfly approached him and requested that Chinya be allowed to travel with them; Le Gendre glanced at him and agreed without hesitation.

Soon after they were aboard, the vessel set off with a shrill whistle.

Once Takao had disappeared, Butterfly and Chinya thanked Le Gendre, who smiled and said, "Ah, but you must be my guides when we reach Sialiao. Carroll just now gave me a map of southern Formosa. We will spend a night in Sialiao and then leave for South Bay. Butterfly, since you have already been there, might I invite you to join us?"

Butterfly declined his invitation immediately. She told him that she had been away from Sialiao for a month, and she wanted to stay there for longer than a single night. Moreover, the fighting last time had been a dreadful experience, and she would not risk repeating it. Le Gendre promised that he did not intend to land, but still Butterfly refused. The consul's face twisted with disappointment.

When the vessel arrived at Sialiao, Le Gendre told Butterfly, "Fine. I shall stay in Sialiao for another day. Tomorrow I will go to Chasiang and look around the town. The ship will set off again the day after that. Please reconsider my invitation. You can let me know tomorrow."

Butterfly smiled at him as she walked off the boat.

Le Gendre spent his first night in Sialiao on board the ship. On deck, looking at the stars, he thought of Butterfly. An intoxication pushed outward from his heart. He did not know if it was caused by the upcoming adventure to South Bay or by something else. Regardless, it was a feeling that had been unknown to him for a long time. It seemed that he had recovered his ambition and along with it, his vitality.

The next day, he rose early and was pleased to learn that Butterfly had decided to accompany him to Chasiang. Mia and Chinya were to join them.

When they got there, Le Gendre was quite surprised; though the people living in Chasiang were mostly Hokkien, a public of diverse ethnicities walked its streets. Apart from the Hokkien residents, there were Hakka people as well as a number of Peppos. Chasiang was not particularly large, but the streets bustled with commercial activity.

Le Gendre paid close attention to the local people. The Peppos were referred to as "tamed savages" by the Qing government, but his guides and the locals called them *tushengzi*. Theirs was a hybrid of plains aboriginal and Hokkien cultures. Le Gendre learned that immigrants from mainland China were divided into the Hokkien from Fukien and the Hakka from Canton. It was easier to recognize *tushengzi*, because they wore head scarves. But Hokkien and Hakka people were difficult to tell apart since their styles of dress were similar. At first it seemed only their languages were different, and as Le Gendre was unable to speak either one, distinguishing between them was quite challenging. However, after he had asked after the identity of several passing people, Butterfly offered a tip to identify Hokkien women from Hakka women: "Hokkien women often have bound feet. Women with feet like mine are certainly not Hokkien."

Le Gendre laughed as he came to understand the distinction. Just then, he saw three strong men wearing red-and-white vests and carrying large bamboo baskets. One of them wore a leopard-fur hat decorated with fangs. The three of them entered a shop. Mia nudged Le Gendre. "Those are raw savages."

From within the shop, the raw savages noticed the strange-looking Le Gendre standing outside, observing them closely. The three of them exchanged a few words and then feigned collective indifference. Le Gendre was overcome by curiosity, so he too entered the shop. He watched as the raw savages opened their baskets. Inside were two pairs of deer antlers and two deer penises. Le Gendre had no idea what these were to be used for. The raw savages and the Hokkien shopkeeper were using body language to communicate; apparently, they barely understood each other. The shopkeeper put aside the antlers and penises, and they all continued chattering. It looked like they were trying and failing to strike a deal. After a while, in what Le Gendre took for desperation, one of the raw savages removed his hat and placed it on the shop's counter. This produced in the shopkeeper a look of satisfaction, and he took out three muskets, six boxes of bullets, and a piece of cloth. After the deal was concluded, Le Gendre continued to eye the raw savages curiously; they forsook their indifference and eyed him curiously in return.

Later, they saw another group of raw savages; these people did not carry any animal parts but rather Hokkien iron pans and cookers. Le Gendre asked, "Are there any Koaluts among them?"

Mia replied, "We're close to the Botan tribe, and people from Baya in the south occasionally visit Chasiang, but Koalut is quite far from here. That said, their languages and clothing are quite alike, so it's hard to tell."

Downtown Chasiang was in fact just a single main street, and when he had walked along both of its sides, Le Gendre asked Mia to take him farther south to Ling-nuang, knowing that beyond it was Koalut. Mia said it was all right for aborigines to go there, but he did not want to risk bringing a foreigner, particularly, he emphasized, in light of recent events. Le Gendre was disappointed, but he understood the logic of Mia's decision.

Back at Sialiao, Le Gendre invited Mia onto the *Ashuelot* to serve as their interpreter. But Mia thought of the battle Butterfly had described to him, and he too declined the invitation. Le Gendre then offered a handsome reward, asking other people in the village to go with him, but still he was unable to find an interpreter. In the end, he left Sialiao and returned to the *Ashuelot* in a bad mood.

But the ship did not set sail. Instead, it stayed moored for a second night in Sialiao port. On the third morning, Le Gendre got off the vessel to look for Butterfly and Mia, but once again both turned him down.

26

Following the map given to them by Carroll, Le Gendre and the crew on the *Ashuelot* easily reached the coast of South Bay, and soon they were at the beach with the ruins of the two small boats.

Le Gendre and Febiger, the ship's captain, withdrew their binoculars and looked at the shore. At first there was almost nothing to see; neither savages nor wild boar were visible. But then they saw four settlers. In a great rush, a few soldiers disembarked to bring the four aboard for interrogation. The men were Hokkien. They said that their family name was Wu and that they had lived in Tossupong for several generations. They had arrived that morning on a small flat-bottomed wooden boat called a *sampan*, which they had left anchored in a nearby bay. They knew nothing of the *Rover*, nor of the raw savages' slaughter of foreign mariners, but admitted that sometimes they would trade with the tribes.

Le Gendre walked away from the four men and, leaning heavily against the ship's handrail, looked to the land. This had to be Turtle Nose Mountain; it was not tall, but its strange formation looked dangerous. Moreover, it was covered by dense woods within which raw savages could easily hide.

Later, after further observation and some hasty calculations, Le Gendre and Febiger reached the same conclusion: at least one hundred soldiers would be required to enter the woods at Turtle Nose Mountain. Of course, they would also need some interpreters to communicate with the savages. Soldiers and interpreters were each indispensable; lacking either group, it would be extremely dangerous to push recklessly into the forest.

Captain Febiger gave the command to return, but Le Gendre bade that they continue south. The vessel passed the southernmost peninsula and then headed north along the east coast of Formosa. Before long, they saw an estuary that flowed through an expansive valley.

This area was not marked on Carroll's map, but from the land's formation and location, Le Gendre thought this river might lead upstream to Tuillassock. He was thrilled. If they entered the valley from this point, perhaps they could invade Koalut directly, unobstructed by the natural barrier that protected the area. Febiger nodded in agreement.

It was now over a month since the sinking of the *Rover*, and about a week had passed since the Qing government had guaranteed that it would deal with the raw savages. Aboard the *Ashuelot*, neither Le Gendre nor the ship's crew could save any of the possible surviving mariners, obtain any of the deceased's remains, or see any of Koalut's raw savages. With an unconcealed sigh, Le Gendre ordered that the *Ashuelot* turn around and head directly to Amoy. For the moment, there was little they could do but wait.

27

With an increasing intensity, Bunkiet found himself missing Butterfly. He had been away from Sialiao for a month, and he wished to return to thank and bid a proper good-bye to Mia. But without confirmation of Butterfly's being there, he was hesitant to make the journey; it didn't seem worth it for a farewell alone. Tauketok had told him that Butterfly would be welcomed if she wished to stay in Tuillassock. However, knowing his sister, Bunkiet felt sure that she would not want to stay in a savage tribe for long.

Tauketok told Bunkiet not to worry. Their ancestral spirits would arrange it. When they were meant to meet, they would meet. After all, their ancestral spirits had prepared it so that the two of them would go on their respective adventures almost on the same day; they arranged everything.

Eventually Bunkiet decided that he had to make the trip. Whatever the outcome, it would take him less than a day to walk from

Tuillassock to Sialiao, and he couldn't put it off forever. Before his sister left, she had told him that she would come back to Sialiao every month. Perhaps she would be there now.

He would walk to Sialiao and spend three nights there. Should he not meet Butterfly, he would return to Tuillassock and wait for Butterfly to find him here. Tauketok agreed to this plan.

On the morning of April 24, Bunkiet dressed as a plains settler and left for Sialiao. For the entire journey, up and down the mountain trails, he thought of Butterfly, hoping—but not quite believing—that she would be there to welcome him when he arrived. That evening, tired and desperate for rest, he arrived in Sialiao. He was ready to sleep and by that time had thoroughly convinced himself that he would not get to see his sister on this visit.

But Butterfly was indeed there! The siblings were thrilled to see each other, and they chatted almost without break until birdsong sounded and light lifted the night.

At the end of it all, after most of the stories had been exchanged, Butterfly told Bunkiet that another foreign ship had left Sialiao for Koalut that morning. Hearing this, Bunkiet thought of Tauketok; his adoptive father had predicted that the foreigners would come again, and they had. He told his sister that Big Head Chief had ordered his people to provide support to Koalut; they were keeping an eye on the sea both day and night.

Butterfly, in response, told him that Le Gendre was quite different from Carroll; Carroll was but a civil official, whereas Le Gendre had fought in many battles.

Bunkiet grew worried.

"But as I said," Butterfly told him, trying to remain positive, "it doesn't look as though Le Gendre wants to initiate a fight . . . at least not at this time."

Bunkiet was quiet; it was time for bed.

In the afternoon, Butterfly told Mia and Chinya that she planned to visit Tuillassock with Bunkiet. She wanted to see the tribe that had once been home to her mother, and she was keen to visit her two uncles and the retired Big Head Chief. She would stay there for a couple of days before returning to Sialiao and then leaving again for Takao.

Chinya seemed weighed down by something. He did not want Butterfly to return to Takao, but he could not give voice to his objection. All he could do was offer to escort Butterfly to Tuillassock and back, to which she happily agreed.

That night, Mia honored Bunkiet with a feast. As a gesture of farewell, he served good wine bought in Chasiang. Bunkiet drank quickly and became quite intoxicated; soon he lay sprawled and unconscious on the floor. This was, as far as Butterfly could recall, the first time her brother had been drunk. Their father had disliked drinking and had done nothing to encourage the habit in either of his children.

Chinya, meanwhile, was lost in thought and barely ate. When he imagined Butterfly's imminent departure for Takao, his heart felt affected by a constricting pain. He often sought connection with Butterfly's eyes, but she wasn't returning his looks. He began breathing heavily, sitting alone in an unnoticed silence.

At the evening's peak, he picked up a chopstick and snapped it forcefully in half. The crack stopped conversations and distilled the air. People stared. The only noises that continued, oblivious of the tension, were Bunkiet's snoring and the insects' chirping outside.

"Get some sleep, Chinya," Mia said forcefully. "You need to be up early tomorrow."

Butterfly spent three nights in Tuillassock. While she was there, she remembered the times her father had told her that many of the immigrants who arrived in Formosa had left a family back home. These immigrants, he had said, came with a dream of making a great fortune, but for only a few people did the dream come true. Butterfly had never dared to ask her father if he was referring in part to his own miserable experience. Nor did she ever ask him if he had been unmarried when he came to Formosa. Now those questions would remain forever unasked, their answers unknown.

Butterfly stared at Bunkiet. He was talking with a member of his new family. How different their lives were from their father's plans and expectations. She wondered: raw aborigines were strict about their family regulations; how was it that Big Head Chief would so freely adopt Bunkiet as his son? She suspected it had something to do with the weight of a long-carried guilt. And perhaps, with the two shells fired from the *Cormorant*, he had been shocked into the realization that the outside world was changing, and he and his tribe had to adapt. Butterfly wondered whether he might have adopted Bunkiet not only with a sense of familial liability but also with some other safeguarding intention.

Indeed, from her brief time speaking with him, Tauketok seemed sensitive as well as sensible. Great numbers of settlers had encroached upon his land, his sister had eloped with a Hakka man, foreign ships arrived more frequently by the month—these factors could well have awakened him to the radical changes of the era. He needed reliable help to cope with the ever-changing situation. And, young as Bunkiet was, he was most certainly qualified for the job.

Butterfly thought of Tauketok's other nephews, none of whom seemed cut out for leadership. Therefore, her brother was endowed with a great mission. The future of their mother's tribe fell on his shoulders. The responsibility was enormous. When they were saying good-bye, she held Bunkiet's hand. "You must stay here. Father and Mother would be happy to see you educated by Big Head Chief."

Bunkiet nodded sincerely.

On the way back to Sialiao, Butterfly was submerged in thought. She walked in silence, her mind churning. As they stepped through an abrupt turn in the trail, she turned to glance at Chinya; his face was scratched with discontent. She quickly turned her head away from his, but he seized the opportunity and asked, "When will you leave for Takao again?"

"Whenever the next ship leaves."

There was a pause. The sound of the forest rose to fill most of the silence, and then Chinya said, "I've made up my mind to seek my fortune with you. When I was in Takao, I saw a lot and I understood a lot of new things. I will remain a nobody if I stay in Sialiao. I can do nothing there but farm, fish, and raise cattle. Big towns give us chances to move ahead. You are right. You have shown me that we don't have to stay in Sialiao."

Butterfly was amazed. Chinya seemed at that moment to be so determined that she began to see him in a different light. She radiated a dazzling smile. "Then, what next?"

"I did not learn to properly read or write, so I am not cut out for jobs like bookkeeping or writing. But ships need people to load and unload goods. I am strong, and I can handle menial work. The problem is, I won't have regular income. And I don't have a place to stay."

"Well, as the foreigners say, God helps those who help themselves. If you are good at your job, you will remain employed. If you really want to find your future in Takao, we can board a ship together."

As they continued their walk home, chatting excitedly about the future, Chinya's bad mood was left abandoned on the forest trail, replaced by a grin that refused for a long time to fade.

28

Tauketok was worried. He confided to Bunkiet that although the Confederation of Eighteen Tribes had been established, the real test was yet to come. He felt almost daunted by the responsibility and was not sure that he could rise to it.

He had told the other chiefs that the foreigners' ships would certainly come again, and after an American ship circled around several spots and then left, many of those chiefs thought the conflict had come to a somewhat anticlimactic end. But Tauketok told them that they should not feel so optimistic as to slacken their alertness.

He warned that the American ship had likely come to survey the area. It had probably sailed south on an exploratory journey in preparation for soldiers to land. Last time, the foreigners were few, so they were easily forced to leave. Whenever they came again, there would be many more to repel.

Nominally, his group was the Confederation of Eighteen Tribes Under One Leader, but Tauketok could only really claim control over the four tribes of Seqalu and Koalut. As for the other tribes, he wanted to make sure that they would not take advantage of any attack to invade Seqalu. Therefore, he told the chiefs of Baya and Ling-nuang that he was afraid the foreign fleet would land and climb the mountain from Ling-nuang or Tossupong. In this eventuality, they would no longer have the advantage of occupying the higher position, so he wanted Baya and Ling-nuang to defend that side of the tribal territory. If the Red-Hairs' troop approached from that direction, they could hold them back for a while.

He then told his own tribe that he was afraid of the foreigners' ships sailing around the island to the east and landing at Tuillassock Creek. He thought they should defend that estuary. He equipped some thirty Tuillassock warriors with thatch, bamboo, and logs. He told them that, should any boat force its entry from the estuary, they were to push thatch and bamboo into the creek to reduce the depth of the water and prevent the boat from sailing upstream. If that did not work, they were to throw logs into the river. This way, even if they could not prevent boats from entering, they would create barriers in the water. Should the enemy boats enter the creek, his warriors were to shoot flaming arrows at the sails. Finally, he ordered that traps be set on the bank, in case the enemies somehow managed to land.

He presumed that the enemies had used the sail-shaped rock as their landmark, and that it would therefore be much more probable for them to attack Koalut from the beach. The enemies were not familiar with the land formation of the whole area, and, he thought, they were as arrogant as they were well armed.

He asked the other chiefs, "If they land at the beach, what can we do?"

"It'll be just like last time," Payarin said. "We will use muskets to shoot at the shore to frighten them off."

Tauketok smiled as one does when explaining reason to a child. "It won't be possible to frighten them off. If they come again, they will bring many more people, perhaps a hundred. They will be here to climb up the mountain in search of our villages, and a handful of dead won't turn them back. Let's count. How many warriors can we send out?"

He looked at Payarin, who answered, "Forty from Koalut."

"Sixty or seventy from Sabaree," said Isa. "Let's say seventy."

"Okay. We Tuillassock can also offer about seventy. But about thirty will be stationed at the Tuillassock estuary. So the total number of warriors we can gather around Koalut to fight will amount to . . ." He hesitated, scrambling to finish the calculation.

Bunkiet leaned in and whispered, "One hundred fifty."

Tauketok looked at him approvingly and said, "Payarin, we will have one hundred warriors gathering at Koalut till the foreign ships come. Most likely within a hundred days the foreign ships and their soldiers will come. If not in a hundred days, then certainly within half a year."

Isa asked, "And what about the other fifty warriors?"

"The fifty warriors will stay in Tuillassock and Sabaree as a relief army. They will support whichever group of warriors encounters trouble.

"Payarin. During this period, Koalut will oversee the feeding of all the warriors. Twenty Koalut will stand vigil at night, and those warriors can rest during the day."

"Right."

The chiefs of Mantsui and Sihlinge then said that since all the men in Seqalu would be away, their tribes could help provide for the women and children who stayed behind.

All those present felt the arrangement was quite sensible. Thus, the eighteen tribes of Liangkiau deployed their warriors.

Later that day, Tauketok led Bunkiet, Payarin, and the other chiefs up Turtle Nose Mountain to pray for victory. This turtle nose-shaped mountain was revered by all the Seqalu people, but for Koalut it was the most sacred of all mountains. People in Koalut always came to Turtle Nose Mountain before and after a battle, whenever they encountered a disaster, or whenever they had a bountiful harvest. When they worshiped their ancestral spirits, prayed for blessings, or looked for atonement, they came here.

Bunkiet stood on the peak. Unsettled winds blew without break. Converging mountains extended inland, carpeted in dense forest that faded to gray in the distant hazy air; streams reflected light from the sky, silver and mirrorlike; here and there were meadows; sea was on three sides. He looked into the distance at Chasiang and Sialiao—Tongling Bo was but a blur—and he vowed to protect all those who lived on this land.

As they walked back down Turtle Nose Mountain, Tauketok asked Payarin, Isa, and Bunkiet to take him to the place where the British had landed.

Early the following morning, when the wind still cut slightly cold against the skin, Tauketok and the other men went to the beach. As they approached, Payarin pointed out the locations where his people had been stationed, waiting for the ambush.

When they reached the shore, Tauketok inspected the land closely. He looked up to Koalut and asked Isa and Bunkiet, "Suppose you were the Red-Hair commander and you landed with not just six, but sixty or even a hundred soldiers, how would you direct your army?"

He turned to Payarin. "And you, if you were waiting for them here, how would you deploy your men?"

Payarin spoke as the others were still considering their answers. "Like last time, my men will hide in the woods near the foot of the mountain. This time, we won't hold back. We will shoot them before they even land. But . . . I wonder if our bullets can go that far."

Tauketok shook his head. "This time, the Red-Hairs will send many people. There will be too many to kill all of them before they land. And anyway, if we reveal ourselves too soon, they will use their bombs. We can't fight back against that."

Isa did not understand. "If the Red-Hair commander brings a hundred soldiers, they will most certainly go up the mountain to search for us. If we let them approach like that, won't the odds be stacked against us?"

"Ah," said Tauketok, "but we *must* let the foreigners go up the mountain. Once they are in the forest, their ship will be unable to bombard us, as they will be afraid of killing their own men. When they are up here, we won't let them see us. We won't engage them directly. We will shoot and then run. They will panic when they can't find us. We don't have to overpower them. We just have to exhaust them, like a pack of dogs fighting a boar."

Isa clapped his hands and laughed. Payarin, in a moment of unusual composure, merely nodded in agreement.

Bunkiet mumbled, "Do we really have to fight them? Is there not another alternative?" Tauketok stared bleakly. "They are the ones who want to fight, not us."

"But when I met them in Sialiao, I didn't feel they were looking for a battle. They just wanted to retrieve the mariners' remains."

"That's just one part of what they want. We killed their people, and they won't stop until they take revenge."

"But suppose we defeat them again. Won't that provoke them further? Make them more furious? Do that, and they'll come again, and again, and again. They won't stop until they win."

Tauketok seemed awakened in that moment to the same realization. "Quite so." He nodded thoughtfully and then fell once more into a quiet contemplation.

In the calm, a flock of birds spooked and took flight from a nearby tree.

"Alas! Alas!"

29

A month or so passed before the foreigners came again.

It was just ahead of dawn when a sentinel ran into the village and reported breathlessly that a large foreign ship had been sighted. Tauketok hurried to the side of the mountain. He saw not just one ship but two; both had three masts. Payarin said that each of them was much bigger than the single ship that came last time.

The day had broken; it promised to be bright with great visibility. Tauketok summoned eighty warriors and told them to divide into groups of ten. "To begin with, you just need to agitate the foreigners as they move through the forest. Remember, watch out for each other. And keep hidden!

"If they do not come into the forest, that would be best. But if they do, we should lure them to the mountaintop, far away from the tribe. The farther, the better. As we planned, the group that is farthest from the tribe will shoot first. After you shoot, change your position. All the groups take turns shooting. Let the enemy wander around lost in the woods. They won't know how many warriors we have, and if they do not hurt us, we won't hurt them.

"They will be easily visible. We will be perfectly able to see their movements. If we are well hidden, they won't be able to fire at us.

118 ᏚᎣ REPULSE OF THE FOREIGN FORCES

We will play hide-and-seek with them. They will wander around in circles, on and on and on. In the end they will retreat after gaining nothing. I doubt they will spend the night in the mountains."

Bunkiet asked, "What if they don't land? What if they use their bombs to blow us and the forest up?"

Tauketok was silent for what felt to Bunkiet like a long time. "In that case, we will retreat."

As they talked, they watched as the two ships moored near the shore and soldiers in uniform boarded a dozen or so boats. They did not have to spend time counting to know that they were outnumbered by the Red-Hair soldiers. Tauketok appeared weighed down with worry. Bunkiet, on the other hand, felt relieved; it was now unlikely that the foreigners would bombard them directly.

Once the soldiers had secured their boats on the sand, the group of warriors farthest from the tribe walked out from the forest and shouted to attract the white soldiers' attention. Immediately the Red-Hairs began marching in the warriors' direction.

30

As soon as the foreign troop was in the woods, the ten groups of warriors took their turns firing toward the invaders. Within the forest, the white army panicked and soon was spread thin, searching desperately for an unseen enemy. Sometimes the tribal warriors would shriek and appear as a flash in front of the soldiers, who would react by firing in wild abandon. But the warriors moved so swiftly that the Red-Hairs' shots always missed their targets. Eventually, once they realized the futility of splitting up to find the enemy, the invading army regrouped into a more unified position, fearing that they might get lost if they went deeper into the woods individually.

It was almost noon, and the sun beat down relentlessly. Though the forest provided almost unbroken shade, the Red-Hairs were not used to exerting themselves in such torrid humidity. There were no well-beaten trails on the mountain, so they had to force their way through thick undergrowth. They started inevitably to tire and wheeze. Some became entangled in vines. Some had their uniform and skin torn by the thorns of poisonous plants.

In a moment of quiet, they sat down to take a rest, opening their backpacks to drink water, eat food, or apply ointment to their wounds. When they got back up and continued into the forest, the white army again started to lose their calm. Tauketok was delighted. He began to consider whether they should capture one or two of the soldiers.

However, at this point, a young man wearing a cap with an embellished rim began working frantically to get the soldiers into line. He spoke in a loud, authoritative voice. Beads of sweat rolled freely down his reddened cheeks as he moved through the forest with a natural, graceful agility. Because of his efforts, the soldiers rallied and realigned; Tauketok could not help but admire the man's command.

Sporadic gunfire continued. Some shots were from tribal warriors, though the majority were fired by white soldiers. The sun was beginning its slant to the west. The white soldiers had been up on the mountain for half the day and had yet to have a head-on encounter with the Seqalu men; nor had they found Koalut. Still, Tauketok started to worry: the backpacks of the foreign soldiers were bulging. Did they plan to spend the night here and continue their search tomorrow? When would they retreat?

If it drags on like this, the battle will turn against us. Sooner or later, the white soldiers will walk out of the woods. Once they discover the tribe, the consequences will be unimaginable, Tauketok thought.

He made up his mind to prevent them from spending the night in the forest; they needed to be driven away before the sun disappeared.

But how to force the white army to retreat? Close conflict would be unfavorable to the warriors. Maybe under the cover of night, they could kill enough of them? But, as Bunkiet had said, the army would certainly come again. And what about next time, or the time after that? He was not sure that they could push them back forever. Should they fail just once, well, it was not wise to dwell on the consequences of that outcome! No. They had to reveal their strength without provoking the Red-Hairs too much.

Aha! Tauketok had an idea. Sometimes, when Seqalu had a dispute with other tribes and wanted to avoid a larger conflict, each side would send out a single warrior to fight, and the defeated would recognize their loss willingly; often it would be the tribal chiefs who fought.

So Tauketok summoned Batai, the warrior recognized as the best sniper in the tribe.

Alexander S. Mackenzie, Jr. led his army into the woods. As they moved slowly forward, the enemy flashed occasionally in front of them, fired off one or two shots, and then vanished into the heavy air.

His soldiers were unnerved. This was a labyrinth without an exit. They had brought compasses, but in this environment, such instruments were of little use. The land here was not flat, nor were there roads; it was a battlefield unlike those with which they were familiar. The woods were deep, and the forest floor was dark. They had never before walked on such rough mountain trails, through such thick woods, in such heat. And to make things even worse, it was almost as if their enemies were playing with them, leading them this way and that. Everything added to their fear.

At some point, their enemies appeared suddenly to leave, so Mackenzie and his men stopped to rest. Originally, he had believed that they could conquer with numerical advantage and superior weaponry. But five or six hours had passed, and they had not killed a single raw savage. This was highly irregular. Nowhere else had they encountered such phantomlike enemies. They had with them four days of provisions. But they could not find any enemies in the day-time; why should they fare any better at night?

Indeed, perhaps the enemies were waiting for darkness to fall, at which point they would begin a proper attack. He knew similar anxieties must be torturing the men, but he put those and other considerations to the back of his mind and yelled loudly that every soldier should take care not to stray from the alignment.

Batai and a few other warriors, their bodies bent low toward an uneven forest floor, rushed through the woods. Tauketok had ordered that they find and shoot the man who wore a cap with an embellished rim. From an oblique angle, they approached the front of the white line and did indeed see someone with a cap different from that worn by any other soldier. It had to be this one. As they were watching from cover, their target stood and, with his back turned, began gesturing to the rest of the army. Batai raised his gun, held his breath, and pulled the trigger.

In that same second, the man spun instinctively to face them, both hands covering his chest, looking almost sorrowful as blood glazed his fingers. He opened his mouth wide and fell slowly forward onto his knees. The white soldiers shot at random into the forest. But Batai and his men had already disappeared.

Soon the army found its structure and signaled the retreat. Its composure, however, was never quite regained, and on their way back down the mountain, the soldiers continued shooting sporadically in various directions.

Before sunset, the two ships left the bay.

Back at the village, Tauketok patted Batai on the shoulder and brought everybody to silence. The battle was over. For the time being they did not have to shoot anymore.

He told the tribesmen, "That white man too was a warrior."

The next morning, Tauketok took Bunkiet, Isa, Payarin, and a few other warriors up Turtle Nose Mountain and, with prayer and song, thanked the ancestral spirits for giving them courage and for bringing them good luck.

31

The call of a bugle and the rolling snap of drums sounded from the nearby consulate. When Dr. Manson heard the bugle, he straightened his back, closed his eyes, and traced a cross in the air in front of his chest.

"An American lieutenant commander was killed yesterday at South Bay by raw savages," he told Butterfly in a low voice. "The funeral is about to start. I need to be in attendance."

Butterfly was worried. A couple of days ago, she had seen two barques enter Takao. As foreign ships mooring in the harbor was a fairly common sight, she had not given their presence much attention. But now that she knew they had returned from an expedition to Koalut, they dominated her thoughts.

She was concerned to the point of distraction. She glanced at Dr. Manson. A similar look weighed on his face as she imagined was shown on her own, though it occurred to her that they were concerned with quite different things.

She sighed deeply.

That afternoon, the two barques fired seven salutes and then sailed out from Takao Harbor. When Dr. Manson returned from the funeral, he told Butterfly that the slain military officer had been buried on the grounds of the British consulate at Takao. But of greater significance to Butterfly was the fact that, according to the American officers with whom Dr. Manson had spoken, not a single Formosan raw savage had been injured or killed, despite there being more than 180 American soldiers in the forest. Dr. Manson spoke in a heavy tone, sighing as one does when delivering bad news; Butterfly, however, felt comforted.

From this day onward, Butterfly's feelings toward Manson became more and more conflicted. Originally her admiration for him had been tempered only by modesty, but now she began to understand that they were separated by a world's distance.

She respected Dr. Manson. He was fairly easy to like, he treated her kindly, and he was a highly accomplished man who, for whatever his set of motivations, nursed people—of all sorts and in all conditions—back to health. Moreover, he spoke well, and—with what seemed at first an unnatural acuity—he could provide explanations of the *reasons* behind many natural phenomena.

In contrast, the straightforward Chinya did not, perhaps, deserve her respect or admiration. But whatever Chinya deserved, whenever she saw him, she was brushed into a light happiness; the feeling of ease and affection was so natural that it was one of release.

That afternoon, she thought of Chinya.

32

On June 19, 1867, Rear Admiral Henry H. Bell, commander of the U.S. Asiatic Squadron, wrote a letter to Mr. Gideon Wells, Secretary of the Navy, giving a report of the Formosan Expedition.

Dispatch No. 53, Series of 1867.
U. S. Flagship Hartford, (Second Rate,)
Shanghae, China, June 19, 1867.
Hon. Gideon Welles, Secretary of the Navy, Washington, D.C.:

Sir: I have the honor to report to the Department that in accordance with my instructions, No. 46, current series, under date of

3d June last, I left Shanghae on the 7th instant in the *Hartford*, accompanied by the *Wyoming*, Lieut.-Commander Carpenter, commanding, for the south end of the Island of Formosa, to destroy, if possible, the lurking places of the band of savages inhabiting the southeast end or point of that island, and who murdered in March last the shipwrecked officers and crew of the American bark *Rover*.

On the 10th of June, on the passage down, I directed Commander Belknap, of the *Hartford*, to have forty sailors armed with Plumaith muskets and forty with Sharp's rifles, and all the marines, with five howitzer-men; and Lieut.-Commander Carpenter, of the *Wyoming*, to have forty Sharp's rifles, and her marines all properly officered ready to land, provided with forty rounds of ammunition and four days' rations and water; in all 181 officers and privates. The service cannot show a better drilled body than these. I stopped on the 12th inst. at Takao, on the island of Formosa, to obtain an interpreter, and Mr. Pickering, a Scotchman, who had seen much of the natives, volunteering his services, they were accepted, he declining pay. I also received as my guests, Mr. Taylor, a merchant at that port, and H. B. M. Consul, Charles Carroll, Esq., who humanely sent out messengers to communicate with the savages with offers of ransom for all the survivors, if any remained of the unfortunate crew of the *Rover*, and afterward went himself in the British gunboat *Cormorant*, Commander George E. Broad, to the bay in question, and was fired upon when attempting to land there. These gentlemen having expressed a desire to be of the expedition, next morning, June 13, at 8:30 o'clock, we anchored within half a mile of the shore on the southeast side of the large open bay indenting the south end of Formosa, a somewhat dangerous exposure at this season of typhoons, though a perfectly safe and convenient anchorage during the northeast monsoon, from October until May. The landing of one hundred and eighty-one officers, sailors and marines, provided with four days' rations and water, was made at 9:30 o'clock, under the command of Commander G. E. Belknap, of the *Hartford*, accompanied by Lieut.-Commander Alexander S. Mackenzie, Fleet Lieutenant, as second in command, who earnestly sought to go on the expedition soon after we anchored. The savages, dressed in clouts and their bodies painted red, were seen through our glasses, assembling in parties of ten or twelve on the cleared hills about two miles distant. Their muskets glistened in the sun, indicating the kind of arms they carried; their movements were visible to us on board during the most of the day. As our men marched into the hills the savages knowing the paths boldly decided to meet them, and gliding through the high grass and from cover to cover, displayed a stratagem and courage equal to our native Indians. Delivering their fire, they retreated without being seen by our men, who charging upon their covers frequently fell into ambush.

Our detachment pursued them in this harassing manner out of sight of the ships until 2 o'clock P.M., when having halted to rest the savages took the opportunity to creep up and fired upon the party, commanded by Lieut.-Commander Mackenzie, and that officer, placing himself at the head of the company commanded by Lieut. Sands, daringly led a charge into the ambuscade that was laid for them, and fell mortally wounded by a musket ball and died while being carried to the rear. The navy could boast no braver spirit and no man of higher promise than Lieut.-Commander A. S. Mackenzie. He was distinguished for professional knowledge, aptitude and tact and suavity of manners which inspired the confidence and affection of the men, while his impetuous courage impelled him along to seek the post of danger where he was always seen in the advance, both a conspicuous mark and an example.

Several officers and men having already experienced severe sunstrokes, and the command being generally exhausted and worn out by their efforts to get at the enemy during four hours' marching, Commander Belknap now thought it expedient to regain this picket on the beach, and during this march of two or three miles many of the men got into such a deplorable condition from the killing heat of the sun that the Commander determined to return with them on board of the ship, which he reached about 4 P.M., after an exhausting march of six hours under the sun at 92 degrees. That afternoon the fleet surgeon reported the casualties of the day—one killed, fourteen sunstruck, four of them dangerously. No sailors, indeed no troops unaccustomed to bush life, ever displayed better spirit, but it was apparent that sailors are not adapted to that kind of warfare against a skillful enemy, and that they could be fitted for it only by a lengthened experience. These considerations, together with the prostrated condition of many of the men and officers from sunstroke, and their inability to stand another such day, decided me not to land them again, particularly as they had already done all that was practicable for them, viz.: burnt a number of native huts and chased their warriors until they could chase no longer, though at a grievous cost of life. Their coverts of green jungle and green grass being fire-proof at this season, cannot be destroyed as I had contemplated. I observed a bamboo hut on every clearing, and several buffaloes feeding in the distance, these indicating that natives are not so wild and ignorant of human comforts as they have been represented. The only effectual remedy against the barbarous outrages on shipwrecked men by this tribe, who are not numerous, will be for the Chinese authorities on the island to occupy this bay with a settlement of their own, protected by a military force, which may be effected through our Minister at Pekin. Having accomplished all that was possible, I got underway at 9 P.M., and returning to Takao on the 14th inst., there buried the remains of the brave Mackenzie, with the prescribed honors, in the garden of the British Consulate,

Mr. Carroll, the British Consul, having kindly proposed his garden for the grave, there being no public burying-ground at Takao. The Consular flags and those of four merchant ships were worn at half mast, and all the foreigners present joined in the funeral procession.

At 6:30 P.M. on the 14th inst., weighed anchor and arrived at Shanghae to-day, expecting to meet the gunboats coming out to this squadron.

Please receive herewith the detailed report of Commander Belknap, marked "A," with the reports of commanding officers of companies, of the occurrences of the 13th of June, marked respectively "B, C, D, E;" also, the report of Fleet-Surgeon Beale, marked "F," as to casualties.

I am, Sir, very respectfully,
(Signed) H. H. Bell, Rear-Admiral,
Commanding United States Asiatic Squadron. (Copy.)

33

In a rage, Le Gendre threw the unfinished letter into the bin.

It had been addressed to Rear Admiral Henry H. Bell, Commander of the U.S. Asiatic Squadron, and its contents had scolded Bell for not informing him of the expedition to South Bay. Now a Western power had once again been defeated by the raw savages, a lieutenant commander had been killed, and they had greatly offended the Qing government.

Le Gendre believed himself the person who, among the American civil and military officers, best understood Formosa. He thought, and indeed had communicated to Bell in an earlier letter, that the best approach for an assault would be from the mouth of the Tuillassock River, attacking Koalut from the rear side of Turtle Nose Mountain.

He couldn't understand why Bell would launch the attack without first informing him. Why had he employed what Le Gendre had identified as the very worst strategy? The retreat was a disgrace. Bell had learned nothing from Carroll's failure.

But as his passion subsided, Le Gendre felt himself begin to understand something of Bell's motivation. He knew that Bell had not secured the official approval of the State Department, and only after the attack did he submit his report. This, Le Gendre considered, meant that Bell had likely intended to give himself more credit—that he was, with this military operation, attempting to assume the title of America's authority on Formosa and to take that title away from Le Gendre. Indeed, if Bell had succeeded, his reputation would surely have risen dramatically; if the State Department ever had need to consult with someone about Formosan affairs, or indeed about any affairs related to East Asia, Bell would have been the natural first choice.

From the time when Le Gendre was first stationed in Amoy as a consul, he had been impressed with the abundance and quality of Formosa's produce. But it was not until he came to the island that Pickering awakened him to the fact that Formosa occupied an important strategic position. It was clear that, compared with European powers, America lacked a footing in the Far East. Formosa, as it turned out, would be the best choice for the United States, perhaps its last chance.

Le Gendre selected some books from his shelf and began reading. He soon discovered that some forward-looking predecessors had already advised that America use Formosa as its bridgehead in the Far East. One of those advocating the policy had been Commodore Matthew Perry, the naval hero who coerced the Japanese into opening their ports to the West.

Le Gendre then found a letter written by Perry to President Millard Fillmore, the thrust of which was that, were an American colony to be established in the northern Formosan town of Keelung, far from aggravating Qing China, it would surely please its government, as the American presence would provide Formosans with increased protection from the pirates that had been harassing the island's seas. Moreover, considering the superiority of the American navy, Perry believed that to make clear the protective intent, only an occasional ship need be sent through the waters.

"Interesting," Le Gendre mused out loud as he finished reading the letter. However, he felt that if, in the current circumstances, America was to occupy Keelung directly, the Qing court would certainly respond unfavorably; it might even result in international interference.

The South Bay at which Bell had landed belonged to Formosan aborigines, not to Chinese settlers. This was why the Qing Empire had been somewhat slow in issuing its protest. Bell, then, was correct in his strategy, but he had used the wrong tactics. He should not have attacked Koalut head on; instead, he should have followed Le Gendre's advice and attacked from the flank. That way he could have taken down Koalut, and perhaps even conquered Tuillassock. Under such victorious circumstances, Le Gendre thought, the Qing might not have complained.

Somehow, as he stood and stretched his legs, he found himself elated by the American defeat. He would put his focus on Formosa, and Bell's failure would be his success. Last time, when he visited Taiwan-fu and met with the Taiwan *daotai* and regional commander, he had heard much about their achievements in defeating the army of the Taiping Rebellion that had turned against the Qing government. Though they did things quite differently from the Westerners, he cautioned himself not to think lightly of them. He would not, in spite of Pickering's insistence, regard them as good-for-nothings. Indeed, at the feast given by the Taiwan *daotai*, he felt sure that Qing government bureaucrats had put careful consideration into the training of their army. He did not know how well it was armed and equipped, but he thought it would be unwise and far too reckless to confront it directly. Moreover, he knew his superiors disliked the manner in which Britain and France bullied Qing China, so he believed such actions would displease Washington.

He needed therefore to develop a good strategy. The immediate priority would be to ensure the future safety of any shipwrecked mariners. After that was achieved, he could shift his attention to promoting America's interests in Formosa without aggravating the Qing government.

Returning to his books, Le Gendre discovered that Dr. Peter Parker, America's ambassador to Qing China, had worked for almost a year to persuade Washington to take over Formosa. Parker had lived in the Qing territory for some three decades, and although he had never been to the island, he was quite aware of its military and commercial value.

Le Gendre was surprised to read, as he flicked through yet another book, that the American businessman Gideon Nye had arrived in Formosa in 1848, earlier even than the British. Nye had immediately recognized the importance of this island and had urged the United States to buy it from the Qing government for ten million U.S. dollars. Reading this passage, Le Gendre smiled; less than two months ago, the United States had signed a contract with Russia to buy Alaska, an area of land forty times that of Formosa, for a little over seven million dollars.

Le Gendre admired Nye. He felt the businessman had a knack for judging an acquisition's value. Compared with the almost barren Alaska, Formosa appeared a much better prospect with its large population, exportable products, and strategic significance.

Caleb Cushing, the U.S. Attorney General to whom Nye had written, had a deep relationship with the Qing government. He was part of the U.S. envoy that had signed the first treaty with the Qing Empire. Parker was his assistant.

Both Parker in Peking and Cushing in Washington had been very enthusiastic about securing Formosa as an American base. Parker had tried to lobby Britain and France, while Cushing had set about persuading President Franklin Pierce to take positive action. Pierce was convinced, but he wished to avoid war. Parker advocated the exchange of interests with Britain and France so that the United States could take possession of Formosa. In 1857 in Macao, Parker met with the Hong Kong governor and British envoy to Qing China, John Bowring, and with the French ambassador, Alphonse de Bourboulon. Parker proposed they distribute their interests: the United States would take Formosa; Great Britain would take the Zhoushan Islands; France would take Korea.

Le Gendre looked up from the book and wondered why the various endeavors had amounted to nothing.

Eventually he found the answer. In 1857, after James Buchanan became President of the United States, the country became immersed in a domestic crisis; the conflicts between the abolitionists and the Confederate states left him no leeway to deal with the Far East. Furthermore, there was some interference from Great Britain. The British were apparently reluctant to let the United States monopolize the interests of Formosa. In the end, John Appleton, America's deputy assistant secretary of state, promised Great Britain that his country had no intention to occupy Formosa. Since then, the American government had retreated from its attempts to seize the island.

What a pity! thought Le Gendre. He did not wholeheartedly support military aggression for territorial expansion, but he believed that the United States should in any case retain its commercial benefits, especially as it had been among the first foreign powers to come to the island.

But sadly, the conservative attitude taken lately by the U.S. government, coupled with the American Civil War, had made a waste of the previous endeavors.

And now the British were taking their place!

34

Le Gendre returned the books to the shelf.

He had decided to negotiate again with the Qing government and persuade them to send troops to punish the raw savages. Some pressure on his part was important; lately Wu Ta-ting had filled his correspondence with little else but prevaricating nonsense.

He would have the Qing government ensure the safety of the Formosan waters. If successful, this would bring him international renown, and the State Department would see how capable he was. His former superintendent, General Grant, would be made to see that he could not only fight but also settle diplomatic disputes.

He wrote a letter to Bell, asking him for use of a ship. Bell's terse reply came on August 20: "I regret to tell you that I cannot dispatch a ship to send you to Formosa; our ships are soon to depart for America."

Le Gendre sneered, staring at Bell's handwriting, resisting the urge to destroy yet another letter. Undeterred, however, he soon came up with a solution and drafted a request for a ship from the Fukien governor. The reply came back quickly in the affirmative; the governor not only lent him a ship but also wrote a letter to his subordinates, the Taiwan *daotai* and regional commander, instructing them to assist Le Gendre in all his undertakings.

Seeing for the first time the newly painted *Volunteer* moored at Mawei Port in Foochow, Le Gendre gloated. "Ah, here she is. The *Volunteer*! You see, the Qing government *volunteered* to let me borrow it. Ha ha ha!"

On September 5, they left for Taiwan-fu. Looking up at the Star-Spangled Banner as the ship cut neatly through calm seas, Le Gendre felt in particularly high spirits. They reached Anping early the next morning after an uneventful crossing.

The officials in Taiwan-fu had prepared a coach to escort Le Gendre and his men to a beautiful mansion replete with a Chinese-style garden. It was a two-story building, constructed in a rare meeting of Chinese and Western styles. Shortly after Le Gendre's arrival, Prefect Ye Zongyuan of Taiwan-fu paid a visit, imploring him to take the afternoon to rest, explaining that the following day another coach would call to take him to where the meeting was to be held. Accordingly, Le Gendre took a stroll on the mansion's grounds.

Walking through the garden—its carefully maintained pathways a vision of gentle serenity—he thought of Pickering. Though he disliked the man's arrogance, he harbored some admiration for his being such an eloquent wanderer of the world. It was a terrible pity that he was so much of a nosy busybody. Nevertheless, before leaving for Anping, Le Gendre had written to him asking for his help.

As he approached one of the distant edges of the garden, Le Gendre stopped in the shade of a pear tree and thought of the well-mannered Dr. Manson, who was likely at that very moment working in the hospital in Takao; the doctor was in truth quite the opposite of Pickering. But then he felt something of a soreness. He missed the Sialiao girl. Why had she shunned him?

A butterfly flew from tree to tree. Its movements were almost like those of a bird; a single flap of its large wings heralded a period of gliding calm. Le Gendre remembered that the girl was called Butterfly. What a beautiful name! Such an attractive girl. Would he see her again? Perhaps there was some way. . . .

But no, he was in Taiwan-fu, not Takao, and the next morning he would have to face the Qing officials and adequately explain how and why it was that Admiral Bell had, without informing them, landed at South Bay. Tomorrow's meeting would be difficult; this was not the time for indulging in forlorn memories, regardless of their provenance.

Contrary to the European style, the garden's pond did not have a fountain at its center. There were instead jagged rocks and a bridge with—at least this was how it appeared to Le Gendre—a highly exaggerated arch. Everything was so small, quiet, and, he admitted to himself, very elegant. He sat on a bench, watching the goldfish swim gracefully, and was reminded of a story told by his Chinese teacher about two Chinese scholars.

> The scholars were watching the fish in the pond.
>
> The first said, "The fish are swimming to and fro. How happy they are!"
>
> The second replied, "You are not a fish. How is it that you know they are happy?"
>
> "And you are not me. How do you know that I don't know that the fish are happy?"
>
> "You are right to say that I am not you, so I don't know how you feel. But I know that you are not a fish. So I am sure that you know nothing of whether or not the fish are happy."

Le Gendre couldn't remember the story's conclusion, but he had left that particular lesson with the impression that Chinese people were wont to engage in pointless debate.

Indeed, his recent experience appeared to confirm these suspicions. From April 19, the Qing government bureaucrats had been procrastinating, sending letter after letter in poor excuse of their inaction. This in contrast with Admiral Bell, who had taken immediate action without informing others of his intentions. Perhaps, Le Gendre thought resentfully, Pickering had something of a point: these different attitudes might be typical of the two cultures.

When Le Gendre last met with them, he and the Qing officials had appeared to reach an agreement. Although General Liu had admitted that his soldiers lacked experience fighting in the mountains and therefore he needed some time to ready them for the operation, Daotai Wu had promised to send troops to punish the culprits "as soon as possible."

Le Gendre had thought that Liu had spoken sensibly, and although the general had not specified how long the preparations would take,

Le Gendre imagined it would be at most a month. But to his frustration, the Qing government had not sent out its troops in anything like a timely fashion. Le Gendre had written a letter at the beginning of June to push them into action, but soon thereafter, Bell took the initiative to fight.

The Taiwan *daotai*'s latest letter had arrived on June 13, just one day before Admiral Bell's attack on South Bay. It described Koalut as completely inaccessible and concluded in a most ridiculous way.

According to the Tientsin Treaty, if your countrymen are injured or killed, local government officials should indeed arrest the culprits and punish them severely. Furthermore, the local magistrate should send out troops to deal with those involved. However, as your countrymen on the *Rover* were not killed on our land nor in our seas, but rather in an area occupied by savages, the Tientsin Treaty does not apply. Those raw savages live beyond our dominion; thus, our army need not take any action in that place.

What nonsense this was! Le Gendre had immediately written a severe reply to Daotai Wu.

Back inside the mansion after his walk, Le Gendre reread a copy of the letter, refamiliarizing himself with its contents and arguments ahead of the meeting. In it, Le Gendre had warned the Qing government that if the savages really did live outside the Qing's dominion, then their land would be open to encroachment from foreign countries, which would greatly affect the Qing's interest in that area. He alluded to the Indians in his own country, telling Wu that, in the nation's interest, the United States had declared that the Indians and their lands fell under the complete jurisdiction of the government. Likewise, the Qing Imperial Court should spare no effort to incorporate the savages' land into its territory.

He had tried also to convince Wu of the necessity to send the Qing army to pacify the savages, as the land was de facto territory of the

Qing government. Elsewhere, the immigrants who continued to arrive from the Qing mainland would further their control of Formosa. He pointed out that the Qing government had already anticipated such development of the savages' land and had responded by enacting strict laws to control the transactions between businessmen and raw savages. He argued that the Qing monopoly over camphor oil—a monopoly enforceable under penalty of death—likewise pointed to Qing control over the entire island of Formosa.

"For the past two hundred years," he concluded, "your government has claimed total jurisdiction and rule over the savages' land; it is the Qing government, therefore, that should answer for any disputes foreign countries have with the natives."

He looked up, feeling very pleased with the contents of the letter, and wondered, with a hint of trepidation, what tomorrow would bring.

6

SERENITY LOST AND FOUND

35

Takao Harbor was divided into two parts—the old and the new. The small isle of Chihou (present-day Qijin), which had been inhabited by Hokkien settlers for almost two hundred years, was home to the old fishing port and the old main street. On the island, the eponymous Chihou Hill looked across the port to Formosa proper. The Hokkien settlers called the island-side mountain Takao Hill. Monkeys lived there in droves, so the seventeenth-century Dutch called it Apen Berg. In 1854, the U.S. Navy arrived, and on the maps they generated from their visit, Ape Hill was specified in English. At its foot was a small fishing village called Shaochuantou.

At the beginning of the eighteenth century, Amoy and Anping were the only ports from which ferries would carry passengers across the strait between the Chinese mainland and Formosa; at that time, Chihou Port was but a small fishing port visited occasionally by smugglers. By the end of the eighteenth century, however, a creek had changed its course, and Anping's port was becoming narrower and narrower due to the slowly depositing silt; when the north winds howled, ships could not enter. Since Chihou Port was nearby, ships coming from Amoy often redirected themselves to anchor there. The cultivation of the plain around Takao Harbor soon began, and Fung-shan New Town and

Old Town were then established. In time, more and more European and American ships came to dock. At this point, when people talked about Takao Port, they were in fact referring to Chihou Port.

In 1854, the first foreign company was established in Chihou by the American merchant W. M. Robinet. The following year, Nye Brothers & Co. and Anthon Williams & Co. were set up. The three foreign companies together purchased a ship called the *Science*, and Captain George Potter signed a contract with Yu Duo, the then Taiwan *daotai*.

According to the contract, in exchange for the right to a monopoly on the production of camphor in Formosa, the U.S. businessmen were to be responsible for the construction of Takao Harbor. They invested a huge sum of money to advance this project in Shaochuantou. They dug a 54-meter-long in-harbor channel and built a bridge, a communications tower, a warehouse, and two houses—all from granite. Afterward, they added a pier on which to load and unload goods. In 1860, when Takao was opened to international trade, the customs house and new foreign buildings were almost all located on the side of Shaochuantou.

In 1866, Maxwell came to Takao to preach and practice medicine. He sought a location similar to Kanxi Street in Taiwan-fu, so he rented a place on the side of Chihou Hill. First he had a church built, and then he set up a hospital with eight beds for patients. He called the hospital Takao Hospital, but most locals called it Chihou Hospital. Maxwell was occupied with preaching, so it was Dr. Manson who oversaw the medical affairs.

Upon her arrival, Butterfly quickly developed a fondness for the environment. Almost half a year had passed since she had first arrived at the hospital, and four months had passed since Chinya returned to Takao and found employment as a quayman. He worked on the Shaochuantou side, carrying goods by day and staying with Hokkien laborers in a corner of a warehouse at night.

As the foreigners all went to church on Sundays, Butterfly and Chinya were able to have the day off as well. Every Sunday, Chinya

would take the ferry to Chihou to walk along Chihou street with Butterfly. Their favorite place was the fair near Mazu Temple, where
they could eat seafood and watch acrobats perform. However, almost
four months of repetition without change had left them somewhat
bored by these activities.

So one afternoon, they decided that Butterfly should come across
to Shaochuantou. Chinya led her along the pier on a stroll in a
delightful sea breeze. As they walked, they passed by heaps of salt
as tall as men, like small mountains shining brilliant and white in
the bright light of day.

They came to the mouth of a river where the water was so wide
that it formed what was almost a lagoon. They had intended to go
farther, but thick woods blocked their way. They found a narrow
trail, and although they could see houses farther on, the ground was
too muddy to walk along easily. Instead they sat and gazed across
the water at a small fishing village, where fishermen were hanging
nets to dry in the sun.

Butterfly looked at the boats, the salt piles, the coral rocks of
Takao Hill where monkeys frolicked; it was different here from
Sialiao, and it was different too from Tongling Bo.

Butterfly and Chinya spent the rest of a pleasant Sunday together
and then took the ferry from Shaochuantou back to Chihou. On the
return crossing, they clung to each other. Butterfly could feel the
length of Chinya's body pressing against her own. She felt nervous—
her heart struck fiercely from within her chest—but she was reluctant to pull away. She stole a look at Chinya; he was looking back
at her.

36

At the hospital, Butterfly grew more and more confident when taking care of patients, and she was also making progress with her

English. She had quickly become the most popular person at Chihou Hospital; Dr. Manson liked her, and many patients asked for her by name, praising both her personality and her skill. Some Hokkien men knew she came from the Puppet Mountains, so they nicknamed her Puppet Flower. Butterfly liked this nickname. Others called her Savage Assistant, and by this she was not offended at all.

Because of Butterfly's presence, some of the locals who in the past had been mistrustful of the hospital ventured through its doors to see the doctor. With Butterfly as an interpreter, they were more willing to be treated; after all, the foreign doctor could speak Hokkien, but not fluently.

Marveling at the success of the hospital, Dr. Maxwell thought back to when he had first arrived in Taiwan-fu two years ago. That time, it had taken just twenty-four days for him to be expelled from the city after rumor spread that he manufactured his medicine out of human livers and eyes. He had taken refuge in the British consulate in Chihou, and it was only when Pickering took him around the plains aboriginal tribes in Siraya to travel and preach that he had recovered his confidence.

One day Mr. Chen, a man in his fifties, was brought to the hospital to see the doctor. When he arrived, his leg was so inflamed with infection that he could barely walk. Dr. Manson cleared the pus and then asked Butterfly to dress the wound. The man groaned, but Butterfly did everything so skillfully and carefully that before long he found his pain subsiding. Once the infection had fully left his body, Mr. Chen invited Butterfly to visit his home.

A few weeks after that invitation, one beautiful Sunday morning, Mr. Chen sent his concubine and a servant to fetch Butterfly. The three of them arrived at Bantan-kang or Bantan port (present-day Zuoying), which was busy with boats of all kinds. They traveled inland to the east and soon came to a magnificent wall no less spectacular than that which surrounded Taiwan-fu.

"This is Koo-sia," Mr. Chen's concubine told Butterfly.

"Why is it called *Koo-sia*?" Butterfly asked. The gate and the wall both looked relatively new.

"I'm not sure," the concubine said with a smile. "Perhaps you should ask our master."

The streets behind the wall were much wider and straighter than those outside the town. It was not, however, a place bustling with people. They stopped by a large temple. The concubine leaned closer to Butterfly. "My master is the keeper of this temple. Whenever we come back from trips outside, we worship Baosheng Dadi, the Deity of Medicine, and pray for our health and happiness. Come, my master is waiting for you inside."

But before Butterfly could enter the temple, Mr. Chen had already walked out through its gate. The people accompanying him appeared surprised at Butterfly's young age as Mr. Chen told them, "This is Dr. Lim. She helped Dr. Manson take care of me."

Butterfly smiled and shook her head. "Please, I am merely Dr. Manson's aide."

Inside the temple, Butterfly worshiped with the three lighted incense sticks given to her by Mr. Chen. When she looked up at the statue, Baosheng Dadi appeared merciful and kindhearted. She did not know the precise origin of this deity, but she was learning medicine, so wasn't she in some way already a follower of this Deity of Medicine?

Butterfly placed her sticks among the many others already in the censer. Mr. Chen looked extremely proud as he told her, "Ciji Temple is the most prosperous temple in this town. We have worshipers coming from as far away as Pitau. Nearby, there is also a famous Temple of the Goddess of Mercy, Guanyin Ting."[1]

When Butterfly heard this, she immediately expressed her interest in visiting the temple. Mr. Chen smiled and said, "Of course.

---

[1] A temple for Guanyin near Fung-shan Koo-sia (now Zuoying District, Kaohsiung City).

there on a sedan chair. My concubine will also accompany us."

Mr. Chen's house was right next to Ciji Temple. During the meal, Butterfly asked, "This town's wall looks quite newly built. Why is it called 'Old Town'? And why don't I see many people here?"

Chen heaved a sigh and said, "Yes, although it is called Old Town, the wall is, as you have observed, relatively recently built. In fact, I watched its construction when I was a child. Afterward, the magistrate and civil officials moved in. But then, decades later, they moved to Pitau. Alas, how can Pitau compare with our town? But regardless of Old Town's greater merits, ever since the government office was transferred to Pitau, this settlement has been declining in population. Now Pitau is home to eight thousand households, while we have only five hundred households left, and those families remain here only thanks to thriving temples like Ciji Temple and Guanyin Ting."

Butterfly probed again with her question. "But why is it called 'Old Town'?"

Chen seemed taken aback. "Miss Lim, you are quite unlike other women. Well then, since you saved my life, I shall take this chance to reveal my identity to you, as well as to my children. I am an old man, as you all can plainly see, and I may never again be gifted such an opportunity to tell these small pieces of history."

Mr. Chen stood up and disappeared into another room. His family members were baffled; in his absence, no one said anything. After a while he emerged holding a yellowed manuscript that, with his eyes closed as if in prayer, he laid carefully on the desk. He said, very softly, "Our family name, Chen, comes from my mother's side. My biological father was Yao Ying, who, almost thirty years ago now, was the *daotai* of Taiwan."

Something very much like disbelief streaked the Chen family faces. One or two even cried out in surprise. Butterfly had never heard of Yao Ying, but she knew that the *daotai* was the highest-ranking government official in Formosa.

Master Chen did little to acknowledge his family's reactions, and he continued speaking. "Yao Ying assisted with the design of the Fung-shan Koo-sia wall, but he did not participate in the construction. When the wall was completed, he wrote an article to mark the occasion."

Chen picked up his cup and sipped; he appeared at this point to be stalling, as if at a loss as to how to begin the story. A silence brushed through the room. After a while he spoke again. "I will start with Yao Ying, my father. He passed the Imperial Civil Examinations and became a *jinshi*[2] at the age of twenty-three. By the time he was thirty he was ruling over several counties in Fukien, and he could speak Hokkien fluently. At the age of thirty-five, he was assigned to be a magistrate in Taiwan. The locals admired him, for he could speak their language. I believe the then Taiwan *daotai* also thought highly of him.

"According to the Qing law of the time, government officials coming to Taiwan were not allowed to bring their wives or children with them. Yao had been in Taiwan for several years, living as a single man, when he took a liking to the temple keeper's daughter. But since he was already married in mainland China, he could only take her as his second wife. Moreover, because his wife in mainland China had forbidden him from taking any concubines, his second wife stayed in her maiden home, even after their marriage.

"Then, quite unexpectedly, Yao's first wife arrived in Taiwan, and she discovered that he had a second wife. The first wife had a fierce quarrel with Yao and asked him to abandon the other wife, who was at that time pregnant."

There was another pause, and then Chen said, "Yes, you are right to guess that I was the baby. In the winter of the twenty-fifth year

---

[2] A successful candidate who passed the Imperial Civil Examinations at the national level.

of Emperor Jiaqing's reign, my poor mother gave birth to me. When I was barely a month old, she went to Guanyin Ting, shaved her head, and became a nun. I was placed under the care of my grandparents.

"But word always spreads, and it spread eventually to the Taiwan *daotai*. He concluded that Yao had disobeyed the law, and he believed it was a sign that Yao could not regulate his own family. He demoted Yao and transferred him far from the administrative center. Yao was sent to Kavalan, an inhospitable place in northeastern Taiwan. This happened in the first year of Emperor Daoguang's reign."

Chen gently shook his head. "Fortunately, the *daotai* knew my father was a capable man, so he did not specify the reason for Yao's demotion in the official records.

"In the second year, Yao's father passed away, so he traveled home to observe the period of mourning. A year later, he returned to Kavalan.

"In the fourth year of Emperor Daoguang's reign, the new Fukien Governor, Sun Erhzhun, visited Taiwan. At that time, rebels were causing a great commotion in Pitau, and the government as well as the residents felt it necessary to construct a stone wall. After much consultation and deliberation, the governor decided to adopt the approach proposed by Yao, and he encouraged locals to donate the funds needed to build the stone wall. The construction began in the fourth year of Emperor Daoguang's reign and was completed the following year. I was just five or six years old, but I can still remember the workers digging out coral stones from Takao Hill and carrying them here on ox carts. When it was completed—this would have been in the fifth year of Emperor Daoguang's reign—it was said that private donations accounted for just over half of the cost, while the rest was supplied by the government.

"By then, Yao had been serving as a government official in Kavalan for five years. The Taiwan *daotai* decided that my father should be given credit for what he had done, so he summoned him from

Kavalan back to Takao. Yao was a renowned scholar known for his elegant writing, so the Taiwan *daotai* asked him to write an essay to mark the completion of the stone wall. Yao wrote 'Reconstructing Fung-shan Koo-sia,' which was to all readers a most eloquent piece of writing. Shortly afterward, the Fukien governor reported to the Qing Imperial Court and suggested that Yao be transferred back to the mainland to serve in Jiangsu Province.

"In the sixth year of Emperor Daoguang's reign, he was promoted out of Taiwan. I imagine he must have had mixed feelings about his stay here. I still remember when he came to see me before he returned to the mainland. It was the first time I saw him. I was just a small child. I had been given my mother's family name, Chen, so I did not feel much affection for him. And anyway, even though he came to see me, he never bothered to take me back to mainland China to be incorporated into his original family. My grandpa here was immensely disappointed. Later, Yao went to Guanyin Ting, asking after my mother, but she refused to see him.

"My father copied his own manuscripts over the years, and he left one set with my grandpa, telling him that his writing would keep me company as I grew up.

"When I was twelve, my mother passed away, and when I was eighteen, my father returned to Taiwan, this time as Taiwan *daotai*. The rest is history that we are somewhat familiar with."

Butterfly asked, "So you never saw your father again?"

"When my father was in office as Taiwan *daotai*, the Imperial Court was having a problem with Great Britain because of opium. In fact, the two countries had a war on that account. Anyway, Yao was dealing with those foreign affairs. After he captured two British ships to stop them from encroaching on Taiwan, the British accused him of slaughtering over 190 sailors. By way of appeasement, Emperor Daoguang transferred him back to mainland China. My father saw me twice during his second stay in Taiwan. The first time was when he took office here, and the second time was when he was about to vacate his position. He summoned me to see him in Fung-shan County Office in Pitau. It was only then that he learned of my mother's death.

"Needless to say, we were not on intimate terms. And neither did we warm toward each other. He gave me some money but did not mention the manuscripts. It was only much later that I learned of them, when my grandpa was dying. By then, my father had been sent to faraway Sichuan and Tibet.

"Finally, in the third year of Emperor Xianfeng's reign, a pageboy came to tell us that my father had died. That was fourteen years ago. . . . The older I get, the more I understand what my father went through."

37

Although Mr. Chen was quite clearly agitated after reliving his life story, he nevertheless remembered to take Butterfly to Guanyin Ting after the meal.

As soon as they entered Guanyin Ting, a nun came up to greet them. A short while later an older nun, the temple's abbess, also came to welcome them.

Chen told the older nun, "This is Miss Lim. She works in the foreign doctors' hospital in Chihou. She came here to visit me, and when she heard me mention Guanyin Ting, she said she needed to worship here."

The abbess, Yizhen, was a slightly chubby nun with an amiable face; Butterfly warmed to her immediately.

"Ah, you work at a foreigners' hospital, but still you come to our temple to worship. It means you are connected to Guanyin!"

"I come from Sialiao, and my father used to live in Tongling Bo. He was a Hakka man who worshiped Guanyin when he was alive. He taught me to chant the Buddhist mantra *Namo Guanyin Bodhisattva*."

"Well, then you are connected to Guanyin by destiny. I will show you around."

Yizhen led her to the main hall, where they bowed three times to the buddha. Butterfly saw the statue, cast in solid glowing gold, of Guanyin seated on the lotus. The first pair of the statue's eighteen arms had a sword in one hand and another sharp tool in the other. Despite the weaponry, the Guanyin did not appear angry; her face looked more grave than merciful.

Butterfly had never seen a Guanyin statue like this. "Is this the Guanyin with a thousand hands?"

"No, this is Cundi Buddha, the Guanyin with eighteen arms on a lotus flower."

Butterfly looked at the statue more closely. "Is Cundi Buddha related to Guanyin, the Goddess of Mercy?"

Yizhen explained, "When Guanyin wants to help the six levels of creatures to transcend, she has six transformations. Cundi is one of them. Each of Guanyin's forms is responsible for helping a specific level of creature. Cundi Guanyin is responsible for delivering human beings from their agony. She is closest to us ordinary humans. That's why we sometimes call her the Buddha Mother."

Butterfly asked again, "Why does Cundi Guanyin hold so many different objects in her hands?"

"These are instruments she uses to help people. The sword is used to cut through perplexity. The purifying bottle is used for catharsis. The lotus is used to cure disease, and the rope is used to link people together. Some pass on knowledge, while others eradicate the karma of vices."

Yizhen floated away to attend to some other matter, and Butterfly was left staring at the statue, thinking about her life and her own shifting place in the world. She felt a growing sense of calm and certainty, even as she considered the unpredictability of each passing week.

After a while, it dawned on her that life is about more than virtue and sincerity; a sword is often needed when hesitation and doubt arise.

38

After visiting Guanyin Ting, Butterfly had so much to share with Chinya, and she was very excited to see him again. However, the following weekend he did not show up. She was a little deflated, but the weather on that afternoon was foul and wet, and she could understand why Chinya would not want to make the trip.

The following Sunday coincided with the Ghost Festival, which was held in the middle of the seventh month on the lunar calendar. People in Chihou set up tables with offerings to comfort and pacify those wandering ghosts. There were all sorts of food, fruit, and pastries on the tables, which, beginning at the Mazu Temple gate, dotted the street's entire length. Again Chinya wasn't on the ferry; how could he miss being a part of such a festive atmosphere?

Butterfly thought of her father as she marveled at the magnificent scene. Dr. Manson, however, merely remarked that she "should have seen it in Taiwan-fu," before asking her, "Why do you people fear ghosts so much?"

"Fear is not the right word, Dr. Manson. We *honor* our ancestors, our ghosts, and our gods."

One week later, Butterfly stood waiting for the ferries from Shaochuantou. Yet again Chinya was nowhere to be seen.

At noon, unable to tolerate the helplessness of not knowing, she boarded a ferry and made the crossing.

She knew where Chinya lived, but she did not want to venture uninvited into the warehouse. What to do?

Back in Tongling Bo, she had learned from her mother to imitate the chirping of all sorts of birds. It was one way they had transmitted important information when in the forest; different birds' chirping, with different combinations of melodies, represented different messages. Later, when she and Bunkiet came to live in Sialiao, they had continued to communicate in this way, particularly when both were in a good mood. Chinya found the technique fascinating, and he had gone to considerable lengths to master it.

Standing outside the warehouse, Butterfly emulated the chirping of Muller's barbet; after a while, Chinya appeared.

Butterfly rushed to greet him, but he was walking very slowly, dragging his feet across the dusty ground. He did not appear happy to see her.

Hours later, back at the hospital, Butterfly sat alone in her room. Night had set in, and her breathing sounded louder now that the world was dark. In the afternoon, she had pieced together something of what had happened from Chinya's fragmented and frequently oblique account.

The Hokkien laborers living in Shaochuantou often gambled together at night, and sometimes they would invite Chinya to join them. At first he had turned them down. But about a month ago, one of the gamblers, a leader figure within the group, won a huge sum of money and said that he would treat them all to a night at the brothel. After some pressure, a reluctant Chinya was persuaded to join them.

Later, this leader became furious when Chinya again refused an invitation to gamble. After all, he fumed, hadn't he paid for all of Chinya's fun? And *still* Chinya was unwilling to gamble. How ungrateful! So, after further threats, Chinya agreed to go with them, "Just once."

The first time he won some money; the thrill was intoxicating, and the bag of coins he took home seemed heavy enough to last forever. The following night he went there again and won more money. But soon his luck ran out and he lost everything, including all of his previous winnings. He upped the stakes, but the more he wanted to win, the more he lost. Desperate, he borrowed money. By the time day broke, Chinya owed more than he could earn from a full three months of work.

Since then, people had been coming to ask him to pay the money he owed. The money Chinya earned during the day was taken away each night. Often he couldn't afford to eat. Finally, one evening a few days before the start of the Ghost Festival, two sturdy men came from the gambling spot and—after listening to Chinya's pleading that he had no money—beat him terribly and then cut a finger from his hand. They left saying they'd be back again in a month. If, come that time, Chinya still did not have the money, they would leave with a second finger.

Since then, until Butterfly found him, Chinya had been in such pain that he was unable to work. He could only hide in the corner of the warehouse, hungry and shedding tears.

Butterfly was angry and upset, but she wanted to help Chinya.

The next day, she asked Dr. Manson for a day off and then took the ferry to Bantan port. When she entered Fung-shan Old Town, she headed directly to Guanyin Ting, where she knelt and prayed before Cundi Guanyin.

As Butterfly prayed, she felt clarity emerge in her heart. After she had analyzed things one by one, a solution loomed.

She got to her feet, bowed three times to Cundi Guanyin, and then returned to Bantan port, where she boarded a ferry to Shaochuan-tou. After landing, she entered Chinya's warehouse—this time without birdsong or hesitation—and practically dragged him back to Chihou, where Dr. Manson agreed to have him at the hospital.

After his wounds were sufficiently healed, Butterfly sent Chinya on a ship back to Sialiao. At first he was reluctant to leave, but eventually, after failing to convince her that he could guarantee his own safety at Bantan port, he agreed to return home. Only when the ship was no longer visible did Butterfly turn, exhale, and walk briskly back to the hospital.

7

TROOPS MARCHING

39

Le Gendre was riding on horseback alongside General Liu. They were in Taiwan-fu, reviewing at a slow walk the seven hundred fifty soldiers of the Qing army who were being sent to South Bay to fight the raw savages. Le Gendre had been told by several people that these were the best Qing soldiers, and indeed he found them well dressed and well equipped; they were in high spirits, and their guns were modern and in good condition—at least on the surface.

General Liu looked quite imposing. He was under thirty years old, but age had not prevented him from rising swiftly to occupy his important position. Le Gendre had heard that Liu distinguished himself when cracking down on the Taiping Rebellion. After that campaign was concluded, his superiors, General Zou Zongtang and General Zeng Guofan, rewarded him with an immediate promotion. Since their first meeting, Le Gendre had been getting along well with this Chinese general, finding him to be a very responsible leader, perspicacious and full of foresight.

Four days ago, on September 6, Le Gendre had met again with Formosan government officials. He asked the Taiwan *daotai* to comply with the Fukien governor's directions and send troops to conquer Koalut in the south. Some of the officials complained immediately

that they were not prepared to send their troops into such an uncivilized place; others said there were more important affairs to which
they must first attend; some even said that they could not take the
risk of having him, Le Gendre, hurt or even—they shuddered physically at this thought—*killed* by raw savages. One came up with the
idea of beheading a few savages by way of retribution. As ever, Le
Gendre was annoyed by their procrastination, and after a period of
unproductive back-and-forth, the Taiwan *daotai* tried to pacify him,
saying, "Sir, perhaps it is time for a break. Now would be an ideal
time for you to try some of the famous food of Taiwan-fu."

Le Gendre sighed. He felt in his heart that these officials were a
disgrace, and he was sure that some of them would take advantage
of the break to slip permanently away from the meeting. But before
it could be disbanded, Regional Commander Liu Ming-teng stood up
and said loudly, his voice cutting through the noise of frivolous chatter, "Gentlemen, the Fukien governor has given his order, and we
should carry it out without question. The amount of time that has to
this moment passed without action is deeply regrettable. Yes, Koalut
is far away. And although it will be hard to provision our troops for
such travels and conditions as they will likely face, we will surely
overcome any and all difficulties. Further talk will not do us any
good. We'd best act at once and finish our preparations. With three
days, everything will be ready." He bowed deeply to Daotai Wu Ta-
ting. "If our honorable *daotai* agrees, I will promise Consul Le Gendre
that on the tenth of September, our army will set off south."

The various officials looked at him in disbelief. Daotai Wu wrin-
kled his brows, but after such a speech, there was no alternative but
to subscribe to the plan.

Le Gendre was surprised but pleased by the sudden twist. The
young general turned to address him. "Your Excellency, please
take your break. In half an hour, we will reconvene and discuss
particulars."

Le Gendre waited in the guest hall. Before long, General Liu joined him.

"As I explained," Liu said, "we will need three days to prepare provisions. For these three days, the *daotai* will assign some escorts to show you around Fu-cheng. That is Taiwan-fu's most prosperous area, with government buildings. I know that this is the second time you have visited Taiwan-fu, and it is not a big place, but still, there are many places worth seeing."

So for the next few days Le Gendre, in the company of Taiwan-fu Prefect Ye Zongyuan, explored the city that was home to some 120,000 people. He visited several temples and spent time at the academies of classical learning. Prefect Ye had prepared a sedan chair, but Le Gendre said that he would prefer walking.

On September 10, exactly as scheduled, General Liu Ming-teng directed his troops to move toward Liangkiau. Le Gendre, gratified by this punctuality, had learned during his time with Prefect Ye Zongyuan that General Liu was not a Han but a Tujia, one of the minority ethnic groups in China. Perhaps, Le Gendre pondered, that was why the general did not display the repulsive adherence to bureaucracy so typical of a Han government official.

In the morning, the troops began their march; Le Gendre rode on horseback alongside General Liu. The road was lined with onlookers, and when they approached the South Gate, drums and gongs sounded. With that, the great procession marched out of Taiwan-fu.

The road—straight, wide, and well maintained within the city limits—quickly deteriorated once they passed beyond the South Gate. It drew so narrow that soon only two ox carts could pass side by side, and weeds rather than trees lined the bumpy path. The weather was very hot, so Le Gendre dismounted from the horse to sit instead on a sedan chair. He felt quite content in the middle of the marching army. His interpreter, Joseph Bernard, was provided with a sedan chair as well. However, to Le Gendre's disappointment, the army moved very slowly; it had traveled just fifteen miles by the time they pulled over to spend the night at Arcontien.

The next day, sitting again on the sedan chair, Le Gendre held a compass in his hand, determining their position and keeping time as if he were a surveyor. For a long while he had been interested in geology and geography; moreover, this was his first time traveling south by land, and he wished to make the most of it.

At noon, Le Gendre saw Banping Mountain, which meant Chihou and Takao were nearby. He thought of Pickering, Dr. Manson, and the girl from Liangkiau. How he wished to see them! Unfortunately, General Liu had told him that they would be heading directly to Fung-shan County Seat without passing Takao or Chihou. What a pity!

When they arrived, they entered Fung-shan County Seat through the North Gate and were greeted by Assistant Regional Commander Ling Dingbang. It was a much smaller and less impressive place than Taiwan-fu. Le Gendre looked at the army. Some of the soldiers appeared tired. He thought perhaps they had lost their morale, and he started to worry.

After a restful night's sleep, Le Gendre was ready to go in the early morning. At noon, however, the army still looked unprepared to set off. Le Gendre found several officers gathering together, talking and laughing; he considered that perhaps they were gambling and left them to it. He went to find Liu but was told that the general had left the camp to feast with some local officials and was not expected to be back until twilight. At that point, Le Gendre stopped feeling anxious to leave; it was impossible for the army to march forward without its general, and there was no point in fretting over something he hadn't the power to change. Deciding instead to spend the day exploring, he left the camp in early afternoon, accompanied by a Hokkien interpreter. On their walk they came across the Fengyi Academy. Inside, students were nodding their heads while reciting ancient poetry. "Cloud-Ascending Road" was written on the plaque mounted outside the building, urging students to study hard so that they could be on the right path that would lead them to distinguished positions.

Le Gendre shook his head as he realized that for the subjects of Qing emperors the shortcut to officialdom was the memorization and repetition of what their ancestors had written. Those Chinese people were so intent on learning about the past that they remained ignorant of contemporary scientific advances. He sighed.

Beside the academy was a new temple. The statue inside looked like a kindhearted government official. The interpreter told him that people came to this temple to worship Cao Jin, who had been magistrate of Fung-shan County some thirty years ago. Le Gendre could not contain his surprise. "He was a magistrate, and now he is worshiped as a deity?"

The interpreter explained that although Cao Jin had been the county magistrate for just four years, he had, during his tenure in office, dug channels to solve the irrigation problem that had beset locals for several years prior to his arrival. With these changes, crops grew well and harvests were handsome. Though he later returned home to Henan, the people of Fung-shan built the Cao Gong Temple to worship him.

Le Gendre was stirred. "Oh, that a man should become a god so soon after his death! If I become a deity to be worshiped like this, then I will not have lived in vain." Afterward he was silent and so clearly immersed in serious thought that the interpreter dared not speak as they walked together through the town.

Later, they came to a lake surrounded by a small number of houses. A handful of men were fishing on its shore, and a few women were doing laundry in its waters. Le Gendre so loved the atmosphere that he sat down in the shade and with his eyes closed, listened intently to the birds singing.

The interpreter spoke gently. "Sir, if you are tired, we can head back."

"Why, I am not tired at all! How can one be tired in a place like this? Let's continue. I want to see more."

Together they visited some more temples, and the interpreter explained as best he could the cultural significance of each. When they returned to the military camp, it was almost dark, and General Liu was back from his feast.

Upon seeing Le Gendre, Liu reminded the consul that it was the Mid-Autumn Festival. He apologized for the lost day but admitted that he wanted to demonstrate his determination to make a success of the mission. With this in mind, he had elected to set off immediately rather than waiting until after the Mid-Autumn Festival to begin the march south. Le Gendre, who earlier had been feeling somewhat frustrated with the day's inaction, suddenly felt indebted to General Liu.

Later, the interpreter remarked that all the troops on the island of Taiwan were sent from the mainland, and whether officers or infantrymen, they had to stay within the barracks; only on festival days like today were they allowed to take a trip outside. As he listened, Le Gendre realized for the first time that the army did not consist of local people. The interpreter told him that these soldiers spoke a Hunan language, and therefore they could barely communicate with the local Formosans. Le Gendre mused, "Now this is truly a colonial world, complicated almost beyond comprehension. The government officials, soldiers, settlers, and aborigines all using different languages."

On September 14, General Liu ordered the troops to resume their marching.

Toward the end of the morning they came upon a river, which the soldiers crossed on light bamboo rafts. That night they were to sleep in the sugar refinery at Tangkang. To get there, they would have to cross three more rivers; the soldiers were having a hard time.

On September 15, the army entered Ponglee. This was the southernmost settlement within the jurisdiction of Taiwan Dao. The land farther south belonged to the raw savages. Le Gendre thought that General Liu was perhaps beginning to look worried.

Moving beyond Ponglee, they reached the Chalatong Pass; on one side was the mountain and on the other side the sea. The pass itself was extraordinarily narrow, with unnamed plants thriving on top of what could barely be called a road. General Liu inspected it and shook his head. "This is a trail fit only for goats or birds!"

He turned to the local guide. "It is like this all the way to Chasiang?"

The guide nodded. Liu winced.

But then Le Gendre told them that six months or so ago, when aboard the *Ashuelot*, he had inspected the shoreline between this place and Koalut. The land was generally flat; it would not, he suggested, be difficult to cut out a road.

Liu smiled. He said that he was in possession of a considerable amount of gold sent by Taiwan-fu as the military provision; with it he could afford not only to pay the soldiers their salaries but also to construct a road. He pointed out—with some pride—that eighty years before, General Fu Kang-an[1] had cut a road from Ali-kang to Chasiang. "What Fu Kang-an could accomplish, we can as well."

So General Liu gave the order, "Begin cutting a road from Ponglee to Chasiang. Finish it within seven days. Once the road is completed, we will march into Koalut and punish those raw savages. We will show them who rules Taiwan!"

---

[1] A Qing general who came to Taiwan to suppress the Lin Shuangwen Rebellion. Lin Shuangwen was a branch head of Heaven-Earth Society (*Tiandi hui*; a secret anti-Qing society). Lin called on people in Taiwan to take arms against the Qing government, trying to topple the Manchu rulers. The rebellion started in 1787 and was suppressed the following year.

40

In Tuillasock, the Mid-Autumn Festival felt especially significant for Bunkiet. Perhaps it was because his father had passed away on this festival a year ago.

Bunkiet had planned to walk to Sialiao on the day before the festival. There he could see Mia and Chinya and spend some time with them. He wished also to meet Butterfly, and he hoped that she too would be returning to worship their parents. After all, the Mid-Autumn Festival had always been a day for family reunion.

As his parents were both buried in Tongling Bo, he would need to set out from Sialiao in the early morning; he could finish worshiping by noon and then head directly back to Tuillassock.

He outlined the proposal to Tauketok, who thought for a while before telling Bunkiet, "The four tribes of Seqalu are our own people. You will visit them on my behalf and thank the chiefs of these four tribes, especially Ling-nuang and Baya, for their recent cooperation. I myself will go north to visit Mantsui, Sihlinge, Peigu, Kuskus, Botan, and Kachilai."

Thus, Bunkiet set out two days earlier than he had planned, flanked by the two warriors Tauketok had ordered to accompany him.

The chief of Ling-nuang gave a big feast to welcome the adopted son of Seqalu's Big Head Chief. At the feast, he said to Bunkiet, "I should say, some people in the tribe have told me this. . . . About twenty days ago, two white men were moving all around here, from Tossupong to Ling-nuang. One of them was hired by the family of the Red-Hair woman killed by Koalut, and he had come all the way from their country to look for the woman's remains. The other one spoke Hokkien, and also some of our language. Apparently he came from Takao. Anyway, it is said that they found the woman's skull and most of her remains. And even some of her possessions! I don't know where they are now or what they are doing."

Bunkiet was taken aback. Six months ago, when the *Cormorant* came to Sialiao, the Hokkien interpreter had told him and the others that the British Consul Carroll wished to retrieve the sailors' remains and the things they had left behind. And even now they were still looking? These whites were very determined; Bunkiet worried that if they intended to take revenge on Koalut, their army would certainly come again.

But where had they found the remains? He didn't believe that many people in Koalut would take the foreigners' things. Payarin had said that the woman who took a necklace from a corpse had died soon thereafter; others were unlikely to follow her. And anyway, they had killed the foreigners because they mistook them for invaders; it had not been a raid. Payarin had told Big Head Chief that when they later returned to the beach, they could see only the boats. Everything else had disappeared, and it was improbable that the things left behind were washed back into the sea.

Bunkiet said, "I can be sure that the foreigners' things were not taken away by Koaluts. They were not interested at all. And it seems unlikely that the other people in Seqalu would take those things. Could it be the Hakka people?"

The chief replied, "Yes, you are right. Peppos and Hakka people were in this together. First the Peppos took the things they wanted to keep. They buried a few of the corpses behind a big red cedar tree, and then they pushed the remaining bodies into the sea. But when they heard the whites had sent a military vessel, they panicked and dug up the corpses and returned the things to the bodies. The Hakka people, however, thought these things deserved a good price, so they began snooping around. Soon the white men came looking too.

"A Hakka man found a plains aborigine who had originally hid those remains and persuaded him that he would serve as his broker and make him some money. But of course, his real purpose was to make himself a profit. This Hakka man was so deceitful. When he met with the whites, he told them that the savages were so ruthless as to kill people at random, and that they were asking a high ransom for the remains. Then, when he saw the plains aborigine, he said to him that the whites were so angry they might decide to send troops in retaliation. Of course, he needed payment to keep his mouth shut, otherwise he might not be able to stop himself from telling the whites where the plains aborigine lived. Finally they all met in a Hakka house in Tossupong to strike the deal. I don't know how much was paid, but I am sure that the one who got the largest sum of money was the Hakka." The chief laughed, but then remembered that Bunkiet's father was Honest Lim. "I'm sorry," he said. "I forgot."

But Bunkiet merely smiled; no offense was taken.

After bidding farewell to the chief of Ling-nuang, Bunkiet and the two warriors continued to Bayaken. The road to the tribe was flat and smooth and the going was easy, but this did little to lift Bunkiet's spirits. The chief of Ling-nuang had told him that the plains aborigine who met the white man in Tossupong had emphasized again and again that the crew of the *Rover* was killed by Koaluts. Since the foreigners now knew who to blame, they would certainly take revenge, and Bunkiet was worried that next time they would attack Koalut directly. In that case, his people would be in great trouble.

The next afternoon, after meeting and thanking the chief of Bayaken, they approached Poliac, a settlement of predominantly Hakka immigrants from Canton. From there, if they continued along the Sialiao Creek, they could reach Sialiao in less than two hours. But as the town drew near, Bunkiet grew timid, and his pace slowed.

He and his two warrior guards entered a Hakka shop to eat lunch. They had changed their clothes that morning to blend in with the local people, but still they felt conspicuous. After sitting down,

Bunkiet heard people at the next table talking in Hakka. "I heard the Qing troops will march into Chasiang. Is it true?"

An older man thumped his palm on the table. "It's the raw savages' fault. They killed those foreigners for no reason, and now the Qing officers and soldiers are ready to attack Koalut. Those Puppet Savages deserve everything they get!"

Bunkiet twisted his body to face the man. His heart thudded loudly in his ears. "A Qing army will attack Koalut?"

"Of course. Posters are up all over announcing that Taiwan-fu will deploy eight thousand five hundred soldiers to the south of Chasiang. They're going to attack Puppet Savages. They asked for local assistance."

"Eight thousand five hundred?" Bunkiet cried out in disbelief.

The old man waved his hand. "If you want to read the announcement, go to the Temple of Three Mountain Lords. There's a poster there."

"Does it say the army will come after the Mid-Autumn Festival?"

"Yes, in fact it does." The old man smiled. "I guess you and your men are somehow related to the tribes in the mountains. It'll be just a couple more days, and then the troops will arrive. They won't just attack Koalut, so tell the other tribes to get prepared!" He sounded very much as if he were gloating.

Bunkiet thanked the old man and then turned back to give the warriors a look. After they had finished their lunch, the three of them walked outside into the sunlight .

Bunkiet said, "You heard that. This time it's not foreigners, but soldiers sent by Taiwan-fu. To them we are outlaws to be dealt with, and they will certainly not be forgiving. You two, hurry back to inform Big Head Chief and tell him to prepare for war. Tell him that after I have worshiped my father in Tongling Bo, I will rush back to Tuillassock."

However, they would not both leave him and instead insisted that one stay with Bunkiet while the other return to Tuillassock.

41

Notwithstanding Bunkiet's rising inner turmoil, Sialiao was unexpectedly calm.

People on the street were surprised to see Bunkiet with a savage; some pretended to ignore him, while others seemed to sneer. Mia, however, welcomed him affectionately. Happily, Butterfly was also there, having made the journey from Takao.

When the warrior guard saw that Bunkiet was reunited with his family he left, telling Bunkiet that he would wait for him in the woods at the foot of Turtle Hill.

Even though it was just the thirteenth day of the eighth lunar month, it was already near a full moon.

Bunkiet, Butterfly, and Mia talked until late into the night, but Chinya was nowhere to be seen. Butterfly wondered where he was, but she didn't ask; after the gambling incident, she wasn't sure if she wished to see him.

Bunkiet told them everything he had heard, and Butterfly readily agreed to leave for Tongling Bo to worship their father one day earlier than she had planned. After he had said his part, Bunkiet was so distracted by worries that he did not inquire about Butterfly's life in Takao. Instead, he asked Mia for his advice about the army of Taiwan-fu.

Mia said that he did not think much of it. He thought that as the Qing army went south, it would certainly cause trouble for Chasiang and Poliac, but Sialiao would be left intact.

"Sialiao is not under the Qing's jurisdiction. The Qing government rules over Hokkien and Hakka people only. We people in Sialiao are *tushengzi*. And Sialiao is farthest away from Puppet Savages. The Qing army won't end up here, as they won't come by sea," Mia answered, chewing on a betel nut.

"That might not be the case." Bunkiet sounded unconvinced. "Chasiang can afford to house and feed two or three thousand people, and Poliac can house perhaps another thousand. If there are really eight thousand soldiers, they will all need to eat and drink, and their horses will need feeding. How can Chasiang and Poliac accommodate that? In the past, hasn't the Qing army asked Sialiao for food and provisions? Can you reject them? Perhaps . . . perhaps you will have to pay taxes to the Qing from now on. And if the Qing sets up an office here, maybe people in Sialiao will choose to follow the orders of those government officials, and you will not be listened to anymore."

This apparently was an outcome not previously considered by Mia; he sat up straight but said nothing.

"From what I saw in Taiwan-fu and Takao," Butterfly offered, "the government officials are really hard to please and will be difficult to deal with."

Bunkiet asked her, "Did you leave Takao by ship? Did you see the Qing army? Did you hear how many soldiers were sent south?"

Butterfly fielded the questions with a practiced expertise. "I saw no army. Chihou was quite calm. Dr. Manson did not mention the army, and he didn't mention General Le Gendre. But he did say that Pickering came to Liangkiau with a British man who was looking for the remains of the captain's wife."

"I know that man," Mia said suddenly. "His name is James Horn. He boarded a ship from Ponglee and showed up here. Then he went to Tossupong. I don't know what happened after that."

"They found the remains of the captain's wife," Bunkiet said coolly.

Mia was surprised. "Really!?"

Bunkiet remembered that Butterfly and Chinya had traveled on Le Gendre's ship to Sialiao. He asked, "Will Le Gendre also come with the Qing army?"

Butterfly shrugged.

"I guess so," Mia reasoned. "Without pressure from Le Gendre, why would the Qing government bother to send its army south to fight a war it may well lose?"

The conversation faded and floated away into the night; Bunkiet thought for a while in the space afforded by the silence. "Sis," he said, "I need to ask a favor."

"What is it?"

"I don't want a war. We need to do everything we can to prevent a war. That's what we need to do."

Butterfly nodded, thinking back to her experience just a few months ago on the beach. She asked, "But do we have the power to stop one? The army is already on its way. . . ."

Bunkiet stared at Butterfly and spoke slowly, as though the words he was forming were recently learned and he was uncertain of their application. "I will ask Tauketok not to launch a preemptive attack. You find Le Gendre and persuade him not to fight, or at least talk him into not attacking without provocation. If Tauketok and Consul Le Gendre both agree not to strike first, I think this war can be prevented."

But Butterfly shook her head. "This is quite different. Big Head Chief trusts you. You have a chance with him. But I barely know Le Gendre. Who am I to persuade him?"

But Mia said, "True, you may be mere acquaintances. But do you recall how he stayed in Sialiao for an additional day for no other reason than to ask you one more time to join him on the ship? I think you should try Bunkiet's suggestion. Nothing is impossible."

"But I don't like talking to him. I avoid his company."

"You should at least try." Bunkiet was using the persuasive tone he knew worked best with his sister.

The silence again descended. Bunkiet and Mia stared at Butterfly with insistent expectation. After a while she nodded and said reluctantly, "Okay. I will stay in Sialiao for a while longer and wait for him to get here. When the army arrives, Mia, can you show me to him?"

"Of course."

Butterfly could only force a smile.

42

The next day, after worshiping in Tongling Bo, Bunkiet returned to Tuillassock. Two days after that a sailboat came to Sialiao carrying freight from Taiwan-fu. Chinya, sitting without a plan at the water's edge, overheard the ship's captain talking about having seen an army at Ponglee, where there had been many locals digging a road and building a bridge.

Chinya, suddenly invigorated, hurried to tell Mia and Butterfly.

"Did they see foreigners in Ponglee?"

Chinya didn't know.

Butterfly said, clearly hinting at a plan, "If Le Gendre is in Ponglee . . ."

Mia smiled. "So you want to take a boat to see Le Gendre in Ponglee?"

"If we rent a ship and set out tomorrow, we will arrive there in the afternoon."

Mia seemed to hesitate. "That will be quite expensive. . . ." But then he laughed. "Of course, if the money will prevent a war, it'll be worth it."

After arriving in Ponglee, Butterfly, Mia, and Chinya walked past the many timber shops and were told by those they asked that the Qing military commanders were staying inside Bao-an Temple. Apparently foreign government officials sometimes appeared on the street seated in sedan chairs. According to a particularly garrulous shop owner, one of the foreign officials had his eye covered by a patch; that had to be Le Gendre.

"Let's wait at Bao-an Temple." Mia sounded excited. "I am sure we can find him there."

The sedan bearers halted outside General Liu's field headquarters and Le Gendre stepped down from the chair. He was about to enter the temple when someone called out, "Consul, Sir, please . . ."

Le Gendre turned around and, to his visible amazement, saw Butterfly, Mia, and Chinya standing in front of him. Butterfly was standing, but Mia and Chinya were kowtowing.

"You two, get to your feet." He turned to Butterfly. "What is this all about?"

"Sir, please stop the war. No war, please." She spoke in English.

"You needn't worry. Sialiao is not in danger."

A Qing soldier stepped forward to prevent them from getting any closer. Butterfly shouted around him, "Consul, a war is no good."

"The general is waiting for me." Le Gendre looked as though he didn't know what else to say. "It is not convenient for you to be here. Go home. When I get to Chasiang, you will see me again. We can talk then." He turned and walked into the temple without saying goodbye, leaving Joseph Bernard to finish interpreting on his behalf.

Butterfly, Mia, and Chinya were profoundly disappointed. After being lucky enough to find him, they had failed miserably to talk meaningfully with Le Gendre. They understood now that words alone could not stop the army; it seemed inevitable that within a few days, the Qing army would continue its march toward Liangkiau.

Thus, the three of them boarded the ship back to Sialiao, looking sullen and speaking little.

43

Le Gendre could not have imagined himself meeting Butterfly in Ponglee, but perhaps even less could he have envisioned seeing Pickering there.

Pickering had come over from Liangkiau. He was one of the two foreigners who purchased Mrs. Hunt's possessions from the aborigine. The other, as identified by Mia, was James Horn, who had been sent to Formosa on commission by Mrs. Hunt's family.

Pickering and Horn had set out from Takao on September 3. They went first to Sialiao, then continued south to Tossupong. Afterward they went deep into Ling-nuang for almost a month. Finally, after much searching, they located and secured Mrs. Hunt's remains and her belongings.

Triumphantly, Pickering described to Le Gendre how they had entered Tuillassock, the tribe led by Tauketok, who was commanding the eighteen tribes in Lower Liangkiau.

Pickering said that while in Ling-nuang they had by chance learned of another recent shipwreck. Someone told them that several Bashi Island (present-day Batan Island) seamen were being kept captive in Tuillassock and that one had escaped to Tossupong. So Pickering and Horn went there to meet with him.

When they found him, he spoke to them in Spanish. "There were nine of us in the canoe. We were blown to the east coast of Formosa. The savages shot at us. Later we found out that they were from Botan, a tribe known for committing the worst kinds of atrocities.

"We struggled south, and the canoe finally went beyond their shooting range. We were somewhat relieved when we came to the mouth of a big river. On its banks grew many fruit trees, so we landed and began to feed ourselves.

"We met an old deaf and mute man. He took us to his house and offered us food. He was very kind to us. But when the other men in the tribe learned that we were being sheltered there, they approached his home carrying knives and sticks. They were threatening to kill us, but the old man barred the entrance, glaring out at his own people.

"The men outside seemed to respect him. They lowered their weapons, bowed to him, and turned to go. Perhaps the old man was from a noble family.

"In the afternoon, the chief of the tribe returned from somewhere else. He had heard of our shipwreck and came to thank the old man for protecting us. Later, the chief had a meeting with his people. It was decided that they wouldn't kill us, or the white foreigners would take revenge. Instead, they were to keep us captive, but they would give us food and treat us well. And if people came to rescue us, a ransom would need to be paid to secure our release.

"We were transferred to an earthen house and prohibited from venturing outside. One day, after we felt sure we had been abandoned, my friend and I tried to leave. Almost immediately my friend was killed by a guard. As I was running for my life, I tripped and fell and then rolled down into the steep valley. I escaped, but my leg was seriously injured. I really need to thank those people in Ling-nuang who brought me to Tossupong."

Pickering and Horn decided to rescue the other Bashi Island seamen, but they needed to send Mrs. Hunt's remains to Takao, so the two of them separated at Tossupong. Horn stayed with the Bashi Islander in Tossupong, while Pickering took Mrs. Hunt's remains back to Chasiang. When people in Chasiang learned what he had with him, they burned incense sticks and would not allow him to carry his luggage into their homes. A few days later, Pickering boarded a ship from Chasiang to Takao. He left the remains in the British consulate, then hurried back to Tossupong to meet Horn.

To show their sincerity, when they made the journey into Ling-nuang, Horn and Pickering had the escaped seaman join them; they were willing to offer to pay the tribe his ransom as well. It was as the group approached their destination that Pickering realized the prisoners were being held in Tuillassock.

Pickering and Horn were made to wait outside the tribe. They did not get to see Tauketok; they were told that he was away from the tribe and that a deputy was acting in his place. Another of the tribal people was to relay their requests to the deputy. The woman who had been appointed to deliver their messages said that the seven Bashi Islanders had consumed a lot of food and that that certainly needed to be taken into account; the tribe was asking for two hundred silver dollars as ransom.

Pickering gave her the money and told her to give the silver dollars to the deputy chief and ask him to release the islanders. If she was successful, Pickering said, he would reward her with two silver dollars.

When the woman returned, she told Pickering that she had seen both the islanders and the deputy chief. The deputy chief had promised to release the captives, but then a merchant had intervened, offering the deputy chief four hundred silver dollars to buy the captives. He told them that he would in turn sell the captives to foreigners. That merchant said that he had read a poster in Poliac, announcing that an army from Taiwan-fu, accompanied by an American government official, was marching to attack Puppet Savages.

According to the woman, the deputy chief was incensed by what the merchant had told them, and he had asked her to tell Pickering that if five hundred silver dollars was not paid, he was inclined to kill the islanders as a gesture of revenge. He accused the foreigners of being not only vicious but also slow-witted; far from solving the problem, involving the Qing army would only further complicate things.

Pickering was left with no other choice; he had to pay the five hundred silver dollars.

They left with the seven Bashi Islanders and returned to Chasiang. The two of them had spent almost all their money, but they had heard that the Qing army would soon arrive in Ponglee. They thought that Le Gendre must be among its number, so they boarded a ship from Chasiang to Ponglee. It was September 20 when they finally found him.

Later that day, Le Gendre presented the Bashi Islanders to General Liu, who promised to reimburse Pickering the ransom money and to send the Bashi Islanders back to Takao, where they could return to their homeland.

General Liu had previously been introduced to Pickering in Taiwan-fu. He was delighted to learn that Pickering had just returned from Liangkiau and keen to know how people there were responding to the news of the approaching army.

Pickering answered that they feared loss of property and life and were almost overwhelmed with anxiety. He then told the general that if the Qing army came to Tossupong to attack raw savages, both sides would suffer significant casualties, regardless of the eventual outcome. The local people had suggested—and this proposal Pickering relayed with a diplomatic impartiality—that with the road finished, they might easily send someone to Chasiang in search of those who were willing to take a risk to earn some money. If handsome rewards were offered, they thought, it would be quite easy to secure the heads of about twenty raw savages. The officers could then send those heads back to Foochow and let the governor know that the raw savages had been conquered and that the army had won a great victory. This way, General Liu could tell his supervisors that he had won the victory himself. The Taiwan *daotai* had surely set aside a large sum of money for this military operation. Even if they returned most of it to the national treasury, the government officials and military officers, as well as some of the soldiers, could receive a significant reward.

When Pickering had finished talking, General Liu demonstrated his contempt with a dismissive face and then told him that the idea had already been proposed and swiftly rejected. He told Pickering that, as ordered by his superiors, he was determined to go south to attack the savage tribes as soon as possible. His army was well disciplined, and the soldiers would not disturb ordinary people. "Mr. Pickering," General Liu punctuated his words with a fist thumping the air, "please return to Liangkiau and tell the residents that the army is coming. Let them know that those who support it will be rewarded, but those who turn against it will be executed!"

44

On September 22, General Liu led his army of over nine hundred soldiers out of Ponglee. It was the first time the Qing army had appeared in Liangkiau since the fifty-third year of Emperor Qianlong's reign (1788).

General Liu rode on horseback, looking down with great pleasure and pride upon the road built in just seven days; he and the army marching along it looked already victorious.

He was in somewhat of a trance. Though he was just a regional commander, he had taken the order to conquer the raw savages who had so disturbed the foreigners. He imagined the swift defeat he would visit upon the Puppet Savages after reaching Chasiang. He believed that the local gentry and a few brave residents would guide him on his way to victory, and he smiled at the thought. Indeed, wasn't he, in his own way, much like the great generals of history? Yes, perhaps he most resembled Generals Wei Qing and Huo Qubing, sent by Emperor Wu of the Han dynasty to conquer the Huns. If successful, he too would deserve a monument erected in honor of his accomplishments.

As for Le Gendre, Liu observed him sitting on the sedan chair, looking very pleased in the middle of the procession. Clearly, he too thought the Qing army was ready to punish the raw savages of Koalut.

However, in truth, Le Gendre felt quite different from the picture of calm anticipation his visage presented.

The previous night Pickering had come to visit him in his quarters and for almost two hours had tried to dissuade him from carrying out the planned attack. The meeting had left Le Gendre with significant doubts as to the merit of their expedition.

Pickering had told Le Gendre that, even after observing General Liu's soldiers and their equipment, he felt sure that the army was no equal to Tauketok's, and more to the point, Le Gendre would not remain safe if he accompanied the army all the way to its destination.

According to Pickering, the combined fighting body of the eighteen tribes of Lower Liangkiau—which had, he stressed theatrically, made a vow to cooperate in collective defense of their distinct lands—consisted of at least 1,200 warriors. They were preparing for the battle, and they were now equipped with muskets, not just the old matchlock guns.

Toward the end of his visit, Pickering had admitted that he held feelings of admiration for those people living in Tuillassock. According to him, the raw savages in Formosa would not kill without reason. They lived according to a strong set of principles, and the killing of Mrs. Hunt was a mistake. They knew they were to blame, so during Bell's attack, they shot just one American as a warning. However, the Puppet Savages had hated Han people for a long time. They believed—quite fairly, in Pickering's opinion—that they had done nothing to aggravate the Qing government. Therefore, if the Qing army entered their tribal land, Tauketok's response would be one of fury.

At this point, Pickering had asked, "How many soldiers has General Liu brought with him?"

Le Gendre was embarrassed. "About a thousand. We left Taiwan-fu with eight or nine hundred, and one or two hundred more were added when we reached Pitau, but they are not as well equipped nor as well attired as those from Taiwan-fu. Perhaps they are not men who are fit for fighting."

Pickering had smiled. "General, do you know how the government announcement puts it? It says that your army is made up of eight thousand five hundred men!"

"What utter nonsense! Are you certain?"

"Of the number, I am sure. Either way, be it an inflation or a bluff, this is the way the Qing government always operates. Even if they manage to recruit some more people when they reach Liangkiau, the attack won't be launched with anything more than fifteen hundred soldiers."

Le Gendre was aghast, and he struggled to reanalyze the situation. When he spoke, it was in a toneless whisper, his sentence trailing off without adequate conclusion, "The Qing's fifteen hundred against twelve hundred of Tauketok's warriors, all of whom are vastly more familiar with the land . . . well. . . ."

From here to Chasiang, the army had to pass by the territory of the Botan tribe, which Liu and the others thought might have joined the alliance with Tauketok. Considering this possibility, they had to be prepared for surprise attacks, so they moved with increasing concern along the new mountain road. Perhaps, Pickering had suggested yesterday with a hint of what might be called glee, the whole army would be wiped out before they reached Chasiang.

That morning, Pickering had again called on Le Gendre. If Le Gendre would not listen to him, he had said, then he would ask General Liu to stay put for a while longer. In those few days, Pickering would go to Takao and send for Carroll, whom he would enlist to come and persuade Le Gendre. With Le Gendre's approval, he believed, General Liu would be willing to withdraw his army.

Le Gendre had not expected that Pickering would attempt to stop the army from continuing its march and had looked at him in surprise, wondering why that this supposedly fearless man should wish to forego the attack.

"Thank you for your advice, Pickering. But I've made up my mind. The army has come this far already. Don't waste your time trying to secure help from Carroll. The army will continue its march as planned." Le Gendre was insistent; he had bit his lower lip, and his working eye appeared to glow as it stared at Pickering.

"First it was the government officials from Taiwan-fu. They said the expedition would be too expensive and they could not be certain of victory.

"Then it was my supervisors in Peking. Every time I mentioned the expedition, it was clear that they regarded me as a lunatic militant.

"Then there was Admiral Bell. I believe he knew that the expedition was the correct strategy, but he initiated the attack without informing me. When I came to Formosa, his fleet was anchored in Hong Kong, but he would not offer me official protection.

"Then I persuaded the Fukien governor to lend me the *Volunteer*. But the ship was prevented from sailing any farther by the customs of Takao. They said, quite implausibly, that the ship would be damaged if it were to sail into the dangerous waters south of their port. The ship's captain anchored the ship in Anping and refused to act upon any of my orders for him to pilot it to South Bay. So I was forced to walk with General Liu's army.

"If I withdraw the army now, at such a critical point, I will certainly find myself the subject of cruel jokes that will no doubt be told by a great many people. No. I will prove to whoever stands against me that I am right!"

At this point, Le Gendre's tone had turned triumphant. "*Veni, Vidi, Vici!*" What Caesar said will again be carried out.

"We are fully prepared. You worry about us being attacked by the Botan tribe, but the Botan tribe have profited from the deals they've struck with the plains settlers in Ponglee and in Chasiang. We will make them understand that should they dare to attack the Qing army, their trade with the coastal residents will be cut off immediately, and they will be unable to buy bullets, weapons, or salt. If they go too far, the army will destroy their homes, and its bullets will tear through their bodies. Do not doubt me, Pickering. I will get this done.

"If, however, they do not bother us, we will reward their tribal chief whenever we arrive at a station point along the coast.

"As far as I know, the Botan tribe, supposedly the most hostile of all the raw savage tribes, has not yet attacked our army. Perhaps this is evidence that the tribal confederation is not all that enduring." At this thought he had smiled arrogantly.

"As for which side will secure the eventual victory, I must say that General Liu is a capable general and a quick-witted leader who knows exactly how to win. I think highly of him. Indeed, the army he is now leading is just the spearhead. After all, he is the regional commander in Taiwan, in charge of all the island's sixty thousand soldiers. I will concede that maybe the raw savages will win the first battle as, yes, you are right, Liu's soldiers are unfamiliar with the land. But things will change later. The raw savages will run short of ammunition. Within a month they will surrender. An army fights with a different discipline. This I know."

Determined as he was, Le Gendre still considered Pickering the Formosa expert, and he was keen to show his diplomatic side; it was important that he be seen as able to compromise and negotiate.

"Therefore, Pickering, go south to Chasiang. Tell the residents there that the government army is coming, and that it will not disturb them unnecessarily. When I get to Liangkiau, meet me at whichever is the largest temple. Though I think the Qing army will win, you are right to think the odds may initially be in the savages' favor. Moreover, should the savages lose the battle, they may be more hostile to us foreigners. We must plan for that eventuality."

Pickering simply chuckled; both Liu and Le Gendre had asked the same of him.

8

PUPPET MOUNTAINS

45

The whole of Chasiang was like a cat trying to walk on a hot tin roof. Though Peppos lived there too, Chasiang was a Hokkien majority town in Liangkiau and was therefore virtually outside the Qing's dominion. But from the moment the official document from Taiwan-fu appeared, announcing that an army would soon come to subjugate the Puppet Savages in the south, the local Chasiang gentry began gathering frequently for meetings at Fu-an Temple.

Now, in its east wing, some twenty landowners sat in a circle, each looking more grave and serious than the last. The town's head, an old man with a white beard, was speaking. "According to the announcement, the army will begin its march south on the sixteenth day of the eighth lunar month. It is presently the twenty-fifth day of the eighth lunar month. Does any of you know exactly where the army is now?"

Someone said, "I know that at least until a few days ago, the advance troops sent by Taiwan-fu were stationed on the outskirts of Chasiang. They recruited local people there to broaden the road in the north to the mountains in Hongkang. If the road can be connected, the army will come. My guess is that they will be here in a couple of days. Mia, village chief of Sialiao, returned three days ago from Ponglee. He saw the military officers there, and from the sea he saw the army preparing to open the road. It will soon be finished."

Another asked, "How are the Qing troops armed? And how many of them are there?"

"The official announcement said there will be eight thousand five hundred soldiers. However big the army, there will be many soldiers. Back when General Fu Kang-an came, there were more than ten thousand. As for their ammunition and equipment, this is the best of the Hunan armies. It is led by General Liu. He and his army famously vanquished the forces of the Taiping Rebellion. They will be more than sufficiently armed. Perhaps they will even bring cannons. That would certainly make the Puppet Savages tremble."

Someone cheered. "Good. We have been intimidated by them for too long!"

But few others were of the same opinion. One even scoffed at the suggestion that the army would bring cannons. "How could they carry cannons and balls up the Puppet Mountains? That's preposterous."

The conversation wound its way toward silence, and then someone said, "My feeling is that neither side has the advantage. It is unwise to think that the Puppet Savages are in any way weak, especially when we know they have guns and a plentiful supply of gunpowder."

The town head asked again, "Gentlemen, how long do you think the war will last?"

A middle-aged scholar spoke up. "If the army defeats them and the Puppet Savages surrender quickly, it will be okay. If the army is at first defeated, however, the government will refuse to lose face. In that case, I think it likely that those in Taiwan-fu will continue providing for the army until it produces a victory. The longer the war lasts, the worse off we will be.

"No matter which side wins, when the army arrives, the first thing we have to do is demonstrate our loyalty. We must make them forget that we helped Zhuang Datian, one of the leaders in the Lin Shuangwen Rebellion, even if that was eighty years ago. We must comply with their every request. This place nominally belongs to the Qing, but we pay them no taxes. Indeed, many of us pay rent to the raw savages. Furthermore, it is our merchants who have provided the raw savages with their weapons. Though the government army is here to attack the raw savages, we must wait to see if it is also hostile toward us. To dispel any doubts, we ought to show our loyalty as soon as possible."

He continued speaking uninterrupted. "The first battle won't affect the war's eventual outcome. The army won't be able to completely conquer the raw savages, who will certainly hide high up in the mountain where they will not be found. It will be impossible for the Qing army to kill them all. When the government troops are here, of course we will aid them. We should offer food and spend money. The troops will certainly ask us to provide for them, and we need to be ready to comply. But when they eventually retreat, the raw savages will blame us for supporting the Qing. They will come into town to take revenge. Alternatively, if the government troops win the decisive victory, they will likely remain stationed in Liangkiau, which will mean our paying all sorts of taxes in the future."

He finished with a sigh. "Either way, the war is sure to lead us toward great misery."

But then, after a pause, he started speaking again, this time with a raised voice. "Gentlemen, we often say, 'Government officials are not terrible. Rather, domination is.' We live here, enjoying our freedom. The emperor is as far from us as the clouds in the sky, and for the most part we can easily appease the raw savages. But suppose the army remains here after the war concludes, whether for victory or for domination, we will be torn between the Qing government and the raw savages. It will not be good for us. Remember what the ancients wrote, 'Terrible governance is worse than a tiger.'"

The town head asked, "Then what shall we do?"

"I hope the troops leave without much fuss or fighting. It will be best if they are just bluffing, trying to scare Puppet Savages into compliance so that they can tell their supervisors they have fulfilled their purpose. But we must be aware that things may end up contrary to our wishes or expectations."

At this point, a servant came in and told the meeting that a foreigner, Pickering, who was quite fluent in Hokkien, had come to them bearing a new announcement from General Liu.

The town head read the announcement aloud. The leading troops consisted of a thousand soldiers, who would set off on the twenty-fifth day of the eighth lunar month. They would spend the night in Hongkang and enter Liangkiau on the twenty-sixth. General Liu promised not to disturb the local people, and he gave assurances that his army would not take things from the locals without paying. Those who complied would be rewarded, while those who revolted against the troops would be executed.

All those at the meeting were relieved to hear that just a thousand soldiers were coming, not the eight thousand five hundred that they had feared. But the town head reminded them that this might be just the leading troops; they could not be sure of how many would come afterward. "Let's discuss how specifically we will receive General Liu and his soldiers," said the scholar. "It seems that the general is not overtly reckless, but we still need to be careful. Let us pray to our Earth God. He will see us through this ordeal."

46

On the morning of September 23, 1867, the Qing army entered Chasiang. The town head ushered General Liu and Consul Le Gendre into Fu-an Temple. Pickering was waiting for them inside; Le Gendre and General Liu were both pleased to see him, and General Liu was satisfied with how he had been received by the town's people.

The town head said that they had made room in the west wing of the temple to serve as both General Liu's command office and his place to spend the night. The foreign government official would be quartered in the east wing.

Le Gendre nodded and then stepped outside, where he marveled at the temple's oriental dragon columns, stone carvings, wooden carvings, and flying eaves. Even though this was not his first time seeing them, he still felt awed by the superb craftsmanship. However, the temple's mural, he felt, could not compare with Western ones.

A Qing guard carrying a gun walked alongside him in escort. People in Chasiang gathered at a distance, looking in Le Gendre's direction. Some recognized him from his last visit to the town, referring to him among themselves as the one-eyed white man.

Le Gendre looked around, but to his slight misery he could not see Butterfly. However, as luck would have it, a small file of Qing troops soon brought her, as well as Mia, to him.

"Mia," Le Gendre spoke authoritatively, "can you arrange a place in Sialiao for us to spend the night? I wish to stay in your village. We'll talk properly when we get to Sialiao."

Mia was surprised, but he quickly regained his composure, answering, "Of course, sir. We can get you a room."

47

Tauketok used the money he had earned from the release of the sailors to purchase two hundred guns and a large amount of gunpower, but he was still waiting on the delivery.

The merchant with whom he had placed the order—the same merchant who had driven up the Bashi Islanders' ransom—was of the opinion that, even if the Qing army arrived at Chasiang directly after the end of Mid-Autumn Festival, it would not launch an attack immediately; after such a long march, he was certain that the soldiers would require a rest of three to five days. Furthermore, they would need time to familiarize themselves with the land and draw up a strategy. The merchant had said, with a well-sold confidence, that the Qing army would not be able to launch an assault before the first day of the ninth lunar month. Perhaps, he admitted, they would send an advance group into the forest ahead of that date, but the purpose would be to explore, not to attack. He advised Tauketok not to kill any members of the advance group, as to do so would likely provoke General Liu into attacking sooner than expected.

All this was his way of saying that, if he made the delivery by the twentieth day of the eighth lunar month, Tauketok would be left with adequate time to deploy his warriors.

The incident with the ransomed Bashi Islanders happened while Bunkiet was traveling in Lower Liangkiau. On his return, as he listened to Tauketok's retelling, he began to develop a clear picture of what had been taking place. Bunkiet said that it was indeed a good thing not to have killed the hostages, and that it would be best if the tribe was rewarded for that restraint. Tauketok then asked Bunkiet if he knew a man called Pickering. Bunkiet replied that he had heard Butterfly mention the name, but he had yet to meet him.

"Is this man trustworthy?"

"I don't know," Bunkiet replied, "but he seems to be on good terms with Le Gendre."

They were both quiet for a while, and then Bunkiet asked, "Which side will win?"

Tauketok smiled. "Remember how we defeated the whites? We played hide-and-seek with them. In the war, if we lose the first battle, we will try to preserve our strength. We will hide, avoiding head-on conflict. Our ancestral spirits will bless us, and time is on our side. Afterward, we will launch occasional attacks on the plains people. If we assault Chasiang and Poliac enough, the *painan* and *nana* will beg the Qing troops to stop warring with us. After that, the army will have to retreat, and things can return to normal."

He handed some muntjac meat to Bunkiet, who chewed it thoughtfully and then said, "I heard the Qing troops have a cannon. If our homes are destroyed, we will have no place to stay."

Tauketok seemed quite unfazed. He said, "You were on the plains for too long. We are nomads; we will move to some other place. Within our lands there are many places suitable for living."

Bunkiet was perplexed. When the foreign gunship was here, his adoptive father was very cautious. But this time, as the Qing troops approached, he seemed almost cheerful; Bunkiet asked him what had changed.

"Ha! Ha!" Tauketok laughed drily, looking up at the stars. "I don't like them. . . . I look down on them. Plains people do not keep their word. They are dishonest and sly. The Qing troops just outnumber us. That's all."

Tauketok stood up. "People say that the Qing government issued a proclamation that they would attack Koalut. I believe they did so under pressure from the foreigners."

Bunkiet nodded. "I guess so, too."

Tauketok asked, "Then how many white troops will come with them? Did they send a ship?"

"I don't know. The notice I read didn't mention any white soldiers."

"How was your trip to the northern tribes?" Bunkiet asked after a period of silence.

"I sent Zudjui instead, as he will be the one to inherit this seat." Tauketok shook his head slowly. "I have done my best to unify the eighteen tribes of Lower Liangkiau. But in truth I am in direct command of only the four tribes of Seqalu and of Koalut. The Botan tribe promised to provide one hundred warriors. With warriors from the other tribes added to our force, I will be in command of about eight or nine hundred people."

Bunkiet sounded alarmed. "The proclamation said there will be eight or nine thousand Qing soldiers!"

Tauketok sneered. "Don't listen to their bluffing. How big is Liang-kiau? How could it feed eight or nine thousand people? And where would they spend the night? There will be six thousand at most, maybe even fewer than three thousand. But you are right to say that they will outnumber us. We must be well prepared. . . . Hmm, I should not underestimate them."

Bunkiet said, "Can I give you some advice?"

Tauketok nodded.

"Be it three thousand, six thousand, or nine thousand soldiers that we face, in no circumstance should we be the first to open fire."

"Bunkiet, you know my plans. I won't attack unless provoked." He stood up and began pacing. "If they are really set on fighting, I will not shy away from retaliation. It is our duty to guard the land of our ancestors. In recent years, more and more of it has been occupied by Hokkien and Hakka people. If they want to live in harmony with us, we can grow to accept that. But if they try to wipe us out," Tauke-tok turned to face Bunkiet, "then we either kill them all, or we all die with them."

48

As they rode on an ox cart from Chasiang to Sialiao, Le Gendre kept reassuring Butterfly and Mia that, should the war arise, he would protect Sialiao and ensure its residents' safety. The very fact that he was moving into the village, he claimed, was to them an invaluable protection.

"When will the attack start? Does the army really have to fight?"

Le Gendre smiled and said, "Butterfly, this operation was started at my request. If we don't fight, how are we to tame the raw savages?

And as for the *when* and *how* of starting the war, those are particulars for General Liu to decide."

In Sialiao, Mia offered Le Gendre the use of his house, but Le Gendre instead ordered his men to erect a large tent in the square in front of Mia's building. For most of each day he stayed in there alone, working and thinking, occasionally calling out to Butterfly and requesting that she bring him tea or food. Only when tired would he emerge from the tent to stroll along the Sialiao Creek. Sometimes he would walk to the foot of Turtle Hill and stand there for a while, looking silently out at the sea.

The sweltering summer had been replaced by rain and the season of typhoons. When leaving Chasiang, Le Gendre had told General Liu that he would not stay there for reasons relating to sanitation and hygiene, because with the sudden boom in population, infectious diseases were inevitable. Instead, he wished to stay in the sparsely populated Sialiao, where the risk of contagion was much smaller. Indeed, in the days after he arrived in Sialiao, there came reports of people suffering from fever in Chasiang, so Le Gendre's excuse seemed justified.

However, more significantly, there had been a recent change in Le Gendre's thinking, which made him reluctant to stay close to Liu; as they had approached Chasiang, Le Gendre had found himself consumed by doubt. *What good would it do to attack the raw savages?* he thought again and again. Perhaps Pickering's words had finally had their intended effect, or in any case, they seemed now to make sense.

General Liu could not speak Hokkien; he spoke only Mandarin and the tribal language of Hunan's Tujia ethnic group. Le Gendre had Bernard with him as a Hokkien interpreter, but Bernard was not proficient in Mandarin. The Fukien governor had provided Le Gendre with an additional interpreter, but Le Gendre disliked and distrusted this appointee, feeling that he was there primarily as a spy.

Therefore, as Pickering could speak not only Hokkien and Mandarin but also some of the Formosan aboriginal languages, Le Gendre had been very pleased to come across him in Ponglee; he finally had an excuse to rid himself of the Fukien governor's interpreter.

This unexpected encounter was highly advantageous, and Le Gendre was confident that it left him in possession of a better understanding than General Liu with regard to Hokkiens, Hakkas, and raw savages. He wanted to take command of the whole situation rather than continuing to let General Liu tell him what to do, and to that end he wished to set up his own headquarters, thereby making sure that this operation would be carried out to his own benefit. The interests he shared with Liu were no doubt similar, but they were not the same.

Moreover, compared with Liu, he now had a much better knowledge of Liangkiau. He had been to South Bay and had sailed along the whole coastline of southern Formosa. He had landed on the beach at the foot of Turtle Nose Mountain and had traveled to the east coast of Taiwan. Liu knew almost nothing of these places; nor did any of the other Qing generals.

In fact, for the most part, the Qing government officials and military officers behaved as if they knew very little of this island that supposedly belonged to them. Le Gendre recalled what Qing government bureaucrats had said and done, and he was baffled. Sometimes it seemed they regarded this place as theirs, and yet at other times they most certainly did not. How did such a country come to exist? Previously Le Gendre had been left with a good impression of General Liu. But as he continued to stew in his own thoughts, he felt he understood Liu's shortcomings.

A few days before setting up camp in Sialiao, on his way from Ponglee to Chasiang, Le Gendre had sat brooding in the sedan chair. It was *he* who had asked for the Qing troops to be sent to Liangkiau, and things were now proceeding as *he* had wished. However, *his* being gifted the glory now seemed an unlikely prospect. "I came,

I saw, I conquered" would instead become "Liu came, Liu saw, Liu conquered."

And what would happen after the Qing army defeated the raw savages? Was that really what he wanted? In what way would that be of benefit to the United States?

In fact, what his country wanted, and indeed what the European countries wanted, was to ensure the safety of the ships that traveled around Formosa; by itself a Qing victory against the raw savages could not ensure this. So what purpose did the war serve? Although he had been the one pushing most ardently for military action, at this late stage he felt an increasing and insuppressible need to reconsider the whole endeavor.

How confounding!

But such bewilderment, he felt, was good for him. Under these circumstances, unrestrained by General Liu, he could implement a strategy that would guarantee the best results for himself and for the United States.

49

At Sialiao, he had resumed his contemplations in the peace of his tent; new concepts and plans took shape in his mind. He scrambled to make the project concrete, writing it down, detailing its procedures. He asked not to be disturbed, and finally, after a long night of consideration, he felt he had things sorted out. He needed more assurances, from government officials, ordinary people, and even the raw savages. He wrote down three primary objectives:

First, the eighteen tribes of Lower Liangkiau must apologize and promise that they will never again murder shipwrecked sailors.

Second, the ordinary people must accept and endorse the raw savages' promise.

Third, the Qing government must erect a watchtower or perhaps even a fort at South Bay, where they must station soldiers and regulate the behavior of the raw savages.

But how could he ensure his plan's realization?

In the present situation, General Liu was in command while he, Le Gendre, was but a toothless consultant. "No, this won't work!" he fumed quietly, driven by his need to be in control. He was determined to use the Qing troops as his pawns instead of being moved around with them.

Indeed, things seemed increasingly to be getting out of hand. In the beginning, when he first visited Taiwan-fu government officials, his goal was simply to hear them admit their own neglect of duty and extract from them a promise to ensure the safety of seafaring in this area. But now, six months later, General Liu carried the order from his supervisors to "vanquish raw savages." This changed everything.

Though he could not order that the army be halted—after all, General Liu remained in command—he would do his best to hamper the troops' advance. However, he still needed General Liu and his troops to apply pressure to the eighteen tribes of Liangkiau and to force Tauketok to accept these new terms.

But new apprehensions were starting to form. Would the mere presence of General Liu's troops offend Tauketok? Suppose the raw savages launched a surprise attack. In such circumstances, things could easily escalate beyond all control. Le Gendre had heard that the raw savages hated the plains settlers. If Tauketok initiated the attack, then the whole issue might well degenerate into a fight between plains people and raw savages. If that happened, then Le Gendre would have no power to change the outcome, and his strategizing would have come to nothing.

In addition, the Hokkien people in Chasiang and the Hakkas in Poliac were all quite hostile toward each other. Those in Chasiang had decided to comply with the Qing army, but what of Poliac? What would happen if the Hakka people decided to take the side of the Puppet Savages? He was sure of this much: he needed to prevent the raw savages from forming an alliance with the Hakkas.

But then suddenly Le Gendre hit upon an idea. He cried out and almost jumped to his feet with excitement. "Butterfly, are you there?"

When Le Gendre came to Sialiao, although Butterfly saw him every day, she did not know what to say; how was she to go about persuading him to stop the war?

Le Gendre would occasionally summon her to his tent to send for food and water. When she entered his quarters, she most often found him concentrating on his own affairs, but he did sometimes pause to smile at her—which caused her discomfort. On such occasions, she continued to endure his eyes' effects as she exited the tent.

"I said Butterfly, are you there?" Le Gendre called out again, impatiently.

Inside the tent, he gestured for her to sit down.

"Butterfly, I need to ask a favor of you."

She sat down after placing onto the table the plates that she had been carrying; despite her best efforts, they left her hands with a sharp clank. Le Gendre grabbed her hand suddenly. She struggled to remove herself from his grip, blushing intensely, feeling unable to look him in the eye.

"I need to ask you a couple of questions." He spoke quickly and seriously. "If I remember correctly, you are half Hakka?"

"Yes."

"Can you speak Hakka?"

"Of course." As she said this, she felt for some reason relieved.

"Do you know how the Hakka people in Poliac are responding to the news of the Qing army?"

"Sorry, I do not." Butterfly shook her head. "But I know the head of Poliac is called Lim Nine. I think he is friendly with Mia."

Later, after he had finished interrogating Butterfly, asking her a series of similar questions from slowly shifting angles, Le Gendre dismissed her and then sat thinking in silence. Eventually, he decided he would have Pickering go to Poliac to meet with Lim Nine and learn how they were responding to this military operation. But Pickering did not understand the Hakka dialect well, so Le Gendre called Butterfly in again and asked her to act as Pickering's interpreter. It was a request to which, after a few moments of consideration, she quietly agreed.

The next day, Pickering and Butterfly went to Poliac to meet Lim Nine. Lim was quite welcoming, as he knew that Butterfly was Honest Lim's daughter. Pickering asked several questions, some of which made Lim Nine smile. In response, Lim said that the Hakka people selling weapons to the raw ravages was just a matter of business, and that they would certainly not work with the raw savages to fight against the government army.

Most of all, he said, he and the rest of the Hakka people hoped for peace. He believed that, according to his understanding of the raw savages, Tauketok would not be the one to initiate the fight. But he warned that once they were attacked, Tauketok would fight until the very end; raw savages would never surrender, for they would be fighting to protect the land of their ancestors.

"Once the Qing troops open fire, the war will go on and on. The army will be unable to completely conquer raw savages, who will likewise find victory very difficult. We Hakka people won't side with the raw savages, but neither would we dare help the Qing troops in their fight. If we did something like that, once the army retreated, the raw savages would come for us." Lim mimed his own beheading.

Pickering said, "Consul Le Gendre and General Liu are set on fighting. Especially General Liu. He marches with an order to 'severely punish raw savages.' He needs to be able to bring reports to this effect to his supervisors, or he himself will be reprimanded. However, if Hokkien people in Chasiang, Hakka people in Poliac, Peppos in Sialiao, and other residents in Tossupong can reach a consensus for peace, then I will beg Le Gendre to rethink his decision."

During the pauses when Butterfly interpreted his words, Pickering looked around, appearing to appreciate the beauty of his surroundings. Afterward he turned again to Lim. "You need to talk to Tauketok and impress upon him the supreme importance of his not being the first to open fire. Ask also that he issue an official apology. If Consul Le Gendre feels that the interests of the United States have been respected, perhaps he can dissuade General Liu from fighting, and then both sides can take their time reaching an agreement."

"I am willing to talk to Tauketok. But I cannot ask him to apologize. Suppose Big Head Chief and the raw savages feel that it is a deliberate strategy to bring humiliation to their tribes? They would fly into a rage. Everything would be ruined."

"In that case, ask Tauketok if he is willing to meet Consul Le Gendre. You needn't mention an apology. When they meet in person, the consul himself can request it."

Lim Nine was relieved. "That I can do."

So they agreed that they would arrange for the head of the whites and Big Head Chief to meet and talk. In three days, they would meet again.

Butterfly was relieved to hear that neither the Hokkien people nor the Hakka people wanted a war, and she knew that Bunkiet did not want a fight either. Surely, with Bunkiet by his side, Tauketok was unlikely to open fire first. But Pickering had mentioned that there were other conditions still to be proposed by Le Gendre. What were they? She started to worry.

50

The army approached like a sharp sword drawn slowly from its sheath. Although there were just a thousand Qing soldiers, the tribes of Liangkiau were very concerned. The latest news was that the army had been recruiting additional soldiers in Chasiang, and maybe some relief troops would come from Taiwan-fu. The situation had all the potential to become desperate.

Although Tauketok agreed with Bunkiet that it would be best to avoid a war, the chiefs all thought that fighting was inevitable. Tauketok was doing what he could to prepare; he had recently distributed the guns bought from the merchant.

Now he gave his order to the other tribes outside Seqalu, instructing them to mobilize their warriors. Long before the Qing army approached their lands, they had discussed and concluded that they would not assemble the majority of their warriors in Tuillassock, since it would be almost impossible to provide food for so many people gathered in a single place. Instead, most warriors were to stay in their own tribes and await further instruction.

But to prove that the alliance remained, Tauketok had asked that each tribe send a small number of men to either Tuillassock or Koalut. The larger tribes sent thirty or forty men, smaller tribes just ten or twenty. All together, they would have four hundred warriors stationed centrally as the main "Alliance Army."

Tauketok summoned the chiefs of the eighteen tribes for a meeting. Reports had come that the Qing army was in Chasiang. To attack, it would probably head first for Monkey Cave, as that road was flat and smooth, and travel would be quick. From Monkey Cave, there were two possible ways to march an army. One option would be to continue south to Tossupong, moving along the southern side of Turtle Nose Mountain, and from there attack Koalut. But that road did not provide easy marching, and moreover, there were many points at which aboriginal warriors could ambush the army. The other option would be to move along the northern side of Turtle Nose Mountain, taking the trail to Volcano and then proceeding to attack Sabaree. If the army took this road, they could quite easily enter Seqalu and attack Tuillassock directly. In that eventuality, the whole of Seqalu would fall apart.

Tauketok assumed the Qing troops would take the road to Volcano. He suggested that the tribes station their main force on Turtle Nose Mountain. Isa would lead about one hundred and fifty warriors as the first line of defense. Another one hundred warriors from Ling-nuang tribe would stay on the beach as backup.

Tauketok himself would lead the core Alliance Army, defending Tuillassock and Koalut. They would be backed up by other tribes whose warriors, if required, would rush to wherever they were most needed. With the plans agreed upon, most of the chiefs believed that the tribes had done all they could to prepare for the war.

That night, leading the other chiefs up Turtle Nose Mountain to pray to their ancestral spirits, Big Head Chief reiterated his strategy. "If the enemies do not open fire, we will not be the first to shoot. And even if they do fire, we will wait. Perhaps one shot is an accident. But if they fire ten shots or more, we can be sure that that they have opened fire on us, and we will fight as best we are able. We will be defending the land of our ancestors. It will be a justified fight. With the blessing of our ancestral spirits, we will prevail."

51

Pickering had decided to spend some time walking around Tossupong. Last time, when he came in search of Mrs. Hunt's remains, he had developed a few connections with the Hakka, Peppos, and raw savages with whom he had interacted. Besides, if the Qing army started their attack, they would certainly pass by Tossupong; perhaps it would be the site of the first battle. He wanted to explore the place some more and to gather news of the raw savages.

So he recruited a couple of bodyguards and then set out. To his surprise, he soon came across a Qing military camp flying Liu's banner just outside of Sialiao. As Pickering and his guards approached, a small group of Qing soldiers walked out of the camp to meet them. With the soldiers was a young officer whom Pickering recognized as Wang Wenqi, General Liu's most important subordinate.

They met on a small plain of well-trodden grass; the day's sun was just beginning to deliver its heat. Wang smiled and bowed, saying, "General Liu is concerned about Consul Le Gendre's safety in Sialiao. Accordingly, he has asked me to station two hundred soldiers here for the consul's protection. We pitched camp last night and are at his disposal. Mr. Pickering, it is early. Where are you going?"

Pickering was a little annoyed. Le Gendre wanted himself rid of the command of General Liu. But clearly, these troops were here to ensure just the opposite. Nevertheless, he told the truth. "I am heading to Tossupong. I wish to refamiliarize myself with that town."

Wang's smile grew larger; it appeared as something of a mask on his face. "Then it is true what they say. Mr. Pickering really *is* an expert on Formosa. Indeed, Tossupong is of great strategic significance. Beyond it begins the realm of the Puppet Savages. Perhaps you have heard the news: my new position, assigned to me by the Taiwan *daotai*, is that of subprefect in charge of aboriginal affairs on the southern border. This means that it is now my responsibility to pacify the raw savages. If it suits you, we will go together. Besides, my guards can ensure our safety."

Pickering was struck by Wang's eloquence. Back in Taiwan-fu he had heard from several sources that though young, Wang was quick-witted, resourceful, and nimble at strategic maneuvering. Now, when Pickering spoke with him, he felt sure that Wang was a man worthy of his fame. He agreed to his suggestion, and they left the camp surrounded by a hundred soldiers.

Along the way, Pickering asked Wang when General Liu would start to attack.

"As I mentioned," Wang responded immediately, "my new position is that of subprefect in charge of aboriginal affairs. As I am sure you know, Mr. Pickering, fluent as you are in several of my country's dialects, *li-fan* in my post's title means to nurse and govern aborigines. So I am therefore here to *protect* the raw savages. If they do not revolt, the government army won't punish them, much less kill them."

Pickering chuckled. "But isn't General Liu here to exterminate them?"

Wang smiled. "It would be best if we can conquer them without fighting a war. Should the raw savages be willing to surrender, well, then no war will be needed."

Pickering said nothing.

When they reached Tossupong the Hokkien head, Mr. Wu, and a Hakka village head, a man unknown to Pickering, were waiting for them. Wang told them what they had come for and suggested that he wish to communicate with the savage chiefs in person. Wu said that they did not associate with raw savages, but the Hakka head said he would take up the task. He sent some of his men out to deliver the message.

Before long, the men came back to report that they had found a tribal chief—one who was related to the chief of Ling-nuang—who would meet them in a plains aborigine's home. They could walk there together now.

The chief was short and sturdy. He leaned against a tree outside the house chewing betel nuts. When he saw Wang, he spat the nuts' blood-red juice onto the ground in a gesture that could, depending on one's disposition, be interpreted as indicating either nonchalance or disdain. Wang looked displeased. Pickering smiled to himself.

A military officer standing beside Wang spoke out. "You should greet Mr. Wang and Mr. Pickering."

The chief breathed a loud *humph*. His eyes remained fixed upon Wang.

Wang gave a signal, and several dozen Qing soldiers raised their guns in such well-timed unison that even Pickering would later admit to being impressed. The chief, however, was unfazed. With a stony face, he looked up to the sky.

Wang seemed enraged. "You people really haven't reflected on what you have done. No wonder the white consul is so eager to kill you."

Pickering interjected, "You were kind enough to return Mrs. Hunt's remains. For that I thank you. Go back and tell Tauketok that Consul Le Gendre wants to meet him and listen to his suggestions. We have pleaded with the consul to delay the attack so that you might have a few more days to think about it."

The chief opened his mouth, "Fight or not, that is up to you. Big Head Chief gave his order very clearly. We owe you nothing. Why should we ask for peace? If you want to fight, we will certainly fight back."

Pickering was able to understand the chief's meaning, so he told him, "We are not bent on fighting. The consul wants to punish you only because you killed those innocent sailors, something for which you have never shown any repentance. But now the consul is willing to offer you some kindness. If he and Tauketok can reach an agreement, perhaps war can be avoided. It would be best for all. . . ."

"If your Big Head Chief refuses to see the consul," Wang began talking and raised his voice effortlessly above Pickering's, "that will leave General Liu with no other choice. Once the war starts, there can be no turning back. General Liu marches with an order to exterminate you all. These soldiers that you see in front of you are just a single column of guards. We have thousands more, and we bring with us cannons that can destroy your houses and land."

Pickering, for some reason finding himself finished with de-escalation, elevated the threat, "If you enrage the consul, he will summon the United States' fleet, the power of which you have already witnessed. If they come again, they won't hold back. And when they come again, they will come with a vow to annihilate you all."

Eventually the bellicosity seemed to sink in. The chief relaxed his tough look and responded, "I'll report this to Ling-nuang's chief, who will tell Big Head Chief."

"Yesterday," Pickering said, "we saw the Hakka Head Lim Nine in Poliac. He will act as the middleman. If Tauketok thinks Lim Nine is a trustworthy friend, can you ask him if he agrees to meet us in Poliac to negotiate?"

The chief left, saying that three days would be needed to wait for a reply.

Wang and Pickering were both satisfied, and together they returned to Sialiao to report to their superiors.

Le Gendre was very pleased. He felt finally that the power of command had been returned rightfully to his hand. General Liu for his part was surprised to hear from Wang that Le Gendre sought a meeting with Tauketok. He had always thought of Le Gendre as eager for war.

He himself also wished for a fight, for, as a general, the most effective way to demonstrate one's ability and worth was on the battlefield. He suspected that defeating the Puppet Savages, who had access to but a few outmoded weapons, would be much easier than defeating the army of the Taiping Rebellion. Still, he had been ordered to comply with Le Gendre as much as possible, so he instructed Wang to visit Sialiao.

When he got there, Wang told Le Gendre that, despite General Liu's being ordered to exterminate the Koaluts, if he were to request officially that the operation be halted, General Liu would be willing to comply. So Wang asked him again if he wished to wipe out the savages.

Le Gendre answered that he had come to the realization that a severe response would offer the savages further excuses to slaughter foreigners, and he was therefore thinking of foregoing his attack in pursuit of a long-term peace, provided the savages promised that they would never again commit the same crimes. Such an outcome, he said, would satisfy the interests of several foreign countries, and would be in line with the United States' generous policy of diplomatic leniency.

If the tribal leader was willing to talk, then Le Gendre hoped both the savages and the Qing government could arrive at an agreement. Still, Le Gendre asked Wang to tell Liu that, should Tauketok refuse the offer, the general could send his troops to attack.

52

Le Gendre seemed to be in a good mood. After breakfast, he did not return to his tent but instead stayed in the house talking with Bernard. Butterfly, sure that now was the time, decided that she would tell Le Gendre everything. When she entered the room, Le Gendre gestured to Butterfly to take a seat. Chinya walked in, and Le Gendre asked him to sit down too. Together, they sampled desserts brought from Amoy and pastries sent by Hokkien people in Chasiang. Butterfly made the tea.

"Butterfly, lately you have been of such great help to me. As you know, we've been terribly busy these past few days, and I haven't been able to thank you properly before now. For that I apologize. In any case, thank you for doing so much."

Butterfly smiled and was suddenly compelled to bow deeply to Le Gendre.

"What is this for?"

Butterfly blushed.

Le Gendre stared at her. He felt that she was extremely lovely, but he sensed that she was here to say something important. He suppressed his desire and asked, "Butterfly, do you have anything you wish to say?"

"Sir, I have something to tell you. I would like to tell it to you alone."

Le Gendre waved Bernard outside. Chinya too was about to leave when Butterfly stopped him.

"Take your time." Le Gendre spoke gently.

Butterfly lowered her head and said, "Sir, please don't tell other people. Don't tell Pickering."

Le Gendre nodded.

"My mother was the sister of the Big Head Chief of Tuillassock. We learned this about half a year ago. My brother had gone to live with Tauketok just before you came to Sialiao. Sir, please don't start this war."

Le Gendre could barely believe it, and for a moment, he did not know how to respond.

In the pause, Chinya added, "Sir, it is true."

Le Gendre smiled, and with a tender look, he said to Butterfly, "Thank you for telling me."

Butterfly then told Le Gendre that she had recently met with her brother Bunkiet. Neither of them wanted the war to happen, so together they made a deal: Bunkiet would ask Tauketok not to fire the first shot, and Butterfly would ask Le Gendre not to send the troops. That was why she had come to Ponglee to see him.

As Butterfly spoke, she trembled a little. Only then did Le Gendre realize that she was there not only for the sake of the people in Sialiao, but also for the people in Tuillassock. Moreover, he understood that she had revealed this information at great risk to her own life; if the secret became widely known, the Qing army might well take her as a hostage. She was burdened with the responsibility of saving her mother's people from extermination.

He was greatly moved, and he swore to Butterfly that he would never divulge her secret, not even to Pickering. He said he would ask General Liu not to attack wantonly, but he stressed that it was up to Tauketok to show his goodwill and agree to the meeting as soon as possible.

As she listened to Le Gendre speak, Butterfly turned aside, tears welling up in her eyes.

53

Bunkiet sighed and welcomed the release that accompanies profound relief.

Yesterday, Lim Nine had come to Tuillassock with the news that Consul Le Gendre from the United States wished to meet with Big Head Chief Tauketok.

Today, a chief from Ling-nuang delivered the same invitation, and he mentioned that a Qing official was present when the request was made.

These messages both conveyed the same happy thing: if a meeting could be arranged and conditions established that were acceptable to both sides, war could be avoided.

Although he had been in Tuillassock for just half a year, Bunkiet felt as much passion for this land as he did for Sialiao and Tongling Bo, both places—incidentally—he could see when on top of the mountain. Whether looking inland or toward the sea, the views up there were breathtaking, and he could not imagine this beautiful place being destroyed in the hellish fire of war.

Too often, it seemed to him, the various groups living in Liang-kiau were split by useless conflicts. Lately, however, the Qing army's presence brought the obvious threat of death and massive destruction, and everybody was united in the wish for it to leave as soon as possible. Indeed, this was probably the first time that Hokkien people, Hakka people, Peppos, and mountain tribes were united by a single hope and goal.

If asked, people on this land would identify themselves as Hokkien, Hakka, raw savages, tamed savages, Tuillassock, Amis, Koalut,

Botan, and so on. Why couldn't they recognize themselves as the "people of Liangkiau"? Bunkiet hoped that after the Qing army retreated, the people here could unite under a common identity. Working himself toward an ever-greater optimism, he stole a look at his adoptive father, who was sitting upright with his eyes closed.

Neither the Hakka head of Poliac nor Ling-nuang's chief had mentioned what conditions Le Gendre had proposed. Such being the case, Bunkiet thought, Tauketok could not refuse the meeting, as he had been presented with no reason to decline the invitation. Bunkiet had heard that Le Gendre was staying in Sialiao; by now, Butterfly must have seen him. He wondered what role she had played in persuading Le Gendre to meet with Tauketok. Whatever had happened, he felt grateful to his sister, and also to Mia and Chinya. They must have worked hard to dissuade Le Gendre from pursuing his revenge.

"Bunkiet." Tauketok had risen silently to his feet and was standing close by; the sudden environmental change shocked Bunkiet free from his thoughts. "Tell Lim Nine we will go to Poliac and meet the consul." Tauketok then summoned Zudjui. "Tell Isa our Alliance Army will set out in the morning. We'll eat lunch at noon in Sabaree and arrive at Poliac in the evening. We will prepare our own food. We won't eat anything served by Lim Nine. We won't even drink his water. I don't want to owe that *nana* anything."

54

Le Gendre, Pickering, and Butterfly were all excited, and Butterfly especially was feeling quite hopeful. Lim Nine had just delivered the message that Tauketok would meet them in Poliac. However, as one of the proposed conditions pertained directly to the Qing government, Le Gendre still had to wait for their assent; General Liu had yet to respond.

Though the Qing government could be very distrustful, so far, Le Gendre considered, he had played the game very cleverly and had not aroused any suspicion. He had used the military threat from General Liu's army to coerce Tauketok into agreeing to meet him, and then he had used the impending meeting to pressure General Liu into agreeing to the two conditions. He was in control.

Le Gendre had told General Liu that he would meet Tauketok in Poliac on October 5. He emphasized that he would not see Tauketok without the Qing government agreeing to his two conditions, which he had laid out earlier in the letter. He also advised Liu, with the softest touch of a threat, that the Qing should send its response in the affirmative as soon as possible, or face the probable consequences of procrastination.

Of course, General Liu was clever as well. When he learned of Le Gendre's conditions, he cursed, "That old fox!"

Certainly, it would be impossible to present Le Gendre's proposal to the Fukien governor within three days. Even if he took it to the Taiwan *daotai* in Taiwan-fu, three days would be insufficient to deliver the reply. He felt Le Gendre forcing his hand.

Sighing, he re-read the conditions; Le Gendre was demanding that a fort be constructed at South Bay. Liu needed to think this over. South Bay was a treacherous place way beyond even Ponglee—the territorial edge decreed by Emperor Kangxi—thus making it quite inconvenient and time-consuming to send supporting troops, should they be required. Furthermore, should Koalut at any point rebel and manage to take control of the fort, the tribe would become almost invincible.

Liu Ming-teng knew that he needed to negotiate with Le Gendre, but in the three days he had been given to respond, this was impractical. After much deliberation, he decided to agree to these conditions in principle, while leaving some flexibility; he would agree to set up a fort, but its location was to be determined after further investigation.

October 5 was fast approaching, and Le Gendre had still not received a response from General Liu. So he asked Pickering to meet with Tauketok and request that the meeting be postponed by one day—two days at the very most.

At Poliac, after being informed that it was not Le Gendre who approached his camp, Tauketok sent a subordinate to see Pickering.

Pickering was impressed by the grand display of warriors there assembled, and when he returned to Sialiao he spoke highly of Tauketok, telling Le Gendre, "You cannot belittle this man. He has brought with him to Poliac upwards of five hundred warriors, each of whom looks, frankly, indomitable. Moreover, he places considerable emphasis on equality and manners. I believe he is a man of principle. He will keep his word. Of that I am certain."

The next morning, after receiving General Liu's cagey reply, Le Gendre took Pickering and Bernard and rushed to the arranged meeting place. Lim was already there, but he greeted them with bad news. "Yesterday, after Pickering's visit, Tauketok and his warriors left and returned to their tribes. Tauketok said you foreigners had not kept your word."

As Lim spoke, his respect for Tauketok was apparent. "Big Head Chief brought some six hundred people here, but they did not drink any of our water, nor did they eat our food."

Le Gendre looked around and asked, "And just where did these six hundred people spend the night?"

"Tauketok found a piece of grassland, and they just slept on the ground."

Pickering was incredulous. "But it rained last night."

Lim replied, his voice warmed by admiration, "They did not mind the rain. They did not take shelter, nor did they place anything on the grass. They just lay there on the ground."

Le Gendre did not know what to say.

Pickering said, "I think perhaps Tauketok thought our request for a delay was made so that the Qing army could attack them at night. He did not fully trust us."

Le Gendre nodded and asked Lim, "Did he say anything else before he left?"

"Yes, in fact he did," Lim appeared increasingly to be suppressing a smile as he answered. "He wanted me to say this to you. 'I thought foreigners were more trustworthy than Qing people, but I see now that this may not necessarily be so.'"

55

Four days later, Lim Nine traveled from Poliac to Sialiao and met with Le Gendre and Pickering.

"Tauketok asked me to tell you that he will meet you at noon tomorrow at Volcano."

"Tomorrow? But isn't Volcano farther away? Why such a hurry?" asked Le Gendre.

Pickering laughed and said, "I was right. In Poliac, Tauketok did not feel secure. Volcano is right inside Seqalu. This means he does not want to fight. Congratulations, consul." He stood up from his chair and walked back and forth as if taken by an insuppressible energy. "I feel sure that you will reach an agreement if you meet tomorrow!"

Tauketok had indeed been cautious, and he had wished to avoid overexposing his army in a place where they could be ambushed. Moreover, Poliac was located on the plain; the Qing bombs could be easily transported there. When the request came for the meeting to be postponed, Tauketok decided that was reason enough to call it off.

Perhaps in part because the raw savages did not live by a system of written words, they placed a high value on oral promises; once a promise was made, it was held to without question. Therefore, when Le Gendre failed to show up, it was received by many as a humiliation. Six hundred warriors had made the trip in vain. That night, when they returned to Sabaree, they were enraged; some even suggested that they attack a village as a punitive measure. This, however, was angrily rejected by Tauketok, "This is the fault of Consul Le Gendre and General Liu. It has nothing to do with the villagers. If you are brave enough, you can attack Chasiang, but can you kill a thousand Qing soldiers?"

As for the second meeting, it was not suggested by Tauketok but by Bunkiet. He told them it was a mistake to blame Le Gendre. "General Liu took the instructions to attack us," he said, "and so far he has held back only because of the consul. It was Le Gendre who insisted on talking to us. Which side do you think is more trustworthy? Which one has been friendlier toward us?"

The next day, when Lim Nine came to the tribe with news that Le Gendre wished to arrange another meeting, quite a few chiefs were opposed to it. At first, Tauketok too was hesitant. He was willing to have a peace talk, but he remained afraid of being trapped and ambushed. Bunkiet, aware of his adoptive father's apprehension, suggested they meet on Sabaree land. To this Tauketok agreed, and the meeting was arranged.

Wang Wenqi and his soldiers were also present and listening as Lim Nine explained to Le Gendre that Tauketok wanted to see Le Gendre at Volcano.

"At noon tomorrow?" Wang did not agree with Pickering's assessment. "This is surely a surprise attack! It's already twilight."

Le Gendre ignored Wang and turned to Lim. "How long does it take to get to Volcano from Sialiao?"

"Four hours if we hurry."

"Then we must set out at seven at the latest. If it rains, we will be in trouble."

"The raw savages are very good at predicting the weather," Lim said. "If Tauketok has arranged it this way, it won't rain tomorrow."

"Very good."

As they were readying to leave, an exasperated Wang Wenqi said that at Poliac it had not been necessary for the Qing army to escort Le Gendre, but if they met at Volcano it would mean venturing into the enemy's territory, and he would be foregoing his sworn duty if he did not provide Le Gendre with adequate protection. He said that the two hundred Qing soldiers presently stationed at Sialiao would escort Le Gendre to Volcano. He would inform General Liu immediately and he could, if needed, deploy four hundred more elite soldiers to meet them at Sialiao by six the next morning.

Le Gendre rejected this offer. After all, he reasoned, Volcano was well inside the realm of the Puppet Savages, and the presence of too many Qing soldiers would pique Tauketok's sensitivity. Should any disagreement arise, it would be not a peace talk tomorrow but a battle.

After some discussion, they finally arrived at a compromise, and it was decided that Le Gendre would bring with him Pickering, Bernard, and two guards. Wang too would go to Volcano, accompanied by fifty Qing soldiers. The other one hundred and fifty would wait at Monkey Cave. Also coming would be Wang's three interpreters, who were Peppos. Mia would have liked to go with them, as he considered himself fluent in the savage language, but he dared not mention anything in front of Wang. Butterfly was also eager to go, and despite the presence of Wang, she told everybody that she could speak the savage language, Hakka and Hokkien dialects, as well as some English.

As she finished speaking, Wang looked at this eloquent young girl and wondered who she was.

"Butterfly," Le Gendre said suddenly, "go to the kitchen and fetch some *aiyu* fig jelly to serve Mr. Wang."

Wang smiled. "*Aiyu*? That would be marvelous."

Shortly after Butterfly had entered the kitchen, Le Gendre flashed in. He whispered sharply in her ear, "Do not arouse needless suspicion in Mr. Wang. If he realizes you and Bunkiet are related to Tauketok, it will do you no good. Do not come with us. Trust me."

He took her tightly in his arms and kissed her, then left without having offered anything in the way of an explanation. Butterfly's face turned hot, and for a while she stood in the room alone, the kiss and its impression fading slowly into what felt like an imagined impossibility.

56

That night, Le Gendre tossed and turned in his tent.

He had often felt like this during the Civil War; on the eve of a battle, sleep refused to be found. And although it seemed unlikely that there would be any fighting the next day, he was still tormented by that familiar suspense. As traumatic memories surfaced one after another, he was transported back to the battlefield, shouts and shrieks drilling through his ears into that part of his brain where fear resided—a part repressed and, to the best of his ability, ignored. Tomorrow, as always, he would be on the front line. After all, it was his style.

The feeling of uncertainty before battle cast many soldiers into panic. Some would use liquor to intoxicate themselves, but Le Gendre never resorted to drink. Many nights on the Virginia prairie, he fantasized about holding and kissing and making love to Clara.

In Sialiao he tried to relive those memories, but the fantasies were snapped by the memory of his wife's betrayal; it felt as though his heart's flesh was being carved at by an old and rusty knife.

The winds suddenly picked up and brought into his room the salty flavor of the sea. How he wished for someone to touch him. It was hot, and he was sweating. He was intensely aroused. He had a strong desire to hold a woman in his arms, believing her warmth could alleviate his anxiety.

His heart and head were filled with Butterfly.

Inside the house, Butterfly too was unable to sleep.

She was confused by Le Gendre's advances, but there was something far more important on her mind.

Wang had said that he would take fifty Qing soldiers to escort Le Gendre to Volcano. Le Gendre had cut the number from an even higher initial proposal, and Butterfly felt thankful for that reduction, but it was not enough. The presence of any Qing soldiers—six hundred, two hundred, or just fifty—would affect the meeting's atmosphere. If this peace talk did not go well, General Liu could easily find reason to open fire. The Qing government would blame everything on the tribes; Bunkiet would be doomed.

She tossed and turned interminably. She had to tell Le Gendre. She could not allow Wang and the Qing army to ruin things; it would be an unpardonable regret.

From her room, she stared out at Le Gendre's tent. When he was in Ponglee, she had rented a boat to travel from Sialiao to see him. Now he was right in front of her, and she had to do something.

She made up her mind, got to her feet, and walked outside. A wintry breeze greeted her. She looked up to the stars and prayed, "Help me, Buddha!"

Butterfly whispered, "Consul, sir."

Le Gendre could barely believe it. He flung open the curtain of the tent.

When Butterfly saw him, she said in a compressed rush, "Consul please don't let Wang and his soldiers go with you. It will ruin everything."

Le Gendre stared at her without offering any indication of his comprehension. A moment passed, and then he came to his senses. "Come inside. Tell me."

Something felt wrong; the chill from outside followed Butterfly into the tent. She stood in front of Le Gendre, continuing to speak in a hurry. "Consul please don't let the soldiers go with you. I promise Big Head Chief will not do anything to harm you. My brother told me Big Head Chief also hopes for peace. Everything will be ruined. Please don't let the Qing army go with you tomorrow."

Le Gendre looked at Butterfly and nodded his head twice. He seemed lost in a faraway place. Butterfly was not sure if the nods were meant as agreement.

She slowed down and tried again. "Consul, please, trust Big Head Chief. Tomorrow you should go only with your men. Go alone. I beg you." She dropped to her knees.

"Okay," Le Gendre said.

He reached down as if to help her to her feet, but then he dragged her up and pressed her forcefully against his body. Her toes scraped at the air above the floor as he smothered her lips with his. Butterfly tried to push herself away but could not match his force; she could barely breathe and began to panic. Le Gendre's hand had groped its way inside her blouse, and with it he was squeezing painfully at her breasts. She closed her eyes and tried again to struggle out of his arms. It was of no use. She felt like a small animal, captured and waiting to be eaten; she burst out crying when he penetrated her.

And then everything stopped; eventually, after a minute or an hour, Le Gendre lay next to her, snoring.

She got up silently—terrified of waking him—put on her clothes, and walked out of the tent. Her entire body was sore. Thick clouds had formed overhead, and the earth was engulfed in darkness. Tears rolled continuously down her face. She wandered around feeling sick, and then lay down in the grass at the foot of the mountain.

Only at dawn did she return to the house. Chinya was awake and seemed shocked to see her. "Where have you been?"

Butterfly just shook her head; she entered the kitchen and started to work.

Later that morning, Wang arrived with his soldiers. Le Gendre was still not up, so Bernard entered the tent to wake him.

Le Gendre opened his eyes with an abruptness located somewhere in surprise. He was somewhat disappointed to find no trace of Butterfly, but felt it was fortunate that he had not been found with her. He dressed himself, then walked out of the tent to apologize to Wang.

In the kitchen, Butterfly was preparing breakfast for everybody while trying her best to behave as if nothing had happened. She wanted to run away, to be somewhere by herself. When Le Gendre entered the house, she lowered her head and walked into an inner room.

Le Gendre suggested to Wang that he sit down and eat, but the offer was politely declined. Le Gendre seemed to hesitate for a moment before patting Wang on the shoulder; although quite taken aback by the intimacy of this gesture, Wang maintained a tight control over his exterior. Le Gendre started to speak. "Mr. Wang, it occurred to me last night that if Tauketok really wants to do me harm, your two hundred soldiers won't help. They will soon be slain by his six hundred warriors. If, on the other hand, he means well, our fifty soldiers will surely arouse in him suspicion, and the peace talk will be ruined."

Le Gendre sat down, apparently relaxed and ready to eat. "Therefore, I am willing to take the risk. I shall bet on Tauketok's goodwill. To win his trust, I will bring neither soldiers nor guns with me. I will go alone with my interpreter and my own bodyguards. As for you and your men, you are to wait for me at Monkey Cave. By sundown today, I shall meet you there."

And that was that; Le Gendre had left no room for negotiation.

57

The October morning was sunny and warm. Gray-faced buzzards flew across the sky, clamoring at the ground below. People in Seqalu loved these birds and saw them as a positive augury. There were so many circling above; it was a spectacular sight. On this, the very day when Big Head Chief was to hold a peace talk, luck was surely on their side.

The shaman danced and chanted to invite ancestral blessings. People chanted with her, and the birds' calls continued. The shaman said that the calling revealed the approval of the tribes' ancestral spirits; it was the greatest auspicious sign.

Tauketok sat on a sedan chair borne by four men. Several Seqalu warriors served as the front lead, and they were followed by warriors and chiefs from the eighteen tribes. As they left, many more people asked to join them; Tauketok allowed it, and a great procession thus set off.

Many of those walking had started the day feeling quite nervous, but the shaman's proclamation had raised their spirits. They were now quite cheerful, shouting and yelling as they watched the birds go with them. Before long, they reached Volcano.

It was a special place; low hills surrounded a clearing of natural grassland. In the middle was a barren and somewhat dusty spot with fire flaring from its center. On the surface of the brook, which flowed beside the grassland, there was another fire that would suddenly vanish or twist unpredictably toward other spots in the water. At night, the flames here moved in a dim and ghostly dance. People in Seqalu held this place in great awe.

Not far from the fire was a platform made up of stone slates. It was constructed at a slight angle and kept very clean. Tauketok sat down in its center. He and the other chiefs formed an outward-facing semicircle, and then almost a hundred warriors sat down around them in a circle. Another hundred men and women stood close behind in a second circle.

Before long, the sentinels reported that the other party was approaching, and that it comprised only eight people. There were only a few foreigners and an interpreter. None of the Qing army could be seen; if it was hiding, it was very well hidden. Tauketok was relieved. But still, he held to his caution.

When the white consul reached the circle, Tauketok used his eyes to signal to the warriors to stand. After Le Gendre and his men had passed, the warriors sat back down and placed their guns on their laps.

Le Gendre stood in front of Tauketok. He nodded, stretched out his hands, and then reached into his pockets and smiled; he had brought no weapons to the meeting. Pickering used the aboriginal language to greet Tauketok.

Le Gendre sat down and looked around, making eye contact with as many people as would receive it, before fixing his gaze on Tauketok. He guessed that Tauketok was in his fifties. He was not tall, but he looked very strong, with broad and well-rounded shoulders. His hair was gray, and, like that of a Qing subject, it was shaved on his forehead and worn in a single long braid down the back. He was dressed in the aboriginal style; he wore a black-and-white coat, but he did not wear the headdress that Le Gendre had until this point thought essential to a chief's ensemble. His face was lined in fortitude. His eyes shone with radiant vigor. He wore a big earring, and his teeth were blackened.

Le Gendre waited for him to speak, but Tuillassock's chief just looked at him with an unmoving face. Eventually, when it became clear that no one else would break the silence, Le Gendre began the meeting. "We held no grudge against Koalut. Why did they kill our people?"

Tauketok answered almost as soon as the interpreter began speaking. "A long time ago, the Red-Hairs came here and acted without mercy. Almost all of Koalut's people were slaughtered. Only three survived. It took their tribe a hundred years to recover. Their descendants vowed to take revenge. This, everyone can understand."

When the interpreter had caught up, Tauketok continued, "But Red-Hairs move on the sea, and Koalut has no boats. All they can do is wait until Red-Hairs come onto land so that they can avenge their ancestors."

Those around him gave shrieks to show their support.

"Nevertheless, the people on that beach didn't kill anybody. Don't you feel regret for the murder of innocent people?" Le Gendre's voice was slightly raised.

Many people began to protest; Tauketok raised a hand to quiet them, and continued to hold the gesture as he answered, "I know. I went to Poliac to show my regret."

"So what do you plan to do?"

Tauketok straightened his back and spoke loudly. "If you want to fight, we will fight. In that case, I cannot know the outcome. But if you want peace, we also hope for peace."

His people cried out again to show their consent.

"If you can guarantee peace, I too would like to see it this way." Le Gendre sounded almost conciliatory.

After the interpreter was finished with this sentence, Tauketok nodded his head. As one, the circle of warriors removed the guns from their laps and placed them on the stone ground with a rich, wavelike click. Le Gendre began to admire these people—they were not "savages" at all.

Since both parties had showed faith and goodwill, the tension between them slackened. Some of those standing in the second circle looked to each other and smiled.

Le Gendre said, "What we care about is the well-being of seafarers. If you promise not to hurt shipwrecked sailors but instead take care of those you encounter, if you agree to provide for them and to send them safely to Liangkiau, then we can let bygones be bygones."

"That we can promise."

Tauketok's people called out again in support.

Le Gendre then said, "In that case, let us move on to the details and arrangements of the procedures. It is inevitable that seafarers sailing in this area will sometimes need to disembark in order to acquire provisions. So if sailors are sent to land to obtain water or other things, they should not be attacked. Rather, you should help them."

Tauketok said he promised to do so, but then he thought some more and added, "But we will be afraid that those who land mean to attack us. We must have a signal. If the ships want their seafarers to land peacefully, they must show a red flag to my people. When we see a red flag, we will wave a similar one in reply and know that they are friends."

Le Gendre considered this proposal and thought it sensible. He said he would specify this requirement in a future written agreement.

Now came the main point of Le Gendre's project. He needed a trilateral agreement. He had proposed it to General Liu, who had seemed reluctant to endorse the plan. He wanted to try his luck with Tauketok; if the chief agreed, then General Liu would be left with no excuse to say no. But if he refused, then it would be Le Gendre giving way.

He cleared his throat and said, "I propose that a fortress be set up in the middle of South Taiwan, close to where Mackenzie and the others were killed."

Tauketok seemed bewildered. "We have no need for a fortress."

"Taiwan-fu will send a hundred soldiers to be stationed there."

The crowd became boisterous, and many of its number raised their hands in objection.

Tauketok rejected the suggestion directly. "We have our land, and the plains people have theirs. If you put plains people on our land, they will certainly find cause to provoke us." Tauketok paused before he went on, "Build your fortress on the land of the Peppos. They have good relationships with *painan* and *nana*. If they don't disapprove, neither will we."

Le Gendre nodded in agreement; he was impressed with Tauketok's quick response.

At this point Tauketok stood up, and the first circle, closely following his lead, also got to its feet. "That's enough for today. We should say good-bye. If you speak more, you may say something that turns us into enemies, and our peaceful meeting will be ruined."

Le Gendre tried for a moment to continue the discussion, but Tauketok was insistent on leaving, so he bowed to the inevitable. These people were sensible, he thought, yet people outside just did not understand them.

He took out his pocket watch. The meeting had lasted only forty-five minutes, but they had talked of so much, reaching several concrete conclusions. He could not help but smile to himself. There was no greeting, no ceremony, no cunning plan. There was just a yes or a no. Even a no was productive, supplied with an immediate alternative to be considered. He thought of other talks at which he had tried to find agreement. Too often each party would beat about the bush, speaking evasively while trying to figure out what the other side was thinking and searching for the greatest profits. An ordinary deal would take days to make.

His interactions with Tauketok had formed a stark contrast with his impression of the Qing government bureaucrats. Tauketok was resolute, sensible, and trustworthy, whereas the Qing officials were fastidious, sly, procrastinating, winding in their thoughts, and in love with the sight of their own faces. No wonder the two parties could not get along.

On the return journey Le Gendre, consulting a map, considered the options and found Tossupong, a place close to South Bay, to be an acceptable location for the construction of a fortress. He decided to travel there for further inspection.

At Monkey Cave they met, as arranged, with Wang Wenqi. Wang knew that an agreement had been made and war avoided; he felt that he, as subprefect in charge of aboriginal affairs, should be given significant credit for the outcome. And so, feeling very pleased with himself, he accompanied Le Gendre and Pickering to Tossupong.

That evening, as he stood on the shore's edge at Tossupong, Le Gendre could see the entirety of South Bay. To the left was the beach where Mrs. Hunt and the sailors were slaughtered. Ahead, the setting sun threw to earth its diminishing evening radiance. The great Turtle Nose Mountain was visible in the distance. Waves broke against a shore of spectacular rocks. Wild boar grazed in the meadow behind him. The breeze pressed hard against his chest. His heart beat with mixed feelings, and he prayed to the Blessed Virgin Mary that no further tragedies would befall this land.

58

On the day of the meeting, after the men had left for Volcano, the silence that replaced them swelled to take on a physical weight. Desperate for some distraction, Butterfly pretended to be busy in the kitchen. She was tormented. She believed that by persuading Le Gendre to dismiss the Qing guards, she had helped her mother's people. But her own life was now overwhelmed by a turmoil against which she could barely struggle.

Before daybreak, she had lain on the grass at the foot of Turtle Hill, praying to the gods for some guidance. Of course, she had known for some time that Le Gendre was attracted to her—it was obvious from his looks, from the target and direction of his eyes. His were expressions quite different from the pure adoration she felt from Chinya.

At that moment, standing in the kitchen, holding objects in her hands for which she had no immediate use, she felt the urge to flee, to run back to Chihou Hospital, where life was fulfilling and where she felt secure. But now this, she knew, was an impossibility.

At noon, she calculated that Big Head Chief must have met with Le Gendre. Silently she prayed for them to avoid conflict and to reach a peace agreement. Afterward her thoughts returned to the previous night. In the evening, she had been shocked by Le Gendre's kiss but felt that it contained at least a hint of sweetness. At midnight, however, he had molested her without affection; he had not asked for consent, nor had he afterward, when she lay trembling and afraid, offered any consolation. Her heart sank to the bottom of an immeasurable abyss.

And yet, she considered that perhaps Le Gendre's decision this morning to forego the military accompaniment, along with his little gestures of thanks and appreciation, showed that he cared for her. *Perhaps he does feel for me*, she thought.

However, in the next moment, she scolded herself for entertaining such absurd ideas. When he forced himself on her last night, he did not yield to any of her protestations. When he got up this morning, he did not bother to talk to her, and he cast but a few stray looks in her direction as she served the men breakfast; what did that signify beyond contempt and aggression?

And then there was Chinya. For the past few months, after sending him back from Takao, she had felt disappointed in him. During the Mid-Autumn Festival she went back to Sialiao, not to see Chinya but to sweep her father's tomb. While there, however, she discovered that Chinya was in possession of a renewed and much improved attitude. He had started to pursue his studies seriously and had become a more stable man.

But now her heart had sustained a wound that she felt certain would bleed without end. She knew Chinya liked her but dared not talk to her about his feelings. And though Mia had always been kind to her and Bunkiet, that was for their father's sake. After all, a boss was supposed to take care of his employees. As she thought about the past, it suddenly occurred to her that she still cared for Chinya. Perhaps . . .

But no. She cautioned herself against becoming carried away by such ridiculous imaginings. There was no possibility for a love between her and Chinya. And anyway, despite their existence being almost self-evident, Chinya had yet to reveal to her his feelings; now, after all this time, he was hardly likely to ever risk disclosing them. As for Le Gendre, how could she let herself be near someone who treated her like that? There could be no future for them.

Anyway, the most important thing right now was to prevent a war.

Le Gendre and his men did not return that evening. At dusk, Mia checked and found that Wang Wenqi had not returned either. As for the Qing army, its soldiers were packing their things, as if readying themselves to move.

Mia needed to find out what had happened, so he sent Chinya to Poliac. People there said they knew nothing of the whereabouts of Le Gendre and his people, but neither had they heard of any fighting. At least, Mia thought, there was no bad news.

After that, Mia went with Chinya to Chasiang, which was as calm as it had ever been. So they came back and told the same to Butterfly, who received the information with reserved optimism. Later, on an unseasonably warm evening, Butterfly looked east to Big Puppet Mountain; its clouded top was now home to Bunkiet. She fiddled with her *yina*'s necklace and said quietly to herself, "I have done all I can."

Finally, the next morning, Butterfly heard the good news.

Le Gendre and Big Head Chief had reached an agreement that had been approved by General Liu. Few details were available, but that didn't matter. As long as there was no war, she was happy.

At noon or thereabouts, Le Gendre's guards arrived in the village to pack away his things. They said that Le Gendre, Pickering, and Bernard had gone to Tossupong and would not be returning to Sialiao.

Somehow, hearing of the peace agreement, Butterfly felt her own agony partly assuaged; at least that suffering had been avoided, and for the time being nothing more would be added to her own.

Unfortunately, although it was now time for her to go back to Chihou, many of the ships previously available had been recruited by the army for transporting troops and equipment, and Butterfly could only wait as time passed, spending the days as if they were years. She wanted so badly to be back in Takao and begin the process of forgetting Le Gendre. But for a while at least, there would be no ships to take her there.

Meanwhile, word kept arriving from Chasiang. It was said that General Liu had also traveled to Tossupong, and that there was to be a new fortress built there; that General Liu had come back to Chasiang, but the foreign consul did not travel with him; that the soldiers from Taiwan-fu would retreat from Chasiang; that the soldiers recruited from Chasiang had received notification that they would be dismissed; that the majority of people in Chasiang praised General Liu for his bravery and his leadership; that the Puppet Savages must have been so frightened at the prospect of war with the Qing army that they were desperate to have a peace talk. Indeed, apparently Tauketok had been so dismayed by the superior power of the Qing army that he surrendered without a fight.

However, this was all merely rumor. . . .

At noon on October 19, Mia returned from Chasiang. "Butterfly," he said as he stepped into the house, "there is a ship in the harbor that will leave for Takao tomorrow morning."

As soon as she had finished cleaning up the remains of lunch, Butterfly rushed to begin packing her things.

That evening, a smiling Mia said, "Butterfly, I have something else to discuss with you."

"What is it?"

He poured her a cup of tea and said, "You have been with us for more than a year. We all like you. It is true, Chinya went astray for a while. But, as you can see, he has pulled himself together, and he has been working hard. What I want to know is, can you accept him? Do you want to consider . . . ?"

Butterfly understood the implication but could not think of an appropriate response. She lowered her head, blinked back tears, and said nothing.

Mia had intended to tell her that if she accepted the marriage proposal, there was no reason she should leave Sialiao. But, taking note of her reaction, he said, "There is no need to hurry to a decision. We can wait till you next come back from Takao."

After a pause he continued, "I am just speaking on Chinya's behalf. Let him go with you to Takao. If you go there alone, I will be worried, and so will Chinya." Butterfly nodded her head.

That night, she held on tightly to her pillow and cried until dawn.

59

It was around seven o'clock in the morning, and dew glistened on the grass. Le Gendre could hardly believe it. Just forty hours ago he had designated the location, and already the wall of the fortress was erected.

General Liu was striding over to greet him. "Consul Le Gendre," he began talking as he completed his approach, "we used whatever we could find. We built the wall with the trunks of palm trees, and then we used sand to fill in the crevices." He knocked a few times on the wall. "What do you think? Is it solid enough? Our supervisors in Fukien have not yet approved this. But to show my sincerity, I have ordered it done."

Le Gendre thanked him, but he felt that this general was entering into some kind of a contest; Liu seemed very much to be implying that he was owed a debt of gratitude. What was that Hokkien expression? Even in a losing game, we still need to win our face.

General Liu held up his right hand with its thumb and fingers splayed. "Give me five more days, and the fortress will be completed. The cannons are already on their way."

"General, I congratulate you! You are indeed swift. When the fortress is completed, I suggest that a hundred soldiers be stationed here. I will return for an inspection at least once a year."

General Liu did not respond directly. Instead, he turned and spoke to his men. They walked off and before long returned carrying a wooden chest.

"These are what we have found, consul. Please inspect them."

Le Gendre opened the chest. Lying beside a mariner's compass and a pair of binoculars was a crumpled photo of Mrs. Hunt. He took it gently in his hands and turned it over to check for any writing, inspecting it closely for a long time without speaking.

The next afternoon, Le Gendre went again to see the fortress. Liu was there and, happily, the cannons had arrived. The two were discussing the new equipment's positioning when they saw Pickering walking alone in their direction along a small road from the east.

Le Gendre grimaced; a few days ago, after the talk with Tauketok had concluded, Pickering had been adamant that to build a fortress at Tossupong or any other nearby place was a bad idea. In fact, he had expressed his belief that the Qing government would do well to leave the whole area alone. He wanted Liangkiau to remain as it was, allowing immigrants, *tushengzi*, aborigines, and raw savages to continue to live as they had been living. He had said a fortress built there would prove redundant, as Big Head Chief Tauketok had already promised to maintain the peace.

Le Gendre had questioned him, "And what will happen should Big Head Chief die?"

Pickering had replied, rather too sharply for Le Gendre's liking, that he believed the raw savages would continue to keep their word, regardless of who was in charge. Little by little, he had said, their ancestral land had been taken from them, until so much of it was gone that they had been forced to hide themselves in the high mountains. If Le Gendre insisted on building a fortress, then he was insisting on helping the Qing government extend its domination into Liangkiau. The raw savages would continue to be pushed farther up the mountains, and they would surely blame this on white foreigners.

Le Gendre had countered, with some deliberate asperity, that he was building a fortress not only to crack down on the Puppet Savages but also to serve as a coastal landmark so that ships could have something to measure themselves against for their navigational safety.

But Pickering had continued to argue, with an increasing belligerence, until eventually Le Gendre had become annoyed and abruptly ended the conversation.

Later that afternoon, Le Gendre had ordered three red banners be made. When they were finished, he had sent Pickering to Tuillassock to present them to Tauketok; they were to be used, as agreed in the peace talk, as a signal to approaching boats.

Pickering had always been prone to exaggeration, and as Liu watched him approach, he realized that it was this aspect of the man's character that annoyed him the most. Back in Taiwan-fu, he had known Pickering to look down on the Qing government bureaucrats, giving voice to his dissatisfaction with Qing China's process and convention as often as possible. Yet, Liu remembered with rising disdain, when referring to Tauketok, Pickering had always done so with respect; perhaps it could even be called admiration. The thought enraged him.

An idea formed in his mind. Since the peace agreement had been made and the Qing army could do nothing substantive to the Puppet Savages, he would instead require that Tauketok acknowledge him as his superior and journey to thank him in person. After all, he, Liu Ming-teng, was an appointed representative of the Qing government; he stood above both Le Gendre and Tauketok, and certainly far above that supercilious Pickering.

But for now, General Liu needed the so-called "expert" on his side. So he congratulated Pickering for his role in the peace treaty and told him that a man of his accomplishments deserved a Chinese name that was beautiful as well as meaningful. He used a brush to write the name of the legendary auspicious beast, Bi Qilin, in beautiful calligraphic strokes, and he presented this to Pickering along with a jade seal engraved with the new name. Pickering received the gift with a generous display of gratitude that pleased Liu to no end.

The following day, Liu asked Pickering to transport some gifts to Tuillassock and while there, to invite Tauketok to Chasiang. General Liu said that as a representative of the Great Qing Empire, it was necessary for him to receive Big Head Chief in Chasiang to mark the signing of the peace agreement. Pickering was delighted, apparently ignorant of Liu's motives.

After Pickering had set off, General Liu bade farewell to Le Gendre, telling him that he was returning to Chasiang, where he would wait for Tauketok. He wished to imply that Le Gendre was on the same level as Big Head Chief, while he, General Liu, was somewhere above them all—waiting, almost regally, for the chief of the Puppet Savages to come and pay homage. It was not clear, however, from Le Gendre's warm good-bye whether he felt slighted.

In Chasiang, General Liu set about arranging the pompous scene he felt befitted the occasion. He imagined Tauketok, insignificant leader of Lower Liangkiau, arriving laden with precious gifts to pay tribute to the representative of the Heavenly Kingdom. He, General Liu, commander of the insuperable Qing army in Taiwan, would surely secure his place in history on this account. He smiled, imagining the contents of these future written flatteries.

However, when Pickering arrived, he was accompanied by two of the chief's daughters; Tauketok had not made the journey.

In the tradition of plains people—both Hokkien and Hakka—daughters had no rights of inheritance, but such traditions did not apply to the raw savages in Liangkiau. Liu was aware of this and, as Big Head Chief had no son, he assumed that one of these two women was the heir apparent. He was willing to receive the two daughters, but he wished badly that it was Tauketok who had come to stand before him. Perhaps, Liu thought, the histories could be written to include the chief's presence. . . .

However, when the two daughters approached, they did not kneel, nor did they bow. "We are here to speak our father's words," they said together, loudly. "Our father, Big Head Chief, was willing to talk with foreigners because he respects them as warriors and as decent men. He witnessed foreign soldiers fighting against our warriors in the mountain forests. They were not afraid of bullets. They were not afraid of heat.

"But our father said that untrue rumor has spread in Chasiang and Poliac that he was afraid of you, and that that was why he surrendered without fighting. So our father wanted us to tell you that the Qing government bureaucrats do not deserve his respect, and that he will never surrender to them. You people living in the plains think you are cleverer than us, but you just brag and boast. You don't keep your promises. That's why he does not want to deal with your people. He will never come to your territory to be received by a Qing government official."

And with that, the two women turned and walked away as proudly as they had come.

General Liu sat with his hands trembling. He wanted to jump up and slice at them with his sword! But he had to show civility. For now, he could vent his anger only at his servants.

These two young women were nothing. What would people think when they learned that he, a magnificent Qing general, had been scolded by two young Puppet Savage women? How they would laugh at his expense. This was more than he could bear.

He talked to himself in a quiet rage, "How dare you! Since I cannot cut you, I will use a brush to show you as clowns to be forever despised."

So he asked his pageboy to prepare ink and paper. He wrote swiftly, as if he were riding a horse.

The emperor ordered I vanquish the bandits;
I conquered those Puppets and stationed in Tossupong.
We opened the road and strained the bows to shoot the arrows;
Those clowns kowtowed to our great power.
We empowered our army and added pools for irrigation.
Stricter governing was enforced here to protect our people.
We assuaged foreign countries as we ensured their navigational
   safety.
What credit do we have? We are deeply indebted to our Great
   Emperor.

WRITTEN BY LIU MING-TENG, REGIONAL COMMANDER OF
TAIWAN AND PENGHU
IN THE AUTUMN OF THE SIXTH YEAR OF EMPEROR
TONGCHI'S REIGN

When he was finished, he ordered that a monument carved with the inscription be installed in Fu-an Temple.

However, even this gesture did not release him from his anger. He blamed the feeling on Pickering. After all, it was Pickering who

226 & PUPPET MOUNTAINS

had escorted the two savage women. He thought perhaps it was Pickering who had encouraged the two women to speak with such breathtaking arrogance. Yes, that would be just like him, like the ever-contemptible "expert."

His thoughts then turned to Le Gendre. "Our Qing army was assembled on *your* account. I'm here for *your* sake. I comply with *your* requests. Now the Puppet Savages say that they respect *you*, but not *me*, a glorious Qing general?"

General Liu began to hate Le Gendre.

60

As in the towns, so in the tribes; everywhere, all sorts of gossip continued to spread.

Many in Tuillassock said that Bunkiet behaved excellently during the whole incident, that Zudjui did almost nothing throughout, and that Tauketok would therefore give his seat to Bunkiet and not to Zudjui. People said that Tauketok sent his two daughters to Chasiang to show his distrust of Zudjui. They reminded each other that the only reason for Tauketok's becoming Big Head Chief was that Majuka had eloped and married a Hakka man, something that greatly depressed Paljaljaus and pushed him to surrender the seat of leadership to his younger brother. Indeed, they also reminded each other that when Tauketok took it over, he had promised that one day he would transfer the seat and title to Zudjui. But it was said that Tauketok had now changed his mind; he wanted to turn over the leadership to his adopted son because Zudjui was too often drunk, whereas Bunkiet was a learned and dependable young man.

Some argued that although Tauketok, by giving his seat to Bunkiet, would be breaking his word, it was not an ignorable truth that Zudjui was not suited for leadership. Besides, it was not just Tuillassock that Zudjui would have to lead, but the whole Seqalu area. The world had changed; was Zudjui capable of facing it? For the sake of Seqalu's future, surely Bunkiet would be a better and more sensible choice.

Nevertheless, some still sided with Zudjui. After all, they said, a promise is a promise, never to be broken. The ancestral spirits would be angry, and then what would happen? And anyway, although Paljaljaus seemed to have lost his sanity, he was still alive. For some, the biggest influence on their thinking was the fact that Bunkiet's father had been a *nana*, and he was therefore not of pure Seqalu blood; Zudjui was the proper choice. Most elders in Seqalu tended toward this thought.

As the rumors fermented, Zudjui became more and more hostile toward Bunkiet. At first he tried to pull himself together to behave as befitted a future leader. However, within half a month he was back to getting drunk every single day. Observing this, some elders reluctantly switched their support to Bunkiet; the future of the tribe was more important than the bloodline or the sanctity of a promise.

People in Tuillassock had felt the tension even before the peace talk, but back then they spoke in secret. After the peace talk, they discussed it in public.

Increasingly, disagreements led to fights. Serenity seemed to vanish from Tuillassock. Even those in Sabaree started to comment and gossip.

61

The sunset, when watched from the cape of Tossupong, was extravagant in its beauty, but Le Gendre longed instead to see Butterfly.

At night he tossed and turned, unable to shed Butterfly from his mind. In his tent in Sialiao, he had not cared about how she had felt. But lying in his cot, deprived of daytime's distractions, he felt guilt gnawing at his heart.

Fierce downslope winds blew through Tossupong, aggravating the socket of his injured eye. He recalled a time in Sialiao when his eye had hurt like this. Back then, Butterfly had used her soft fingers to stabilize his forehead while massaging the area around his eyes with cool, wet gauze. Remembering that afternoon, he felt that it was from that moment that he began to fall for her.

He had to admit that he had been abusive. He remembered her tears, her wet cheeks, her initial struggle, and her body's eventual desperate, twitching submission. He regretted not saying any loving words. He hoped that she could be by his side. He needed her. After all, his love was—he was sure—a fact of undeniable being. He began to think of her more and more, not just at night but throughout the day as well; soon he had convinced himself that it would be best to take her back with him to Amoy and to begin his second life there.

Yes, he was positive; this was how his second life would commence. His life in America had come to an end with Clara's callous betrayal. Now was the time for renewal. Butterfly had aroused his lust and reawakened his vitality, and now he again yearned for a family life. Since he was Catholic, divorce was unthinkable. But he wished never again to see Clara. Perhaps he could have a family with Butterfly in Amoy. They would be so far away from Clara that she would not figure in their life at all. Yes, that would be an excellent compromise.

Though at first Butterfly had seemed to shun him, most of the time he had found her to be open-minded and approachable. This last time, when he visited Liangkiau, she had no longer fled from his presence. For half a month or so, she had kept him company and dutifully served him food and tea. Gradually he had become overwhelmed with the desire to embrace her, to take her as his own. And then, that night, it was as if heaven had arranged it . . . that she should enter his tent and beg. . . .

He decided to visit Sialiao.

62

The next morning, Le Gendre ordered his men to pack his belongings and ready for departure. They began without a fuss, long since having become used to his erratic and unknowable impulsions.

Le Gendre hoped to arrive in Sialiao by dusk. He longed to see Butterfly as soon as possible, to tell her all of what was on his mind. However, things would not go to plan, and he was instead doomed to suffer a most unfortunate few days.

After his possessions were fully packed, he walked to the fortress for a final inspection and there saw a British gunship, the *Banterer*, passing in the shallows. The previous month, the ship had left to return the imprisoned Bashi Islanders to their homeland, and now it was on its way back to Amoy.

When he saw Le Gendre and his men, the *Banterer*'s captain waved at them warmly, and soon the ship shifted its course and began moving toward the shore. Le Gendre, despite his other more pressing concerns, could do nothing but wait for the ship.

Seeing Le Gendre already packed, the captain offered to take him back to Amoy. Le Gendre's men were delighted; they had been in Taiwan for more than a month, and they wished to return home, or at least to return to a more familiar place. Le Gendre, however, rejected the proposal without consideration; he had to say good-bye to Mia in Sialiao. And anyway, he said, the *Volunteer* was waiting for them in Takao.

His men could not understand why that was necessary. If Le Gendre intended to bid farewell to General Liu at Chasiang or to Daotai Wu at Taiwan-fu, they could make sense of it, but why Sialiao, why Mia? However, as they all expected, Le Gendre was not forthcoming with an adequate explanation.

After the *Banterer* had left, Le Gendre and his men set off on their march. Almost immediately they encountered severe headwinds that slowed their progress, and in total darkness they reached Sialiao.

Mia was asleep in bed when Le Gendre entered his room without knocking. As Mia blinked back considerable surprise, what came into view was a desperate face, one eye covered and the other red and inflamed; Le Gendre looked quite terrifying.

"Butterfly, Butterfly, where is Butterfly?" Le Gendre demanded in a hoarse whisper that kept cracking into fully voiced sound.

"Butterfly went back to Takao at noon today. Did she wrong you, sir?"

Mia's tone and facial expression alerted Le Gendre to his own indiscretion. He sat down, breathed deeply, and tried to calm his voice. "My eye is in intolerable pain. I wish for Butterfly to look at it, to wash the eye for me."

Mia was relieved.

Le Gendre asked him to serve food, water, and fruit to his men, while he strained to steady his mood. He regretted not coming back to Sialiao one day earlier. He needed to touch Butterfly. He wanted to persuade her to join him in Amoy. He would never let her leave him.

The next day, Le Gendre rose early in the morning. He had decided to travel to Chasiang to say good-bye to General Liu. While there, he would ask Liu to set aside some sedan chairs for the journey to Takao.

However, as he stepped away from Mia's house, a surge of anxiety grabbed him as he realized that, once back in Amoy, he would not be able simply to come and go to this island as he pleased. He would need the approval of his supervisors and also the approval of the Qing government. How much time would pass before he could again see Butterfly? He had lost Clara through distance. He could not afford to lose Butterfly for the same reason.

His anxiety refused to subside, and soon after he set off to see General Liu, something came over Le Gendre. He ordered his men to halt and rushed back to Mia's house alone. He barged in and began speaking immediately. "Listen, Mia. Butterfly is my woman. I will be back soon to take her to Amoy. Take good care of her. For your help I will thank you handsomely."

He thrust a small bag into Mia's hand before turning suddenly to go. The bag was heavy, and Mia knew without checking that it contained a huge sum of money.

He called out, "Consul! Sir!" But Le Gendre was already gone.

General Liu, who had talked and laughed with Le Gendre in Tossupong so merrily just a few days ago, now offered him a distinctly cold shoulder. It was only later that afternoon, when he met with Pickering, that Le Gendre learned how terribly General Liu had been offended by Tauketok's daughters.

That same day, the interpreter brought a piece of bad news to Le Gendre: the lease duration originally agreed upon for the *Volunteer* had expired. The ship could not wait for him any longer, and it would sail from Takao to Foochow at seven o'clock on the morning of October 25.

"It never rains but it pours," Le Gendre said angrily. But what use was groaning? He could do nothing about it; this was not his country, and that was not his ship.

He and his men were exhausted. It was sundown of October 21, and it would take two and a half days to march to Takao, provided the going remained favorable. In that case, he would have only a little time with Butterfly. Worse still, General Liu had given them just two sedan chairs—one for Le Gendre, the other for Bernard. Pickering and the other men would have to walk.

Such being the case, Le Gendre elected instead to go to Takao by sea, ostensibly so that his men could rest—although the increase in speed may also have influenced his decision. He returned the sedan chairs to Liu, and they boarded a small sailboat. However, bad luck continued to haunt Le Gendre; that night they fought against fierce winds, and the boat made little progress toward Takao. At dawn they gave up, landed at Chasiang, and decided to make the journey by land after all.

When they met again with General Liu, he told them that he too was traveling to Taiwan-fu. For some strange reason, Liu was unwilling to re-loan them the two sedan chairs from yesterday. However, if they went together, he would reserve one for Le Gendre's use. In fact, Liu said, it would be much safer for Le Gendre if he traveled under the guard of Qing soldiers. So they joined with General Liu's army and spent the night at Hongkang. It was October 22.

The following afternoon they arrived at Chetongka. Le Gendre calculated that the army would reach Ponglee by nightfall. Once there, he would no longer have to worry about his safety. He could rush on alone, without the protection of the Qing army, and be at Takao by dusk on October 24, perhaps even earlier. With this timing, he would be afforded some private time with Butterfly—a few hours in which to talk and persuade her to join him in Amoy. But then he remembered Dr. Manson; he hoped that the doctor would not get in his way.

Perhaps, should things not go smoothly and Butterfly not immediately make up her mind, he could find a position for her at the hospital of Amoy Customs. At some later date he could fetch her from Takao to Amoy.

However, as he was indulging in these and other thoughts, feeling more and more convinced that everything would, for him, work out very well indeed, the sedan chair came to a lurching halt, and its carriers walked away unencumbered, leaving both Le Gendre and the chair helpless in the middle of the road.

He waited and waited. Nearly half an hour passed, but still the bearers did not show up. Finally, a man came to inform him that General Liu had decided to spend the night here. Le Gendre sent Bernard to talk to Liu, but Liu said that the sedan carriers had worked hard and needed rest.

Le Gendre flew into a silent fury. He cursed General Liu, who he was quite sure had never been a man to consider the condition of any of his laborers. Indeed, those Liu had conscripted to build the road to Chasiang had worked solidly without break. Le Gendre sat under a mulberry tree by the roadside in a horrible mood; the setting sun hung heavily over the horizon.

He decided that in such dire circumstances he could count on only himself; it was *he* who would have to get things done. So he sent his men back to Chetongka to ask for help.

Before long, Pickering returned with good news: a small sailboat was unloading freight in the harbor. Le Gendre practically shouted at him that he was willing to pay whatever it took to rent the boat. Pickering replied calmly that he had already made a deal with the boat owner; once the last of the logs and boards were unloaded, Le Gendre could set off.

When they were all aboard, Le Gendre felt relieved, and he soon fell into a deep sleep. He trusted that the boat would be at Takao by sundown the next day.

But still bad luck would not let go of him. The following noon, when the boat had reached Tangkang, the winds suddenly reversed their direction, and the boat could go no farther north. So Le Gendre and his men disembarked at Tangkang and began walking to Takao at a high speed.

In the final hours of the day they reached Takao, hungry and exhausted, and there they found the *Volunteer* moored, as expected, at Shaochuantou.

In the darkness of the night, Le Gendre stood at the shore, looking across the harbor at Chihou. There were dim lights flickering in several of the buildings, but—despite knowing its location—he could not place Chihou Hospital. His chest seemed burdened with an overwhelming heaviness. He had rushed almost without pause for four days and three nights, and yet, despite all his efforts, he had not managed to see Butterfly. He hesitated, wondering whether he should even board the ship. Perhaps he could head to the hospital and see her now. But what could he say by way of explanation both to Manson and to his own men? No, it was too late now. Just a few more paces and they would be on the deck of the *Volunteer*. His feet were leaden; every step felt impossible. How he hated fate for playing him this way! What would Butterfly think of him? Apprehension took hold; would he ever see her again?

There were many foreign sailors aboard the *Volunteer*; most of them were British. They crowded around and congratulated Le Gendre on his great achievement. They said that they no longer had to worry when sailing around Formosa, and it was all thanks to him.

As if he had been awakened from a dream, Le Gendre's face split into a broad smile. He greeted everybody and accepted their congratulations heartily, as if he were in fact the triumphant returning hero he suddenly believed himself to be.

So later that night, alone in his cabin after regaling the men with tales of his adventures, Le Gendre started working on a letter to his supervisor in which he bragged, for several prolix pages, about his marvelous achievements in Formosa.

9

PRAYING TO GUANYIN

63

Five days before Le Gendre left Formosa, Butterfly sat on the deck of a boat. She was traveling from Chasiang back to Takao, her mind cycling through a series of increasingly worrying thoughts.

She looked to Sialiao and thought of Le Gendre, remembered him forcing himself upon her. From that night on, she had felt nervous whenever she saw Mia and Chinya. Of course, she could not bear to tell them any of what Le Gendre had done to her.

She was sinking in a sea of contradictions. She hated Le Gendre for taking advantage of her, and yet for some unknowable reason she found herself almost wanting to see him again.

Forget him. Forget all about Le Gendre. Butterfly lowered her head and watched the seawater rise and fall against the side of the boat. She prayed silently, *Goddess of Mercy, bless me and help me forget all about Le Gendre. Let him retreat from my heart like the waters vanishing into the sea. Let him disappear from my life!*

Chinya was on the boat as well. Mia had given him enough money to pay off the gambling debts. He wanted to find a job in Takao and re-establish himself there; he would stay away from Shaochuantou and instead move to Chihou, where he would be closer to the hospital and to Butterfly.

Although Butterfly had been feeling somewhat uneasy around him, she did not object to Chinya's traveling with her to Chihou; with his company, the journey would certainly be more comfortable. From Chinya's perspective, although Butterfly had not immediately accepted the marriage proposal, neither had she turned it down. Even more promising was that she did not object to his moving to Chihou. He committed himself to a reflected glimmer of hope.

Chinya walked across the deck to stand next to Butterfly. After a moment, he nudged his right hand against her thigh. She did not step away, so he worked up the courage to touch her hand. Butterfly did not recoil, nor did she want to; Chinya, in response, held her hand tighter. Butterfly had not felt such a warm feeling of security in a long time. The sea winds blew on them and through them. She closed her eyes and sighed.

The winds and waves were favorable, so they arrived at Chihou before dark. When they landed, Chinya wanted to accompany Butterfly all the way to the hospital, but she refused. "The sun is still up. I can get there by myself. You should look around to see if any boats or shops need a helping hand."

Reluctantly, Chinya agreed.

Butterfly was back to working hard in the hospital. She fed the patients, washed them, combed their hair. When she was done with her own tasks, she would lend a helping hand to her co-workers. Her colleagues liked her, and her patients adored her. Dr. Manson was delighted, telling her that he and many of the patients had been afraid that she would never come back.

Butterfly loved the hospital; when she was there it felt like she was standing on solid ground. Nevertheless, she was sometimes revisited by the appalling memory of that night at Sialiao. Whenever she recalled it, she felt her heart snap out of its normal rhythm; it was as though the attack were happening again.

One afternoon, she noticed that the ship with the Star-Spangled Banner that had been anchored in Shaochuantou was no longer there; she knew that meant Le Gendre had finally gone. Good. She hoped he would never again come to Taiwan.

On the second Sunday after they returned to Takao, Butterfly and Chinya visited Fung-shan Koo-sia together. Butterfly wanted to thank the Cundi Buddha in Guanyin Ting for helping them to avoid war, as well as for blessing Chinya with good luck after he came to Chihou. He had been hired by the captain of a fishing boat.

Butterfly remained kneeling in front of Cundi Buddha for a long time. In her prayer, in addition to expressing her gratitude to the Buddha, she mentioned Le Gendre, who continued to bother her day and night. She prayed to Cundi Buddha to grant her wisdom and courage to dispel his shadow. She wondered if she should tell Chinya what had happened.

She looked at the sword held by the first pair of the Buddha's hands, and suddenly a clarity blew through her mind. Whatever existed between Le Gendre and herself was not supposed to be, so she should wield the sword of wisdom to cut it off and let it go. Once she had done that, it could no longer exist, and there would be no need to tell Chinya about any of it. After all, she thought, if she was selfish enough to tell him, she would be dumping her own worries and anxiety into his heart. Silently she prayed to the Buddha to help her sever any connection between her and Le Gendre, and then she got to her feet.

Chinya had been standing behind her, waiting patiently for her to finish her prayer. She smiled and told him, "You know something? Whenever I come here, I find peace and serenity. My mind is clear, and my heart is emptied of worries. Chinya, can we come here on every other Sunday to pray to the Buddha?"

"Of course, Butterfly. Whatever you say."

64

On the fourth Sunday after Butterfly and Chinya arrived at Chihou, Mia showed up at the door of the hospital.

When told by the doorman that someone was outside looking for her, Butterfly had guessed that it would be Chinya, and she was quite startled to see Mia.

He did not smile at all; it was certainly not as though he was visiting by way of presenting her with a pleasant surprise. He simply told Butterfly that he had come to Takao to see Chinya, but he did not know where to find him.

On the way to Chinya's lodgings, Butterfly told Mia excitedly that Chinya had found a job and rented a good place to stay, but Mia just grunted a brief response that effectively ended the conversation.

Fishermen did not have fixed holidays, and Butterfly thought Chinya might be out at sea. This morning, however, they were in luck; Chinya was sleeping at his place.

The younger brother was, as usual, excited to see the older. "Let's go to Koo-sia," he suggested. "It's wonderful there. There's a hill inside the town and a lake just outside it." Mia did not appear interested, but he agreed to go anyway.

When they were in Koo-sia, Mia conceded that it was indeed magnificent, but he was not much impressed by Guanyin Ting. As usual, Butterfly and Chinya worshiped and prayed to the Buddha. Mia did not pray but instead wandered about; his pacing sounded impatient. A couple of times he seemed about to say something, but he never did. Chinya kept emphasizing that he and Butterfly really loved it there. Mia was somewhat surprised when he heard Chinya effusing about the Buddhist temple and its statue, but he understood that Chinya had come to love these things under Butterfly's influence.

Butterfly had noticed that Mia was acting strangely. He was not in the least bit excited as they traveled around Takao—indeed, he rarely talked. She wondered if it was because she had not responded in the affirmative to his proposal, made a month or so ago now, that she get married to Chinya. Back then, Mia had said that perhaps she needed time to think, but he did not mention how long he would wait. Had he come to ask again? Perhaps he was worried that Chinya might slip into some of his past bad habits. But whatever his reason for visiting, Butterfly thought it better not to question him about it.

Although she hadn't told anyone, perhaps not even her own self, somewhere in her heart Butterfly had agreed to marry Chinya. But, the shadow of Le Gendre was yet to be completely dismissed. And moreover, was she willing to go back to Sialiao, where she would be asked to find satisfaction in a life of keeping pigs and catching river fish? She hesitated, reluctant to leave Chihou Hospital; she loved working there.

Apprehension gnawed. If Mia asked her, how would she answer?

It was getting late, and Mia suggested that they return to the hospital. Butterfly was perplexed. Did he come all the way to Takao just to look at Chinya? Again, Mia seemed to be about to say something, but then . . . nothing. What was it that he wanted to say?

When the three of them got back to Chihou, they began the familiar winding walk to the hospital. It was almost time to say good-bye when Mia slowed to a stop in the middle of the road. He looked first at Chinya and then at Butterfly. His face was oddly contorted, as though it was being controlled by two opposing forces. Finally he said, "Butterfly, congratulations! Consul Le Gendre told me everything. You should have let us know. I will take Chinya with me back to Sialiao."

Butterfly didn't know what to do. She looked at Mia and then at Chinya; now it was her turn to be unable to speak. Chinya tried to remain composed, but when he spoke it was in an agitated yelp. "Mia, what do you mean by that?"

Mia looked like a child who had, mostly without thinking, created an unresolvable problem. "Just after you left," he said, "Consul Le Gendre came to find Butterfly. He told me that she was his woman, that he would come back to take her to Amoy as soon as possible."

The air froze. Butterfly stood still, fixed like a nail hammered into hardwood. Her face emptied itself of blood until she was sheet-like pale. Her eyes lost their shine, and her mouth remained closed.

Chinya glared at Mia and then howled, "Nonsense! I don't believe it!" He turned to Butterfly. "Tell me. Butterfly. Please. What Mia said is not true, right?"

Butterfly was trapped in a nightmare from which she could not awaken. She smiled in an almost pathetic way, looking at Mia with profound anguish. Her head felt only loosely attached to her neck; it wobbled—shaking, nodding. She remained silent, and then turned around to walk slowly up the steps of the hospital as if struggling up a steep slope.

"Butterfly! Butterfly!" Chinya shouted after her.

But she didn't react; it seemed as if she heard nothing. Chinya tried to follow her into the hospital, but he was prevented from entering by the doorman.

A moment passed, and then Butterfly opened the door to stand at the threshold. "Chinya, I'm so sorry. Go back to Sialiao. Mia, thank you for taking care of me this past year."

And with that she turned around to shuffle back inside.

Chinya fell to the ground and burst into tears. Mia patted him on the shoulder. "Come on. Get up, Chinya. Let's go back to Sialiao."

65

It was not until she had closed the door to her room that Butterfly began to cry.

She had, of course, been unaware of Le Gendre's visit to Sialiao. Nor did she know anything of what he had said to Mia. But even if she had known about it, little would have changed; Mia had already made his decision.

For the past few days, she had been wrestling with the *if* and the *how* of whether she should confess everything to Chinya. But now that she was severed from the Yang family, such worries seemed irrelevant.

She lay down in bed. In a peculiarly tragic way, her burden had been deprived of its weight, and she identified a sense of relaxation in the emptiness; it was no longer necessary for her to care about those many teeming thoughts.

Mia clearly felt that she had betrayed Chinya, that she had developed a love with Le Gendre in secret. Oh, how badly she had been wronged! She had been getting along well with Chinya for the past few weeks. But now everything was over.

Mia said that Le Gendre had intended to bring her back to Amoy. What did that mean? How should she feel about that?

The emptiness was replaced by contradiction and worry. Would Le Gendre come again? Would she have to go with him to Amoy?

No. How ridiculous that would be! She hated him, and to judge from his actions, he clearly thought similarly of her. And anyway, what would she do in Amoy? It was such an unfamiliar place, even if it was quite close to her father's homeland. Moreover, Le Gendre had told her that he lived there with his son; he was a married man.

She thought of Chinya. What would happen to him? He would most likely be mocked by the people in Sialiao, perhaps so much so that he would no longer be able to hold himself together. She felt her heart being pressed; tears rolled freely down her cheeks. She had done too much harm to Chinya. And he had been so nice to her.

Even though Mia had wanted Chinya to return with him to Sialiao, she felt it was she who had inflicted the fatal wound. When she told Chinya to go back home, it was as if she had let him know that she had chosen Le Gendre. It was such a misunderstanding.

Suddenly she felt empty again, but it was no longer liberating. Chinya had been forced out of her life. Perhaps she would never see him again.

She tasted and recognized bitterness. Her parents were both dead. Her brother was far away in a savage tribe. She had only just begun to accept that she would live with Chinya for the rest of her life and that the Yang family would become her family. But now all of that was impossible.

She missed her brother and wanted to visit him at Tuillassock, but she was afraid to set foot in Liangkiau. Her only available choice was to wander around town. She could not even stay in the hospital, as she was worried now that Le Gendre would try to find her there.

Could she still go to work the next day? Would she feel timid when she saw Dr. Manson? How could she explain to him the fact that she would never again visit Sialiao? And it was not just Dr. Manson; perhaps she would feel guilty in the presence of any and everybody else. She was afraid of being abandoned by the world, and yet she wanted more than anything to hide from it.

But whatever happened, she would certainly not go to Amoy with Le Gendre. He had violated her in a most terrible way, and then he had once more not sought her consent when deciding that she was to go to Amoy with him. It was clear that he did not respect her at all. He had attacked her, he had assaulted her physically, and now, without even seeing her, he was continuing to assault her mentally. How she hated him!

She thought of Mr. Chen, the temple keeper she had visited in Fung-shan Koo-sia, and remembered him speaking of his mother's becoming a nun; perhaps there remained a spark of hope, unextinguished in the surrounding darkness.

She left the hospital before dawn the following morning, carrying her baggage and waving a good-bye to the doorman. Day had not yet broken; the moon was floating silently in the diluted night sky.

The sea winds blew, and her heart shriveled as tears left cold streaks on her face.

The world had refused her, and the only place of refuge she could think of was Guanyin Ting, temple of the Goddess of Mercy.

She thought of her mother. All those years ago, when her mother was fleeing from her tribe, had she felt like this? At least, Butterfly thought through another shot of pain, her mother had been able to count on love. But what about her, what love did she have?

66

Butterfly sat in Abbess Yizhen's room. Walking into the temple an hour ago she had blurted out—before Yizhen had time to even offer a greeting—that she wished to have her head shaved and become a nun. Yizhen had calmly refused her request and suggested instead that Butterfly take shelter in the temple. After a modest lunch, she had led her here.

It was a simple room, with just a single bed and without any table, chairs, or other furniture. On a board that protruded from the wall was a statuette of Cundi Buddha. There was no other decoration.

After listening to Butterfly talk about all that had happened, Yizhen smiled lightly and asked her what she would do after she became a nun. Butterfly said, "I want to be here in the company of the Buddha, chanting the sutras, growing vegetables, doing whatever I can for the temple. I will spend the rest of my life here, safe and away from everything."

Yizhen shook her head gently and said, "When a person becomes a nun, she does so because she wishes to learn the Buddha's way. It is not an escape from the world."

Butterfly started to cry. "But the world has no place for me. I am homeless."

Yizhen smiled. "Everywhere is your home. This place or that place, it really doesn't matter. Think of your father. Wasn't he making a home somewhere close to nowhere?"

Butterfly's eyes widened.

"Presently you are in the thick of karma. I will help you through it, but you have to believe in the mercy of the Buddha. With that belief, you can overcome the difficulties that lie ahead." She patted Butterfly gently on the shoulder. "Now rest, and let your mind find peace. If you are tired, sleep. I will come to see you again after the afternoon sutra."

It was dark when Butterfly opened her eyes. She could hear chanting and guessed it was the nighttime sutra. The hall of the temple was dimly lit. Yizhen was seated in front of everyone else, knocking on a wooden fish as she chanted. Butterfly stood at the back of the hall and bowed to Cundi Buddha before kneeling down. A nun passed her a book, and Butterfly started chanting along with the others.

After they had finished, she bowed to Yizhen, telling her, "Mother, I am confused. I don't know what to do. . . ."

Yizhen said simply, "Stay in one of our rooms for three days, and then tell me your decision."

Butterfly could not push Chinya from her mind. It seemed impossible to disentangle herself from the lingering connection that existed between them. How she wished Chinya would come to find her! As she sat alone in the temple, she felt willing to traverse the world with him, just as her mother had wished to do with her father. She was not sure if Chinya would marry her, if he still even wanted her. If he went back to the hospital and found her missing, would he know that she had gone to Guanyin Ting? If he came to find her, they could make a living together somewhere, somehow.

She wanted to work with what she had learned at the hospital. South of Takao, there was no one else with her knowledge of foreign medicine. She planned their future: Chinya would continue working on the boat, and then, after saving enough money, he would ask the boat owner for help, carrying freight from other places for them to sell. They would open a small shop somewhere to sell those goods; the shop could serve also as a little clinic. Even if Chinya did not come back for her, perhaps she could open a small clinic by herself.

Suddenly, just as she felt herself breaking free from perplexity and inaction, something rushed into the front of her mind that threatened to put an end to that hard-won progression. She remembered telling Le Gendre about Guanyin Ting.

It had been a Sunday, and Le Gendre had just returned from his Sunday service. Butterfly had asked Le Gendre why his cross did not look like the cross in Dr. Maxwell's and Dr. Manson's church. He had praised her for her cleverness and keen observation and then asked her if she had ever attended the service at Chihou Church. She had said she had, and then she told him about Guanyin Ting, where she said she went often to worship the Buddha. "It is similar to foreigners' church services," she had said. "And we can talk directly to our gods, who will answer our questions and give us answers." Le Gendre had been very interested to hear of Fung-shan Koo-sia and had wondered out loud why Carroll or Manson never bothered to mention these things to him. From his luggage he had taken out an ancient-looking map of Taiwan, on which he had found Guanyin Ting; he had made Butterfly promise that she would take him there someday.

Recalling this conversation, Butterfly became worried that, should Le Gendre really wish to find her, he would know to look here. But then she scolded herself for thinking too much. And anyway, if she became a nun, she would certainly refuse and ignore Le Gendre, should he ever come to the temple.

Thus, after the evening's chants, Butterfly again told Yizhen that she wanted to become a nun. She requested that Yizhen assign her some jobs; she was determined to take on more work than could ever be finished so that she would be left with little time to think of anything else.

Yizhen offered her an understanding smile. "It won't be hard to find jobs for you. But the point is, you need to understand the essence of Buddhism and aspire to become a well-established soul on your own."

Butterfly got up early the next day and sat with the Buddhist beads in her hand, chanting the morning sutra. Her head-shaving ritual was scheduled for mid-morning. As the time drew near, she appeared to be calm, but her heart was agitated, beating what felt like an irregular rhythm. She prayed to the Buddha to grant Chinya the good luck to find a wife. She also prayed that Bunkiet and Tuillassock would be blessed with a lasting peace. Perhaps, now that life was filled with bitterness and pain, it would be an impossible dream to hope for the eradication of worry and anxiety.

Life . . . it was for her a word contaminated with sorrow and cynicism. She would spend the rest of her time in Guanyin Ting. The least complicated existence turned out to be the one inside the temple, far away from her past. She tried to feel ready to bid farewell to the outside world.

But then, a fit of commotion began outside. Someone was calling her name, "Butterfly! Butterfly!"

She recognized Chinya's voice immediately; it was as familiar and as sweet as a sound could possibly be. A flurry of steps followed, and he burst into the temple.

67

On the morning of October 21, when Le Gendre had requested that he take good care of Butterfly until his return, Mia was put in shock. He figured that Le Gendre and Butterfly had developed their relationship in secret. No wonder Butterfly had not looked happy when he suggested that she marry Chinya.

After the shock came the fury. It was stupid of him to propose the marriage to Butterfly, and pointless therefore to send Chinya to Chihou. And he had given Chinya a large sum of money; what a waste that was!

The issue was further complicated when he opened the bag Le Gendre had left with him. He was quite taken aback; the money was enough to build a new house! He dared not write to Le Gendre in request of the details, so instead he vented his anger onto an imaginary Butterfly. Why had Butterfly given neither of them any hint of her feelings? "Hakkas, humph! They are never good!" He murmured to himself, "And she is half savage . . . *of course* gratitude is foreign to her."

He thought next of Bunkiet; how was it that brother and sister were both so lucky? One was in love with a wealthy foreign diplomat, and the other was adopted and highly thought of by Big Head Chief. His anger turned into jealousy. It was all so unfair!

He sighed. "I'd better bring Chinya back to Sialiao as soon as possible." He thought Le Gendre must have noticed that Chinya was fond of Butterfly. Maybe that was why the consul had reminded him to take good care of her. Or was it actually a warning? In any case, he understood well that he could not afford to offend Le Gendre, who at this point was practically his patron.

However, it was November, and the northwestwardly winds had started to blow, making it difficult to sail from south to north. Besides, Mia was occupied with festivals in the temple, so he did not board a boat to Tangkang until almost a month later. Once there, he changed to a boat bound for Chihou. It was Friday night when he arrived, and he waited till Sunday to find Butterfly and Chinya.

When he saw Butterfly, he could not show his anger. Consul Le Gendre himself had asked him to take care of her. If he offended

Butterfly, he would be offending Le Gendre, something that would surely do himself much more harm than good.

He had intended to speak with Chinya before mentioning anything to Butterfly. But he had been unable to find him, and then how happy and excited Chinya had looked by her side! He could not bring himself to talk until the very last moment, just as Butterfly was about to enter the hospital. He had anticipated Chinya's agitation, but Butterfly had responded in a most unexpected way. It seemed that at first she was not aware of the existence of any agreement between her and Le Gendre. However, when she reemerged briefly from the hospital, she had asked Chinya to go back to Sialiao. What was this all about? Mia was baffled.

The next day, Chinya was a puppet with no soul, completely at his brother's disposal. Mia had heard that there was a freight boat sailing for Tangkang in the evening. When they got there, thankfully, the boat's owner agreed to have them on board.

On the ship, Chinya stood at the stern, rolling his back forward as if distancing himself from those behind him; his shoulders trembled.

It was a calm night lit by a full moon, so the boat continued sailing after dark. At midnight, Mia decided that he could no longer stay on the deck and went to the cabin to sleep. Before he left, he patted Chinya on the shoulder and said, "Come inside. Get some sleep." Chinya did not reply.

Mia fell asleep quickly and then was shaken awake from a dream. He opened his eyes to see Chinya.

"I am not going to Sialiao. I'm going back to Takao. I've talked to the boat owner. He said they'll unload the goods at Tangkang and then, if the weather stays like this, they'll leave again for Takao at night. I will be back by the morning."

Mia was stunned into clear-headedness. "You're going back to Takao for Butterfly?"

Chinya nodded. "I've made up my mind."

When the day broke, Mia found that the depressive scowl from the previous evening had disappeared from Chinya's face. As they both walked out of the cabin, Mia asked, "Are you sure?"

"Brother, please forgive me. This time I will go to Takao without your money."

"The money doesn't matter, but Butterfly . . ."

Chinya didn't let him finish. "I've thought it over. Butterfly does not want to go to Amoy with Le Gendre, or she wouldn't have looked like that yesterday. I don't believe I will lose her to him."

Suddenly a pain pressed itself against Chinya's voice. "I don't know what happened between her and the consul. But I believe in Butterfly. Besides, I myself did something terribly wrong to her."

Mia thought of the money Le Gendre had given to him and he mumbled, "What if Le Gendre . . ." But he did not know how to finish the thought.

The sun had risen, and the boat was nearing the shore. Mia saw that Chinya's resolve was unshaken and he said, "Okay, as you wish. Go back to Takao. But I have a request for you. On the fifteenth day of the first month next year, come back to Sialiao for the festival *Laozu Tiaoxi* and receive our tribal ancestress's blessings."

Before they parted, Chinya took out the remainder of the money Mia had given to him. But Mia shook his head. "Keep it. You will need it."

Chinya bowed. "Thank you."

A little while later, alone on the deck, he looked upward and whispered, "Butterfly, I hope our future will be like the rising sun, like the cloudless blue sky."

68

Yizhen and the other nuns were very happy for her, but Chinya's sudden appearance had left Butterfly feeling intensely embarrassed. She knelt in front of Yizhen without knowing what to say.

Yizhen laughed. "Come. Get to your feet. Thank the Buddha, and then you can leave."

Chinya knelt next to Butterfly and said, "Mother, please preside over our wedding."

Butterfly lowered her head and stared at the ground; her face was burning, but Yizhen was pleased. "Good, good! I will be happy to. Your wedding will be witnessed by Guanyin and Mazu. The two of you will be immensely blessed."

Butterfly looked back on the past few days. The thick fog of misery had been quite implausibly cleared. Everything had happened so quickly, and she was scrambling to find some order and understanding. She looked up at Cundi Buddha with tears shining in her eyes.

"Thank you. Thank you for blessing me. I will be forever indebted to you."

After their wedding at Guanyin Ting, Butterfly and Chinya bade farewell to Yizhen and the other nuns. As they walked away from the temple, they wondered where they would settle down. Butterfly had decided not to go back to Chihou Hospital. She was very fond of the place, but both she and Chinya knew that she had to stop working there. And although she wanted to return and say a proper good-bye to Dr. Manson, she was worried that he might talk to Le Gendre. If Le Gendre came in search of her, he would be informed by the doctor of their whereabouts. She wanted nothing to do with him. Sadly, she thought, it was better that Manson knew as little as possible.

"Where can we go now?"

Chinya thought for a while, but then, before he could answer, Butterfly added resolutely, "I want to do something in a big town. Something I like doing. I don't want to go back to Sialiao." Chinya smiled and said he enjoyed being in Fung-shan Koo-sia. Bantan port was there; he could work as a fisherman, and Butterfly could open a small clinic.

But Butterfly rejected his idea. "If I open a clinic around there, Dr. Manson will soon learn about it. No. I will not stay in Takao, nor in Fung-shan."

"If not Chihou, not Shaochuantou, not Koo-sia, not Bantan port, and not Sialiao, where else is there to go?"

Butterfly was for a moment plunged into a pensive mood.

Chinya told her, "It doesn't matter. You don't have to consider me. Wherever you want to go, I'll go with you. I can find a job anywhere."

Butterfly looked up, smiling after Chinya's reassurance, and said, "Then let's go to Taiwan-fu. I love the area around Shuixian Temple. It's always busy, and I know that many people miss the medical care provided by the foreign doctors. We can try our luck there."

So they went to Taiwan-fu. Butterfly found the kindly woman she had met when she was last in town, and from her they rented a small room. Chinya managed to secure a job at the market, but it was not easy for Butterfly to open a clinic. Fortunately, a traditional herbalist doctor was looking for an aide, so Butterfly went to see him. When the young doctor heard that Butterfly had learned some medical skills from a Western doctor, he was surprised, but he did not reject Western medicine outright. He said instead, quite diplomatically, "Han Chinese medicine is better than Western medicine in its philosophy. It is better than Western medicine in treating sprained ankles or injured bones. But, frankly, foreigners can treat wounds, stomachaches, or fevers better than we can." Thus, Butterfly was hired.

By and by, Chinya and Butterfly settled into life around Shuixian Temple. It was convenient to live and work there, and they felt very comfortable.

They arrived at Taiwan-fu at the end of the tenth month on the lunar calendar. The Lunar New Year was just around the corner, so they soon left town to visit Mia. They boarded a ship on the fifth day of the first lunar month and arrived at Sialiao two days later.

For the most part, those in Sialiao were quite excited when they learned that Butterfly and Chinya had been living in Taiwan-fu, although a few of them, for some reason, affected indifference. Mia had not expected them to get married so soon, but he was happy to learn that they had established themselves in the city, and that his little brother had returned a changed man. Chinya now moved and spoke with the confidence of someone who had seen enough of the world to know their place in it.

More delightful still was the news of Butterfly's being pregnant. Chinya was overjoyed at the prospect of becoming a father. Mia wanted them to give a wedding feast. But according to custom, the Lunar New Year holidays, which lasted from New Year's Eve to the Lantern Festival, were not an appropriate time.

It was the day of *Laozu Tiaoxi*, the most significant ritual passed down by the ancestors in Sialiao. Before it became dark, many people in the town were busy with festival preparations. The ritual was to be held at an ancestral hall of the Huang family, quite close to Mia's home.

The previous year, Butterfly and Bunkiet had looked on as mere observers. But this year it was different. Bunkiet wasn't there, and Butterfly was now one of the Yang family members; she felt herself a part of this community of *tushengzi*. Especially after the signing of the peace treaty, people here had tried to rid themselves of previously held enmity. Regardless of their origins, they sought harmony. Despite these positive changes, however, she missed her brother.

Chinya looked so happy as he told many different people that his child would be blessed with the combined blood of *tushengzi*, Hokkien, Hakka, and raw savages. He and Butterfly, he said, would have a child whose blood was so thoroughly mixed that people anywhere could claim to be its relatives. Whenever he finished telling this little tale, he would burst out laughing.

As the moon appeared, everybody placed their offerings to Laozu in the center of the hall. Along with various fragrant flowers and betel nuts, a large bowl of millet wine was in place. Beside these offerings was a round wooden table laid with twelve sets of bowls and chopsticks, meant to be used by ancestors and ancestresses.

Sialiao's inhabitants gathered in a big circle. Everybody was singing. The shaman danced on the altar as an avatar of the ancestress Laozu. She wore a tall crown of flowers and an affectionate smile on her face. She balanced on the balls of her feet and then danced her way over to the table. She picked up one offering and, to show her appreciation, raised it to the height of her head while looking at the people around her. Afterward, facing the altar and its urn, she danced with her hands, moving forward and then backward. She repeated this sequence several times, until all the offerings had been raised.

Laozu then used her left hand to hold a gourd filled with millet wine. In her right hand she held a wooden spoon. Dancing around the people of Sialiao, she would offer each of them a small spoonful of millet wine and bless them with auspicious words. Fed with wine and blessed by Laozu, people returned her favor with an ecstatic bow. Elderly people would sometimes direct a question at her; Laozu would offer them a solution, and they seemed satisfied with her proposals.

Butterfly stood by Chinya and watched Laozu's delicate dancing. In keeping with her father's Hakka tradition, Butterfly had long worshiped Guanyin, and she also believed in her mother's ancestral spirits. In Takao she had encountered Christianity, and although she was impressed by its believers' lifestyle and their religious fervor, she was not touched by Christian sermons and services. What she liked most was the Cundi Buddha in Guanyin Ting. Now she had a close encounter with Laozu for a second time; she was greatly affected.

Because Laozu was goddess and ancestress combined, she was the deity closest to the people in Sialiao. She possessed the solemnity of a deity alongside the affection of an ancestress. And once a year, she would show up in front of her descendants in this combined guise. As she watched, Butterfly realized that every group had their own way of worship, and that no religion or culture was superior to the others.

When Laozu faced her with a smile, Butterfly felt as though she was bathing in spring sunlight. Unwittingly, she closed her eyes and lowered her head. Laozu caressed Butterfly's hair and then gently nudged her chin. Butterfly swallowed a spoonful of the millet wine. When she tasted the liquid, she was reminded of her mother; millet wine had been her favorite. She opened her eyes. Laozu smiled. She reached out and touched Butterfly's belly, and then she leaned in and whispered in her ear, "Host a banquet on the first of the fourth lunar month. Remember, the first day of the fourth month."

Afterward, as Laozu danced up to Chinya, she turned her head again, with a smile lingering on Butterfly.

When the festival was over, Butterfly and Chinya told Mia that Laozu wanted them to hold a banquet.

Mia was surprised. "You must be favored by Laozu. She will take special care of you, Butterfly."

The three of them found the first day of the fourth month on the lunar calendar; they would come back to Sialiao for that day.

69

Le Gendre took a deep breath as he stepped once again onto Formosa. This time, he had come to deal with a conflict that had escalated between Qing China and Britain over a dispute related to camphor.

After the *Rover* incident, his reputation had risen, and he was now internationally acknowledged as the best man to deal with Far Eastern affairs.

Perhaps fittingly, the present dispute had in large part been provoked by Pickering, who in February 1868 had negotiated the purchase of camphor, on behalf of McPhail & Co. (now under different ownership), from the Salach and Attabu tribes in central Formosa. Such private trading was illegal, and he had instigated a local militia to turn against the Qing army. The two sides had come close to war, which placed additional strain on the already tense relationship between Qing China and Britain. Under such circumstances, Le Gendre was sent for to mediate between the two sides.

As he was making final preparations for the crossing, a letter arrived from Clara asking for his forgiveness. Le Gendre had no idea how to react; he had done his best to forget all about his wife. In mid-February he had sent his son back to the United States, perhaps as part of arrangements for bringing Butterfly to Amoy.

But he was annoyed. He did not know how to contact Butterfly. He had considered writing to her at the hospital in Chihou, but he didn't believe she was proficient enough in English to read a letter. Moreover, if Dr. Manson and other people learned of his writing to her, they would think it very strange, and he should not like to become the subject of gossip.

And even if he did take Butterfly to Amoy, it would be impossible for him to take her out on public occasions; she would instead be a precious object to play with while no one was around. In truth, though he did feel a sense of guilt regarding his behavior toward Butterfly, more potent was the compulsion to see her. How he longed to go back to the night, to savor the felicity of holding Butterfly's body in his arms!

Another thing bothered him. About half a month ago, Dr. Manson had sent him a letter in which he mentioned off-handedly that Butterfly had left the hospital. It was just as well that he had not written to Butterfly at the hospital; still, he was too embarrassed to ask Manson where she was.

He had written previously to Manson in early January. In that letter, which was sent primarily to convey his New Year's greetings, he had quite nonchalantly asked about Butterfly. But around that time, Dr. Maxwell had left Formosa for Hong Kong, and Manson, having taken on much of Maxwell's work, was very busy. He had put off replying to Le Gendre's letter until late February, and when Le Gendre received the reply, it was already March.

But just a few days later Le Gendre received another letter, this one from the new British Consul to Formosa, George Jamieson, requesting that he travel to Formosa to help end the discord between Britain and Qing China.

Jamieson's invitation delighted Le Gendre. After receiving the reply from Manson, Le Gendre had been agitated, distracted by speculations. He wanted to go to Formosa and search for her, but he could think of no reason to travel to the island. Although he assumed she had nowhere to go but Sialiao, he felt that Butterfly was somewhat unpredictable, and he could by no means be sure of her actions. Regardless, Jamieson's letter provided him with the perfect excuse.

The relationship between Qing China and Britain was worsening. First Pickering and his men had killed a few Qing soldiers and then, on his way back to Taiwan-fu from Takao, the British manager of McPhail & Co. had been beaten up by a lackey of the Formosan government. The church in Fung-shan had been set on fire, and Maxwell's assistant, a Hokkien member of the church's clergy, had been beaten up by someone there. That same assistant was later accused of poisoning one of his female neighbors.

And yet, at such a sensitive time, quite incredibly, the highest-ranking government officials on both sides were changing. The British Consul to Taiwan had been replaced by Jamieson, and the Taiwan *daotai* was replaced by Liang Yuangui—someone with no experience dealing with foreigners—who was so stubborn and arrogant as to refuse to recognize Jamieson's position. Jamieson was enraged; he

asked Amoy to send more gunboats to Formosa. It was then that he
wrote to Le Gendre, asking him to negotiate with Liang.

On April 22, Le Gendre reached Taiwan-fu and met with Liang
Yuangui and Jamieson. They quickly reached an initial agreement;
both sides settled for compromise.

The Qing government was to return the confiscated camphor to
McPhail & Co., and the British government was to order McPhail &
Co. to put a halt on purchases of camphor until such time as Peking
reached a final agreement with the British consul. It took just a
single day, and Le Gendre was now free to deal with his personal
affairs.

His ship left Anping early the following morning. The *Aroostook*
moved swiftly through the water, and Le Gendre had already planned
his itinerary. He was working under the assumption that Butterfly
had returned to Sialiao, and it was essential that he get there before
sundown. He had to see Butterfly today. It must not be like last time;
he could not miss her again. Of course, he had told those who cared
to know that he was visiting Tauketok for the purposes of maintaining their friendship. Le Gendre smiled at his own cunning. However,
just to be on the safe side, the ship was to stop first at Takao; there
he would ask Dr. Manson, delicately of course, if there was any news
of Butterfly.

After anchoring at Shouchuantou, Le Gendre disembarked and
went directly to the hospital. Almost immediately after they
exchanged hellos, Le Gendre asked the doctor if he knew anything
about Butterfly's whereabouts. Dr. Manson stared at Le Gendre in
surprise. When he saw him striding up the hospital's steps, he could
not have guessed that Le Gendre had come to inquire about Butterfly. But, Le Gendre's comportment, in particular the almost burning
ferocity of his stare, was such that Manson dared not joke. He told
Le Gendre that Butterfly had left without saying good-bye, and that
in the past five months she had not once been back to visit him; this
behavior puzzled Manson, as it was not her way.

Le Gendre was worried. After talking a little more with Manson, changing the subject multiple times to avoid arousing suspicion, he turned to leave. Having boarded the ship, he asked Captain Beardslee to set sail as soon as possible. The captain and his seamen were disgruntled. Many had stepped on land for a stroll only to be immediately summoned back. Nevertheless, per Le Gendre's orders, the *Aroostook* sailed out of Takao at half past ten, bound for Liangkiau.

The ship went as fast as possible; it passed Lambay Island (present-day Xiaoliuqiu) at two in the afternoon. Thomas Dunn, the U.S. consul to Foochow, was also on board. He had heard that there was a ghost cave on Lambay Island and said that he would very much like to see it, but Le Gendre replied derisively that there was no possibility of the ship stopping for such inconsequential trivialities. Consul Dunn was offended. Le Gendre was not his supervisor; indeed, they were of almost the same rank. In fact, Le Gendre had never been to Lambay Island, and, but for the fact that he was in such a hurry to find Butterfly, he would have been only too willing to stop at the cave. He needed to see her that evening. If there was time, he would visit Tauketok tomorrow.

In February, a British ship had malfunctioned and found itself stuck at the southern tip of Formosa; food and water had been running low. The captain, in accordance with the "South Cape Agreement," had waved a red banner to appeal for help from the raw savages, who, in time, had provided assistance to the ship. Le Gendre therefore really did need to visit and thank Tauketok. If possible, though it had not yet been a year, he would like also to go to Tossupong to inspect the fortress.

At around four in the afternoon, Sialiao came into sight. Le Gendre felt his heart thrashing to escape from his chest whenever he looked to Turtle Hill.

Their destination drew closer and closer. The *Aroostook* was a big ship, and people in Sialiao would undoubtedly have seen it approaching. Someone must have told Butterfly. And Mia, who had always been so compliant, would certainly come to the shore to greet him.

The winds started to blow harder and the waves became fierce. Still, the ship continued at full speed, and it reached Sialiao by five o'clock in the evening. How strange! There was nobody in sight. Last time, as soon as the ship had made clear its intention to dock, a large group of people had gathered to watch its approach. Today, however, there were just a few children playing. When they saw the ship, they ran into the village, perhaps to tell the adults. But where *were* the adults?

Shortly after Le Gendre stepped ashore, Mia appeared. He was so drunk that to remain standing he required the constant support of another person's shoulder and neck. He reeked of alcohol. Words came out in odds and ends. "Consul, I . . . I, have been. Butterfly's . . . It is Butterfly's wedding . . . her banquet."

Le Gendre felt sick. "What do you mean, Butterfly's wedding?"

His question seemed to have a profoundly sobering effect on Mia, who practically fell to kneeling. He was almost prostrated when he said, "Consul Le Gendre. It is Butterfly and Chinya's wedding banquet. It's all my fault. I will give back your money."

Fire seemed to flare from Le Gendre's single eye. "What nonsense! Shut up!"

He had not expected to be faced immediately with such an awkward scenario. Fortunately, in anticipation of at least some embarrassment, he had asked the interpreter to stay behind on the ship. Consul Dunn, standing nearby, could not fathom why Le Gendre seemed so overwhelmed with both rage and disappointment. He asked, "Are you all right, Charlie?"

Things had the potential to get out of hand. But in front of his colleague, Le Gendre could not afford to lose his composure.

"It is nothing. He said there is a plague in the village. Let's go. Let's not land." He turned around and cried out, "Make fire and set sail!"

Thus, the *Aroostook* blew the bugle three times and returned to the sea in a twilight of winds and waves.

On the shore, Le Gendre had been so incensed as to be almost trembling. But once back on the ship, he regained his commanding stance. The ship carried a large group of people, but they had accomplished nothing in Sialiao. Dunn had wanted to land on Lambay Island, but merely for the purposes of sightseeing. That was not enough to warrant their sailing south. Even the trip's original stated purpose, that of visiting Tauketok, now seemed unsatisfactory.

Le Gendre needed to think of something else for them to do, something worthwhile. Otherwise this expedition would be thought of as an embarrassing waste of time and resources. He remembered General Liu mentioning that the Botan tribe, fiercest of all the Formosan raw savages, lived in the mountains beside the road they had opened all those months ago. *If I can visit the Botan tribe on a goodwill trip, it will bring credit to my career*, he thought.

So the next day, Le Gendre ordered that the *Aroostook* drop anchor outside Ponglee. He went ashore with Dunn and Captain Beardslee—escorted of course by a few soldiers—and found a Hokkien village head with whom he had become acquainted almost half a year ago. He asked the head to guide them up the mountain to see Botan's chief. The man readily agreed. He said that of late he had been on good terms with the nearby chiefs of the raw savages. His land was leased from them, he paid the rent on time, and he often bartered with them, exchanging Hokkien goods for the raw savages' products and wood. He said that it would not be hard to get along with the raw savages for the foreseeable future, as long as everyone kept their promises. "However," he said, "the Puppet Savages do not like outsiders stepping into their territory. We barter with them or pay our rent at the 'earth-cow trench,' that is, the territorial borderline between the aboriginals and Han Chinese immigrants."

"If they refuse us entry to their tribe, then we can invite them onto our ship," Le Gendre said.

Captain Beardslee laughed loudly at what he took for a joke, but Le Gendre was serious.

The Hokkien head showed them to the "earth-cow trench," where they were met by a Botan sentinel. Afterward the sentinel left and soon returned in the company of about seven people, one of whom was pompously attired. Le Gendre, assuming this man must surely be the chief, invited him and his men onto the ship. The chief seemed interested, but at the same time deeply cautious. To persuade him, Le Gendre suggested that the tribe keep Captain Beardslee as a hostage.

With this, the raw savages became more animated. They spoke excitedly, not able to decide who would be so unlucky as to stay behind with Beardslee.

Eventually the two parties walked together to the shore, where they climbed into a small boat and then boarded the *Aroostook*. On the ship, the guests looked around with a guarded inquisitiveness, sometimes sighing in disbelief, sometimes giggling among themselves.

Le Gendre ordered his men to fire a blank shell. The raw savages were almost knocked down by the massive thundering jumpback of the cannon's recoil, and afterward all of them were for a long time stunned.

At the end of their visit, Le Gendre entered his cabin and came back out with a delicate wooden box. Inside were women's accoutrements, including a necklace, a bracelet, a mirror, and a needle and thread. There were also some cosmetics—lipstick and face powder—as well as perfume and a music box. Le Gendre told the chief, "You can have these. Take them as gifts from the United States, on the condition that you treat our seamen in a more friendly way from now on."

The chief could not believe it. He kept saying, "Masalu. Masalu," meaning "Thank you. Thank you."

Dunn was amazed to see so many items intended for a woman. He asked, "Charlie, why was it that you thought it necessary to take with you so many of these things? Exquisite though they most certainly are, I cannot guess at their usefulness to you."

Le Gendre laughed the question away, but his heart was bleeding. He had purchased these things in Amoy, and it had taken him a long time to acquire them all. He had intended to give them to Butterfly as a betrothal gift. Never once had he considered that she would get married.

The raw savages, on the other hand, were overjoyed; when they landed on the shore, they continued to thank Le Gendre as they walked away up the mountain. In the afternoon, Captain Beardslee returned to the ship, whereupon he made it clear that he thought Le Gendre was truly a first-class diplomat, who had managed to exchange a small chest of womanly things for many years of peace and safety in southern Formosa.

As the *Aroostook* moved slowly away from the land, Le Gendre looked at the shoreline and at the mountains. For the past few months, he had always thought of Butterfly as belonging rightfully to him. But now she was married to Chinya, an ignorant fool who was not in the least bit outstanding.

His love, which had been simmering unrequited, now boiled over into indignation. Never had he felt more humiliated. Clara had betrayed him, but Butterfly had insulted him without any reserve. Who could tolerate this? Since his first visit, he had felt quite positively toward the Formosans, but now he thought of them with revulsion.

He withdrew a small box from his pocket. Inside was the ring that he had intended to put on Butterfly's finger. He looked at it with hatred and dismay before throwing it far out into the sea.

With a splash that very quickly vanished, the ring and its box were engulfed and then forgotten by the sea's eternally churning waves.

10

EPILOGUE

70

Wang Wenqi sat on his sedan chair. He had been summoned to
Anping by General Liu and the newly appointed Taiwan *daotai*, Liang
Yuangui. They wanted him to shoulder the blame for the Qing army's
defeat at Anping.

Half a month ago, the Qing navy at Anping had been defeated by
the British warships. Lieutenant T. Philip Gurdon, captain of the
Algerine, had led another officer and twenty-three soldiers to land
on Anping. Regional Vice Commander Jiang Guozhen, who was in
charge of that section of the Qing navy, had deserted his post and
committed suicide the following morning.

What a great disgrace!

But as it turned out, this was just one of many humiliations. Two
nights before, Fort Zeelandia, built by the Dutch in the seventeenth
century, had been bombarded by Gurdon and swiftly turned to rubble. It had stood by the shore of Taiwan-fu since 1643, and it was
indeed magnificent. Even though the Dutch had long ago left Formosa, and although the mud had piled up in Anping port, this magnificent fort had always stood facing the tides. Whenever he traveled across the Black Water Channel to Anping, Wang Wenqi would
watch it come into view from far away, marveling all the while at the

ancient gigantic structure. It had stood for over two hundred and forty years; it was as old as Taiwan-fu itself and had witnessed all of the city's twisting history, only to be destroyed without reason by a brutal British captain.

Indeed, two days before its destruction, the peace agreement had finally been made. The Qing government was to open business to foreigners, who would be permitted to collect and deal in camphor. By agreeing to these terms, the Qing government could take back control of Anping, which had been occupied by the British for over half a month. Wang Wenqi was assigned to oversee the handover.

Earlier that morning, as he strolled aimlessly through the fresh rubble, his heart had felt truly broken. How relentless fate was! Simply because of the camphor trade dispute, this fort had been destroyed. That which had represented Taiwan-fu was now crumbled. He considered it something of an omen: the city was falling apart.

After he had finished lamenting in the ruins, he and his sedan-chair carriers returned to the Five Channels Zone in Taiwan-fu. As they passed the Shuixian Temple area, Wang glanced into a medicine shop. His eye was caught by a young woman who stood inside, holding a little baby. She wore a long blue skirt and a red-and-white blouse with close-fitting sleeves. Her attire stood out from that of the typical Hokkien woman, who dressed mostly in gray or black. He felt sure that he had seen someone wearing similar-looking clothes in Liangkiau last year. But where? He tried for a moment to arrive at a convincing answer, but memory failed him. In any case, he did not bother to think about it for long; soon enough, he directed his thoughts back toward himself.

As Taiwan *Daotai* Liang Yuangui wanted him to shoulder the responsibility for the Camphor Incident, after taking over Anping from the British, Wang was to go from Taiwan-fu to Chiayi. There he would serve as the county magistrate. It was quite a demotion.

Although he had distinguished himself throughout last year's *Rover* Incident, and despite the fact that General Liu had spoken

highly of him, Liang Yuangui still blamed Wang for failing to protect the Qing territory in the south of Taiwan. Indeed, because of his
failure, Anping fell to a foreign force and General Jiang Kuozhen
committed suicide.

As he thought back to the *Rover* Incident, Wang suddenly remembered where he had seen clothes like those worn by the young
woman. It was at Sialiao. Inside that village head's house, before Le
Gendre left for the peace talk with Tauketok, he had seen a young
girl dressed like that. He remembered that Le Gendre was on intimate terms with the girl, and whenever with her, he behaved much
less seriously than he did ordinarily. He had at first thought the girl
was a maid, but Le Gendre had treated her differently than he might
treat a maid or a servant. Wang was at the time quite curious as to
the nature of their relationship. He thought about it again now; it
was indeed strange. But then he remembered Pickering, who had
been standing beside Le Gendre at the house. He was the one who
had caused this mess; he was the reason for his demotion, these fail-
ures, this camphor war. He hated Pickering beyond measure, and he
knew that General Liu hated him too.

But in any case, the girl inside Le Gendre's house and the young
woman with the baby could not be the same person. It was simply
impossible. Besides, tomorrow he had to go to Chiayi to assume his
new position; he had no time to think about this now. And anyway,
it was hardly respectable to go around asking for information about
randomly encountered women. He laughed out loud at the ridiculous idea.

Later that day, on the way to Chiayi, Wang Wenqi again found
himself immersed in deep thought. He was a positive man, and he
had quickly come to believe that, despite it being a lessening of his
position, he could find pleasure in the fact that his new post was
something of a sinecure; he could live a more relaxing life for a while,
and it would give him time to think of how he might start his rise
again. He felt sure he would emerge as a winner even though at

present he appeared as anything but. In any case, taken to a faraway place by those and other thoughts, he failed to notice the conversation between the two men who bore the front half of his sedan chair, a conversation that certainly would have been of great interest to the new magistrate.

"The woman with a baby, right? I burned my hand quite badly a couple of months back. I saw several herbalist doctors. Nothing worked. But in the end, after I went there, she cured me. Such a careful and skillful woman!"

"Really? How can a woman be so good at healing?"

"Who knew? Anyway, she is famous. I have a relative living near here. He says everyone goes to her if they are sick or injured. Though she is just an assistant in the shop, more people want her to treat their wounds than want the herbalist doctor. The shop's owner is happy, though, since business runs so high. Ha ha!"

The sedan-chair bearer spoke with an acute admiration. "She is really good at curing people. Also, apart from wounds, she can cure people of their diseases. The medicine she gives works better than herbs. I wonder where she learned to do all that."

"Hey, did you notice her dress? And she always wears a bead necklace, like a Puppet Savage. She tells people that her mother was a Liangkiau Puppet Savage. She is very proud of that fact. I hear many patients call her Doctor Puppet Flower, or Lady Butterfly. . . ."

71

Bunkiet slumped farther into the chair, his tears channeling through the grooves of an age-lined face.

He could never have predicted that, after thirty years of complying with those in power, he would be dismissed as Big Head Chief of Seqalu by those he considered his friends, the Japanese.

They may not have used humiliating language—indeed, they beautified their words, saying that people in this area were so civilized that they should no longer be called "savages"—but oh, how the Japanese took advantage of the people in Seqalu. The latest infliction: the title Big Head Chief would no longer be used as, apparently, there was no need to use it. And the place name of which he was so proud, Liangkiau, well, it too no longer existed. Tuillassock, Sabaree, Baya, Koalut, and Seqalu: these places were together called Hengchun Sub-*ting*, Fung-shan *Ting*.[1] Mantsui was obliterated. Now it was called Manzhou. Only Ling-nuang Lake carried the aural trace of its past.

He remembered all the honors conferred on him and all the presents given to him. But without Tuillassock and without Seqalu, those honors brought him only pain. And anyway, he had been blind for almost ten years and had never even seen the more recent gifts.

He thought of his adoptive father, and his heart was stabbed by a still-fresh pain: he had let him down; he had failed to live up to his expectations. Tauketok had placed a great responsibility on his shoulders, and for a long while, Bunkiet had thought himself capable of carrying it. But eventually he was found wanting.

That year, when he had been taken in by Tauketok, his adoptive father's wisdom and determination had helped avoid a war. But that agreement they made was merely an oral understanding; it could be broken at any time. Bunkiet had seen how cunning and sly people on the plains were, and he knew that a written agreement was needed for it to matter to the foreigners. Therefore, two years later, when Le Gendre had again visited Tauketok, Bunkiet had composed a written agreement in Chinese, which was combined with Le Gendre's English version to become the official document. Tauketok admired him very much, and Zudjui had begun to trust him.

---

[1] *Ting* (or subprefecture) and sub-*ting* are administrative divisions.

Four years later, Tauketok passed away and was succeeded by
Zudjui. Less than a year after that, Liangkiau was invaded by the Japanese, and Bunkiet served as a mediator in the conflict. At that
time, the Kuskus tribe, who had triggered the Japanese invasion by
killing some sailors from Ryukyu, still existed. As did the rebellious
Sihlinge tribe. Now all three were lost.

What an irony it was!

The Japanese had attacked and forced their way through tribal
territory, defeating the Botan tribe, the Tjaliunay tribe, and the
Chicksia tribe. Bunkiet was just twenty-one years old, but he knew
very well that this was a war fought at the behest of Le Gendre. As
some kind of pitiless insult, the Japanese army had Mia as its guide.
It was all so ridiculous.

During that conflict, Bunkiet had asked Isa to represent Seqalu.
Isa was the leader, but Bunkiet was the one planning everything. Isa
was willing to listen to Bunkiet, who thought people in Seqalu should
protect themselves instead of getting involved in the fighting. Later,
when the Japanese appeared to demonstrate lenience, the Seqalu
tribes were seduced by their friendliness. But looking back now,
Bunkiet realized that the Japanese were more aggressive than any
other foe he had faced.

Thirty years have passed by so quickly, Bunkiet thought with a sigh.
Throughout those decades, in order to protect the Seqalu people and
their land, he had involved himself in almost every battle. But now
he questioned whether he had done the right things.

To deal with the Japanese, the Qing government had deployed the
elite Anhui Army to Taiwan. However, the army did not fight the Japanese but instead began fighting Formosan aborigines. They, as did
the Japanese, spoke euphemistically of their operation, claiming that
they were there to "pacify" the savages.

Soon after the Qing government came, Isa died. Zudjui did not
want to deal with the turmoil; he found escape in the analgesic welcome of alcohol. Under those miserable circumstances, Bunkiet

became the representative of Seqalu and of the eighteen tribes of Lower Liangkiau.

Although Bunkiet assisted the Qing government as they tried every means imaginable to pacify the tribal chiefs, the other tribes refused to comply. Of the eighteen in Lower Liangkiau, only the Seqalu tribes were submissive.

In the winter of 1874, high-ranking Qing officials came to Liangkiau. They discovered Monkey Cave and planned to build a large city there. But this city was not to be called Liangkiau, nor was it to be called Monkey Cave. It was called Hengchun, meaning "Everlasting Spring."

Later, because of his role in recruiting people from Seqalu to help build the Hengchun city wall, Bunkiet was granted an honorary Chinese surname. Growing up, he had used his father's Chinese surname, Lim. But, when he became the leader of Seqalu, he had dropped it. What would the ancestral spirits of Seqalu think now that the Qing imperial government had officially bestowed upon him a new surname, Pan? And what would his Hakka father say?

The aborigines had not anticipated the ferocity of the Qing army. In the spring of 1875, the Acedas and Uwaljudj tribes as well as three others in Tjaquvuquvulj were slaughtered. However, more than two thousand Qing soldiers were also killed. So many died that the Taiwan *daotai* had a shrine built in their memory. But so what? No matter how many Qing soldiers they killed, there would always be more that could be sent from the Chinese mainland. Before long, the aboriginal territory became the territory of Qing China.

After that, the tribes became used to the way the plains people addressed them—by then, Zudjui and his brothers were all dead, their lives shortened by alcoholism—and people in Liangkiau began calling their village group *sia* or "community," in the manner of Qing immigrants. Bunkiet had become something like a Qing bureaucrat; indeed, he had been given the position of Grade Five Government Official, with his own official residence. It was just as his father had hoped for him. He started to put on airs, and though it now brought him shame to admit it, he had been proud of himself and of his role. Bunkiet, half Hakka and half aboriginal, had ended up as Big Head Chief of the Lower Liangkiau, and more important, as a Grade Five Qing-dynasty official. How his father would have smiled had he still been alive!

And then, nine years ago, the Japanese army came again, this time to drive away the Qing government. Guangxu Year 21 suddenly became Meiji Year 28.[2]

At first he felt positively toward the Japanese. He thought they were at least better than the murderous Qing Chinese, and he had welcomed them when they began their colonial rule. He established a school in Tuillassock, the first of its kind in Taiwan to teach the new official language, and he did whatever he could, as leader of the eighteen tribes in Lower Liangkiau, to help the Japanese take over the land. When the Qing General Liu Deshao refused to surrender in Puyuma, Bunkiet recruited aboriginal warriors to help the Japanese.

When Mizuno Jun, the supervisor of civilian affairs, came to inspect the area, Bunkiet felt as though his old friend had come back, for he had known him for twenty-one years. By the time of Mizuno Jun's return, Bunkiet was completely blind; although he was just forty-three years old, the heavy burden of twenty-nine years as leader of Seqalu had left him looking like an extremely old man.

He had extended his calloused hands to Mizuno Jun. The white people were gone. The Qing people were gone. And now here came the man whom he had known for over twenty years. He was overjoyed.

But in the years since, the Japanese had left him feeling despair. At one point, he had been so furious that he had asked his son to accompany him to Taipei so that he could talk with Mizuno. But his

---

[2] 1895, the year the Qing Empire lost Taiwan and Penghu at the end of the first Sino-Japanese War.

fourth son, the twenty-five-year-old Pan Abei, had refused. "Mizuno has returned to Japan," he said. "And even if he is still there, what's the use of reasoning with him?"

For so long, Bunkiet had done his best to comply with every power that had tried to occupy this place. How subservient he had been! Though he had secured several decades of peace for his people, and he himself had certainly gained much in the way of material wealth, it was in exchange for his tribe's autonomy. And eventually he too was deprived of his leadership.

It occurred to him that if things continued like this, someday he and his people might all be well fed, but they would lose their souls and their spirits. They would lose everything that they had inherited from their ancestors. Should that day come, what good would life be?

He thought of his adoptive father, braver and smarter than he had ever been. Sometimes Tauketok would seek reconciliation, but not always. His integrity had won Le Gendre's admiration. Tauketok had sustained Seqalu, and he kept his "self" intact.

Yes! If they sustained the ancestral spirits, they could preserve their independence. But if they continued living like this, Seqalu would fall apart and become wiped out. Bunkiet knew that their ancestors had come from Puyuma; they should return there, or as near there as possible. So he summoned Pan Abei, whom he regarded as his most capable son, and instructed him to take action.

And so it was, two months later, that Pan Abei took half the people in the tribe, and, with some cattle and the blessing of his father, set out from Tuillassock. They walked north along the coast until they reached the big meadow near Botan Bay. This place looked across the shore of Alanyi to Kadibu. They could feel the breath of their ancestral spirits, so they stopped, and there they continued with their lives.

The following year, on December 12, 1905, fifty-three-year-old Bunkiet died with memories flooding his mind, made somewhat happier by the knowledge that his people were, for the time being at least, safe.

72

The building of the Taiwan governor-general's office was glamorously decorated for the occasion. In the well-kept garden, maids dressed in colorful kimonos floated through the scattered and mostly static guests. Invitees from various countries raised cups to lips to enjoy the wine and sampled a wide variety of delicious food. They congratulated their hosts on the speed of Taiwan's development over the past forty years.

It was October 10, 1935, and the Taiwan governor-general's office in Taipei was holding a rather self-important ceremony to celebrate "the fortieth anniversary of Japanese colonial rule in Taiwan." Elsewhere on the island, there was an international fair, all sorts of athletic activities, dance parties, temple parades, and dramatic presentations. The festivities were to last for more than a month.

In the middle of this party, the governor-general stepped onto the podium. Chatter faded until just one or two conversations remained, their concluding words individually distinguishable. "For this celebration of ours," the governor-general began, "I have invited a performer of honor to further add to our enjoyment. Miss Sekiya Toshiko, please. . . ."

A young lady in a magnificent Western-style dress walked onto the stage. She was the soprano who had caused a sensation in Tokyo the previous year with her performance of "Asha Frenzy." The applause she received was louder even than that given the governor-general, but, clapping along with the rest of the guests, he showed no signs of minding.

Sekiya sang the Japanese song "Yoi Machi Gusa," then the English song "The Last Rose of Summer."

The audience marveled at her voice, her beauty, and her quite undeniable talent. Even those who had heard her sing on previous occasions were wowed afresh.

After the outdoor celebration was over, the governor-general invited Sekiya and a select few of the more renowned guests to join him inside in one of the building's Western-style living rooms.

A square-faced man with big ears approached Sekiya and said, "My lady, you sing even better than Sensei Miura Tamaki."

Sekiya shook her head and answered with a weightless smile, "No, no. That's impossible. Sensei Miura Tamaki is my teacher. How could I possibly surpass him?"

The director of general affairs in the governor-general's office introduced them. "This is Mr. Koo Hsien-jung. He is the first Taiwanese appointed to the Japanese House of Peers."

Koo bowed.

Sekiya bowed in return, and then she smiled and asked, "Do you come from Tainan?"

Koo replied, "No, not from Tainan. And I am not from Taipei, either. I come from Lukang."

"I will soon travel to Tainan," said Sekiya. "I have a student there. It's a pity that I don't have enough time, or I would visit Takao and Liangkiau."

"Liangkiau?" Koo was surprised. "How do you know that name? It has not been in use for over thirty years."

"My late grandfather called it by that name. It was later changed to Hengchun Sub-*ting*, Fung-shan *Ting*, correct?"

Even the director of general affairs looked surprised. "Who could imagine that Miss Sekiya would understand Taiwan so well? You are correct. Hengchun now belongs to Checheng Township, Hengchun County, Takao Prefecture."

Sekiya said, with a touch of melancholy, "These were places visited by my grandfather, who came here on many occasions. He stayed in Takao and in Tainan, but I think he spent his time mostly in Liangkiau."

Sekiya looked around at the perplexed faces. She tried to explain, "My grandfather was Le Gendre. My mother is General Le Gendre's daughter."

For the most part, those present remained puzzled when they heard the name. But the governor-general clapped his hands and cried out, "No wonder you can sing English songs so beautifully. You are of European descent." He turned to his secretary. "This is too good to be true. Master Mori Ogai's son happens to be inside the governor-general's office right now. Find Professor Mori and bring him here."

The director of general affairs, who also recognized Le Gendre's name, was more than excited. "We owe you a debt of gratitude, Miss Toshiko. Our great nation can celebrate its fortieth anniversary of ruling Taiwan only thanks to the help of General Le Gendre. He was the strategist behind the attack launched by General Saigo Judo sixty-one years ago. It is to him that we owe what we have now."

The director then proceeded to tell everybody about the contributions made by General Le Gendre to Japan.

Sekiya was saddened. Her grandfather, who had been instrumental in developing the Japanese plans to invade and conquer Taiwan, was now barely known to Japanese officials. *No wonder he died in Seoul. Poor Grandpa!* she thought with a sigh.

Presently a middle-aged gentleman, who had the definite appearance of a scholar, entered the room. The governor-general introduced him. "This is Professor Mori Oto from the Medical School of Tokyo Imperial University. Next year he will come to Taipei Imperial University to teach anatomy. I invited him here as our guest so that he might become more familiar with Taiwan. Professor Mori's father is the renowned author Mori Ogai, who was here on this island for several months in Meiji Year 28."

Mori Oto answered respectfully, "The governor-general is truly a dear friend of my father's. When I was little, my father often mentioned Taiwan to me. Its people and culture left a deep impression on him. He had a very sweet memory of this place. It was on this account that I volunteered to teach at Taipei Imperial University."

The governor-general smiled and said, "If my memory serves me right, our professor's grandfather was the famous Admiral Akamatsu Noriyoshi?"

Professor Mori was delighted, if a little taken aback by the governor-general's depth of knowledge. "Correct!"

The director of general affairs said excitedly, "Is that so?! Admiral Akamatsu was second only to Marshal Admiral Saigo Judo when we fought in Taiwan in Meiji Year 7. What a coincidence! In this room we have a granddaughter of General Le Gendre, and also a grandson of Admiral Akamatsu. This gives us a unique chance to review the history of Japan's conquest of Taiwan. Without the expedition in Meiji Year 7, we wouldn't have taken up the colonial rule of Taiwan in Meiji Year 28, and we wouldn't be celebrating the fortieth anniversary here today!"

When the other guests had departed, the governor-general asked Sekiya, Mori, and the director of general affairs to stay behind a little longer—though he himself soon retired to another room. Mori became sentimental as he said to Sekiya, "My mother died when I was very little, and I was brought up by my grandpa. I remember one thing in particular. I was nine, or perhaps ten, when my grandpa learned of General Le Gendre's death. That afternoon he seemed to be in a very bad mood. He kept drinking, downing one cup of sake after another. I was sitting beside him, and he told me the story of General Le Gendre's first years in Japan. He said that since General Le Gendre was a foreigner, even though he had made many contributions to our country, he nevertheless suffered a lot. My grandpa thought Japan owed a great debt to your grandpa."

Sekiya said, "Five years ago, when I went to Seoul, I visited my grandpa's tomb. For the whole day, snow fell. Standing in front of my grandfather, whom I had never seen when he was alive, I could not help but remember some conversations between my grandma and my mother, those times when they had spoken about him.

"Apparently, in his later years my grandpa became somewhat of a cantankerous old man. To help Japan win Taiwan, he had served as the advisor to the Japanese government. Afterward he could not return to America, so he never had a chance to see his son, who was living there. And although the Japanese government for a while thought highly of him and his opinion, this period lasted less than three years. Later he continued to offer his strategic advice to the Japanese government, but he was mostly ignored. He was offered a lowly and poorly paid position, which left him in financial difficulties, unable to provide support to his son. This really tormented him. He turned to Seoul, but by then he was sixty years old, quite an elderly man. Alas! My grandpa was ambitious. But his dreams were never fulfilled."

Mori said, "I still remember that afternoon vividly. My grandpa sighed and said that Advisor Le Gendre was the one who had first drawn up a plan for conquering Taiwan. That's it, I remember now, my grandpa used to call your grandpa 'Advisor.' He mentioned that Advisor Le Gendre had intended to take Taiwan as a piece of U.S. territory, but that the U.S. government would not listen to him. In December 1872, when he was on the way back to America, he stopped in Yokohama. He talked to Soejima Taneomi, then Minister of Foreign Affairs, and decided immediately to stay to help Japan. He ended up staying there for most of the rest of his life. According to my grandpa, Advisor Le Gendre always thought that the Qing did not deserve to have Taiwan, that the aborigines in Taiwan deserved to be managed by a more civilized government.

"His career did not go so smoothly in the United States. Many people there still saw him as a Frenchman. He went to Japan, hoping to be able to become King of Taiwan, or at least King of Liangkiau. But the odds were against him, and he failed to become either. At last, he hoped to be Japanese, but they always thought of him as an alien."

Sekiya nodded. "Indeed. My grandma was not married to him. Though they loved each other, my grandma was afraid of being laughed at. Even their children, that is, my uncle and my mother, were adopted by others after they were born. He did not enjoy the warmth of a family in Japan. That's why he went to Seoul alone. Poor Grandpa!"

Mori Oto looked thoughtfully at the floor and then said, "My grandpa said that after Japan took over Taiwan, Advisor Le Gendre went back to Japan. He visited my grandpa, who asked him, 'When will you go again to Taiwan? You always liked it there.' My grandfather said Advisor Le Gendre had reacted very strangely. He had said dimly, after seeming to be lost for a while in thought, 'There's no need.' My grandfather said that he felt Advisor Le Gendre always had some complicated, unresolved feelings toward this island and its people."

Sekiya sighed and said, "He did not have a good time in Japan, and he was even gloomier in Seoul. The most successful period in his life lasted from 1867 to 1875, when he was engaged in Taiwan affairs. Sadly, that period was, if one takes the length of the rest of his life into consideration, rather short. He spent his life wandering around, working for foreign governments. But in the end every nation regarded him as an outsider. I believe that was his greatest pain."

There was a sudden silence; no one knew what to say.

The director of general affairs had been listening, and now he spoke. "Advisor Le Gendre signed a peace agreement with the Eighteen Tribes of Lower Liangkiau. It was a great achievement at that time. But now the Eighteen Tribes of Lower Liangkiau no longer exist. Those raw savages have been assimilated into Hengchun County and are governed by us."

Sekiya Toshiko forced a smile. She raised her cup to sip the tea and tried to swing the conversation somewhere else. "This Taiwan oolong is really choice tea," she said. "Truly it is excellent."

But that topic proved difficult to sustain, and soon the three of them were silent once again.

Finally Sekiya got politely to her feet. "Thank you, Professor. And thank you, Director. I am so glad that at least in Taiwan, some people still remember my late grandfather."

She walked out of the house, looking at the stars flung like glitter across the sky. "Grandfather," she mumbled to herself, "you *will* be remembered!"

MAPS AND ILLUSTRATIONS

FIGURE 1 Map of Fukien Province drawn by Jean Baptiste Bourguignon d'Anville, first printed in 1735. At that time (1735–1750), only the western part of Taiwan was under the jurisdiction of Fukien Province.

Courtesy of National Museum of Taiwan History

FIGURE 2 Map drawn by Charles W. Le Gendre in 1870, entitled
"Formosa Island and the Pescadores, China." Le Gendre specified
that the land east of the red line was aboriginals' land,
not part of the Qing Empire's territory.

Courtesy of SMC Publishing Inc.

FIGURE 3 Part of "Kangxi Taiwan Map" (康熙台灣輿圖, 1699–1704), with the Puppet Mountains in the background

Courtesy of National Taiwan Museum

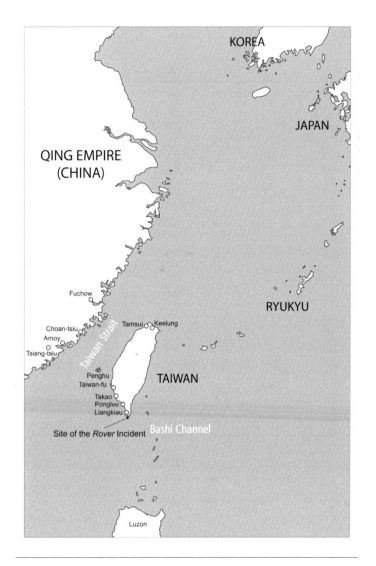

FIGURE 4 Map of East Asia around 1867

Jasper Huang

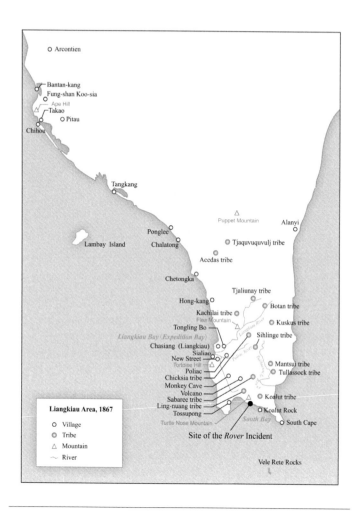

FIGURE 5 Map of southern Taiwan around 1867

Jasper Huang

CONFLICT BETWEEN H.M.S. CORMORANT AND THE SAVAGES OF FORMOSA.

FIGURE 6 "Conflict between HMS Cormorant and the savages of
Formosa." Engraving from a sketch by W. N. Fencock.

Illustrated London News, June 15, 1867, 600

ATTACK OF UNITED STATES MARINES AND SAILORS ON THE PIRATES OF THE ISLAND OF FORMOSA, EAST INDIES.

FIGURE 7 "Attack of United States Marines and sailors on the pirates of the island of Formosa, East Indies." Drawing of the 1867 American Expedition to Formosa by an unknown artist

Harper's Weekly, September 7, 1867, 572

FIGURE 8 Photo of Lieutenant Commander Alexander S. MacKenzie, U.S. Navy, who died in Kenting, Taiwan, at the age of twenty-five

https://en.m.wikipedia.org

FIGURE 9 The warship USS *Hartford* (1864), a flagship of the fleet
on the 1867 American Expedition to Formosa

https://en.m.wikipedia.org

FIGURE 10 Photo of (left to right) Charles Le Gendre, an unidentified
chief, Captain Wallace, and Mia, among a group of natives
in the Sabaree settlement.

Notes of Travel in Formosa by Charles Le Gendre, ed. Douglas L. Fix and John Shufelt
(Tainan: National Museum of Taiwan History, 2012)

General Le Gendre (U.S. Consul) M⁺ Dodd, and aborigines of south Formosa

FIGURE 11 General Le Gendre (U.S. Consul, seated in the center),
Mr. John Dodd (British tea merchant in Taipei, fourth from right),
and aborigines of South Formosa

Courtesy of National Museum of Taiwan History, Tainan

GLOSSARY

Names of persons, places, and aboriginal tribes in this glossary are chiefly based on those in *Notes of Travel in Formosa* by Charles Le Gendre, edited by Douglas L. Fix and John Shufelt (Tainan: National Museum of Taiwan History, 2012). For others, the Hanyu Pinyin system is used to transliterate Chinese characters, with some exceptions. Variants, if any, are inserted within square brackets.

Acedas tribe　內獅頭社 (在屏東縣獅子鄉)
Akamatsu, Noriyoshi　赤松則良
Alanyi　阿塱壹 (在屏東縣牡丹鄉)
Alcock, Rutherford　阿禮國
Ali-kang [Ah-lu-kang]　阿里港 (今屏東縣里港鄉)
Amoy [Xiamen]　廈門
Anping port　安平港
Anthon Williams & Co.　威廉士洋行
Ape Hill [Ape's Hill; Apen Berg]　猴山 [柴山] (今高雄壽山)
Arcontien　阿公店 (今高雄岡山)
Aroostook, the　「阿魯斯圖號」
Aruqu [Aluqu]　阿祿古
Ashuelot, the　「亞士休落號」
Attabu　阿罩霧 (今台中霧峰)
Banping Mountain [Mount Banping; Pan-ping Mountain]　半屏山
Banta-kang [Bantakang; Bantan port; Wandan port]　萬丹港 (今高雄左營軍港)
Banterer, the　「班德勒號」
Bao-an Temple [Pao-an Temple]　保安宮

Baosheng Dadi [Pao-sheng Ta-ti; Deity of Medicine] 保生大帝

Bashi Channel 巴士海峽

Bashi Island 巴士島

Baya tribe 猫仔社 (在屏東恆春仁壽里)

Bayaken 猫仔坑

Beardslee, Lester A. 畢斯禮

Bell, Henry H. 貝爾

Bernard, Joseph 竇內

Black Water Channel 黑水溝

Botan tribe [Mudan; Mutan; Sinvaudjan] 牡丹社

Botan Tribe Incident [Mutan-she Incident] 牡丹社事件

Bowring, John, Sir 寶寧

Broad, George D. 布羅

Buchanan, James 詹姆斯·布坎南

Bunkiet [Jagarushi Guri Bunkiet; Bungekaic Garuljigulj; Wenjie] 文杰 [潘文杰]

Burlingame, Anson 蒲安臣

Butterfly [Tiab-moi; Tiap-moe; Diemei] 蝶妹

Canton [Guangdong; Kuangtung] 廣東

Cao, Jin [Tsao Chin] 曹謹

Carroll, Charles 賈祿

Chalatong [Jialutang] 加祿堂 [加洛堂] (今加祿，在屏東縣獅子鄉)

Chalatong Pass 加祿堂隘口

Changhwa [Zhanghua] 彰化

Chasiang [Checheng] 柴城 (今屏東車城)

Chetongka [Citongjiao] 莿桐腳 (在屏東縣獅子鄉)

Chiayi [Jiayi] 嘉義

Chicksia tribe 竹社 (在屏東縣車城鄉)

Chihou [Qihou] Hospital 旗後醫館

Chihou [Qihou] Port 旗後港 (今高雄旗津)

Chihkan [Chikan] 赤崁 (今台南市區)

Chinya 松仔

Choan-tsiu [Quanzhou] 泉州

Ciji Temple [Tzu-chi Temple] 慈濟宮 (在高雄左營)

Confederation of the Eighteen Tribes of Lower Liangkiau 下瑯嶠十八社聯盟

Cormorant, the 「鸕鷀號」

Cundi Buddha 準提菩薩

Printed and bound by CPI Group (UK) Ltd, Croydon, CR0 4YY

大沽口

Daoguang, Emperor [Emperor Tao-kuang] 道光皇帝

Dawu Mountains [Tawu Mountains] 大武山群

Dodd, John 德約翰 [陶德]

Dunn, Thomas 鄧恩

earth-cow trench [borderline] 土牛溝 [土牛界線；土牛紅線]

Expedition Bay [Liangkiau Bay] 探險灣 [瑯嶠灣]

Febiger, John C. 費米日

Fengyi Academy 鳳儀書院

Fillmore, Millard 米拉德·費爾摩

Five Channels Zone 五條港區 (今台南市中心)

Flea Mountain [Stone-Gate Mountain] 蝨母山 (今石門山，在屏東縣牡丹鄉)

Foochow [Fuchow; Fuzhou] 福州

Fu-an Temple 福安宮 (在屏東縣車城鄉)

Fu-cheng [Prefectural City] 府城 (今台南市)

Fu Kang-an [Fuk'anggan; Fu-K'ang-an] 福康安

Fukien [Fujian] Province 福建省

Fung-shan [Fengshan] Hsien [County; District] 鳳山縣 (今高雄市和屏東縣)

Fung-shan Koo-sia [Old Town] 鳳山舊城 (今高雄市左營區)

Gao, Chang [Kao Chang; Ko Tiong] 高長

Garuljigulj 卡珞利谷家系

Gibson, John 吉必勳

Gulangyu [Kulangsu] 鼓浪嶼

Guanyin Ting [Kuan-yin Ting] 觀音亭 (今高雄左營興隆寺)

Gurdon, T. Philip 茄嘮

Hakka people 客家人

Heaven-Earth Society [Tien-ti hui; Tiandihui] 天地會

Hengchun [Monkey Cave] 恆春

Hengchun Peninsula 恆春半島

Hengchun Sub-*ting*, Fung-Shan *Ting* 鳳山廳恆春支廳

Hokkien [Minnan; Hoklo; Holo] 福佬話

Hokkien people [Hokkiens; Hoklos] 福佬人

Honest Lim [Lim Mountain Products] 林老實 [林山產]

Hongkang [Fenggang] 風港 (今楓港，在屏東縣枋山鄉)

Horn, James 洪恩

Hunt, Joseph W. 杭特

Hunt, Mercy [Mrs.] 杭特夫人

Huo, Qubing [Huo Chu-ping] 霍去病

Isa [Yisa] 伊沙

Mantsui tribe 蚊蟀社 (在屏東縣滿州鄉)

Manzhou [Manchou] 滿洲 (屏東縣滿洲鄉)

Maxwell, James L. 馬雅各

Mazu Temple [Matsu Temple] 媽祖廟

McPhail & Co. 天利洋行

McPhail, Neil 尼爾·麥克菲爾

Mia [Miya; Yeu Tick Tchien] 棉仔

Miura, Tamaki 三浦環

Mizuno, Jun 水野遵

Monkey Cave [Kootang; Koutang; Hengchun] 猴洞 (今屏東縣恆春鎮)

Mori, Ogai 森鷗外

Mori, Oto 森於菟

nana 倈倈 (客家人)

Nanking [Nanjing] 南京

New Street 新街

Nye, Gideon 吉頓·奈伊

Nye Brothers & Co. 奈伊兄弟洋行

painan 白浪 (福佬人)

Paiwan tribe [Paiwan people; Paiwan group] 排灣族

Paljaljaus 朴嘉留央

Pan, Abei 潘阿別

Parker, Peter 伯嘉

Payarin 巴耶林

Peking, Treaty of 北京條約

Penghu [the Pescadores] 澎湖

Peppo [Pingpu; Pingpuzu; plains aborigines] 平埔族

Perry, Matthew C. 培里

Pickering, William A. 畢客淋 [必麒麟]

Pierce, Franklin 皮爾斯

Pitau [Pitou] 埤頭 (今高雄鳳山)

Pingpuzu [Pingputzu; Peppo] 平埔族

Poliac [Baoli; Paoli] 保力 [在屏東縣車城鄉]

Ponglee [Pang-lia; Pangliau; Fangliao] 枋寮

Provintia, Fort [Providentia] 普羅岷遮城 (今台南市區，赤崁樓)

Puppet Mountains 傀儡山

Puppet Savages 傀儡番

Puyuma 卑南地區

Qianlong, Emperor [Emperor Chien-lung] 乾隆皇帝

Qing China [Qing Empire; Ch'ing China]　大清國

raw savages [wild savages; *shengfan*]　生番

Red-Hairs [red-haired people]　紅毛人 [洋人]

Robinet, W. M.　羅賓奈

Rover, the　「羅妹號」

Rukai tribe [Rukai people]　魯凱族

Ryukyu [Okinawa]　琉球

Sabaree tribe　射麻里社 (今屏東縣滿州鄉永靖村)

Saigo, Judo [Tsugumichi]　西鄉從道

Salach [Shalu]　沙轆 (今沙鹿)

Saliling　莎里鈴

Saracen's Head [Chihou Hill; Qihou Hill]　薩拉森山頭 (今高雄旗後山)

Science, the　「科學號」

Sekiya, Toshiko　関屋敏子

Senggerincin　僧格林沁

Seqalu [Seqalu people]　斯卡羅族

Shaochuantou　哨船頭 (今高雄鼓山區哨船頭里)

Shiwen Creek　士文溪 [率芒溪]

Shuixian Temple [Shui-hsien Temple]　水仙宮 (在台南市)

Sialiao [Sheliao]　社寮 (今屏東縣車城鄉射寮村)

Sichuan [Szechuan]　四川

Sihlinge [Chinakai] tribe　四林格社 (在屏東縣牡丹鄉)

Siraya [Siraya people]　西拉雅族

Soejima, Taneomi　副島種臣

South Bay　南灣 (在屏東恆春墾丁)

South Cape　南岬 (今屏東恆春鵝鑾鼻)

Sun, Erhzhun [Sun Erh-chun]　孫爾準

Swinhoe, Robert　郇和 [史溫侯]

Taiping Rebellion　太平天國之亂

Taiping Tianguo [Tai-ping Tien-kuo]　太平天國

Takao　打狗 (今高雄)

Taiwan-fu [Taiwan Prefecture; Taiwanfu; Taiwanfoo]　台灣府 (今台南)

Tamsui [Danshui]　淡水

Tangkang [Donggang]　東港

Tangkang River [Donggang River]　東港溪

Tauketok [Tou-ke-tok; Toketok; Tokitok]　卓杞篤

Temple of Three Mountain Lords　三山國王廟

Tientsin, Treaty of [Treaty of Tianjin]　天津條約

Tjaliunay [Niinai] tribe　女乃社 (在屏東縣牡丹鄉)

Tjaquvuquvulj [Tjakuvukuvulj; Tacobul] tribe　大龜文社 (在屏東縣獅子鄉)

Tok Kwang [Deguang; Te-kuang]　德光

Tongling Bo　統領埔 (今屏東縣車城鄉統埔村)

Tossupong　大繡房 [大樹房] (今屏東縣恆春鎮大光里)

Tujia ethnic group　(湘西) 土家族

tushengzi [*tu-sheng-tzu; hybrids*]　土生仔 [混種，混生]

Tuillassock [Tuilasok; Cilasoaq] tribe　豬勝束社 (今屏東縣滿州鄉里德村)

Turtle Hill [Guishan]　龜山 (今屏東縣車城鄉射寮村附近)

Turtle Nose Mountain [Dajianshi Mountain]　龜鼻山 [大尖石山] (今墾丁社頂公園)

Uwaljudj tribe　外獅頭社 (在屏東縣獅子鄉)

Vele Rete Rocks　七星巖

Volcano [Chuhuo]　出火 (在屏東縣恆春鎮)

Volunteer, the　「志願者號」

Wang, Wenqi [Wang Wen-chi]　王文棨

Wei, Qing [Wei Ching]　衛青

Wu, Benjie [Wu Pen-chieh]　吳本杰

Wu, Ta-ting [Wu Dating]　吳大廷

Wu, Tang　吳棠

Yang, Bamboo [Yang Zhuqing; Yang Chu-ching]　楊竹青

Yao, Ying　姚瑩

Ye, Zongyuan [Yeh Tsung-yuan]　葉宗元

Yizhen [Yi-chen]　乙真

yina [*ina*]　伊那 (母親，排灣語)

Zeelandia, Fort　熱蘭遮城 (今台南市安平古堡)

Zeng, Guofan [Tseng Kuo-fan]　曾國藩

Zheng, Chenggong [Koxinga; Cheng Cheng-kung]　國姓爺 [鄭成功]

Zhuang, Datian [Chuang Ta-tien]　莊大田

Zou, Zongtang [Tso Tsung-tang]　左宗棠

Zudjui [Cudjui; Cudjuy]　朱雷